RED ICE

Other Books by William C. Dietz

AMERICA RISING SERIES
Into The Guns
Seek And Destroy
Battle Hymn

MUTANT FILES SERIES
Deadeye
Redzone
Graveyard

LEGION OF THE DAMNED SERIES
Legion of the Damned
The Final Battle
By Blood alone
By Force of Arms
For More Than Glory
For Those Who Fell
When All Seems Lost
When Duty Calls
A Fighting Chance
Andromeda's Fall
Andromeda's Choice
Andromeda's War

RED ICE

WILLIAM C. DIETZ

This is for my lovely wife Marjorie.
Thank you for, well, everything.

CONTENTS

ACKNOWLEDGEMENTS

I would like to thank the following people for their advice concerning the military aspects of
RED ICE. I couldn't have written it without them. All technical errors, if any, are mine.

Robert Crichton, Electronics Technician First
Class, US Navy Submarine Service

Major Troy C. Bucher, USA

Lieutenant Colonel Dane Franta, USAF

Major Matthew T. Kealy, USAF/TACP

Major Brian "Bear" Privette, USAF

And many thanks to my editor, Marjorie Dietz

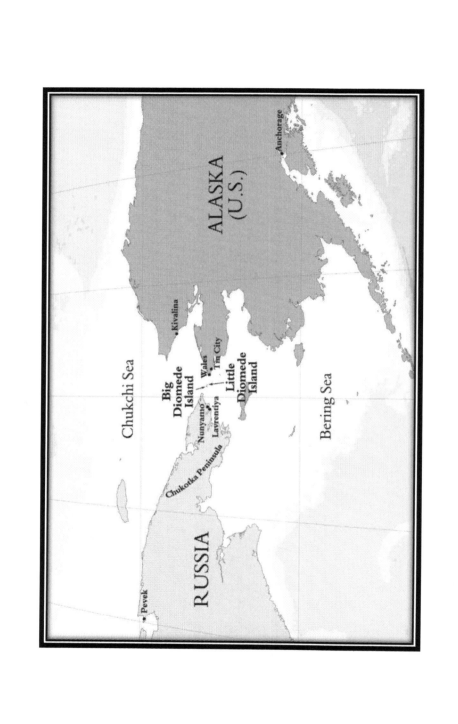

CHAPTER ONE

**South China Sea, aboard the Zumwalt Class Destroyer,
USS *Stacy Heath***

It was a bright sunny day, the sky was achingly blue, and fluffy white clouds were reflected in the waters of the South China Sea. There were no whitecaps, just an orderly procession of gentle swells, each following the rest south. So as the USS *Stacy Heath's* inverted bow sliced through the water, Captain Mary Franklin felt nothing other than a slight vibration. Franklin was five foot eight and slim. She had short rusty red hair, most of which was covered by a navy ball cap. A spray of freckles crossed the bridge of her nose prior to spilling down onto her cheeks. Franklin had graduated from Annapolis eighteen years earlier, and been in the navy ever since.

To port and starboard two dozen nearly identical Chinese fishing trawlers could be seen. The rusty boats were about 75 feet long, had open bows, and two story superstructures. Some of the vessels were uncomfortably close to the *Heath* despite repeated warnings. Were spy ships hiding among them? Sent to track the warship's movements? Yes, of course. Such was the way of things, and had been for a long time.

As for the *real* fishing boats they were an international source of concern due to their well-documented tendency to hoover up fish at a rate that the world's oceans couldn't sustain.

But fishing was only a small part of it. There were indications that substantial reserves of oil and gas were waiting to be plundered beneath the seabed. And *that,* many analysts believed, was the real reason for Chinese expansionism. The *Heath's* mission was to "... challenge the Chinese government's claims of sovereignty in the entire South China Sea," as part of the ongoing effort to prevent China from annexing the entire area.

The immediate source of concern was the smudge of land visible up ahead. It was called Mischief Reef. And, having spent hours studying satellite photos of the circular coral formation, Franklin had a mental image of it. The passageway to the inner lagoon had been enlarged to a width of 900 feet so that Chinese dredgers could pass through. Dredgers the Chinese had been using to pump white sand up onto the existing land. Enough sand to support buildings. And Franklin knew that similar reclamation efforts were underway elsewhere.

According to the Chinese government all of the projects were peaceful in nature, like the airstrips that could be used for "... search and rescue missions." A pretense that no one believed. Least of all the men and women who ran the Pentagon, and wanted to reaffirm America's right to send ships through international waters "... any fucking time we want to," as one admiral put it.

Franklin approved of the mission. But, like her peers she understood how uncertain the current political situation was, both internationally and at home. Part of that stemmed from the fact that the president of the United States was notoriously unpredictable. On Monday he might be in favor of lifting sanctions on Russia. By Tuesday he could oppose it. And the president's posture regarding China was no different.

According to Hayden's supporters it was all part of a clever strategy to keep opponents off balance. Those on the other side of the aisle suggested that the lack of clarity resulted from a short attention span, and a tendency to follow whatever advice he'd heard during the last ten minutes, including that provided on FOX News.

Franklin's thoughts were interrupted by the shrill sound of a whistle, followed by an announcement over the ship's PA system. "Man overboard! Man overboard! Starboard side! This is *not* a drill... This is *not* a drill."

Franklin felt something like cold water enter her blood-stream as the OOD (Officer Of the Deck), Lieutenant Commander Lambert began to issue orders. Some idiot had fallen into the drink... And, given the ship's circumstances that could be disastrous. What if the Chinese managed to get their hands on him? *Shit! Shit! Shit!* They would use the sailor for propaganda purposes at the very least, and might take the opportunity to harass the ship with flybys, or other forms of intimidation. After reducing power, and checking to make sure the man in the water was well clear of the destroyer's screws, Lambert ordered "Slow astern," followed by "Standby."

"Launch a boat," Franklin ordered. "Put an officer on board, and arm the crew. Who's the floater? Do we know?"

"Seaman Larry Wilson, ma'am," the navigator replied.

"What the hell was he doing?"

"We don't know, ma'am."

"Is he okay?"

"As far as we can tell... He's wearing a life jacket, and swim-ming toward the ship."

"Sound general quarters... This might turn into a shit show."

"Aye, aye, ma'am."

Franklin heard a shrill whistle, followed by a klaxon, and the announcement every sailor was familiar with. "General quarters! General quarters! All hands man your battle stations!"

That was little more than a formality in this case, since all the ship's sections were closed up, and on high alert. "Tell Lieutenant

Chow to get on the horn, and warn the trawlers off," Franklin ordered. "They are not, I repeat *not*, to approach Wilson. I'm going aft."

The *Heath's* Mission Center had been compared to something from *Star Trek*. Huge flat panel screens were mounted against the starboard bulkhead. Rows of computer stations faced the monitors, and the twenty people stationed in front of them were trained to handle all of the ship's communications, weapons, and engineering functions.

TAO (Tactical Action Officer) Chow was waiting for Franklin. She was short and intense. "I can't raise any of the trawlers, ma'am. But they're gabbing with each other."

"Keep trying," Franklin ordered. "Maybe we can herd them like cattle."

The *Heath* was equipped with two Northrop Grumman MQ-8 Fire Scout unmanned helicopters which could be launched and controlled from the Mission Center. She leaned in between the UAV pilots. "Are your birds ready to lift?"

"Yes, ma'am," Lisa Rafferty replied.

"What kind of loadout are they carrying?"

"Hellfire missiles," Derek Foster answered. "Two each."

"Excellent. Put 'em in between the trawlers and Wilson. See if you can push the fishing boats away from him." The techs said "Aye, aye," in unison, and went to work.

Franklin's next stop was the com section. The lead Information Systems Tech was a woman named Sims. "There's bound to be at least one spy ship out there," Franklin said. "They'll start squawking soon. ID them if you can, and pass the information to the weapons officer. We'll kill them if we have to."

Sims had short hair, dark eyes, and mocha colored skin. "Aye, aye, Captain. We'll find 'em."

Franklin heard her name, and pressed the transmit button on the radio. "This is the captain."

"Lambert here," the XO said. "One of the trawlers is trying to cut us off from Wilson. A second boat is moving in to pick him up."

Franklin swore silently. So much for her plan to scare the trawler captains. They were calling her bluff. Franklin found herself in a no-win situation. She could destroy both trawlers in seconds. But, *if* she did, China would accuse the United States of attacking peaceful fishermen as they attempted to rescue an American sailor. Not the sort of story the president or the chairman of the Joint Chiefs would want to see on the front page of the *New York Times*.

And, if Franklin allowed the Chinese to grab Wilson, the bastards would parade him in front of cameras in Beijing as "proof" that the U.S. had violated Chinese waters, or some equally ridiculous bullshit like that. And Franklin had seconds in which to decide. Lieutenant Chow was watching her. "Fire a warning shot in front of the first boat," Franklin ordered. "And prepare to do the same with the second. Execute."

A rating named Rigg had control of the ship's six-inch guns. Franklin went over to stand beside him. "Don't hit the bastards," she cautioned. "Just scare the shit out of them."

Video and targeting data was visible on the screen in front of Rigg. He used a joy stick to swivel a deck gun around. Franklin watched the crosshairs settle on a patch of open water. A key clicked and there was a muted thump as the gun fired. A column of white water shot up in front of the incoming boat. It veered away. "Good work," Franklin said. "What's the other target up to?"

"It's still coming our way," Chow replied.

"Fire *another* warning shot," Franklin instructed. Then, as Rigg tapped a key, Franklin spoke into her radio. "Lambert? Is the boat in the water yet?"

"Yes, ma'am. But it's going to take at least ten minutes to reach Wilson, and take him aboard."

"Tell them to hurry," Franklin said, and immediately came to regret it. The boat crew knew they were supposed to hurry—and unnecessary orders were self-indulgent. "Belay the last order," Franklin added. "They know what to do."

"One of the trawlers is talking nonstop to what might be a shore station," Sims interjected. "And the transmissions are encrypted."

A fishing vessel carrying military grade com gear. That served to confirm Franklin's suspicions. "Put in a call to the *GW* (*USS George Washington*) and tell them we need air cover ASAP." The carrier was just over the horizon, and sure to have at least two planes in the air.

Franklin could have called on the fighters earlier—but had been hoping to keep the rescue low key. That was impossible now, and if the military trawler was calling for help, the situation was going to get worse. A lot worse. "Yes, ma'am," Sims replied, and went to work.

"They're pulling Wilson out of the water," Lambert announced over the radio. "We'll have him back aboard in fifteen."

Fifteen minutes! Franklin thought to herself. That was like an eternity.

"We have four, repeat *four*, bogeys inbound from the north," Operations Specialist Cory Moore announced. He was seated in front of a SPY-3 radar screen and could monitor everything for miles around. "I have confirmation from the *GW's* Super Fudd," Moore added. "The ETA for the bogeys is five minutes."

Franklin knew that Super Fudd was a nickname for the navy's E-2 Hawkeye airborne early warning aircraft. Five minutes wasn't a whole lot of flight time, and a good indication that the Chinese planes had taken off from the base on Hainan Island. "They probably have orders to buzz us," Franklin told Chow. "But you never know."

"We're ready," Chow assured her. "The boards are green, and the ESSM system is hot."

ESSM stood for the Evolved SeaSparrow Missile System, also known as the RIM-162. The SeaSparrows were "quad packed" in Mark 41 vertical launchers, and capable of destroying all of the incoming planes. That offered some comfort, but not much. The *Heath* was virtually dead in the water, and the very definition of a sitting duck.

"I have the *GW* on the horn," Sims announced. "The admiral is waiting for you on a secure video link."

Franklin was surprised to say the least. "You must be shitting me."

"No, ma'am, and they say it's urgent."

"I'll take it in the booth."

"The booth" was a small enclosure where it was possible to have a private conversation. Franklin had no idea what Admiral Geary would say, and didn't want the bridge crew to listen in. She stepped into the cubicle and closed the door.

Geary was visible on the screen. He had a buzz cut, hollow cheeks, and an uncharacteristically dour expression. "I'm sorry Mary," he said, "but I don't have enough time to grease this up for you. Don't fire on the Chinese regardless of the provocation. That's straight from the commander-in-chief. Hayden is trying to reach Premier Lau. He says the premier is a 'good guy.' And the two of them can do a deal."

Franklin could hardly believe her ears. Yes, she understood the stakes involved, but what about "Peace through strength" and all the rest of the campaign bullshit? Now, based on Geary's comments, it sounded as though the president was going to cave. Franklin struggled to maintain her composure. "Even if they fire on us?"

"Even then," Geary said grimly. "And I can't send the planes you requested. Not until I get the green light from Washington.

The National Security Adviser fears that the planes might be seen as provocative."

"*Provocative?*" Franklin demanded. "Who cares? What about my *crew*? And my ship?"

"I'm sorry," Geary said miserably. "Those are my orders."

Franklin heard a muted roar. "Chinese fighters are buzzing the ship, Admiral ... I have to go." And with that Franklin broke the connection.

Another roar was heard as she left the booth. "They're looping us," Chow said, as Franklin reappeared. "But that's all so far."

Franklin spoke into her radio. "Lambert? Is Wilson aboard?"

"Yes, Captain."

"Change course and head for the *GW*. They can't send planes, but we can go to them."

"They can't send planes?" Lambert demanded. "Why not?"

"Because the president said so. Full speed ahead. Take evasive action."

Lambert liked that. "Yes, ma'am!"

Franklin could feel the additional rpms through the soles of her shoes as Lambert demanded more speed. The destroyer was capable of 20 knots and could clear the area quickly. The deck started to slant as the *Heath* made a turn to the east. Franklin felt better. The Chinese had driven the American destroyer off, taped it, and could feed the video to the world. But the *Heath* and her crew were safe.

"Here comes another one," Chow said.

Franklin looked up just in time to see the laser guided bomb drop free of the J-8 fighter plane's belly, and head straight for the *Heath*. Franklin opened her mouth to shout a warning but it was too late. The 1,000 pound bomb hit the destroyer's superstructure and exploded. The jolt threw Franklin and Chow to the deck. Fortunately the *Heath's* armor was thick enough to withstand the blow. The Chinese had been planning to attack all along. The initial flybys were intended to put the Americans at ease.

"Engage those planes!" Franklin ordered, as she scrambled back to her feet. "Kill them!" The response was instinctual, and made without regard to Admiral Geary's orders. *Fuck Geary and the president,* Franklin thought. *There's no way in hell that the Heath will go down without a fight.*

The ship shook as a *second* bomb struck the superstructure, damage control parties rushed to respond, and Rafferty spoke up. "The Fire Scouts are still airborne, ma'am ... Can we kill the trawlers? The ones that called the planes in?"

"Smoke 'em," Franklin ordered. "And recover the Scouts if you can."

The ship's ESSM system was firing on the Chinese planes. "Six missiles, four kills," Chow reported calmly.

"*More* bogeys on screen," Moore announced. "Six targets inbound from the north."

Franklin swore. It was clear at that point ... The attack on the *Heath* was more than a misunderstanding. The Chinese were all in. They were going to war ... And sinking the *Heath* would give them a Pearl Harbor like victory right off the top.

The planes weren't likely to make bomb runs this time. They would use standoff weapons instead. Franklin gave the order, "Shoot them down," and heard Chow pass it on.

"Missiles fired and tracking," a tech said.

"I have an additional target," Moore said. "It's inbound from the north ETA two minutes. My guess is a cruise missile."

Franklin knew the Chinese had a subsonic cruise missile called the CJ-10. It had a range of more than 900 miles, was equipped with a wide variety of guidance systems, and could deliver a 1,000 pound payload. Odds were that it had been launched from the mainland. "Knock it down if you can," Franklin ordered.

"Three kills," Chow put in, but that wasn't enough.

"Missiles incoming," Moore reported. Then they hit. It was like taking two blows from a gigantic hammer. One of the weapons blew a hole in the port side of the superstructure, a second struck only yards away from the first point of impact, and sprayed the Mission Center with shards of shrapnel. Chow died instantly. Her blood sprayed across Moore who was dumped out of his chair. By some miracle Franklin was still on her feet. She helped the tech up off the deck. His hand was slick with blood. A petty officer was screaming for his mother, and another sailor kept calling for a corpsman over and over again.

"Systems down," duty Chief Atkins said thickly... "Rerouting... Rebooting... We're back up."

Franklin's head was spinning. There was so much to think about, and so little time in which to do so. The good news was that the *Heath* was resilient, and her self-healing systems could reroute critical functions, but the destroyer was taking casualties. Lots of them. And the crew was small. Critics said, too small. How long before Franklin ran out of bodies?

Chief Atkins stepped in to replace Chow. He was standing in a pool of the dead officer's blood. "We nailed the missile, ma'am... There are *two* planes on the screen. They're well out of range and circling."

They're waiting, Franklin thought. *For what?* The answer came quickly. "One-one high-speed surface targets," Moore announced. "Inbound from the north."

RIB boats, Franklin decided. *Based at Mischief Reef? Yes. To keep nosey neighbors away. Fortunately we have an app for that.* "Standby on the MK-46 gun system," Franklin ordered. "Engage the intruders the moment they come into range."

"Aye, aye," Chief Atkins replied. The 30mm chainguns could fire 200 rounds per-minute, and were fed by 400 round magazines via dual feeds. Their effective range was 2,200 yards.

Sims had been wounded. A bloody bandage was wrapped around her head. "The *GW* is on the horn ma'am. We have permission to engage. Fighters are inbound."

Franklin couldn't help but laugh. It had a shrill sound. "Tell them to fuck themselves."

Franklin allowed herself a moment to think. She had disobeyed a direct order. Her career was over. The only thing that mattered was saving her crew and ship.

"Targets are in range," Atkins intoned. "Firing." The chainguns produced a sustained bang-bang-bang sound as the automatic tracking system sought the RIB boats out and destroyed them.

Franklin eyed her watch. Less than twenty minutes had elapsed since Wilson had been brought aboard. It didn't seem possible. "I have radio contact with a flight of four Super Hornets," Sims announced.

"The J-8s are running for home," Moore added.

"That's it," Franklin said. "I think we're in the clear. Lambert? Do you read me?"

"Five by five."

"I need damage assessments, pronto."

"Aye, aye."

Franklin took a moment to look around. The Mission Center looked like a slaughter house. Foster was curled up on the deck, clutching his gut, and whimpering. Franklin wanted to cry. And later, once Franklin was by herself, she would.

Meanwhile a rivulet of blood ran out of the black-rimmed hole in the destroyer's side and trailed back along her port flank. The South China Sea was waiting to receive it.

***

Aboard the Chinese submarine, *Great Wall-009,* the South China Sea

The Yuan class sub was 254 feet long, about 27 feet wide, and cruising 200 feet under the surface of the South China Sea. The dimly lit control room was located directly below the conning tower. Indicator lights glowed red, green, and amber. The air was heavy with a miasma of diesel fuel, cooking odors, perspiration, and the fishy smell of Amine—a chemical used to remove carbon monoxide from the air. That was the atmosphere that Lieutenant Commander Chang Jing and his crew had to breathe as they waited to die.

Like his peers Chang was something of an expert on American warships and their capabilities. That included Zumwalt class destroyers like the *Heath*. So Chang knew that the ship that he'd been ordered to sink was equipped with the latest detection gear and vertically launched anti-submarine rockets.

According to Chinese intelligence agencies as well as Wikipedia.com, the ASROC anti-sub missiles carried by the *Heath* were designed to deliver Mark-54 torpedoes to a pre-calculated point, where they would home in on the 009 and destroy her. That's when Chang would die.

As for the thirty-seven men under Chang's command, the only thing they knew was that the 009 had been sent to find and shadow an American ship. The kind of mission they'd carried out on previous occasions. Why trouble them with the truth? Nine was a lucky number, but their submarine was in the wrong place, at the wrong time.

It's the sort of mission that a nuclear attack boat should carry out, Chang thought. *But they're out in deeper water playing with themselves. Ta ma de tamen* (fuck them).

The bitterness stemmed from the fact that Chang had applied to the school for nuclear submarine commanders and been denied. *Twice.* That didn't bode well for his career. *But,* Chang told himself, *test scores aren't everything. I will prove myself by dying well.*

Chang's ruminations were interrupted by Sonar Operator Ku. "I have a contact, sir."

Ku was employing passive, rather than active sonar, to avoid detection. Chang felt his heart beat start to increase. "What have you got?"

"*Two* screws, sir ... Turning at high rpms. The acoustic signature is similar to that of a *Los Angeles* class submarine, but it *isn't* a sub, so there's a high likelihood that we have our target."

Stealth, Chang thought. *Zumwalt class destroyers are supposed to be stealthy, just like submarines.* "Well done, Ku. Take her up to periscope depth Lieutenant Shan. I want to confirm the ship's identity."

Rather than blow the sub's tanks, Shan chose to "drive" the boat to the surface using a combination of control planes and propulsion. Once the 009 arrived at the correct depth, the diving officer began to raise the periscope even as he used the sub's low pressure blower to eject water from the ballast tanks.

Then Shan stood to one side so that his commanding officer could look through the scope. What Chan saw was too good to be true! There was no mistaking the *Heath's* katana-like bow and streamlined appearance. Two overlapping black-edged holes could be seen on the ship's port side. Gray smoke streamed back along the destroyer's flanks. The damage was consistent with the urgent message Chang had received twenty minutes earlier.

Judging from the size of the destroyer's bow wave, and what Ku had told him, the warship was operating at flank speed. In the distance Chang could see the glint of sunlight reflecting off metal as a fighter circled the enemy ship. The Americans had control of the air then ... So, why hadn't the *Heath* attacked and killed him?

"Ku," Chang said, without turning away from the periscope. "Are they pinging us?"

"No, sir."

Thanks to our air-independent propulsion system the Americans can't hear us, Chang concluded. *Or, all of their sonar operators are dead, and some of their systems are offline. Maybe I'm going to survive after all.* "This is not a drill," Chang announced. "Prepare to fire torpedoes one through six. Set to acoustic homing. Confirm."

"One through six, acoustic," the weapons officer replied. "Confirmed. All weapons ready to fire."

"Fire one, fire two, fire three, fire four, fire five, and fire six," Chang ordered.

"Torpedoes away," the weapons officer replied stoically. What was the man thinking? That Chang was insane? It didn't matter. An order was an order.

Under normal circumstances Chang would have given orders to dive deep to escape a counterattack by the target's escorts or allied aircraft. But the *Heath* didn't have any surface escorts to rely on. And, while the planes circling above the destroyer could be carrying standoff anti-sub weapons, they were unaware of the 009's presence.

Chang pulled a quick 360 but didn't see any threats. "All torpedoes running straight and true," the weapons officer reported. All Chang could do was watch and wait. Five long seconds passed. Finally, after what seemed like an hour, the first torpedo hit the destroyer just aft of her bow. The second, third, fourth and fifth weapons were equally spaced along the length of the ship's hull. The sixth missed by a few yards.

Wherever a torpedo struck there was a bright flash, followed by an upwelling of spray, and a puff of smoke. There was no sound. Not for Chang. But the explosions would be quite loud on the *Heath*, and Chang couldn't help but smile.

The destroyer's speed dropped from 20 knots to nothing in less than a minute. The *Heath* wallowed and began to sink as water surged in through a dozen holes. Chang saw two international orange life rafts appear near the stern.

Then with no additional drama the *Heath* slipped under the surface and disappeared from sight. Huge bubbles rose to the surface, followed by scattered debris, and a series of radiating waves. The *Great Wall-009* was victorious.

A dozen American sailors were rescued by Chinese fishing trawlers, handed over to the navy, and paraded in front of cameras in Beijing. Captain Mary Franklin was not among them. But, by some miracle, Seaman Larry Wilson was.

CHAPTER TWO

Forward Operating Base Hope, Khost Province, Afghanistan

Blackhawk helicopter clattered overhead as Air Force Major Dan Falco followed Broadway south to the command bunker. Forward Operating Base (FOB) Hope was a sprawling affair that consisted of perfectly aligned tents, a navy field hospital, a civilian run chow hall, an army motor pool, and the roughly four-hundred men and women who were stationed there. With the exception of the CIA's spooks all of the personnel were part of the Joint Special Operations Command or a support group.

World War III was about a month old. And, like everyone else, Falco was acquainted with both versions of how the conflict began. According to the account put out by President Hayden, he'd been on the phone with Chinese Premier Lau, cutting a deal to avoid bloodshed, when a renegade naval officer named Franklin attacked a fleet of civilian fishing boats.

But that story was an out-and-out lie according to Admiral Frank Geary who, after flying home from the Pacific, went on CNN to explain what *actually* happened. And that was a badly bungled attempt by the president to negotiate a deal while the *Heath* was being fired upon.

Then, in response to the shame he felt, Geary blew his brains out on camera. A tragedy which, according to the president's loyalists, proved that Geary was batshit crazy.

Falco was doing his best to ignore the politics of it. His job was to control and direct ground-attack aircraft, although very few missions were underway, as Hope's personnel worked day and night to pack everything up. The need for that was obvious. Pakistan was only thirty miles away and, after the so-called "*Heath* incident," the Paks had decided to side with China.

Why? Because the Pakistanis hated the Indians that's why... After sinking the *Heath* the Chinese invaded India to gain control of the Buddhist Monastery in Tawang, Arunachal. That's where the *next* Dali Lama was expected to incarnate. An event that could trigger an insurrection and threaten China's grip on Tibet.

All three countries had nuclear weapons. In hopes of scoring a quick victory over India, Pakistan made use of tactical nukes. India responded in kind. And, as eight-hundred tanks clashed near Wazirabad, thousands died.

While the major powers focused their attention elsewhere, the Kurds took the opportunity to create a new state called Kurdistan, which laid claim to large chunks of Turkey, Syria, Iraq, and Iran. The resulting chaos provided remnants of ISIS and Al-Qaeda with an opportunity to slaughter thousands of "disbelievers" in order to create a caliphate. Then, in a breakthrough piece of diplomacy, the Israelis chose to form an alliance with Saudi Arabia—even as the oil rich country attacked Iran.

Meanwhile, in an effort to restore the Soviet empire to its former glory, the Russians invaded Ukraine. NATO had no choice but to respond, and it wasn't long before the resulting conflict spilled over into Belarus, Poland, and Romania. That raised the threat of an all-out nuclear war.

So, since Afghanistan shared a border with Pakistan, American troops needed to get out while the getting was good. Afghanistan would have to fend for itself and, if history was any guide, Pakistan and China would be well advised to leave the country alone.

That's why Falco expected base commander, and army colonel Lloyd Campo, to hand him a "pack everything up" shit detail. As Falco approached the JOC (Joint Operational Center) he saw that a battlefield fashionista was guarding the ramp that slanted down into the underground bunker. Like his peers the operator was armed with an exotic rifle, was decorated with tats, and wore a beard. Salutes get old when people see each other every day, so the men nodded to each other. A corporal left the JOC as Falco entered.

It was like a madhouse down below as soldiers, sailors and airmen sorted documents and packed them into boxes. A senior airman spotted Falco and came over. "The colonel is in the briefing room, sir. Do you need anything?"

"No, thank you," Falco replied. "I'm good."

The briefing room was an island of serenity in a sea of chaos. Campo was there, along with an Afghan national, and they were poring over a map as Falco entered. "There you are," Campo said. "This is Mr. Jawan Mohammadi. He'll be your guide. Jawan, this is Major Falco. He's a JTAC (Joint Terminal Attack Controller) and a dammed good one too... If Hashemi shows up, Major Falco will send him straight to *Jahannam* (hell)."

Falco felt his pulse quicken. Campo was going to hand him a mission rather than a chore! He stepped forward to shake hands. Mohammadi was clean shaven, and dressed in the usual outfit of vest, long shirt, and baggy trousers. As their hands made contact Falco noticed that the Afghani's palm was soft, rather than callused, and his English was exceptionally good. An educated man then. "It's a pleasure to meet you, Major," Mohammadi said. "With your help we will rid ourselves of the goat turd named Noor Mohammad Hashemi."

Falco looked at Campo. The army officer had a white sidewall haircut, blue eyes, and a lean body. He smiled. "That's right,

Falco ... We're going to give the people of Khost Province a going away present. The Taliban sent Hashemi to the area ... And he uses murder, kidnappings, and gang rapes to keep people in line. That alone is enough reason to cancel his ticket. But, according to our Intel people, he's the bastard who conceived and orchestrated the Valentine's Day attack."

Falco had been inside the wire the day that a "farmer" drove his truck into the fence and blew himself up. A squad of hadji had been hiding in a streambed nearby. They rushed through the hole and opened fire. Five soldiers were killed during the ensuing gun battle. "That works for me, sir," Falco said. "One question though ... Could we use a pred?" (Predator drone.)

"Hashemi likes to surround himself with civilians," Campo replied. "So we haven't had a good opportunity to use a drone. But a wedding is going to be held in the village of *Em Bal* two days from now and, assuming that Jawan's sources are correct, Hashemi will attend. Both he and his bodyguards are legitimate targets. But we'll need more than a pred to wipe them out. The trick is to grease the bastard without killing any civilians."

"He murdered my sister," Mohammadi added tightly. "For going to school."

"I'm sorry," Falco said. And he was. And, like Campo, Falco wanted to kill the man behind the attack on FOB Hope. That would be an excellent way to end his tour in Afghanistan.

The next thirty minutes were spent discussing the particulars of the mission. Under normal circumstances Falco would have been part of a two, three, or four man team. But Campo was sending him to *Em Bal* alone. "This a unique situation," Campo explained. "The mission will require a person with eyes-on to ID the target, and given how exposed the OP (Observation Post) is, a larger group would be too conspicuous. A quick reaction force will be on standby if the shit hits the fan."

Falco nodded. "Yes, sir."

"One more thing," Campo added. "I'm delegating On Scene Commander authority to you... You'll have the best vantage point, and I trust you to make the correct call."

So Falco and Mohammadi were going in by themselves. And rather than enter the operational area during the day, they were going to infil during the hours of darkness.

After discussing the weather forecast, enemy activity, and close air support Falco returned to his tent. His first task was to select the right com equipment and to check it over. His choices included a tablet computer, plus an AN/PRC-117G radio, with a PRC-152 as backup.

Other than the com gear, Falco didn't plan to bring much. Just his weapons, ammo, one MRE, a Jetboil stove and a hydration pack.

After prepping for the mission there was only one more thing to do, and that was to take a nap, because Falco was slated to depart at 2000 hours. Sleeping could be difficult with helos roaring overhead, vehicles growling past, and people shouting orders. So earplugs were helpful. But it was Falco's capacity to sleep anywhere, and at any time, that came through for him.

Falco's alarm went off at 1830. He rolled out of bed, took a hot shower, and got dressed. The routine never varied. The ritual began with checking to make sure his TAC vest was properly loaded with a Ruger Silent-SR .22 pistol, extra magazines for his carbine, and the all-important first aid kit. Then it was time to load his pockets. Power bars were important... As were packets of instant coffee.

Then with the pack on his back, and his M4 carbine in hand, Falco left for the mess tent. It was open 24/7. And Falco ordered his favorite pre-op meal, which consisted of a double cheese burger and chili fries.

Various people said "Hello," but left it at that, since they could tell that Falco was outbound. Some people were gregarious prior to departing on a mission, but many weren't. So it was SOP to give operators like Falco plenty of space.

After finishing his meal Falco stopped by Operations to make sure that the weather forecast and the overall strategic situation were the same as they had been earlier in the day. Then he left for the motor pool where Mohammadi was waiting. If the Afghan was nervous Falco couldn't detect any signs of it. Mohammadi was dressed in the same outfit Falco had seen earlier, plus a nondescript pack, and a night vision headset. The device was new to Mohammadi and he was fiddling with it. "You look green, Major ... But I can see you quite clearly."

"Good," Falco said. "Let's mount up."

The Taliban didn't like to fight at night. But they could. So the Americans were forced to choose. They could cede the night to the enemy, which would allow the hadji to plant IEDs, move supplies and intimidate the locals—or they could conduct patrols. *Unpredictable* patrols that left the base at all hours, followed random routes, and were targeted to different objectives.

One element *was* predictable however—and that was the choice of vehicles used for nighttime operations. In spite of their efforts to change things up the Americans knew they'd come under fire occasionally, and be targeted with IEDs. So the Mine-Resistant Ambush Protected trucks called MRAPs were the best way to go.

The boxy trucks came in a variety of configurations. The one looming over them had a fifty mounted up top, and firing ports along both sides. And to give the patrol even *more* firepower Ops was sending a Stryker vehicle along.

The MRAP's engine was running and a squad of soldiers was seated inside. A staff sergeant nodded to Falco. "Good evening, sir. Where's the rest of your team?"

"They're goofing off," Falco replied. "It's just the two of us tonight. We need to stop at the gate on the way out."

"Roger that," the sergeant said. "Okay, Morris… You heard the major, let's roll."

There was a slight jerk as Morris put his foot down. A series of turns took them to Hollywood Boulevard which led to the gate. An MP stepped up to the driver's side window as the MRAP came to a halt. "Tell him that Mr. Mohammadi is aboard," Falco instructed.

The driver relayed the message and the MP disappeared. When the soldier returned he was carrying an AK-47 and a canvas bag full of spare magazines. Mohammadi accepted both without comment. "Don't load your weapon," the sergeant cautioned. "Not until you're clear of the vehicle." The gate swung open.

Maybe Mohammadi's feelings were hurt, and maybe they weren't. But the Afghan understood. In the wake of various green-on-blue shootings Afghan nationals weren't permitted to carry weapons inside the wire. And the sergeant was determined to protect his soldiers. Falco stood next to the driver. "You know where the drop point is?"

Morris nodded. "Yes, sir. It was in the briefing."

"Good. Make it quick," Falco said.

"I will," Morris promised. Both of them knew that what appeared to be empty farmland frequently wasn't and, if the men were spotted, that could be disastrous.

The MRAP's armor was superior to the Stryker's, so it took the lead. The route had been allowed to cool for a week. The road passed between two fields of wheat, through the small village of *Hadit*, and across a swiftly flowing river. There was a bridge. But that was a natural place to place an IED, so Morris drove the MRAP through the waist high water, and up onto the opposite bank.

After fifteen minutes of uneventful driving the vehicles arrived at an intersection where the MRAP paused. That too was a likely place for an IED, and Falco waited for an explosion that didn't come. "This is where we get out," Mohammadi informed him.

Falco thanked Morris prior to exiting the vehicle into the cool night air. Mohammadi followed him. The first thing the Afghan did was to load his AK-47. Falco was ready to fire if the AK's barrel began to swing his way. It didn't. The assault rifle had a sling which Mohammadi hooked over his shoulder.

"I will lead the way," he announced, and that was logical, since the Afghan was what Brits would call a farmerbarma. Meaning a local guide. And if there were traps ahead Mohammadi would trigger them. Falco had to watch his six however ... That meant glancing back over his shoulder at regular intervals.

Mohammadi led Falco across the road to a path that wound up along the side of a hill. Falco could see quite well thanks to his vision gear, but there wasn't much to look at. Their surroundings consisted of boulders, scrub, and the occasional wind-twisted tree. There were stars however ... *Thousands* of them. They twinkled and were a good source of ambient light.

Falco was in good shape, so the climb was easy at first. But he was breathing heavily by the time they arrived at the village of *Em Bal*. Mohammadi was unfazed. "This is where the wedding will take place," he whispered. "We will be up *there*." Mohammadi pointed up into the darkness. "You will see everything."

Falco knew that. And the fact that his surroundings matched his expectations was a source of comfort. The egress route was on the opposite side of the hill. If everything went well the Taliban fighters would be disorganized during the minutes immediately after Hashemi's death. That would help them escape. But if things went badly? He'd call for help. "Okay," Falco said. "Lead the way."

The second trail was less worn than the first, and likely to be the province of goats and the boys who were in charge of them. It zigzagged back and forth for a while, circled around a pinnacle of rock, and petered out. "This is it," Mohammadi said, as he came to a halt. "Wait until the sun rises! Everything will be visible. Including the road into *Em Bal*."

Falco nodded. "That's good, Jawan. But people will see us."

"Not so," Mohammadi replied. "Come. I will show you."

After turning their night vision gear off, and their headlamps on, the men entered a jumble of rocks. Falco followed Mohammadi through a narrow passageway and into the cave beyond. It was large enough to stand in, but far from secret, judging from the litter that covered the ground. "Look!" Mohammadi said proudly. "Water! I brought it here two days ago."

Falco looked, and sure enough, two one-gallon containers of water were hidden behind some rocks. "Well done," Falco said, even though the previous visit was a source of concern. Had the Taliban been tracking Mohammadi's movements? Bad things would happen if so.

"Alright," Falco said. "Let's take five." Mohammadi hadn't seen a Jetboil before, and was amazed by the speed with which the device could boil water. The Afghani made green tea while Falco poured his half of the hot liquid over two packets of instant coffee. Then, with a power bar each, they settled in.

Mohammadi told a story about staying in the cave as a child, while Falco listened to a report from a drone operator, via the earbuds hooked to the 117G. There were no heat signatures in the immediate area, other than those generated by goats, and Falco let Mohammadi's words wash over him.

When the sun rose the men went outside to greet it. The sound was faint, but Falco could hear the pre-dawn call to prayer or *Salat al-Fajr* being broadcast from the village mosque, and knew the faithful were up and about.

The men lay flat on their stomachs as the sun continued to rise behind them and they glassed the village with binoculars. Falco was using a GPS enabled portable range finder (PLRF), which provided coordinates for whatever he looked at. "Start on the left," Falco said, "and give me a tour. I want to know what each building is used for."

Falco took notes as Mohammadi ran through the list. There was a shoe store, a barber shop, a fabric store, what had once been a movie theatre, an outdoor restaurant, the wedding hall where the nuptials would take place, a hole-in-the-wall pharmacy, a school and the mosque.

Once the review was complete Falco read his notes back to Mohammadi and confirmed that they were correct before uploading them via the tablet and an uplink. Falco was putting the computer away when Mohammadi spoke. "Two men left the village and are climbing the hill. They're hidden now ... But they will reappear soon."

Falco swore. "Are they armed?"

"Yes," Mohammadi replied. "Most men are."

That was true. And Falco felt sure they were Taliban. Why? Because if the hill was a natural vantage point for *him*, it was a natural vantage point for the hadji too, and Hashemi was coming to town. Falco hadn't given any thought to the possibility of an enemy overlook and felt stupid. The realization was humbling. But, thanks to Mohammadi, there was time to prepare. "Okay," Falco said. "We'll kill them. Here's what I want you to do."

The better part of twenty minutes passed before the Taliban fighters arrived on the hilltop. Mohammadi was there to greet them. He was seated on a boulder drinking tea. A scene so innocent that the hadji didn't bother to unsling their weapons. "Jawan," one of them said in Pashto. "What are *you* doing here? Shouldn't you be kissing some crusader's ass?"

Falco was hiding in the jumble of rocks. The special issue .22 was in his hand. So long as he did the job correctly the *Mujahedeen* wouldn't have a chance. Nor did the murderous bastards deserve one. Falco stepped out into the open, took aim, and shot a man in the back of the head. The .22 made no more than a clicking sound as two bullets struck home. The *second* hadji was turning as the body fell, and fumbling with his assault rifle.

Falco shot him in the temple. Twice. The man collapsed. Mohammadi went over to spit on the body. "I know them ... These pigs eat from Hashemi's trough."

"The second one has a radio," Falco observed. "I want you to monitor it."

"And if someone calls?"

"Try to make it sound as if the lookouts are trying to respond but can't," Falco told him. "Press a lot of buttons, but don't say anything. That's the best we can do."

Most Afghan weddings began at roughly 1700 and, according to Mohammadi, this one would as well. That meant hours would pass before they could expect to see Hashemi. But what if he arrived early? *Assumptions are bad*, Falco reminded himself, *and vigilance is good.*

So they took turns scanning the village square as the minutes crept by. There was some traffic on the *Mujahedeen* radio, but no calls to the dead men, for which Falco was grateful. People came and went. A dog dozed in the sun. An elaborately decorated bus arrived and five well-dressed passengers got off. They were carrying packages. Wedding guests? Probably. Boys were dismissed from school. Men entered the mosque for *Asr*, or the midafternoon prayer, and filtered out half an hour later.

Then Falco heard it. A laconic message from a drone pilot who was sitting in front of a screen at Creech Air Force Base back in the U.S. of A. "We have five vehicles approaching *Em Bal* from the west."

Falco turned his binoculars to the road, and was watching when the first vehicle appeared. It was an ancient Mercedes convertible. The top was down and a passenger could be seen in back. As Falco focused his glasses he expected to see Hashemi.

But the man in the Mercedes *wasn't* Hashemi. Falco didn't think so anyway, although the photos he'd seen were two years old. "Jawan ... The man in the Mercedes ... Is that Hashemi?"

Mohammadi looked, and shook his head. "No. I've never seen him before."

Falco's mind was racing. What the hell was going on? Had Hashemi been replaced? Was the man in the car an envoy? Sent to represent the Taliban leader? Or was Hashemi playing games? To fool *him?* No, Hashemi didn't know about the trap. He was worried about predator drones. And trying to confuse the people who flew them.

"There he is!" Mohammadi exclaimed. "Right *there!* Standing in front of the wedding hall."

Falco shifted the range finder to the left, and sure enough, Hashemi was there surrounded by a half dozen fighters. Hashemi had arrived under the cover of darkness. And now he was making his presence known. Not just anywhere ... But at the center of *Em Bal* where a UAV operator would be hesitant to strike without a positive ID. And faces were difficult to make out from drone footage.

So Hashemi believed himself to be safe. But *was* he? Falco figured that a carefully targeted missile could take the bastard and his entourage out while causing minimal damage to the village. The first step was to pass the targeting data to a pilot who was circling an area north of them. Falco felt a terrible tightness in his chest as he eyed the prospective blast area. Maybe the locals were afraid of the Taliban, or maybe it was happenstance, but the area around Hashemi was clear. Falco made the call. "Bring it."

Falco heard a burp of static followed by a laconic, "In from the north."

"Cleared hot."

The fighter entered a steep dive. A missile flashed off the plane's starboard wing. The pilot said, "Rifle," which indicated that he had released a missile rather than a bomb.

Falco was waiting for the explosion when the door to the wedding hall opened, and three burqa clad women emerged. Falco yelled, "Shift cold! Shift cold!" Hoping there was enough time for the pilot to direct the missile away.

But it was too late. Falco watched in horror as the missile struck. There was a flash of light, a loud BOOM, and an upwelling of smoke. Mohammadi shouted: "Praise be to Allah!"

There was nothing Falco could do except deliver a formulaic report. "Good bombs, target down, mission successful." Even though it *hadn't* been entirely successful. The target was dead all right, but so were three civilians, and that sucked. Falco stood and shouldered his pack. "It's time to go. Lead the way."

Falco could have led the way himself, but it made sense to put Mohammadi out front, rather than expose his back to the Afghan. The second trail was steep, and treacherous in spots. Falco did his best to avoid thinking about the women including who they were, why they'd been there, or anything else about them. His job was to focus on the exfil. Check the back trail. Call for a helo. Run, and run some more. And, when Falco fell, he got back up. His ankle hurt. He ran anyway.

The process was automatic and seemed to take care of itself. A Blackhawk helicopter swooped in to pick the men up as they arrived on the flat ground at the foot of the slope. The rotors blew dust in every direction and a door gunner was eyeing the hill behind them.

Mohammadi boarded first followed by Falco. The JTAC fell into a seat and stared at the floor as the helo lifted off. It took fifteen minutes to reach Forward Operating Base Hope. Colonel Campo was waiting next to the pad as Falco dropped to the ground and winced. The ankle hurt like hell. The men shook hands. They had to yell in order to be heard over the racket. "Congratulations!" Campo said. "You nailed the bastard."

"I also killed some civilians," Falco replied darkly.

"There was some collateral damage," Campo admitted. "But it couldn't be helped. The missile was on the way when the civilians entered the kill zone. And that, Major, is what you will tell the investigation board."

"I'm being grounded?"

"It's SOP. You know that."

"Yeah," Falco agreed. "I know that."

"Don't worry," Campo assured him. "You'll be fine. Hell, I'm putting you in for a medal! Come on ... There's a bottle of Jack in my desk. We're going to have a drink."

"Thank you, sir ... I'll meet you there."

Falco turned, saw that Mohammadi was standing by himself, and went over to shake hands. "Thank you, Jawan. You're a brave man. And a good brother. We're pulling out ... You know that. Go away from here. Far, far away."

"I will," Mohammadi replied. "As for the women, do not worry, they are in *Jannah* (paradise) with my sister."

After parting ways with Mohammadi, Falco crossed the camp to the headquarters bunker, and followed the ramp down into the murk. If there had been a worse day in his life he couldn't remember it. People stared, radios murmured, and the air force swallowed him up.

CHAPTER THREE

Eielson Air Force Base, Alaska, USA

Eielson Air Force Base was located 26 miles southeast of Fairbanks, Alaska. The primary purpose of the base was to host an allied forces training exercise called "Red Flag Alaska." And, because of the war, such efforts were even more important than they'd been before.

So when Red Flag pilot Kathy Parker requested permission to go home for her grandmother's funeral, she'd been granted *three* days rather than the five she'd requested. And as the SUV entered the base, Parker felt lucky to get that.

After thanking a fellow Red Flag pilot for the ride, Parker made her way into the terminal, and went to check in. "Yes, ma'am," the sergeant behind the desk said, as he eyed her paperwork. "Your Mighty Mouse will board in 15 minutes. Have a nice flight."

Parker knew there wouldn't be any amenities on the plane. So she went to get a Grande coffee and some candy bars. She was eating one of them, and sipping coffee, when a captain sidled up to her. He was in uniform and wearing a Judge Advocate badge. That meant he was a lawyer. *Here we go*, Parker thought. *Maybe I should put the ring back on.* "Hi," the JAG said brightly. "Are you on the flight to Fairchild?"

"Yes," Parker replied. "I am."

"Work or pleasure?"

"Neither one. My grandmother died. I'm going to her funeral."

Parker knew some men would hit on her anyway. Fortunately the lawyer wasn't one of them. "I'm sorry to hear about your loss," he said. And, after chatting about how difficult such times were, he drifted away. And that was fine, because Parker wasn't ready for another man yet.

Once they called the flight Parker followed a line of people out through a door and onto the tarmac beyond. The C-17 Globemaster III, or "Mighty Mouse," was 174 feet long and had a wingspan of nearly 170 feet. The plane was powered by four Pratt & Whitney engines. They would get Parker to Spokane, Washington in five hours give or take.

As Parker followed the line out to the plane she was struck by how normal everything appeared. Even though battles were raging in Asia, the Middle East, and Europe, Eielson remained an island of tranquility. And that was good because the next Red Flag exercise was coming up fast. Some people thought the program should be cancelled so that the participants could join the fight. Others believed that cross-unit training was a critical investment that would payoff later on. Parker was one of them.

Parker followed the line up a ramp into the C-17's cavernous interior. Crates occupied the center of the cargo bay and inward facing seats lined both bulkheads. Open seating allowed Parker to grab a spot in back which, as every pilot knows, is the safest place to be in a crash.

Not that Parker expected a crash. But who knew? The truth was that Parker didn't like to fly, not unless *she* was at the controls. Did that make her a control freak? Probably.

Once Parker's seatbelt was fastened, and her earbuds were in, she closed her eyes. Would anyone notice the way her hands gripped the seat as the transport took off? No, she didn't think so.

The flight was uneventful—for which Parker was thankful. Security had been increased since the beginning of the war which meant her mother couldn't drive a car onto the base. After the plane put down Parker had to take a shuttle from the terminal to the off-site parking lot where her mother and other civilians were waiting.

Mary Parker had been pretty once. Parker knew because she'd seen the photos. But a marriage to a bad man, followed by decades of drudgery, had left their mark. Now she looked puffy and tired. After a brief embrace Mary pushed her daughter away. "Look at you... So pretty! Even in a pair of overalls."

"It's a flight suit, Mom."

"You won't wear it to the funeral will you?"

"No," Parker said patiently. "I brought a dress. It's in my carryon."

"Good. Let's go home and change. The service is at 4:00 PM. I told your uncle to push the time down in case your plane was late."

The next half hour was spent catching up. Life in Spokane was increasingly difficult. Mary had been planning to retire from her administrative job at a local tech company. But the corporation had a "mission critical" contract to assemble components for a top secret weapons system. And the company's CEO wanted Mary to stay on.

There was rationing too, on everything from gas to eggs, so Mary was considering the possibility of building a chicken coop. Then there were the relations. Parker was an only child, but part of an extended family, most of which was dysfunctional in one way or another.

And as Parker listened to her mother describe the latest goings on, she was reminded of why she had joined ROTC. A free education was part of it, but so was the opportunity to escape her family. College was followed by flight school, a tour in the Med flying missions over Syria, and a handsome pilot named Greg. There was a whirlwind romance, followed by marriage, and a return to civilian life. "Major Mom." That's what Greg called her.

But Greg's death in a car accident left Parker without him, without children, and without a job. And that's where the offer from a company called OpenAir came in. OA had a contract to supply the air force with so-called "Aggressor Squadrons," which could replicate what it was like to engage Russian aircraft like the Su-30. And, in some cases, OA could provide actual aircraft for American pilots to hone their skills on. The company's collection of MiG-21 fighters was a good example of that.

Of course the Red Air planes were worthless without pilots who knew how to fly them. So after Greg's death Parker signed with OpenAir, spent three months in training, and was rewarded with a "graduation ceremony" held in a bar. That's why she was living and working at Eielson. The Red Flag exercise was coming up, and OpenAir was going to supply "bad guys" such as herself. "Here we are," Mary announced, as they pulled into the drive. "What's it been? Six months since you were here?"

"Something like that," Parker agreed, knowing that her mother wanted her to come home more often. The ranch style three bedroom house was more than twenty years old, but well maintained, and a symbol of what Mary had accomplished all on her own. "I like the red geraniums," Parker said. "They make for a wonderful splash of color."

The interior of the house was clean, tidy, and frozen in time. Pictures of Parker hung everywhere. There were photos of Parker as a cheerleader, Parker as a ROTC cadet, and Parker as a pilot. But there were no pictures of her with Greg. Why was that? Mary claimed to like him. Yet not a trace of her daughter's marriage could be seen.

Had Mary been lying? Or was she hoping that a *new* man would appear? One who wouldn't want to see pictures of his predecessor. There was no way to know other than to ask… And Parker wasn't about to open that door.

"You can change in your room," Mary told her. "We'll leave at three."

Parker walked down the hall and into a room that was decorated high school style. Lady Gaga posters were taped to the wall next to a montage of jet fighters. Pom Poms hung from the bed frame, glassy-eyed animals stared at Parker from a bookcase, and running trophies lined a shelf. How many times had she urged her mother to get rid of that stuff? Dozens. But nothing changed.

After shedding her flight suit, Parker slipped into the simple black dress she'd brought for the occasion, plus some matching heels. Then she looked in the mirror. A pair of green eyes stared back at her. They were steady, and what else? Wary? Yes. And for good reason. The only thing she was sure of was war—and the part that she would play in it.

The weather was good—and Parker's family had agreed to a graveside service. It took thirty minutes to reach the cemetery. It was well kept and surrounded by an eight-foot tall wrought iron fence. A gently curving street led them through an acre of grave markers to the point where a hearse and a line of cars were parked.

Maddie Struthers had been Mary's mom, and a positive force in Parker's life. "You can ride a bike, you can pull a 4.0, and you can get through college."

It didn't matter what Parker aspired to, Maddie was sure that her granddaughter could achieve it. Or said so anyway. And Parker loved her for it. Now after 84 years of life, it was time to say goodbye.

Relatives were there to greet Parker, to tell her how good she looked, or to inquire about her job. And Parker did her best to be sociable. But it was difficult. They were part of the past. And if Parker *had* a family other than her mother, it consisted of the pilots and ground crew she worked with.

The minister was a middle-aged man who, to his credit, had actually taken the time to learn something about Maddie's life. Family anecdotes had been woven into a well-constructed eulogy that brought people to tears. Then, at Maddie's request, he read a poem titled "And you as well must die," by Edna St. Vincent Millay.

> And you as well must die, beloved dust,
> And all your beauty stand you in no stead;
> This flawless, vital hand, this perfect head,
> This body of flame and steel, before the gust
> Of Death, or under his autumnal frost,
> Shall be as any leaf, be no less dead
> Than the first leaf that fell, this wonder fled,
> Altered, estranged, disintegrated, lost.
> Nor shall my love avail you in your hour.
> In spite of all my love, you will arise
> Upon that day and wander down the air
> Obscurely as the unattended flower,
> It mattering not how beautiful you were,
> Or how beloved above all else that dies.

There was more. But nothing so moving. Once the service was over people mingled for a while, traded stories about Maddie, and shed an additional tear or two. Then came the awkward hugs, the inevitable goodbyes, and the silly stuff. "We'll see you soon! Send me a picture of your plane ... Dress warmly!"

Mary appeared at her side. "Are you ready to go?"

"No," Parker replied. "I want to visit Greg's grave."

Mary nodded. "I'll meet you at the car."

Parker knew the way by heart. Greg's resting place lay outside the boundaries of the family plot, but not far away. Parker knew that if her husband existed, he was elsewhere, and free to live whatever kind of life was available to him.

"Until death do us part." That phrase seemed like a not so tacit admission that regardless of what people might hope for—relationships *weren't* forever.

Would there be another? *Could* there be another? Yes. A year and a half had passed since Greg's death. And, if the right person appeared, Parker would welcome that. *But not now,* she told herself. *Not until the dying is done.*

Parker knelt in front of the headstone, kissed her right index finger, and placed it on her husband's name. "Watch your six, baby … Fly safe."

Mary eyed Parker as she entered the car. Looking for tears? Probably. And a lot of them had been shed during the months since Greg's death. But an equilibrium had been reached. And when Parker returned to Eielson she'd be looking forward, rather than back over her shoulder.

Mexican food, especially *authentic* Mexican food was hard to come by in Alaska. So Mary took Parker out to eat at Mama's, which was one of their favorites. The restaurant was crowded and noisy, but the food was wonderful.

The initial conversation centered around Mary's job, and her decision to put retirement off for a year. Then the discussion turned to Parker, and her situation. "Where will they send you?" Mary wanted to know. "Will you be an instructor? Like you are now?"

Parker knew that was what her mother was hoping for. So she said, "That's a possibility. I should know more within the next thirty days."

"What have you got planned for tomorrow?" Mary inquired.

"Nothing much. I thought I'd sleep in and goof off. Why do you ask?"

"Danny called. He heard you were in town...I said you'd have dinner with him."

"You *what?*"

"You dated him in high school, so I figured you'd like to see him."

"You figured wrong," Parker replied. "Danny is a nice guy, but I don't have those kind of feelings for him."

Mary looked aggrieved. "So you're going to dump him?"

Parker sighed. It was impossible to dump someone she didn't have a relationship with. Parker didn't want to hurt Danny's feelings though. And that put her in a difficult spot. "Okay, I'll go to dinner with Danny. But stay out of my love life. Do you read me?"

Mary made a face. "You sound like a military officer."

"I *am* a military officer."

"You'll have a good time," Mary promised. "I know you will."

Parker made no reply. The conversation felt forced after that, and Parker was happy when the dinner ended. True to her word Parker slept in the following morning. Then, after a shower, she made her way to the kitchen. A note was taped to the fridge. "There's plenty to eat, take whatever you want. Love, Mom."

So Parker fried some bacon, scrambled some rationed eggs, and sat down at the kitchen table. A small TV occupied one corner of it. Mary's dinner companion? Yes, and that was sad. *But no different from the way you live,* Parker thought, as she turned the set on.

CNN appeared. And, not surprisingly, the news was focused on the war. Thanks to the use of drones the networks could show their viewers what was taking place in ways that hadn't been possible before. So the public could watch from above as an American tank company ground forward, artillery shells rained down around them, and a battalion of infantry followed behind.

"The Russians are waiting just over the next rise," the narrator said. "The Russians have more tanks than we do ... But allied planes own the sky. And that should make an important difference. Casualties are expected to be heavy as NATO forces attempt to push the *Kantemirovskaya* Tank Division out of Latvia..."

A shell scored a direct hit on an American M1. Parker watched in horror as the tank exploded, the turret lifted off, and a gout of flame shot straight up. She couldn't stand anymore and turned the set off. Would *she* wind up in Europe? She'd do her part if so. And the allies would win if they could control the skies.

Parker's food was cold by then, and her appetite had disappeared. Parker took the plate to the garbage. She felt guilty about the eggs.

Later Parker took a cab to the mall, went shopping for things that were hard to find in Fairbanks, and was shocked to see so many empty shelves. She'd heard about hoarding, and widespread shortages, because of the war. Car companies were producing army vehicles. Clothing companies were sewing uniforms. And decaying steel factories were coming back to life. Parker left the mall with half the items on her list.

After eating lunch at the mall Parker returned home and took a nap. When she rose it was time to get ready for the date with Danny. He was right on time. After a polite chat with Mary the couple left.

Danny had always been into sports and cars. So Parker wasn't surprised to discover that he was driving a Cadillac Escalade. "The war started three weeks after I took delivery on it," Danny explained sheepishly, as he opened the passenger side door for her. "And there's no market for SUV's now. So I ride my bike to work."

"That sounds like fun if the weather is good," Parker replied. "Where do you work?"

"At the Cadillac dealership," Danny replied with a smile. "I sell Escalades."

Danny closed the door and went around to the driver's side. Parker watched him get in. He was in good shape. Danny had been a standout football player, and that's how they met. Parker was a cheerleader, and Danny was the team quarterback, as memorialized in lots of teen movies. Except that Danny wasn't an egotistical jerk, and Parker wasn't a mean girl.

They'd never been close though... Not the way some high school kids were close. Maybe that had to do with the fact that Danny had plans to stay in Spokane, while Parker wanted to leave.

The dinner went better than Parker thought that it would. Danny was still nice, if somewhat unsophisticated, and getting ready to enter the Marine Corps. "I'll be heading off to boot camp in a week," he told her. "How 'bout *you*? You're on active duty I suppose."

Parker explained that no, she wasn't, but soon would be. The conversation turned to old friends after that, what they were doing, and what they wanted to do. Danny was still in touch with the old crowd, which made him a font of information. Most were supporting the war effort in one way or another. One girl however, the one everyone called "The drama queen," had made a place for herself in Hollywood.

When dinner was over, and they were about to leave, Danny cleared his throat. "Thanks for coming. I just wanted to say how special you are, and that the times we had together meant a lot to me. I should have told you that back in high school, but I was afraid to. Now, well, it's time to tidy up."

Parker felt a lump form in her throat. Danny had been in love with her. And, as he entered the marines, he was saying good-bye. *Why?* Because he expected to die. "Thanks, Danny... That means a lot to me. I'll be thinking of you. Do you like pushups? I hope so."

Danny forced a smile. "You're going to outrank me."

Parker nodded. "Yes, I will... So watch your step."

They laughed and Danny took her home. Parker waved as he drove away. Would Danny survive? And how about *her*? Parker pushed the thought away as she turned and entered the house. Mary was seated on the couch in the living room. "So," she said. "How did it go?"

"It was good to see him," Parker replied. "He's joining the marines."

"*And?*"

"And nothing," Parker replied. "I'll see you at five in the morning...My plane leaves at seven."

Morning arrived all too soon and, due to gas rationing, traffic was light. As before Mary was forced to enter the off base parking lot. Her eyes brimmed with tears. "I love you, Kathy...Take care of yourself."

It had been no different when Parker had left for the flight school and the Middle East later on. Parker leaned in to kiss a cheek. "You too, Mom. Don't worry, I'll be fine."

Then, knowing that short goodbyes were the best goodbyes, Parker got out of the car. She waved as Mary pulled away. Parker looked up as a delta winged F-15 Strike Eagle roared overhead. The weekend was over. The war was waiting.

CHAPTER FOUR

Chantilly, Virginia, USA

Mornings were always the same, and Lori Okada liked it that way. With rare exceptions she awoke three minutes before the alarm went off, rolled out of bed at exactly 5:00 AM, and was out the door by 5:15. Her run was five miles long. That put her back in the apartment by 6:00. Then it was time to check for text messages and email. Not the ones from her mother in San Francisco. Those could wait.

The messages Okada looked forward to were from the mysterious PaulT. They'd met on line, but had never met in person, and Okada wasn't sure why. Was it the way she looked? Something she'd said? Or was PaulT a jerk? Whatever the reason the sonofabitch had her on an intermittent reinforcement schedule, and it was working.

But, maybe there was a reason for PaulT's frequent absences. Maybe he was a spook. CIA (Central Intelligence Agency) headquarters weren't that far away, and a war was raging, so anything was possible. *No,* Okada told herself. *Chances are that he's a professional gambler, a drug dealer, or an escaped convict.* Her mail came up. Nothing. She sighed.

The rest of the routine consisted of taking a shower, getting dressed, and eating a quick breakfast. Then she left for work. Okada's car was the same six year old KIA her mother had given her as a high school graduation present, and she'd driven throughout college. It would have been nice to have something newer, but NRO analysts weren't overpaid, and the Washington D.C. area was an expensive place to live. So the KIA would have to do.

Okada had been able to minimize her commute by living close to work. The National Reconnaissance Office was located just south of Washington Dulles International Airport, in a group of unassuming office buildings.

But even though the complex didn't *look* important it was. Because the National Reconnaissance Office (NRO), the National Geospatial-Intelligence Agency (NGA), the Central Intelligence Agency (CIA), the National Security Agency (NSA), and the Defense Intelligence Agency (DIA) were the so-called "big five" U.S. intelligence agencies. And Okada was proud to work at the NRO, if only as a junior analyst in the Imagery Intelligence Systems Acquisition Directorate. A name which had a strangely Russian feel to it.

Okada took the usual turn, got in line behind some other cars, and waited to show her ID. After parking the KIA in the usual spot Okada made her way across the parking lot to the building she worked in. It was a nice spring day, and there was no need to take her umbrella.

Once inside Okada had to pass through *another* checkpoint before making her way up to the third floor, where she waved her card at the reader mounted next to the office door. There was a click, followed by a green indicator light, and Okada went inside.

Okada was typically the first person to arrive. And that day was no exception, although some of her peers had been forced to pull an all-nighter. Her boss Duane Blakely was one of them. He was tall, rumpled, and badly in need of a shave. "Good morning, Lori," Blakely said gravely, as he turned his back on the communal coffee urn. "No, that's bullshit. There ain't noth'in good about it."

Okada frowned. "What's wrong?"

"You haven't heard? North Korea attacked South Korea an hour ago."

"Shit. Did they use nukes?"

"Not yet... But they're pounding Seoul with long range artillery. Thousands of civilians have been killed. And the Russians overran Estonia."

"Is there anything I can do to help?"

Blakely took a sip of coffee, made a face, and poured what remained into the sink. "No, thanks. I know it isn't sexy, but I'm counting on you to keep an eye on everything north of Shenyang."

That was bullshit of course. The truth was that Blakely didn't *trust* Okada to handle the important stuff—because she was the departmental newbie. That's why she had responsibility for one of the few areas in the world where everything was calm. But Okada understood, and nodded her head. "I'm on it, *and* I'll make some coffee."

After making coffee Lori took a cup to her cubicle which, in keeping with her lowly status, was the worst work station on the floor. Her cube faced a wall rather than a window, and was two square feet smaller than the rest. It *was* located in a corner however, and Okada liked that. There were three monitors on her desk, plus a terminal, and a Snoopy mug filled with colored pens. Okada put her purse in a drawer and sat down.

Like other intelligence agencies the NRO had its own highly secured computer network consisting of fiber-optic and satellite communication channels which couldn't be accessed via the public Internet. The network allowed NRO personnel and civilian and military intelligence analysts all over the world to access the agency's systems and databases.

Internet access was monitored, controlled, and handled separately. As Okada entered her password, she knew that every keystroke she made would be logged, and her activities would be audited on a regular basis.

Okada spent the first fifteen minutes plowing through routine emails and submitting reports. Once her chores were complete she went to work. Except it *wasn't* work. Not to Okada. The process of analyzing images was part science, part art, and endlessly engaging.

So it was with a sense of anticipation that Okada began to review the most current imagery for her corner of the world. Most of the photos were from satellites, but others had been acquired by high-flying spy planes, and a variety of drones.

The first area Okada wanted to examine was the 284,000 square mile Chukotka Autonomous *Okrug* (county). The area had a climate similar to that of western Alaska. So why, given how remote the Chukotka was, had the Russians sent a division of motorized troops there? Especially given the fighting in eastern Europe? That was the question Okada had voiced two days earlier at the directorate's 5:00 PM scrum.

And the answer, according to a well-coiffed rep from the Mission Integration Directorate (MID), was widely available on the Internet. A snarky comment that generated titters and made Okada blush. "According to the press release that the Russian *Stavka* (high command) put out," the rep intoned, "the troops are in Chukotka for a winter training exercise called 'Red Ice.' The folks at the pentagon figure that the Russians are preparing for what is sure to be a hellacious winter. Even if some of us have forgotten about what happened to Napoleon's troops in 1812, and to Hitler's armies in 1941, the Russians haven't. They call the winter 'General Frost,' and plan to take full advantage of it."

And that was that. Or it should have been. But Okada remained unconvinced. World War III was underway, and the *Stavka* chose to announce what 15,000 troopers were up to?

Seriously? But junior analysts were to be seen, not heard. So Okada was forced to back off.

That wasn't the same thing as giving up however. Okada put a sat image taken 24 hours earlier up on monitor one, and the most recent version on monitor two, and compared them. Then she repeated the process using thermal imagery. It was easier to read, but still inconclusive. Russian army vehicles were moving around. "So what?" That's what Blakely would say.

Okada chose to look at the same area from a higher altitude while using a program that could not only compare before and after images, but flag the differences between them. And there were lots of differences. Icebergs had moved. So had ships. And thousands of vehicles. All of which was normal.

But there were other objects too … Identical constructs that were moored in the Russian ports of Anadyr, Petropavlovsk, and Magadan. They were rectangular in shape and highly reflective. Okada thought they were floating docks at first.

But, after enlarging the photos and running a reverse image search, Okada realized her mistake. She was looking at concrete pontoons! Dozens of them. After additional analysis Okada estimated that each pontoon was roughly 360 feet long, 75 feet wide, and nearly 30 feet tall. To be used for *what?* After back searching three days' worth of data Okada realized that the constructs were multiplying during the hours of darkness. As if more of them were being launched every day.

Okada ran a comparison search, discovered that nearly identical pontoons had been used to construct the 520 floating bridge in Washington State, and began to work a variety of related search terms. It took less than a minute to find a Wikipedia article titled: "Bering Strait Crossing." The first sentence read: "A Bering Strait Crossing is a hypothetical bridge or tunnel spanning the relatively narrow and shallow Bering Strait between the Chukotka Peninsula and the Seward Peninsula in the U.S. state of Alaska."

Okada felt a sudden surge of excitement as she read the words. *A bridge!* The Russians were going to build a freaking bridge across the strait! And, since the strait was only 53 miles across at its narrowest point, the feat could be accomplished with 777 pontoons. Except that Okada's data included *850* pontoons. Why so many? Because the Russians were manufacturing spares, that's why. They knew the Americans would try to stop them— and some of their pontoons would be destroyed.

The discovery was so amazing, and so important, that Okada felt compelled to find Blakely and tell him about it. He was in his office, and preparing to go home, when Okada entered. He frowned. "Hi, Lori ... Can this wait?"

"I don't think so," Okada told him. "I came across something big. *Very* big."

Blakely sighed. "Okay, give me the five second version."

"The Russians are going to build a floating bridge between the Chukotka Peninsula and Alaska."

Blakely blinked. His eyes were rimmed with red. "What makes you think so?"

Okada told him. And, to Blakely's credit, he let her finish before dropping the hammer. "Look, Lori ... I appreciate your enthusiasm. But here's the situation. The United States is fighting on three continents. We're stretched to the limit. So we have to prioritize. And this qualifies as a one on a scale of one to ten. Continue to monitor it. And, if you see a smoking gun, let me know. I'm going home." And with that, Blakely left.

Okada was more than disappointed, she was pissed. If 850 fucking pontoons didn't constitute a fucking smoking gun, then what the fuck did?

But orders were orders, and Okada had hers. The search began. Okada spent the rest of the day and half the night searching, enhancing, and cross indexing images without success. Was that because the information didn't exist? Or because she didn't know what to look for?

The second possibility followed Okada home, and was foremost in her mind when she returned to work the next morning. After wading through the usual to-do's Okada launched an Internet search for people who might be able to help her. There were lots of hits. But, after fifteen minutes of analysis, Okada narrowed her choices down to three engineers: Alan Reeves, Mitchell Conway, and Carol Simms.

All three had been involved in the 520 project in Washington State, and could theoretically answer her questions. But that was as far as Okada could take it without straying from her box. Something Blakely would almost certainly object to.

So Okada took an early break, and went out to the KIA, where her cellphone was hidden under the front seat. By checking Facebook and LinkedIn Okada developed leads that eventually produced phone numbers for two of the three engineers. And, by entering "67" before dialing each number, Okada could place anonymous calls. Simms failed to answer. But the call to Reeves went through. "Hello? This is Alan Reeves."

"My name is Mandy Howell," Okada lied. "I'm doing research on floating bridges, and I wondered if you'd be willing to answer a few questions."

"About the 520 bridge? That's old news ... And there's plenty of stuff on the Internet."

"Not exactly," Okada replied. "I'm writing an article about the feasibility of building a bridge across the Bering Strait."

Reeves laughed. "Okay, I can imagine that on the cover of Popular Science, but the concept isn't practical."

"Why not?"

"Who would pay for it? There's no economic demand for a shortcut between Chukotka and Alaska. Never mind the fact that we're fighting Russia in Europe. Problems like that don't bother pie-in-the-sky Conway though … He wrote a self-published book on the subject. You can buy it on amazon. It's a buck ninety-nine if I remember correctly."

"What you say makes sense," Okada told him. "And I'll be sure to include your perspective in the article. But I'd love to get a couple of quotes from Mr. Conway too … Have you got a number for him?" Okada held her breath. *Did* Reeves have the number? And would he share it if he did?

"Sure," Reeves said. "Hang on … I'll dig it up." He returned moments later, and Okada could hardly believe her good luck. Conway's area code was 202! That meant the engineer was living in Washington D.C., even though he was a resident of Seattle, according to LinkedIn. "Thank you," Okada said. "I really appreciate it. Can I call you back if I have more questions?"

"Sure," Reeves replied. "Say hello to Mitchell for me. The Bering Strait thing is whacky—but he's a good engineer."

Okada was twenty minutes into a fifteen-minute break, and had to hurry back to the office. There was regular work to do—and plenty of it. As a result Okada wasn't free to call Conway until noon. The call went to voicemail. "Hello, this is Major Mitchell Conway, with the U.S. Army Corps of Engineers. I can't take your call at the moment, but leave a message, and I'll get back to you. Thanks."

Okada broke the connection. Now she knew more. Or thought she did. Based on the content of Conway's voicemail message, it sounded as if his National Guard unit had been called to active duty. She would try him again.

It was 3:30 by the time Okada could return to the KIA and place another call to Conway. It went through. "This is Major Conway."

After lying to Reeves Okada was tempted to lie again, but knew that would be stupid, since it might be necessary to contact

Conway again. She played it straight. "My name is Lori Okada, and I work for the NRO."

"A sky spook," Conway said. "Cool."

Okada had never heard anyone refer to NRO personnel as sky spooks before. "I'm calling in regards to your work with floating bridges," Okada told him. "Would you be willing to answer some questions?"

"I would if you're who you claim to be," Conway replied. "How 'bout I call the NRO and ask for you?"

Okada wanted to avoid that if she could, since Blakely would object. "That would be fine," she assured him. "Or, we could get together for a drink, and I'll show you my ID."

"Works for me," Conway responded, before naming a bar near the Pentagon.

The last thing Okada wanted to do was battle rush hour traffic. But the opportunity was too good to pass up. She agreed to meet Conway, and returned to the office.

There were advantages to being the departmental newbie, one of which was to leave work on time, because Blakely invariably assigned the high priority stuff to senior analysts. So Okada was free to sign out and hit the road.

The drive was every bit as bad as Okada expected it to be, but she managed to make it on time. As Okada entered the bar she saw military paraphernalia on the walls and uniforms all around. "Ms. Okada?"

Okada turned to find that Conway had approached her from behind. He was tall, with graying hair, and a friendly manner. "How did you recognize me?" Okada inquired.

"You were the only Asian American female to enter the bar at precisely 1800 hours," Conway replied. "Follow me, I have a table in back." After working their way through the crowd, they arrived at a tiny table with two chairs leaning against it. "I was serious," Conway said, once they were seated. "I need to see some ID."

Okada offered her NRO identity card and her driver's license. Conway grinned as he gave them back. "Okay, sky spook, what's shaking?"

Okada met his gaze. "According to Alan Reeves you are not only an authority on floating bridges—you are an ardent proponent of building a span across the Bering Strait."

Conway stared at her. His eyes widened. "Holy shit! The Russians are going to build one!"

The speed with which Conway arrived at that conclusion surprised Okada, but shouldn't have. He knew who she worked for—and what she wanted to discuss. "Maybe," Okada allowed cautiously. "Please remember that this conversation is classified."

Okada didn't have the power to classify the discussion—but Conway didn't question the pronouncement. He nodded. "Of course. So, tell me … What are the bastards up to?"

Okada told him about the pontoons, the way they continued to multiply, and the similarities between them and the ones used to construct the 520 bridge. Conway listened intently. "Okay, I agree. Based on your description, it sounds like they're going to throw a span across the strait during the ice melt. But you know that. What do you want from me?"

"I know it," Okada agreed. "But my boss is skeptical. So I need more evidence. Maybe I have it, but don't know that I have it, if that makes sense."

"It does," Conway assured her.

"Tell me what to look for," Okada said. "What kind of things would the Russians do before the construction process can begin?"

"Everything you need to know is in chapter three of my book," Conway replied. "It was number 1,365,296 on amazon earlier today. But here's the summary: It's safe to assume that the Reds have contour maps of the sea bottom that were originally created for their submarines to use. However … Because the area we're talking about is notoriously hard and uneven, it's possible that they used a survey ship to remap the section of the sea floor that will lie directly beneath the bridge.

"Before starting construction the Russians would drop sea anchors at carefully chosen locations. The anchors will play a critical role in keeping the bridge where it's supposed to be. There are winds to worry about, tides to consider, and huge chunks of drifting ice to contend with.

"And finally," Conway added, "I would expect to see a military dimension to the construction effort. I didn't cover that in my book for obvious reasons. But once the Russians make a start, they'll have to defend what they build. So it's logical to assume that you'll be able to identify military preparations over and above the troop concentrations you mentioned earlier. Their efforts may be subtle—but they'll be evident."

"They'll be evident." Those words were still ringing in Okada's ears as she returned to the office. She could tell that some sort of hush-hush operation was underway, because two of Blakely's top people were huddled with the director as she passed his office.

The conversation with Conway had been an eye opener. Okada knew what to look for now—and couldn't wait to go after it. Had the plans for the bridge been sitting on a Russian hard drive? Waiting for the right set of conditions to come along? Yes, Okada concluded. They had.

But the earliest start date would have been the day the war began. Because up until that point the Politburo had no reason to begin work. So Okada took that as the starting point for her search. She was looking for a vessel which would have been cruising back and forth between Chukotka and Alaska.

By accessing the NRO's databases Okada was able to determine that the Russians had an Ivanov class "research" vessel operating off the east coast and, according to the data summary, the *Yantar* (Amber was equipped to carry out subsurface mapping missions—as well as gather Intel on American submarines. That made the *Yantar* the ideal ship for the sort of mission Conway envisioned.

But after reviewing all of the relevant data regarding the spy ship's movements Okada came up empty. The *Yantar* had been in the area, and passed through the strait. But the ship had been cruising north to south rather than east to west. That was disappointing to say the least.

Okada got up and took a trip to the vending machines, where she purchased a Pepsi. That's when she had an epiphany. The Russians *knew* that the Americans knew about the *Yantar!* Therefore they wouldn't use the spy ship for their survey. No, they would use some other vessel. One that had the necessary equipment but a lower profile.

Moments later Okada was back at her desk entering new search terms. And it didn't take long to come up with a trawler called the *Sea Harvest*. There the ship was, two weeks into the war, cruising east to west along the path the bridge would have to take!

Could Okada *prove* that the *Sea Harvest* was mapping the sea floor? No. But if she managed to acquire a sufficient number of supporting data points, Okada would be able to pitch Blakely without embarrassing herself.

Locating the sea anchors used to secure the bridge should have been easy, since each would be marked with a buoy. The problem was that both American and Russian fishermen used hundreds, maybe thousands, of buoys each year. Most of them were recovered, but some broke free. That meant there were drifting, as well as stationary targets to track.

Still, even with those variables to deal with Okada was able to succeed by setting up a search based on the type and size of the buoys used for the 520 project in Washington State. They were larger than standard fishing floats, and made of metal.

Once the computer knew what to look for it could produce a map overlay. The buoys were like a string of beads that ran from Chukotka to a point just east of the Diomede Islands. And that was as far as the trawler could go without attracting the attention of the U.S. Coast Guard. *I'm two for two,* Okada thought, as she went to work on Conway's third indicator, which was military preparations over and above the Red Ice exercise. She lost track of time.

***

Okada was walking on a beach. Waves rushed in to break around her ankles, gulls wheeled above, and she could feel the sun's warmth on her face. It was a beautiful place, and she didn't want to leave. But a voice was calling to her. "Good morning, Lori … It's time to rise and shine."

Okada opened her eyes to discover that she wasn't on a beach in California. She was face down on a desk. *Blakley's* desk. Okada sat up to discover that her boss was seated across from her. He smiled. "You look like hell."

Lori ran fingers through her hair. "I *feel* like hell. But I'm first in line to see you."

"Yes, you are. What can I do for you?"

"It's about the bridge," Okada told him. "The one I mentioned the other day. It's real, and I can prove it."

Blakely's eyebrows rose. "Okay, lay it on me."

Okada brought up the necessary visuals on his monitors and took him through the process. That included the secretive mapping, the sea anchors, and how Conway said they would be used. Then Okada brought up images of two rusty freighters. One was docked in Petropavlovsk, and the other was moored in Magadan. "They're Q-ships," Okada told him. "Like the special services ships that we used against the Germans and the Japanese during World War II. They *look* normal—but looks can be deceiving.

"According to the CIA both ships were overhauled and retrofitted with vertical missile launchers. The people in Langley didn't know why of course... They assumed that the freighters would be sent south to attack allied shipping. But I believe their actual purpose is to defend the bridge against American planes."

"There are a lot of assumptions in your case," Blakely observed. "You *assume* the trawler was mapping the sea floor, you *assume* those buoys are connected to bridge anchors, and you *assume* those freighters will be used to defend the bridge."

Okada felt her spirits plummet. Even with all of the additional evidence she'd fallen short. Blakely grinned. "Don't look so glum. I'm sold. Those bastards plan to build a bridge across the Bering Strait, and invade North America! That's a big deal... And the DNI (Director of National Intelligence) is going to go ape shit."

Okada sat up straight. "Does that mean I can have a cube with a window?"

Blakely formed a steeple with his fingers. "That would be nice, wouldn't it? But what about the fact that you ignored my instructions and ventured off on your own? Yes, you lucked out, but what about the next time? Enjoy your wall."

Okada left. What she needed was a shower and some sleep. She was in the KIA, and about to pull out, when her phone chirped. "Hello?"

"This is Paul."

"Paul, *who?*"

"Paul Thomas... You know, PaulT. I realize this is short notice, but would you have dinner with me?"

"That sounds like fun," Okada replied. "Tell me something, Paul, if you don't mind. Where have you been?"

"I'm a pilot. I was working for Federal Express, but the air force called me up. I'm flying tankers now. I just got back from, well, somewhere. What kind of work do *you* do?"

"I'm a data manager," Okada replied.

"Cool. Let's meet at Jakes' in Centreville. Is six okay? I sent a photo so you can pick me out of the crowd."

Okada brought it up. PaulT was easy to look at. "Six is fine," Okada told him. "I'll see you there." Then she drove home. Suddenly, out of nowhere, there was something besides work to look forward to.

CHAPTER FIVE

Somewhere over Canada

Falco was seated with his back resting against the port side of the C-17 Globemaster, as the transport flew north to Eielson Air Force Base in Alaska. The plane was carrying forty-one passengers, plus thirteen pallets of cargo, one of which was strapped to the deck in front of him.

Falco closed his eyes and let the strains of Haydn's Symphony No. 100 surge through his earbuds. The title of the piece was, ironically enough, "*Military.*"

But soothing though the music was, it couldn't wash away the emotions associated with the decision rendered the previous day. "It is our finding that the missile fired by Lieutenant Ted Cavanaugh was already on its way, when the civilians appeared, and Major Falco attempted to abort the mission. However," the report continued, "Major Falco's decision to call in a strike on a spot where civilians could suddenly appear shows a lack of good judgement. Based on our findings we recommend that Falco review the rules of engagement, standard operating procedures, and SPINS (special instructions)—and adhere to them in the future. Major Falco is cleared for a return to duty."

It could have been worse. Everyone said so. And Falco knew they were correct. In retrospect Falco realized that his desire for revenge for the so-called "Valentine's Day Massacre" at Camp

Hope had clouded his judgement. The finding was a stain on his record, and he wanted to erase it. But his new job, which was to take command of the JTAC training detachment at Eielson, wasn't likely to provide that kind of opportunity.

Hours passed. Falco awoke to the sound of the pilot's voice. "We're ten minutes out from Eielson Air Force Base. Please stow your personal items and check your seatbelt. You can expect broken clouds and a surface temperature of 40 degrees. Have a nice day."

Falco had done his homework. Eielson was located 26 miles southeast of Fairbanks and was host to the 354th Fighter Wing which had primary responsibility for the Red Flag-Alaska training exercise. And that was coming up in a week. So JTAC trainees would be arriving from all over the world. Some would speak English and some wouldn't. *Oh, goody*, Falco thought. *That'll be fun.* Falco felt little more than a gentle thump as the 585,000 pound transport touched down. That was the end of the trip— and the beginning of the check-in torture.

Thanks to Falco's rank he was allowed to skip the generic "Welcome to Eielson" orientation lecture scheduled for the next day. But he was required to visit personnel, and fill out a dozen forms. Then it was off to finance, followed by a quick stop in the chaplain's office, and a trudge to medical. That was where Falco discovered that his medical records had been lost. Would the air force find them? Yes, but only after Falco completed a three page form.

It was late afternoon by then, and time for Falco to collect his luggage and call a cab. The driver took him to the hotel most people stayed in while coming or going. His room was worn, but clean, and the staff was helpful.

A call was enough to schedule a meeting with Colonel Ricardo Austin for the following day. What kind of officer was Austin anyway? All Falco knew about his new commanding officer was that the pilot had a rep as "a tight ass."

Falco left his bags in his room and went to eat at Burger King. It was one of the few restaurants within walking distance. Transportation was something he would have to make arrangements for. There hadn't been enough time to drive his car up from his parents' place in Eugene. What he needed was a beater...A truck with four-wheel drive would be ideal.

Then it was back to the hotel for what he hoped would be a good night's sleep. It wasn't. Falco had suffered through various versions of the same dream for weeks by that time. There were slight differences but the basic components never changed. He was on a high point looking down. A man appeared. Then, as Falco gave the order, the man morphed into a woman. Or a child. That was when Falco warned them. Or tried to. Except he had no voice. The missile hit, the innocent died, and he awoke drenched in sweat.

"Shit happens." That's what other JTACs told him and Falco knew they were right. Anyone who chose his line of work had to accept the fact that there were too many variables to fully control. So the truth was that what Falco acknowledged to be his own poor judgement bothered him more than the civilian deaths. Would that look good in a newspaper? No. But it was true.

Falco still felt tired when the alarm sounded. But the appointment with Austin was set for 0830, so Falco had to roll out of the king sized bed, and get his butt in gear. He took a shower, got dressed, and walked to Burger King. There was a high overcast, and the temperature was barely over forty. Falco heard a sustained roar as an F-16 took off.

Once breakfast was over Falco set off on foot. After getting lost, and asking a civilian for directions, he spotted the correct building and went inside.

A senior airman sent Falco down a hall to a small waiting room located outside a door with Austin's name on it. A captain and a chief were already there, and both of them were allowed to see Austin before Falco did. Was Austin running late? Were the other two men working on mission critical tasks? Or was Austin mind fucking him? There was no way to know.

Finally, after Falco had been waiting for thirty minutes, Austin came out to greet him. The colonel had "the look." He was tall, slim, and handsome. But not *too* handsome.

Falco figured Austin was on the short list for a star. And, given the number of causalities the United States was taking, he wouldn't have to wait long.

"Welcome to Eielson," Austin said as they shook hands. "Please follow me."

There were no pleasantries, just "please follow me." Austin led Falco down a hall, and into a small conference room. It was decorated air force style with plaques, photos of planes, and government-issue furniture. "Take a load off," Austin instructed. "Two members of your team are going to join us—but I'd like a word with you first."

Here it comes, Falco thought, *the shit bomb is about to fall.*

"I'm familiar with what took place in the village of *Em Bal*, and the findings that came through yesterday," Austin began. "The air force has processes, procedures, and protocols for a reason Major ... And as the officer in charge of JTAC training it will be your responsibility to ensure that students understand the three Ps and follow them. A task made all the more important by the fact that some of your students will be from other countries."

Austin paused as if to let Falco process the words. "What they learn, or *don't* learn, could cost lives when the time comes to fight next to them," Austin cautioned. "Do I make myself clear?"

"Yes, sir," Falco replied.

"Good," Austin said. "Enough of that. I'll see if the others have arrived."

Once Austin left the room Falco discovered that he had a death grip on his chair. He forced himself to let go. The lecture had been difficult to listen to. But it was understandable. For all

Austin knew Falco was a careless piece of shit who might contaminate every student he came into contact with.

Falco's thoughts were interrupted as a first lieutenant and a master sergeant entered the room. Falco stood as Austin followed them in. "This is Lieutenant Carrie Johnson," Austin said, "and this is Master Sergeant Greg Oliver. Both of them have been through the Red Flag wringer before. I suggest that you follow their advice. Lieutenant ... Sergeant ... This is Major Falco. Please treat him gently."

It was a joke. But Johnson nodded as if coddling majors was a sensible thing to do. She wore her hair pulled back into a bun. Her face was long, narrow, and serious.

Oliver on the other hand had a big grin on his face. He had black hair, broad shoulders, and dark skin. "No problem, sir," Oliver said. "We'll return Major Falco in good condition."

"Excellent," Austin replied, as he turned to Falco. "I have a meeting to attend. Johnson and Oliver will take you on the tour, and introduce the rest of the team. Red Flag is almost here and I'm depending on you. Let me know if you run into any problems." And with that he was gone.

Johnson led the tour which took them to a building half a mile away where there was a small office with Falco's name on the door, a maze of cubicles for use by JTACs who weren't in the field, and a workroom where a tech was busy working on a radio.

Falco did his best to remember names and job titles as he was taken from place to place. The final stop was a conference room with a map mounted on one wall. Johnson was ready with a rather pedantic presentation. "Eielson is home to a large number of wings and squadrons," she said. "Including the 354th Fighter Wing. Our mission is to prepare U.S. and allied aviation forces for combat in a variety of environments. An important part of that effort is hosting joint forces combat training events on the Joint Pacific-Alaska Range Complex.

"There are three tactical ranges including Blair Lakes, Yukon, and Oklahoma. Taken together they incorporate more than 68,000 square miles, 28 threat systems, and 225 targets for range and exercise operations. Do you have any questions?"

"Yes," Falco said. "The colonel mentioned that we will be training foreign nationals as well as American personnel. What can you tell me about that?"

The answer was a lot. For the next half hour Falco listened as both Johnson and Oliver told war stories about Japanese JTACs who could barely speak English, Brits who drank too much, and a Mongolian who insisted on sleeping outside.

That was to say nothing of the complexities of dealing with pilots from Australia, Canada, France, Germany, India, Italy, Malaysia, the Netherlands, New Zealand, Norway, Poland, the Philippines, Singapore, South Korea, Spain, Sweden, Thailand, and Turkey. All of which served to emphasize what Austin had told him earlier: "What they learn, or *don't* learn, could cost lives when it comes time to fight next to them."

Even though Falco would have preferred to stay, and deal with the shitload of paperwork that was multiplying in his inbox, he had to find a place to live. And start looking for a vehicle. The answer to the first problem was a complex called Randolph Pointe. It was located on-post and close to his office. The perfect place for a bachelor.

After signing on the dotted line, and exiting the manager's office, Falco ran into an old friend. News traveled quickly in the air force, and Falco could tell that Major Ron Randal knew about the *Em Bal* airstrike, and the resulting investigation. The pilot made no mention of the incident however, and was quick to extend an invitation. "I'm going into Fairbanks this evening... Would you like to come? We could have dinner and catch up."

"That would be great," Falco told him. "Where should I meet you?"

"Right here," Randal said. "We're going to be neighbors. Would 1730 be okay?" It was.

Falco spent the rest of the afternoon checking out, hauling his gear to the apartment complex in a taxi, and looking at trucks online. There were two possibilities on base. Falco made appointments to inspect both the next day. Then, at the agreed upon time, he went to meet Randal. Both wore civvies.

The pilot had a bus sized Lincoln Navigator which he had driven to Alaska from Fairchild Air Force base in Spokane. His wife was going to fly in later that week, so Randal was baching it until then. They drove up Richardson Highway with the turgid Tanana River flowing past on their left. As they entered Fairbanks Falco saw that the city was mostly flat. And thanks to the time of year, Alaska's third largest city was free of snow.

After exiting the highway Randal drove to a bar called "The Prop Wash." It was located next to Ladd Army Airfield, and a favorite among military and civilian pilots. A propeller was mounted over the front door. As Falco followed Randal into the converted warehouse he saw a plane dangling from the ceiling. "It's a Cessna 165 Airmaster," Randal said. "One of the prop jobs bush pilots used back in the thirties."

"Kathy Parker and her pilots are at the bar," Randal added. "They're going to play the part of aggressors during the Red Flag exercise. So you'll be working with them. Come on, I'll introduce you."

Falco noticed that one of the male pilots had a ponytail. "Are they air force?" he inquired.

"Most of them are in the reserves," Randal explained, as they crossed the room. "Which means they will be called up. But for the moment they're civilians working for a company called OpenAir. It's been supplying rent-a-pilots to Nellis for some time. Now, what with the shortage of qualified aggressor pilots, OA is under contract to support Red Flag too."

As Falco got closer he couldn't help but notice the way half a dozen men were clustered around Parker. The reason for that was obvious. Parker had strawberry blonde hair, a softly rounded face, and a figure that even a flight suit couldn't conceal.

Parker turned as Randal called her name. And that was when Falco saw a pair of green eyes pivot his way. It sounded as though Randal's introduction was coming from a long ways off, and Falco felt like a schoolboy as he shook Parker's hand. "This is Major Dan Falco," Randal said. "Otherwise known as Wombat."

"It's a pleasure to meet you," Parker said. "What do you fly?"

"Falco isn't pretty enough to be a pilot," Randal interjected. "He's a JTAC."

The civilian pilots laughed, and Falco forced a smile. "I washed out of flight school. So I spend my time telling dot chasers like Major Randal when to pickle the bombs."

Parker smiled. "While getting shot at … It's a tough job. Can you join us for a beer?"

Randal said, "Yes," and Falco was struck by the skillful way in which Parker had covered for him. But rather than stand there, and gape at her, Falco was careful to pull back to the edge of the crowd where three pilots were seated at a table.

The group included a civilian named Dennis Lynch. He was three sheets to the wind, and bragging about his sexual conquests. The latest being an E-4 at Eielson. "That's one of the things I like about being a civilian," Lynch exclaimed. "Military regs don't apply! I can screw as many enlisted women as I want."

Most of the people in the group laughed. Falco was the exception. And Lynch took notice of that. "What's the problem, Major? Do you fuck women? Or do you prefer to blow them up?"

All the conversation came to a stop. It seemed that everyone knew about Falco's error, civilian pilots included. Falco rose, turned away, and was walking towards the men's room, when a heavy hand fell on his shoulder. "Don't turn your back on me, coward," Lynch grated.

Falco turned. His voice was icy. "You're drunk. I suggest that you stand down."

"Oh, *really?*" Lynch demanded sarcastically. "Well, I *suggest* that you kiss my ass."

"Lynch!" Parker's voice cut through the country western music that was playing in the background. She shouldered her way through the crowd. "Back off... That's an order."

"We're off duty," Lynch replied thickly. "So you can take your order and shove it up your awesome ass."

And with that Lynch launched a roundhouse right. Falco saw it coming, turned his head, and felt it whizz past. Falco's move morphed into a spin, followed by a kick. He felt the impact, and heard something crack, as his boot struck Lynch's knee. The pilot screamed as he collapsed. "Uh, oh," Randal said unsympathetically. "Asshole down."

Medics came to cart Lynch away. The police arrived shortly thereafter. They interviewed a number of witnesses including Parker and Randal. Once they collected the facts Falco was permitted to leave. And, after returning to base, he wound up having dinner at Burger King again.

Falco didn't have any bedding, so he slept in his air force issue sleeping bag, and woke feeling reasonably good. A shower followed by a shave made him feel even better. He hadn't had time to buy groceries. So rather than have another BK breakfast Falco stopped at the commissary, where he bought a breakfast sandwich, and a large cup of coffee. The food was still slightly warm when he arrived at his desk.

A priority voicemail and matching email were waiting for him. Both said the same thing. He was to report to Colonel Austin at 0900. Falco sighed. Austin knew about the fight. Falco ate the sandwich, chased it with coffee, and began work on the inbox. The pile of paper was an inch lower by the time he departed.

The streets were busier than they had been, and Falco knew why. More and more people were arriving each day. He didn't know what to make of the foreign uniforms he saw. One of the people who saluted Falco was wearing enough gold braid to put a general to shame—but could have been a lieutenant for all he knew.

Falco entered the building, took a left, and made his way down the hall to the waiting room. It was 0858 and a staff sergeant was present to show Falco into the colonel's office. He took three steps forward and came to attention. "Major Dan Falco, reporting as ordered, sir."

Austin was seated on the other side of a scrupulously clean desk. He allowed the salute to hang, which forced Falco to hold it, and remain at attention. After ten seconds or so Austin returned it. "At ease." Falco spread his feet and clasped his hands behind him.

"You're starting to piss me off," Austin said. The remark wasn't framed as a question, which meant there was no need to reply. Falco didn't.

"Let me tell you something," Austin said. "Lynch won't be able to fly for six months. And there's a shortage of pilots who can fly Russian MiG-21s, Czech L-159Es, and Italian MB-339 CB trainers. So when you kicked Lynch in the knee—you kicked the war effort in the balls."

Falco opened his mouth to object but had to close it when Austin raised a hand. "Shut up. Here's the deal. I know Lynch took a swing at you, and I don't care. Each aggressor pilot is worth *ten* JTACs. So if one of them wants to kick your ass, then bend over. Do I make myself clear?"

"Sir, yes sir."

"Good. Get the hell out of my office." Falco came to attention, did an about face, and marched out. The day was off to a great start.

Falco made his way outside, zipped his jacket against the cold, and walked toward the commissary. The plan was to buy a cup of coffee and return to the office. Then he would meet with Johnson and review the personnel assignments for Red Flag.

That's what Falco was thinking when a siren began to bleat, and the trailer mounted C-RAM installation at the end of the block swiveled toward the west. The acronym stood for Counter Rocket, Artillery, and Mortar. The system consisted of radars linked to a 20mm Phalanx weapon system. The gun produced a sustained roar as it threw 4,500 rounds per minute into the air.

There was a loud BOOM as something ran into the curtain of shells and exploded. Unfortunately the incoming weapon was only 200 feet away by then ... And the explosion combined with the damage done by flying shrapnel destroyed the C-RAM. Falco was stunned. What the hell?

More explosions were heard. They came in quick succession. Eielson was under attack! But by *what?* Falco looked up half expecting to see Russian bombers passing overhead. But no, the sky was empty. Missiles then, fired from who knew where.

Columns of smoke were rising beyond the buildings to Falco's left. It seemed that most of the missiles were targeted at the runways ... And that's where dozens of Red Flag planes were parked! What remained of the C-RAM was on fire. It blew up as the flames found the reserve ammo supply.

Falco turned and ran toward the airstrip. It was only a block away. And Falco's worst fears were realized. At least a dozen fighters had been demolished. Firefighters were spraying foam on them. A nearby building was on fire too, and as three airmen arrived on the scene, Falco waved them forward. "Come on! There could be people in that building!" Sirens continued to bleat as the men ran. North America was under attack.

CHAPTER SIX

Pevek, Chukotka Autonomous Okrug, Russia

Then city of Pevek was many things—including Russia's northernmost town, an administrative center, and a fading seaport. But Pevek was something else too. It served as the temporary headquarters for General Anatoly Baranov's New Dawn Brigade. The unit that was going to step off the Bering Strait bridge, and plant the Russian flag on U.S. territory.

Baranov and his staff were seated in the army's regional command center. It was located underneath Pevek's government building. The original construction effort had been carried out by prisoners drafted from gulags back in the late 1950s. A time when the USSR faced the threat of nuclear war. According to local legends some of those political prisoners were buried under the floor. But so what? They had to be somewhere. "Play the recording again," Baranov ordered, and the technician obeyed.

The attack had been carried out by two of Russia's *Akula*-class multi-role nuclear attack submarines. Each was armed with twenty 3M-54 *Kalibr* missiles. And from their positions in the Bering Sea the boats had been able to strike at both Eielson AFB outside of Fairbanks, and Elmendorf AFB in Anchorage.

The purpose of the attacks was to destroy as many planes as possible prior to the invasion. And, thanks to the wonders of technology, each cruise missile was equipped with a video camera. That allowed Baranov and his aides to see what each weapon "saw" as it fell from the sky. The officers had seen the montage before. But they still cheered every time an American plane exploded. "That'll teach the bastards," a crusty major growled, as an F-16 was vaporized. "We're going to beat them like a drum."

Baranov agreed but knew it wouldn't be easy. How would the Americans respond? With violence of course. But where would it fall? On Anadyr? Petropavlovsk? Magadan? Or on all three locations? There was no way to know. Meanwhile American attack submarines would be searching for the boats that launched the missiles. And the Russian subs would be waiting. Baranov wished them luck.

Baranov stood as the montage ended. He turned to the slightly built civilian who had been shadowing him for days. "Well, Boris ... What will you scribble?"

Boris Dudin was a correspondent for the Russian News Agency, TASS. He'd been sent along to cover the eastern front for the citizens of the newly reconstituted USSR, and for the sake of history, which was very much on Baranov's mind. "I will tell them about our victory, Comrade General."

"But not *too* much," Baranov replied. "The missile attack, yes, but nothing more."

"Of course," Dudin said. "We must maintain the element of surprise."

"Good. Grab your bag ... We're going to Petropavlovsk."

After leaving the government building Baranov and his party were taken to the airport where they boarded a military version of the Yak-42 three-engined passenger jet. There was a communications section up front, backed by a tiny galley, and rows of leather upholstered seats. The flight to Petropavlovsk would take five hours. Time Baranov would use to cope with the never ending river of effluent that flowed from the Ministry of Defense.

Russia's greatest general had been Alexander Suvorov back in the 1700s. Had Suvorov been forced to write endless reports? Of course not. His job was to win battles. More than sixty of them. But no sooner had Baranov opened his laptop than Major Gotov came back to speak with him. Gotov was a big man with bushy eyebrows, a shaved head, and an eternally sorrowful expression. "Excuse me Comrade General... We have a report from the naval command in Petropavlovsk. The Americans are bombing the city."

"That isn't surprising Valery. They're after the Rybachiy Nuclear Submarine Base."

Gotov nodded. "Yes. But, it's likely that the American B-2 bombers are based at Whiteman Air Force Base, in the United States."

With the exception of American ships, Baranov was familiar with every weapons system the enemy had. So he knew that the stealth bombers could carry an enormous payload of missiles and bombs. Baranov also knew that the planes had a top speed of 628 mph. Call it 550 mph since the planes were unlikely to fly long distances at their top speed. And that raised an interesting question.

Baranov did the math in his head. Whiteman was something like 4,500 miles from Petropavlovsk. So that, divided by 550 mph, equaled a little over eight hours. Yet only *three* hours had passed since the submarines launched their missiles. The realization came as a shock. The American bombers had taken off *prior* to his missile attack! They knew... Somehow the bastards knew. But they hadn't known for long. The strike would've been launched earlier if they had. That meant Baranov no longer had the advantage of surprise. He needed to get on the ground where he could push, and push hard.

A communications officer appeared. He had blond hair and a slight build. "The American B-2s unloaded two Massive Ordinance Penetrator (MOP) bombs on the sub base, sir. And the airport in Petropavlovsk is under attack. Our people believe the Americans are dropping *Matra Durandal* runway penetration bombs on it. The pilot requests permission to divert."

"Tell him to continue on," Baranov replied. "Tell him that I have faith in his skills."

The lieutenant looked doubtful. "Yes, sir." He disappeared.

Dudin was seated opposite Baranov and had witnessed the whole thing. "Your dedication to duty is most impressive, Comrade General."

Baranov shrugged. "A great deal is at stake, Boris. It's clear that the Americans know what we're up to. And I need to be in Petropavlovsk in order to ensure that our plan is successful. Write this down. We have three reasons for invading Alaska. The first is to seize control of the American oil and gas wells. Armies *feed* on oil, Boris. It's like mother's milk."

Dudin had a laptop and his fingers flew. "And the second reason?"

"American forces are fighting in Asia, in the Middle East, and in Europe. Every soldier, every tank, and every plane that they send to Alaska will weaken their forces elsewhere."

Dudin looked up. "And the final reason?"

Baranov glanced out the window and back again. His eyes were bright. "The third reason is the most important of all," he replied. "And that is to reclaim the vast piece of land that Alexander II foolishly sold to the Americans in 1867, god damn his soul to hell. Like Ukraine, it is part of mother Russia, and it *must* be restored."

* * *

Keys clicked as Dudin typed. Baranov's views regarding the reunification of the socialist republics were very much in line with those expressed by the president of the reconstituted USSR.

Thus both he and the general would be standing on firm ideological ground when the story was published. And that was a requirement that *every* TASS reporter had to keep in mind.

***

Reports continued to trickle in and they ran the gamut from good to bad. One of the submarines involved in the missile attack had returned to Petropavlovsk unharmed. But the other was missing. Maybe it too would return to the badly ravaged base, but Baranov had his doubts.

As for the air war the B-2s had escaped unscathed. But now enemy B-52s were sweeping in over Petropavlovsk. All but two of them had been intercepted by surface to air missiles (SAMs) and shot down.

On the other hand the four outdated F-22 Raptors that the Americans had sent to escort the B-52s had been able to eliminate three Russian fighters before running for home. One American fighter had been destroyed by a SAM, but the rest had escaped. And so it went.

The sun was low in the western sky by the time the Yak-42 neared Petropavlovsk. And as Baranov peered out through the window he could see that hundreds of fires were burning. His first thought was for his wife, Katya. For more than thirty years she'd followed him from station-to-station and Petropavlovsk was no different. Their rental house was in a nice neighborhood, and well away from the submarine base. Would that be enough to protect her? Baranov hoped so. His thoughts were interrupted when Major Gotov appeared. "The pilot refuses to land, General. He says that it's his patriotic duty to protect your life."

Baranov felt a surge of anger and stood. "It's *his* life that the weak kneed sonofabitch is worried about," Baranov said. "The man isn't fit to wear a uniform. Give me your pistol."

Gotov doubled as one of Baranov's bodyguards, and was carrying an army issue MP-443 *Grach* pistol under his left arm. He drew the weapon and offered it butt first. "There is a round in the chamber, Comrade General."

"Thank you," Baranov said, as he accepted the weapon and made his way to the front of the plane. Technicians turned to look as Baranov went forward to open the cockpit door. Two steps carried him to the spot that was centered between and slightly behind the pilots.

Baranov chose to ignore the pilot, who was seated on the left, so as to focus his attention on the copilot. He was young and had high Slavic cheekbones. "How many hours have you flown?" Baranov wanted to know.

The lieutenant looked nervous. "About fifteen hundred, sir."

"Excellent!" Baranov exclaimed. "So, you can land a plane like this one?"

"Yes, of course," the copilot replied.

"And that includes a wheels-up emergency landing?"

"Y-y-yes, sir."

"Then prepare to do so," Baranov said, before turning to his left.

The pilot saw the nine millimeter pistol swivel in his direction, and like everyone else on board, he was aware of Baranov's reputation. His voice quavered. "Please, sir . . . I'll do whatever you say."

"It's too late for that," Baranov said. "The chain is only as strong as the weakest link . . . And *you* Captain, are a very weak link. Never fear, I understand the need to maintain the plane's cabin pressure, and I will take that into account as I shoot you."

The pilot was struggling to release his harness when Baranov fired. There was a loud bang, followed by an eruption of bloody brain tissue, as the bullet traveled down through the pilot's skull to lodge somewhere below. The dead man slumped forward as the copilot flew the plane. He was looking straight ahead.

Gotov was waiting outside. Baranov returned the gun. There was blood on the barrel. "Pass the word ... Tell everyone to strap in. It's going to be a rough landing." Then Baranov entered a lavatory to wash his hands.

"What happened?" Dudin inquired, when Baranov returned to his seat.

"The pilot fell ill," Baranov said. "But never fear ... The copilot can land the plane."

Dudin didn't believe it. He'd heard *what?* A dull bang. Could that have been a gunshot? He didn't want to know. "I see," he said. "How unfortunate."

"Yes," Baranov agreed. "Most unfortunate indeed."

"This is the copilot," a voice said over the intercom. "Check your seatbelts and brace yourselves. We are going to land wheels up in order to skim across the craters in the runway. You may feel some bumps. Then we will come to a stop. All personnel will leave the plane via the emergency exits. We consumed most of our fuel during the flight—but the possibility of a fire remains. So move away from the plane quickly. Thank you."

Baranov liked what he heard, and made a mental note to hang a medal on the boy, assuming he survived the landing. Runway lights flashed by. The Yak hit hard—but Baranov's seatbelt held him in place.

The copilot said the plane would slide and it did. But what the youngster *hadn't* predicted was the horrible screeching sound, the avalanche of belongings that fell out of the overhead bins, and the fact that the right wingtip would scrape the surface of the tarmac.

The brief moment of contact was enough to spin the Yak around, even as it continued to surf the runway and throw showers of sparks into the air. The flight ended with a groan of tortured metal. "Everyone out," Gotov ordered. "Go! Go! Go!"

"Shall we?" Baranov inquired, as he released his seatbelt.

Dudin did his best to imitate Baranov's nonchalant manner, being careful to bring his carryon, and the laptop stored inside. Gotov was there to help both men onto the emergency slide which carried them to the ground.

The airport's fire department arrived three minutes later and began to foam the wings. But despite their efforts witnesses saw a flash of light inside the cockpit which erupted into flames. No one would bother to examine the pilot's badly burned body. Why should they? The man was a hero ... And that was that.

But what about the copilot? Would he file a report with authorities? Gotov would find out. And when Baranov saw them leave the plane together he knew the answer. The boy was no fool—and likely to go far.

A three vehicle motorcade was waiting in front of the terminal. It consisted of a well-armed GAZ Tigr (Tiger) 4X4, a ZIL limousine, and a second Tigr. Baranov entered the limo with Dudin and Gotov. As the vehicles made their way through Petropavlovsk's twisting-turning streets Baranov felt the steadily growing pressure. He regretted the damage done to the city, but his responsibility lay elsewhere. The bridge was everything. Without it there would be no invasion, and Alaska would remain in enemy hands.

Had the tug boats departed on time? Towing the pontoons behind them? If so, there was an excellent chance that Baranov's plan would succeed. But, if the vessels had been in port when the bombing began, some might be resting on the bottom of the bay.

Such matters were best kept to himself however ... Especially with a TASS reporter sitting beside him. So Baranov made no mention of his concerns as the convoy neared the sub base. It was dark by that time, but fires lit up the night, and the motorcade was forced to circle around them as refugees streamed past. That served to remind him of Katya. But, when he tried to call her, Baranov got a frustrating "All circuits are busy" message.

A great deal of defensive weaponry had been added to the area surrounding the inner harbor since the beginning of the war. Not due to the Red Ice initiative—but to defend the sub base. So they passed a number of SAM sites, some of which had seen action only hours earlier. After reaching the base, and passing through security, Baranov and his companions were taken to a nondescript two-story brick building. Gotov and Dudin accompanied Baranov into a sparsely furnished lobby, where it was necessary to show ID before boarding an elevator.

It took them down four stories into the Pacific Fleet's hardened command center. Vice Admiral Maxim Zharkov was waiting to greet them. He was a short, balding man, who was more scholar than sailor. And no wonder. When it came to operating nuclear submarines brains were worth more than brawn. The two men embraced each other like long lost brothers. "Anatoly!"

"Maxim!"

"You grow uglier every day."

"And you smell like a goat!"

Dudin watched in amazement as both men laughed. Gotov was expressionless as usual.

"So, tell me," Baranov said. "How are we doing?"

"Follow me," Zharkov replied. "I will show you."

The war room occupied a huge U-shaped space that was equipped with two dozen flat screen monitors, and an equal number of computer terminals, all manned by headset wearing techs. The combined murmur of their interactions reminded Baranov of prayers in a Russian Orthodox Church.

There were seats for visiting VIPs but the men chose to stand. "I will give you the good news first," Zharkov said. "Anadyr, Magadan, and Petropavlovsk were hit—but we managed to send some of our subs out to sea, and move others into hardened pens. The rest are hiding in the bay. Meanwhile the tug *Hercules* towed ten pontoons out to sea, followed by the *Titan* with an equal number, and the fishing trawler *Zest* with five more. Plus twenty-five pontoons left the harbors at Anadyr and Magadan for Lavrentiya."

Baranov did the math. Based on Zharkov's report a total of 50 pontoons were on their way to the Bering Strait! That was enough to begin construction. The rest would arrive in carefully timed waves during the days ahead. "Good. *Very* good. And the bad news?"

"The Americans knew what your Q ships were intended for … Both were destroyed. I will do my best to provide naval support—but most of my assets are in the South Pacific."

The news came as a blow. The Americans didn't have a navy base in Alaska … Or any surface ships in the area. But Baranov had been counting on the anti-aircraft Q ships to defend his construction crews from American fighter planes. What to do?

An idea came to him. "Barges," Baranov said. "Find me some barges. I will equip them with army Buk missile carriers—and *they* will keep the enemy at bay."

"I can find some barges," Zharkov assured him. "But the ships to tow them? That will be more difficult. There is an acute shortage of seagoing tugs. That's why we're using fishing boats to drag some of the pontoons north."

Baranov's voice was like steel. "I need them Maxim … Don't disappoint me."

Zharkov frowned. "I will do what I can for mother Russia, Anatoly."

Baranov knew that the rebuke was justified, and wished Dudin had been elsewhere. Baranov knew that while his passion was a virtue, it was a flaw as well, and could cause him to be impetuous. There had been no need to kill the pilot, yet he'd done so. And the loss of control troubled him. "Of course Maxim," Baranov said. "Forgive me, I'm tired."

"There's nothing to forgive," Zharkov said. "Come ... A shot of Vodka will set you right."

"I'd like to," Baranov said sincerely. "But I need to check on Katya ... I need to make sure that she's safe."

"Of course," Zharkov replied. "We will talk in the morning. I will have more information by then."

Baranov released Gotov and Dudin and assigned a vehicle to each. Then, in the remaining Tigr, he set off for home. It was a frustrating journey. A blackout was in place, there were lots of roadblocks, and traffic was backed up in front of each.

According to Baranov's driver, a battalion of American paratroopers had landed in the city, and were committing atrocities. That was ridiculous. But the driver believed it, and it appeared that the local officials did as well, because Baranov had to prove his identity again and again.

Finally, after forty-five minutes of torture, the 4X4 followed a winding road up to the top of the hill where Baranov's rental house was located. Much to Baranov's horror he saw that two fire trucks were parked at the summit—and an aid unit as well. A generator had been brought in to power a cluster of work lights. And there, in the harsh glare, was the wreckage of what *had* been his house. Baranov's heart sank as the Tigr came to a halt. He had to find Katya.

Baranov threw the door open and got out. He saw a neighbor and went over to speak with him. "Dimitri! What happened?"

Dimitri was an executive for a mining company. He was dressed in a robe and slippers. "We aren't sure, General ... But it looks like one of the American planes dropped a couple of bombs in the wrong place. Unless they were after *you* that is."

Baranov felt his blood run cold. The possibility that the Americans would target *him*, the same way they targeted terrorist leaders, had never occurred to him. Such a thing was possible though... He knew that. And if that was true, Katya would qualify as collateral damage. "My wife," Baranov said. "Have you seen her?"

"No," Dmitri said. "I'm sorry."

"I'm sorry too," Baranov said. "For you, and your family. Is everyone okay?"

"Yes, thank god," Dimitri replied.

"Good," Baranov said, and turned away. The work lights threw his shadow over the remains of his house. Firemen were searching the wreckage. A dog sniffed around. Baranov stepped forward, and was about to clear debris with his bare hands, when he heard her voice. "Anatoly? I knew you would be here. I came as quickly as I could."

Baranov whirled. "Katya! Where were you?"

Katya had a high forehead, big eyes, and an oval shaped face. And, after more than thirty years of marriage, Baranov was still hopelessly in love with her. "I was at Marta's house," she said. "I left as soon as I could. But there are so many roadblocks... And I had to leave the car at the foot of the hill. Look what they did to our house."

As Baranov took Katya into his arms he reveled in the smell of her. "I don't care what they did to the house. You're safe... That's the only thing that matters."

That was a lie of course... The Americans had attempted to kill him. *And* Katya. They would pay.

CHAPTER SEVEN

Joint Base Elmendorf-Richardson, Alaska, USA

Everything had changed. What had been a backwater in the war was being referred to as "the northern front" by the news media, the Red Flag exercise had been cancelled, and Falco was working with the 4th Brigade Combat Team located at Joint Base Elmendorf-Richardson near Anchorage.

The brigade had been systematically stripped of personnel during the early months of the war to reinforce other units worldwide. So rather than the nearly five-thousand soldiers the 4th was supposed to have, the combat team was down to less than three thousand. That's why "available" air force personnel were being sent to fill in. And, due to Colonel Austin's low opinion of Falco, he was available.

Fortunately the Randolph Pointe apartment complex was both understanding, and willing to return Falco's deposit. Now, only two days after the devastating attacks on Eielson and Elmendorf, Falco was going to attend the mission briefing for "Operation Shortstop."

The gathering was about to take place in a large auditorium on Elmendorf AFB with about one-hundred officers and senior enlisted people seated in front of the stage. Their newly announced commanding officer was a tall, lanky man named

Colonel George Waya. And, according to what Falco had heard, "Waya" was the Cherokee word for "wolf."

If so, Waya certainly looked the part. There was something wolfish about his broad forehead, prominent brow, and aquiline nose. "Okay," Waya told them. "By now all of you know about the Russians plan to put a bridge across the Bering Strait. We believe the purpose of the span is to move an entire division of troops into Alaska before winter comes.

"If the Russkies manage to complete the bridge, and invade Alaska, they could try to defend it with icebreakers. But our experts don't expect them to do so. They believe the enemy will allow the ice pack to destroy the span rather than commit the resources required to maintain it. If that's true they will resupply their forces by air. Something they could theoretically do using *our* airstrips. But that shit ain't gonna happen."

That announcement brought cheers and cries of "Hooah!" The latter being an army expression used to celebrate just about anything. Waya grinned. He had a lot of white teeth. "Listen up ladies and gentlemen ... Because here's how we're gonna stop 'em."

Video blossomed on the screens located above and behind Waya. An outline was visible on the left, a map could be seen in the middle, and a photo of an icy headline occupied the far right screen. "After manufacturing hundreds of concrete pontoons," Waya told them, "the Russians towed some of them out into the strait, where they are can be connected to prepositioned sea anchors. More are on the way. We will try to stop them, but they own the air for the moment, so that's a bit iffy. Assuming they manage to get a sufficient number of pontoons into place, the Russians will build a twenty-five mile long span running from the mainland to Big Diomede Island."

The map over Waya's head morphed to show a computer generated bridge that ran from the Russian mainland to a blob-shaped chunk of land. "The Russians own Big Diomede," Waya said. "And a battalion of Russian Border Guards were stationed there until recently.

"But according to recently gathered intelligence, members of Russian's Spetsnaz, or Special Purpose Forces, were infiltrated onto Big Diomede dressed as border guards. That means we'll be going toe-to-toe with a force made up of soldiers like our Rangers or Green Berets. But, we're airborne, so fuck them."

That produced more Hooahs, and shouts of "Geronimo!" which had been the rallying cry for the World War II paratroopers who preceded them.

Who dropped the ball on the Spetsnaz thing? Falco wondered. *The CIA? Yes, and military intelligence as well.* But he knew that kind of deception would be relatively easy to pull off, especially in a shithole place that no one was paying attention to.

"So," Waya continued, "our job is to land and seize control of Big Diomede. Once we do the Russians can't complete their bridge. Game over.

"*And,*" Waya added, "we're going to do it soon. *Not* next month, *not* next week, but the day after tomorrow…So pay attention. And remember that this presentation is classified."

The session lasted for an hour and a half. Falco was suffering from information overload by the time it came to a close. He had notes, but they looked like Egyptian hieroglyphics, and it would be necessary to rewrite them prior to briefing Master Sergeant Greg Oliver and Staff Sergeant Jason Lee.

But Falco's team wasn't going in with Waya's troops…No, the motto of the USAF Combat Control Team was "*First There.*" So Falco and his people were slated to parachute in twelve hours *before* the main attack, find a place to hide, and be ready to call in airstrikes by the time the army arrived. Would the Spetsnaz object to that? Most certainly they would. But only if they knew. There were lots of things to do. Falco followed the flow to the double doors. That was where he ran into Kathy Parker.

She was as pretty as he remembered her to be, and dressed in what looked like the same olive drab flight suit. A government ID card dangled from her neck. Falco saw what looked like amusement in the pilot's green eyes. "Major Falco."

"Ms. Parker ... Or are you back on the air force payroll?"

"Soon, once the paperwork comes through. Have you crippled anyone today?" It was said with a smile.

"No, never before noon. How *is* Mr. Lynch?"

"Do you care?"

"No," Falco answered. "But there's the possibility that you do."

"I *don't*," Parker replied emphatically. "Lynch is a moron."

"So we agree on something."

Parker nodded. Her expression was grave. "I read the plan. You're going in first."

"Yup, that's the job."

"We'll be there. Call on me if I can help."

Falco frowned. "Civilians? Flying combat missions? It's that bad?"

"Yes," Parker answered soberly. "It's that bad."

Falco winced. "Roger that. What's your call sign?"

"Stripper."

Falco's eyebrows rose. "Seriously?"

Parker nodded. "Yes."

"You were one?"

"Briefly, while in college. I was broke."

"And word of that got out in flight school?"

"Exactly," Parker replied. "And Wombat? Where did *that* come from?"

"Wombats are slow," Falco replied. "And so, according to my instructors, was I. That's one of the reasons I washed out of flight school."

Parker smiled. "Of course wombats are kind of cute too ... Watch your six Wombat." And with that she was gone.

The plan looked simple on paper. At 0100 on the day of the attack a submarine would launch cruise missiles at key targets on the Big Diomede. That would serve to distract the Russians as Falco and his team jumped out of a plane at 25,000 feet, plunged toward the ground at 126 mph, and opened their chutes at 3,500 feet. *If* everything went perfectly the high altitude-low opening (HALO) freefall would last less than two minutes and allow the JTACs to land undetected.

There were dangers however ... Lots of them. Starting with the possibility that the high-flying C-130 would be spotted and shot down. Then there were the risks associated with HALO jumps including hypoxia and freezing temperatures. All of the team members had made HALO jumps—but never under combat conditions. And, because special operators were in short supply, the JTACs were going in by themselves.

So the rest of that day and most of the next were spent checking gear, *rechecking* gear and, as Oliver put it, "shit proofing my pants."

Falco knew he should sleep prior to the insertion but couldn't. A hundred possibilities crowded into his mind, all of them bad. So he tossed and turned for a while. Then he gave up and listened to the *Moonlight Sonata* until sleep carried him away.

Once the alarm sounded Falco felt better than he thought he would. His camos and HALO jump suit were waiting. He left the BOQ forty-five minutes later. A blackout was in effect, so it was dark outside. A vehicle was waiting. The short ride took him to a hangar where coffee, sandwiches, and the rest of his team were waiting. "And a good morn'in to ya," Oliver said, in what he fancied to be an Irish brogue.

Thanks to the black drop suit, Sergeant Jason Lee looked bigger than he actually was. He shook his head. "Make him stop, Major ... He's driving me crazy."

"Ignore 'imself," Oliver said. "Yer man 'ates de Oirish."

"Put a cork in it," Falco said. "It's too early for impressions. Let's eat."

After the meal was over the men ran a final check on their gear. Once the free fall was over the controllers would use special parachutes to glide in. And it was important to land in the same area for the purpose of mutual defense and to get the job done.

Their radios, weapons, and other gear had been apportioned to balance everyone out. Oliver was the heaviest, so he carried the least. Lee was the lightest which meant he had to carry more. Once on the ground the gear would be redistributed.

After the check was complete, and the men had fastened their helmets, specially trained Physiology Technicians (PTs) led them out to a C-130. Once inside the plane's cargo bay it was time for everyone, crew included, to don oxygen masks for use above 13,000 feet.

The jump suit wasn't made for sitting, but Falco did his best. A PT helped him strap in. Falco let his helmet rest on the bulkhead behind him and closed his eyes. He wasn't scared—he was terrified. The HALO jump was bad enough. And the knowledge that he was going to land in Russian held territory boosted his fear index from 8 to 10.

Falco felt the plane lift off, and tried to think of something other than dying. Parker came to mind. There was something about her half smile... The slight lift at both corners of Parker's mouth made it seem like she was perpetually amused. At what? Life? *Him?* Why was she single anyway?

A PT interrupted his thoughts. "We're going on inline aircraft oxygen now." Once the proper adjustments were made Falco could relax again. Oliver offered him a thumbs up and he returned it.

The distance between Anchorage and Big Diomede was 666 miles. Six-six-six. The number of the beast. And, since the C-130 was doing about 320 mph, the drop zone was roughly two hours away. Falco closed his eyes for the second time. And the drone of the engines helped put him to sleep. So when the voice spoke into his helmet it seemed as if less than a minute had passed. "We're ten minutes out, Major ... It's time for the gear-up and pre-jump check." He was alive! The C-130 was still in the air.

The "gear-up" involved connecting to his own oxygen supply, clipping a low-hanging front-pack to his harness, and checking to ensure that all the straps and hooks were properly secured. The jumpmaster held his arm out at shoulder height before bringing his palm up to touch his helmet. That meant "shuffle to the rear." The ramp was down, and the darkness was waiting to swallow them up. Falco didn't want to go. Nor did he want to remain behind as his team fell into the night. The light blinked green, and the jumpmaster yelled, "Go!" over their radios.

They waddled forward and fell. And fell some more. Falco felt the slipstream tug at his jumpsuit, as the rush of frigid air searched for a way to get in. His arms were back, and his legs were straight. Taken together they caused his body to pitch forward. An altimeter was strapped to Falco's left wrist. But he put his trust in the main chute's automatic activation device knowing the others would as well. And that would help to keep them together.

As Falco fell he saw flashes of light and knew that the incoming cruise missiles were striking their targets. *That'll keep the bastards busy*, he thought.

Then came a powerful jerk as his chute opened and pulled him upwards. It was designed to glide for considerable distances, and would, so long as Falco did the right things. Making use of lights entailed some risk, but so did operating without them. A chute-to-chute collision could be disastrous—and there was the risk of getting separated as well. Falco kept it brief. "Lights."

Two strobes appeared. Both were a safe distance away. "Confirmed. Form on me."

Falco glanced at his altimeter. Three thousand feet. Good.

Big Diomede was shaped like an oval, with high bluffs all around, and a mostly flat top. There were some low hills though... Two in particular. The team called them "Alpha" and "Beta." Their target was Alpha.

Falco had an internally lit GPS on his right wrist. The controller used it to steer as he lost altitude. "Alpha is directly ahead. Get ready."

The ground came up quickly, his boots hit, and Falco hurried to dump the air out from under his chute. It billowed before it collapsed. "Down."

Oliver echoed the word, as did Lee. Falco couldn't see a damned thing. He removed his helmet. Cold air stung his cheeks. He pulled a black balaclava on over his head, released the pack, and opened the flap. The high priority items were on top. Falco's night vision rig being the most important. He pulled it on.

With his "eyes" on, Falco removed the compact Heckler & Koch MP7 submachine gun from the bag, and put a round into the chamber. The weapon was threaded for a suppressor—and equipped with a laser sight. Falco was ready to fight.

The next task was to grab a pair of thermal imaging binoculars and perform a slow 360. Had the team been able to land undetected? Or were Russian troops closing in? Falco felt a sense of relief. The immediate area was clear.

Now it was time to communicate. Oliver was on it. "This is Sinker-Two... We're down. Zero contact. Over." The message was encrypted, and too brief for the enemy to get a fix on.

The reply was equally short. "This is Redwood. Roger that. Out."

"Okay, Lee," Falco said. "We're going to stick out like a sore thumb once the sun rises. Let's dig in."

A thick layer of permafrost made it impossible to dig a true fighting position. The best they could do was to scrape troughs out of the crusty ice, each pointing away from the others, to form a three pointed star. That meant each team member would be responsible for a 120-degree swath of the surrounding countryside.

After that it was a matter of taking a pee, erasing their footprints, and pulling artic camo netting over their positions. The well insulated jumpsuits would have been a liability somewhere else. But they were perfect for lying on a field of ice, and Falco felt thankful for his, as he checked the time. It was 0516 and the airborne assault was scheduled to begin at 0600. Were the Russians expecting one? Or did they view the cruise missile attack as a one-off?

No, Falco decided, the Russian CO couldn't allow himself to make that kind of assumption. So, what was he doing to prepare?

Falco began a slow painstaking examination of the countryside in front of him. He was facing west, but he couldn't see the buildings there, because they were hidden by the high bluff. He'd been able to study satellite imagery however, and knew that a new "port" had been constructed on that side of the island. That's what a six-month old TASS story called it. And the U.S. Intel community hadn't seen any reason to contradict the claim back then.

But now, after closer scrutiny, it was clear that the "port" was actually designed to anchor the east end of the floating bridge. So preparatory work had begun well before the *Heath* incident" in the South China Sea.

As the sun rose higher the recently constructed "service road" was revealed. Falco could see where it surfaced on the plateau and ran west to east across the island's midriff. Miniature mountains of rock and soil marked the road's route as it passed south of the team's position, and made its way to the "new research station" on the east side of the island.

Except the research station was actually intended to serve as the starting point for the short span that would connect Big Diomede with the American island of Little Diomede a few miles away. All of which made sense, from a Russian perspective anyway.

What *didn't* make sense was the fact that Falco hadn't seen any enemy troops yet. Where were the fire breathing Spetsnaz? The team was equipped with low power, encrypted radios for interpersonal use. Falco spoke into a BOOM mike. "I have zip over here ... Have you seen anyone?"

"Nada."

"Zilch."

"Okay, radio it in. But keep scanning. This doesn't feel right."

"Don't move," Oliver said. "Drone at two o'clock north."

Every fiber of Falco's being wanted to turn and look. He didn't. Thirty seconds passed. "Clear," Oliver said. "I'll call it in."

He did. But then it was Lee's turn. "Hold still ... We have *another* drone to the south. Nine o'clock."

Falco waited for Lee to give the all clear. He didn't and the reason was obvious. Falco could hear the machine whirring directly overhead! "We're busted," Falco said, as he rolled over onto his back. The device was small by military standards, but large enough to carry a camera, and held aloft by four rotating blades. "Call it in." The MP7 produced a soft clacking sound as the green dot wobbled on the drone. The 4.6X30mm slugs tore it apart. Pieces of plastic rained down on them. "Holy shit," Lee said. "You nailed a drone! That's amazing."

"He got lucky," Oliver put in.

Falco's attention was elsewhere. Would destroying the device bring the Russians down on them? Falco didn't have time to worry about that as the steady drone of engines was heard, and a fleet of prop planes appeared. Falco spotted C-130s, Beech King Airs, a CASA C-212, and a menagerie of other civilian aircraft that Colonel Waya and his staff had pressed into service. Chutes blossomed as tiny figures poured out of them. The 4th Brigade Combat Team had arrived.

Falco felt a sense of jubilation. But the feeling was short lived. Eight Russian SU-34 fighters appeared out of the west and Falco watched in horror as the sleek planes fell on the defenseless transports. Missiles destroyed some, while guns tore the rest to shreds. *It's a trap*, Falco concluded as a C-130 caught fire. *They knew we would come, and they were waiting.*

The transport wanted to nose over. But if the pilot allowed the plane to do that the parachutists wouldn't be able to jump. So he or she was battling to keep the burning plane level as paratroopers spilled from the back. Then the transport exploded. A lump formed in Falco's throat as pieces of flaming debris fell from the lead gray sky.

"Heads up," Lee said. "There are at least six-zero bad guys coming our way... They're boiling up around those mounds."

Falco looked, saw the black dots hurrying his way, and something more as well... SAMs sleeted into the air as pop-up missile launchers appeared. A Beech King was replaced by an orange flash and a puff of black smoke.

Falco keyed his mike. "SAM launch! SAM launch!"

"Here comes the cavalry," Oliver said, as four American fighters bored in from the east. Except that *two* of them were Russian MiG-21s! Falco thought of Parker. Was she flying one of them? Of course she was... The MiGs were notoriously difficult to control, had a limited range, and were equipped with outdated avionics. The fact that the brass had sent Parker out in a 21 demonstrated how desperate they were.

Still, the MiG pilots had *one* advantage, and that was surprise. Their Russian counterparts mistook the 21s for allies at first, failed to engage them, and paid the price. *Two* 34s were eliminated in a matter of seconds. One blew up, and the other corkscrewed into the strait. But Falco had his own job to do, and things were heating up. "Hey, Major," Oliver said. "We're going to be ass deep in Spetsnaz two minutes from now."

Falco swore. Oliver was correct... Russian troops were a thousand yards away, and closing. He'd been watching the air war—and his situational awareness had suffered as a result. Falco's breath fogged the air as he spoke into the mike. "Any available aircraft, this is Wombat. Our position is about to be overrun! Requesting close air support. Enemy troops are a thousand yards west of our position and closing fast. We're popping smoke."

Oliver heard the comment and tossed a canister toward the Russians. Red smoke boiled up into the air.

"Wombat, this is Stripper and Slowboy inbound. We see your smoke."

Falco turned to look. "Stripper, you are cleared hot."

Help was on the way, but Falco knew it wouldn't arrive quickly enough to solve all of their problems. Fortunately the Russians were concentrated on the team's western flank.

Geysers of ice jumped into the air, as some of the enemy fired their AK-47s in an attempt to suppress fire, while the rest of them surged forward. One of the Russians fired a RPG and it landed just short of the American position. There was a flash of light, followed by a BOOM. A column of dirty ice shot up into the air— and Falco felt some of it land on him.

Falco knew the MP7s were worthless at the present range, and instructed the others to keep their heads down. "Save your ammo for when they get closer," Falco said. "What have we got? Two grenades apiece? Throw them downhill on my order."

It took a tremendous amount of self-discipline to withhold fire as Russians spread out and ran up the slope. But then, when they were about 50 feet away, Falco gave the order. "Grenades!" He threw his in quick succession, and opened fire once they were in the air.

Half the grenades exploded without doing significant damage, but Falco saw two enemy soldiers fall, as shrapnel cut them down. Then it was time to fire the MP7. The submachine gun's high rate of fire was perfect for the situation. More Russians fell, and the rest were forced to hit the dirt. And that was when Parker's voice came in over his headset. "Stripper is in with guns, Slowboy with bombs, from the east."

As Falco went face down on the ice the MiG-21 came in from the east. It was fitted with twin Gryazev-Shipunov 23mm autocannons. And, when Parker fired them they plowed a bloody trench through the Russian ranks, leaving little more than chunks of raw meat behind.

Slowboy's 500 pound gravity bomb was like an afterthought. It hit, took a bounce, and exploded over the soldiers in the rear. Those lucky enough to survive turned and ran.

Hundreds of American soldiers were on the ground by then, slugging it out with the Spetsnaz troopers who had been hidden underground. As a pair of F-15 Strike Eagles arrived overhead, the air war shifted in favor of the invaders. The controllers spent the next hour calling in strikes on troop concentrations, popup missile launchers, and the mortar tubes that seemed to materialize out of nowhere.

It took the rest of the day for Waya's soldiers to hunt the surviving Russians down, fight their way into clusters of underground bunkers, and secure them. Then came the task of processing prisoners—and making preparations for what promised to be a cold night.

Some of the Americans could flake out in cleared bunkers. But there was the chance that the Russians would launch a nighttime counterattack. That meant Colonel Waya had to keep half his force up on the surface and ready to fight.

Having completed their mission, for the moment anyway, the JTACs went looking for a place to take refuge. The signals company took them in … And that meant they had a relatively cozy underground bunker to sleep in. The conveniences included some crudely constructed bunk beds, floors that consisted of wooden cargo pallets, and light bulbs that dangled from the ceiling. There were personal belongings too, including sleeping bags, uniforms, bottles of vodka, and a wealth of pornographic magazines.

After eating most of an MRE, and using gritty Russian soap to wash with, Falco chose a lower bunk. The mattress was thin. And when Falco looked up the photo of a Russian girl was looking down at him. She had a pretty face. Was her soldier dead? Or had he been taken prisoner?

Falco closed his eyes. There was so much pain in the world. Sleep found him ... And so did the dreams. None of them made sense. And that was the way of things.

CHAPTER EIGHT

Chukchi Sea, 25 miles northwest of Wainright, Alaska, USA

Captain Marvin Soto stood with his feet spread as the Coast Guard icebreaker *Northern Dawn* shouldered her way between two looming icebergs, and pushed them aside. The helmsman stood a few feet to Soto's right with both hands on the chrome steering wheel. It was wrapped with white cord and looked very retro in an age when joysticks were used to steer large vessels. But even though the *Dawn* had been launched back in 1976, and refitted more than once, the old lady still retained some of her original elements. And Soto liked it that way.

He was looking out over a layer of so-called "steam fog," which occurred when a layer of cold air slid in over warmer water. "Warmer" being a relative term where the Beaufort Sea was concerned.

Soto felt the *Dawn* shudder slightly as powerful engines drove the ship's steel reinforced bow through a four-foot thick chunk of floating ice. The icebreaker could break through sheets of ice up to twenty-one feet thick if she was required to. *But that won't be necessary today*, Soto mused. The skeptics could say whatever they wanted to, but Soto had *seen* the ice pack shrink year-after-year, and he knew that global warming was to blame. Not that anyone was focused on *that*...They were too busy killing each other.

Thinking about the war caused Soto to shift his attention to what he thought of as "the abomination" mounted on the icebreaker's bow. A wisp of fog was blown away to reveal the five inch MK-45 deck gun. The weapon had no place on a ship like the *Northern Dawn* to Soto's way of thinking, but had been added a few weeks earlier nevertheless.

There had been a time when *all* icebreakers were armed. That was during and immediately after WWII. But things had changed since then. And by the time the *Dawn* put to sea in '76 icebreakers were no longer viewed as warships. The *Dawn's* purpose was to keep shipping channels open—and to serve as a platform for scientific research.

Now everything was turned on its head. The *Dawn* still had an obligation to keep shipping lanes open. But the icebreaker had been given a second and equally important mission ... And that was to serve as a submarine tender for the navy's nuclear powered ballistic missile submarines, at least two of which prowled artic waters at any given time. They, along with twelve sister subs, carried fifty percent of the country's thermonuclear warheads.

The other components of the so-called "nuclear triad" included long range bombers and land-based intercontinental ballistic missiles. Taken together those capabilities served to prevent countries like China, Russia, and North Korea from launching preemptive strikes against the American homeland. But even though Soto understood the strategic importance of his ship's new role he didn't have to like it. Soto's reverie was interrupted by the *Dawn's* second officer, Lieutenant Linda Penny. "We're coming up on Point Barrow, sir ... Requesting permission to turn onto heading 70 degrees north."

Penny was wearing a Coast Guard ball cap, and had her hair pulled back into a short pony tail. She was waiting for Soto to approve the change in course. He went over to take a look at the chart and the GPS. Not because he didn't trust Penny, but because the check was SOP. Soto nodded. "That's correct."

"Prepare to change course," Penny said, for the benefit of the helmsman.

"Very well," the helmsman said, in the time honored fashion.

"Change course to heading 70 degrees north," Penny said formally.

The helmsman turned the wheel to the right, met the turn, and made a slight correction. "Very well, ma'am. We are on heading 70 degrees north."

Soto eyed the chart. His orders were to rendezvous with the ballistic missile submarine *Nevada,* 75 miles north of Kaktovik, Alaska in the Beaufort Sea. And Soto knew that even though he wasn't excited about the trip—the *Nevada's* crew was looking forward to the fresh food, spare parts and most of all the mail that his ship was bringing to them. The poor bastards. Spending up to seventy days locked in a 560 foot long pipe with 155 other people was Soto's idea of hell. He turned to Penny. "I'm going on the tour." He held the radio up for her to see. "Call if you need me."

Penny treasured the moments when she was in command, and the last thing she wanted to do was call Soto and request help. But she would if it was necessary. "Aye, aye sir. And remember your diet."

"No cinnamon rolls on the mess deck."

"Yes, sir. That's what you said."

Soto made a face. "I hate you."

The bridge crew chuckled as he left.

The tour was a daily ritual and Soto's opportunity to check with the various departments aboard his ship. The inspection included a peek at the fitness center, a pause in front of the ship's tiny store, and a moment in the barber shop.

Other departments came in for greater scrutiny. They included the mess deck, where the smell of freshly baked cinnamon rolls called to him, and the sickbay, where Dr. Nelson had his feet up on a stool and was reading a book.

Then Soto was off to visit the engineering control room. That was the long narrow space from which the so-called "Snipes" controlled six diesel powered service generators and three propulsion gas turbines, not to mention all of the *Dawn's* critical subsystems.

Six flat screen monitors were mounted on the bulkhead, over an equal number of control panels. It was the heart of the ship, and therefore of particular interest to Soto. The Chief Engineer was off duty, which meant his number two was on, and Soto could feel the tension in the compartment.

Lieutenant Fred Norris was in his late thirties which made him old for his rank. *So* old that the engineer would have been pushed out of the service had it not been for the war. As a result the ship was stuck with the man generally referred to as "His Highness." Fortunately Norris was a competent engineer, even if his interpersonal skills were lacking. "Good morning," Soto said, as he entered the room. "How's it going?"

"All systems are performing within normal parameters," Norris answered pedantically. "Although shaft three is running two degrees hotter than optimal."

A chief petty officer was seated behind Norris. He rolled his eyes. Soto refused to take the bait. Norris was an officer, and Soto wasn't about to undermine his authority. "Thank you, Lieutenant. Let's keep an eye on that. I assume that all of the off duty engineering staff will attend tonight's showing of *Beach Blanket Bingo.*"

A cheer went up. Most of the crew loved to watch any movie that had to do with sun, beaches, and scantily clad women. Even if the movie was more than fifty years old, and most of the actors were dead. Soto waved as he left.

Soto's final stop was in what had previously been designated as the ship's science section. But rather than the marine oceanographers, biologists, and climate scholars of the past the *Dawn* was now host to a navy chief petty officer, and his band of piratical gunners mates.

Chief Wright and his men were convened in a large work room which was serving as a makeshift armory. A sailor shouted "Attention on deck!" as Soto entered, and all of them came to attention. Soto didn't get that level of respect from his own crew, nor did he feel a need to. A partially disassembled fifty-caliber machine gun was laid out on a stainless steel table like a patient in surgery. "As you were. What are you people up to?"

Chief Wright had dark slicked-back hair, a pencil thin mustache, and a square jaw. He radiated physicality. "We're going over all of the ship's small arms, sir. And, because regular lubricants can't retain the level of viscosity required in sub-zero temperatures, we're applying a product called 'Bio Artic.' It's a blend of synthetic materials and vegetable oil. Then, after lunch, we're going to do an hour of PT, and run drills on the five. *Sir.*"

Soto assumed that "the five" was a reference to the abomination that was bolted onto the forward deck. As Soto scanned the faces around him he saw that the sailors were staring at him like a band of inquisitive meerkats. And every single one of them had a mustache! Was that a sign of solidarity? A navy thing? There was no way to know. "Yes, well," Soto said awkwardly. "That sounds like a full day."

Soto's radio produced a squawking sound. He keyed it on. "This is the Captain."

"Penny here ... Can you join me on the bridge?"

Soto, who was happy to escape the armory and its mustachioed crew, was quick to agree. "I'll be there shortly."

Soto issued a cheery, "Carry on!" and left. A series of ladders took him up to the bridge where Penny was waiting. There was a frown on her face. "Petty Officer Monk is up in the crow's nest sir ... The fog parted for a moment, and she spotted a ship. Then it disappeared."

The crow's nest was an enclosed box mounted halfway up the *Dawn's* single mast. The purpose of the perch was to provide a ship's officer with a vantage point from which he or she could navigate the ship through a maze of pack ice.

But now the crow's nest had a secondary purpose, and that was to maintain a sharp lookout for enemy ships. Chances were that the vessel Monk had seen was a friendly tanker on its way south from Prudhoe Bay. But anything was possible. "Did Monk ID the ship?"

"Yes, sir. She snapped a picture." Penny pointed to a computer screen, and Soto went to take a look. Most of the other vessel was obscured by fog. But her bow was clear to see. Soto recognized the ship immediately and knew Penny had too. That's why she was worried.

The *Narwhal* was a Russian icebreaker of roughly the same tonnage as the *Northern Dawn*, but she had a very different appearance. While the *Dawn* had a white superstructure and a red hull, the Russian ship had a red superstructure and a black hull.

The *Narwhal* had something else as well ... And that was a gaping mouth complete with shark-like teeth painted onto her bow. To symbolize *what?* An appetite for ice? Or something more sinister? Whatever the reason the gaping maw gave the *Narwhal* an ominous look.

Soto went over to look at the radar screen. There were dozens of blips. Most of them were icebergs—but one of them was a ship. Which one? And *why?* Was the Russian icebreaker clearing a path for a particular ship? A convoy of ships? If so, the United States Pacific Command (PACOM) would want to know.

Or, what if the *Narwhal* was on a reconnaissance mission? The kind that only an icebreaker could carry out. Had the *Narwhal* been sent to shadow the *Dawn?* If that was the case Soto could inadvertently lead the enemy vessel to the submarine *Nevada*. The sub could take care of herself while submerged. But once on the surface, in order to load supplies, the *Nevada* would be extremely vulnerable. It was time to pass the buck. Soto turned to Penny. "Notify PACOM of the sighting, send them the photo, and provide our position. Oh, and request instructions."

Penny nodded and made her way back to the com shack. Soto poured himself a cup of coffee, climbed up into the elevated chair labeled "Captain," and stared at the whiteness ahead. Icebergs slid past to port and starboard. Some were the size of ships. That made them large enough to *hide* ships. It was a scary thought. Penny appeared at his side. "PACOM got back to us, sir."

And? Penny handed him a piece of paper. The text read: "PRIOR TO COMPLETING YOUR ORIGINAL MISSION, YOU WILL INTERCEPT AND SINK THE *NARWHAL*."

Soto could hardly believe his eyes. He read the message again. He looked at Penny. "That's *all?* There's nothing more?"

"No, sir. Nothing other than the usual mumbo jumbo."

Soto felt a rising sense of panic. The people at PACOM clearly saw the *Narwhal* as a threat. To the ship's mission? Or for some other reason? It didn't matter. The order was clear. He'd been trained for ship-to-ship combat twenty years earlier at the Coast Guard academy.

But, unlike most Coast Guard officers, Soto had never served aboard an armed cutter. So he lacked any relevant experience. An icebreaker attacking an icebreaker? Had the world gone mad? Yes, it had.

Don't panic, Soto told himself. *Think. The first step is to find the Narwhal. So do it.* Did he look confident? Soto hoped so. "Call Lieutenant Riker," Soto said. "Tell him we're going to launch a helicopter. Then I want you to summon all of the department heads to the bridge. That includes Chief Wright."

Penny nodded. "Yes, sir."

"And one more thing," Soto added. "I can't believe I'm saying this, but sound general quarters."

Penny gave the order and a klaxon began to bleat. A prerecorded voice said, "This is not a drill! This is not a drill! All hands to their battle stations!"

What ensued wasn't pretty. Most of the *Dawn's* crew assumed that some idiot had pressed the wrong button, and immediately phoned the bridge to complain, or simply ignored the announcement. That forced Soto to get on the PA system and tell the ship's company that the order was for real, and to get their asses in gear. And, since none of them had heard the captain swear before, they took the admonition seriously.

Meanwhile the ship's department heads had arrived on the bridge. All of them tried to ask questions at the same time, and Soto felt sure that such briefings were handled differently on true warships. He raised a hand. "Listen up! The Russian icebreaker *Narwhal* is somewhere nearby, and we have orders to sink her. Please don't ask me to justify that ... We have our orders and we will follow them.

"The first step is to find her. Lieutenant Riker will handle that. Once we know where the *Narwhal* is, we will close with and engage her. And be advised ... She *is* armed. Lieutenant Penny informs me that, based on the photo Petty Officer Monk took, the Narwhal has a 57mm twin-barreled AK-725 gun mounted in her bow. So once we trade shots with her we're likely to take casualties and suffer damage. That means we are likely to make extraordinary demands on our damage control parties and the medical department. So communicate with your people, and get ready. Chief Wright and Lieutenant Riker will remain. That is all."

"Okay," Soto said, once the others had left. "This won't be easy."

Chief Wright nodded. "No, it won't. But my boys are ready. You'll need to get in close though... We can only fire twenty rounds before reloading. And, since the *Dawn* isn't equipped with an automated reloading system, we'll have to do it by hand. That means humping five-inch rounds up from below, while the Russkies pound us with 57mm shells. We need to kill that bitch with twenty rounds if we can."

That was news to Soto. It shouldn't have been, since the information had been there for the asking, but the possibility that he would actually be called upon to use the deck gun had never occurred to him. "Thank you, Chief... That brings us to you Lieutenant. Lift off as soon as you can. We need to find that ship and get in close."

"You have *two* helos," Wright interjected. "Are they armed?"

"No," Riker replied. "We're flying HH-65A Dolphins. They *can* be armed. But it didn't seem necessary. Not on an icebreaker."

"Well, let's arm them," Wright responded. "Just say the word, and my boys will mount a fifty on each bird."

"I don't know," Riker said doubtfully. "What about the recoil?"

"What about it?" Wright replied. "Would you like to defend yourself or not?"

"Hold on," Soto interjected. "How long would it take to mount those guns?"

"An hour," Wright replied. "Give or take. We'll have to find a way to nail them down."

"That's too long," Soto objected. "Go ahead and install a gun on bird two. But we need to put the first helo up ASAP."

Wright nodded. "Aye, aye, sir."

"Okay," Soto told them. "Make it happen."

Riker and his copilot departed twenty minutes later. Since Riker's two person crew wouldn't be needed, they remained on the ship.

If there was anything that Riker and Lieutenant JG Mary Zimmer knew how to do, it was to find things, because that's what search and rescue helicopters do. And if they could find a swimmer in the water, then they could sure as hell find a mostly red ship. Or so it seemed to Soto. Thanks to the video feed from Riker's helo, Soto could watch as the pilot made use of the time honored expanding square search pattern. Soto saw what he *expected* to see. And that was drifting ice separated by patches of gently heaving water.

Monk had seen the *Narwhal*... But had the Russians spotted the *Dawn*? And if they had, were they following the American ship? Or on an errand of their own? *What difference does it make?* Soto thought. *We have to attack them either way. It's too bad we can't sneak up on them. But they'll spot the helo, and that will be that.*

"Bird-Dog-One to Bird-Cage...We have a visual. Standby, we're going to circle them."

Soto watched the screen with great interest as the hulking icebreaker appeared. He saw sparks of light originating from various locations on the *Narwhal's* superstructure and decks. "They're firing on us," Riker observed calmly. "The *Narwhal* is fifteen miles astern of the *Dawn* and on the same heading."

Soto took that in. It appeared that the Russian vessel *had* been following the *Dawn* and accidentally drawn even with her earlier that morning. Furthermore it seemed logical to suppose that the Russians had been tracking the *Dawn* for some time. From space at first? Possibly. And they knew the icebreaker was serving as a sub tender.

That, Soto surmised, was why PACOM had given the orders they had. The *Narwhal* was a danger to the *Nevada,* and any other sub that the *Dawn* might have to rendezvous with in the future. "Roger that, Bird-Dog-One. Well done. Return to the ship. Over."

"Affirmative," Riker said. "We are ..." And those were the last words he said. Soto saw a flash of light followed by static. The Dolphin was no more.

"Shit," Penny said. "That was a shoulder launched missile."

Soto was a peaceful man. Or he *had* been. But something changed during that brief moment of time. Something primal. He felt a sudden surge of anger, followed by an overwhelming need for revenge. "Put the ship about, Lieutenant. We're going to find those bastards—and we're going to kill them."

A sheet of ice cracked and parted as the *Dawn* began to turn. Then, as the ship came onto the new course, her speed increased. The icebreakers were approaching each other at a combined speed of 10 knots, or 11mph, at that point. That would bring them into range of each other very quickly.

Soto spoke over the PA. "We are going to engage the Russian icebreaker *Narwhal* in a few minutes. They shot one of *our* helicopters down, and killed two members of our crew. This is for our country, but it's for each one of us as well. I expect every man and woman to do their part. Remember our motto, *Semper Paratus*. Always Ready. That is all."

"The second helo is ready to depart," Penny said, as Soto returned the mike to its hook.

That meant a lieutenant named Maggie Olson was going up along with copilot Tom Drake. "What's the status on that machine gun?" Soto inquired.

"It's aboard, along with a navy gunner, and his assistant," Penny said.

"Good," Soto replied. "Clear them for takeoff."

Penny did so, which meant a second video feed was available for Soto to watch, as the Dolphin left the helipad on the ship's stern. He keyed the mike. "Bird-Cage to Bird-Dog-Two ... Stay well back from the *Narwhal*, and out of range. Your job is to show us what's going on. Over."

"This is Two," Olson said. "Roger that ... But we have a visual on a Russian Mi-17. It's airborne and headed our way. I will engage."

Events had overtaken Soto yet again. All he could do was watch helplessly, as the Dolphin turned, and the enemy helicopter came into view. And there, in the distance, was the *Narwhal* herself. Mouth agape, steaming straight at him.

Why hadn't he thought about the possibility of a Russian helicopter? *Because you're out of your league*, Soto thought. *You need to focus.*

"The lookout in the crow's nest has visual contact with the Narwhal," Penny informed him. "And the navy spotter says that we're in range."

Soto remembered what Wright had told him. "You'll need to get in close."

"Tell the gunners to hold their fire," Soto said. "We can't afford to miss."

As Soto turned his attention back to the monitor he discovered that the aerial battle was underway. Puffs of dirty gray smoke blew away from the Mi-17's belly-mounted gun pod. The camera swung to the left as Olson turned. The fifty! They were about to fire the machine gun out of the Dolphin's side door. The one they normally used for rescues.

"We're taking hits," Olson said grimly. "But we're fighting back."

Then the scene changed as the Dolphin turned. That was necessary so that the helicopter's gunner could track the Mi-17. And Soto could hear Olson shouting instructions. "*Lead* the bastard!"

Soto heard a whoop of joy from what he assumed to be the helo's copilot, followed by a terse announcement from Olson herself. "The Mi-17 is trailing smoke ... We're in hot pursuit." As the camera swung around Soto saw that it was true. His initial impulse was to call Olson off, and allow the Russians to land if they could. Then he remembered Riker and Zimmer. "Roger that, Bird-Dog-Two. Finish them off."

"The *Narwhal* opened fire," Penny announced. And when Soto looked up from the monitor he was shocked to see how close the other ship was! Soto saw twin flashes and felt the impact as Russian shells struck the lower part of the *Dawn's* superstructure. "This is the captain ... Return fire, and make every shot count!"

Soto felt the *Dawn* lurch slightly as the five-inch gun fired, and heard a muffled BOOM. A waterspout appeared off the *Narwhal's* starboard bow. "Up!" Soto said, even though the gunners were getting their orders from the crow's nest, and couldn't hear him.

Then there was a loud bang and the world seemed to explode. Soto was thrown to the deck as a razor sharp piece of shrapnel took the helmsman's head off, and someone began to scream. "I have the con," Penny said, as she stepped over the body, and took hold of the bloody wheel.

Soto struggled to his feet and looked down at his body. Was he wounded? No, there wasn't any blood. The five fired again. "A hit!" one of the watch keepers said, and that was good. But the Russian guns were firing even more quickly now, and Soto felt the *Dawn* shudder, as shells hammered her hull.

"Look!" Penny exclaimed. "*Above* the *Narwhal.*"

Soto looked. And there, tracking the enemy ship's progress, was the Dolphin! "Bird-Dog-Two to Bird-Cage," Olson said. "Chief Wright is about to drop a M3A1 shaped charge on the *Narwhal* ... Standby. Over."

Soto was astounded. Chief Wright was on the helo? Shaped charge? *What* shaped charge?

The question went unanswered as the Russians fired small arms at the Dolphin and a speck fell away from it. The charge? Yes. Then the helo was gone as it swooped out and away. Soto saw a yellow-orange flash of light, followed by a thunderous BOOM, as the upper part of the Narwhal's red superstructure exploded into flame. Pieces of fiery debris were thrown high into the air, and came twirling down to splash into the frigid sea.

The Russian icebreaker turned to port at that point, suggesting that no one was at the helm, or that the helm didn't exist anymore. The *Narwhal's* bow gun fell silent as her klaxon began to bleat. It was a plaintive sound like that of a dying beast. The *Dawn's* windscreen had been destroyed, and Soto heard a loud bang, as the five-inch fired again. He saw the shell hit the enemy icebreaker's stern and explode.

A seaman had relieved Penny on the wheel. "Order the gun crew to cease firing," Soto said. "And contact the *Narwhal* if you can. Tell them to abandon ship. We'll rescue survivors if they do. But we're going to sink their ship either way."

Penny nodded. "Aye, aye, sir."

Suddenly Soto felt cold. Was that because of the air pouring in from outside? Or an emotional reaction? He continued to shiver until someone threw a parka over his shoulders. "Always Ready." His crew *had* been ready, and Soto was proud.

The Russians decided to surrender, lowered their boats, and had no choice but to follow orders as the *Dawn's* helicopter hovered above them. Once the 67 survivors had been searched, and brought aboard, they were placed under guard in the aircraft hangar.

The Dolphin was low on fuel by the time it put down on the helipad, and Soto sent for the crew. Olson was tall, lanky, and a bit cocky. Drake wore a perpetual grin, and Wright looked the way he *always* looked, which was wound tight. His assistant stood at the back of the group.

Soto came forward to shake hands with each person. "I'm going to put all of you in for medals," he told them. "That said, I'd like a word with you Chief... What were you doing on that helicopter?"

Wright came to attention. "I was the best qualified person for the job, *sir.*"

"And the shaped charge?" Soto wanted to know. "Where did *that* come from?"

"From the magazine, sir. We brought six of them on board. They're on the inventory, sir."

Soto had been required to sign for Wright's arsenal, but hadn't studied it, and could hardly complain. "I see. Turning the charge into a bomb was very clever. *Six*, you say... Could you and your assistant use some of them to scuttle the *Narwhal?*"

Wright stood a little bit straighter. "Yes, sir."

"Good." Soto turned to Olson. "After the Dolphin has been refueled I want you to take the Chief, and his assistant over to the *Narwhal.* Then, once the charges are in place, you will fly to Prudhoe. Dinner will be on me."

"What about the *Dawn?*" Olson inquired.

"We're going to Prudhoe as well," Soto told her, "assuming the Russians don't send any planes to hunt us down. I asked PACOM to provide air cover, but they said, 'no.' Some sort of battle is taking place in the Bering Strait, and their assets are committed there."

Later, as the *Dawn* forced her way through an ice floe, Soto was able to watch live as Chief Wright pressed a button and the *Narwhal* seemed to shudder. There wasn't any audio. But Soto could imagine a series of dull thumps as the charges went off and broke the ship in half. A raging fire was revealed. The *Narwhal* was consumed by a huge cloud of steam as the wreckage slipped below the surface. "Send a message to PACOM," Soto ordered. "Tell them that the Russian icebreaker *Narwhal* has been sunk."

It was dark by the time the *Dawn* docked in Prudhoe Bay. A team of MPs had been flown in to receive the Russian POWs, and a civilian shipyard stood ready to make temporary repairs to the *Dawn's* badly battered superstructure. They did their best, but the process still consumed a day and a half, which meant the icebreaker would be late for its rendezvous with the *Nevada*.

It took ten hours of steady steaming to reach the spot where the ballistic missile submarine was supposed to meet them. And, thanks to the long artic days, the sun was still up when Soto ordered Penny to cut power. A low frequency signal was sent.

Time passed but there was nothing to see. Had something gone wrong? *Could* something go wrong? Hell yes, it could. The *Dawn* was a sitting duck for any Russian plane that came along. Such were Soto's thoughts as a report came down from the crow's nest. "A submarine is surfacing off the starboard bow."

Soto brought his glasses around just in time to see the submarine's "sail," or conning tower, rise through a hole in the ice. The rest of the boat followed and soon sat gleaming in the bright sunlight. "I have the *Nevada's* skipper on the horn, sir," an electronics tech announced. "He wants to know what took so long."

Soto thought about that. Should he tell the other officer about the way that Lieutenant Riker and his copilot had been killed? About the battle that ensued? No, Soto decided. It wasn't relevant. "Tell him we're sorry… Tell him that since the *Nevada* has been at sea for more than 45 days, the crew is entitled to a beer day, and the cold stuff is on us."

"I can hear cheering," the radioman said.

"Good," Soto replied. "Tell him that we're going to come alongside."

"We made it," Penny said, as she appeared at his side.

"Yes," Soto replied soberly. "This time."

CHAPTER NINE

Big Diomede Island, the Bering Strait, Russia

When the Russians came, they came hard. The day began when a noncom entered the underground bunker where the JTACs were sleeping. "Everybody up! Grab your weapons... The Russians are coming our way."

The announcement set off a confused frenzy of activity as soldiers hurried to pull their boots on, and make what might be critical decisions. Was it best to pack up? And take all of their gear along? Or did it make more sense to leave excess stuff in the bunker, so as to be more mobile?

The JTACs by contrast, were packed, and ready to go. That was SOP. Falco led them to the surface. The sun was up, the sky was clear, and the outside air felt cold compared to the fuggy warmth of the bunker.

In order to escape the cold breeze blowing in from the north, the team took shelter behind a cairn of frost covered rocks. Once the radios were running Staff Sergeant Lee used his Jetboil to heat water, and it was only a matter of minutes before JTACs were enjoying mugs of coffee. "Wow," Falco said gratefully. "That's good."

"It's Starbucks," Lee explained. "That's how I roll. Here, have a trail bar."

"Okay," Oliver said, as he removed one ear bud. "Here's what I have so far. The Russians are about fifteen minutes out—and coming in fast."

"Coming in *what?*"

"That's the thing," Oliver answered. "The bastards are smart, or the general in charge of them is…Because the first wave is going to arrive in roughly 100 nine-man RIB (Rigid-Hulled Inflatable Boats) boats. And the second wave will consist of three *Aist*-Class hovercraft carrying four tanks each and *more* troops."

Falco did the math. Based on Oliver's report 900 enemy soldiers were about to arrive on Big Diomede. But more importantly, from a tactical perspective, was the *way* the enemy soldiers were going to come ashore. The RIB boats would allow them to land all along the coast, rather than in concentrated groups that the defenders could go after. And the zigzagging targets would be difficult for the American pilots to hit.

Once the boats arrived the attackers would have to climb cliffs to reach the plateau. That would force Colonel Waya to divide his forces into at least a hundred small detachments in order to stop the Russians before they could regroup.

Then, while Waya's combat team was spread out, the Russian tanks would arrive. And, with no American armor to oppose them, the machines would climb up onto the plateau and wreak havoc. The thought was punctuated by the scream of jet engines as a MiG fighter passed overhead and released a pair of gravity bombs. The explosions shook the ground, and threw gouts of dirty ice up into the air, but did very little damage.

That wasn't the point however…No, the purpose of the attack was to create confusion which it certainly did. Soldiers ran every which way. *Shit, shit, shit*, Falco thought. *The person who conceived this plan is a fucking genius.*

There was no place to go, so the JTACs remained where they were. "Where's Waya?" Falco demanded. "That's where we should be." And that was true, because in order to be effective, the team needed to take orders from someone who could see the big picture—and provide guidance.

"Other people are asking the same question," Oliver replied. "And all of them get the same answer. Wolf-Six is on Big Diomede island."

Falco could understand that. Was the army's radio network 100% secure? Hell, no. Nothing was. So, in order to keep the colonel safe, his staff was being coy.

But the lack of a coherent command structure made it damned near impossible for Falco and his team to function. So what to do? One thing for sure ... Standing around sipping coffee wasn't the answer. "Okay, pack up. We'll find the colonel later. In the meantime let's make ourselves useful. We'll head for the water and give the doggies a hand."

As the men jogged towards the water they fell in with a platoon led by a youthful 2nd lieutenant. Ice crunched under their boots and the bright artic sun threw long shadows toward the west as they crossed a field of white. The JTACs stopped short of the bluff rather than silhouette themselves against the sky. As they looked out over the water they could see two dozen RIB boats bouncing over the waves as they paralleled the coast. Were others beached below?

The lieutenant went forward to peer over the bluff. Falco yelled, "Hey! Don't ..." But it was too late. A shot rang out and the officer pitched forward. "Grenades!" a sergeant yelled. "Roll them off."

After a series of explosions were heard, the noncom crawled forward to take a peek. There were no additional gunshots. "We got 'em," the sergeant said, as he stood. "But more of the bastards are on the way."

Falco saw that the statement was true. Three RIB boats had turned toward shore, and were headed for that section of the coast. Why so many? Falco went forward. "I'm sorry about the lieutenant, Sergeant. Why is this spot so popular?"

"There's a small beach down there, sir. And the slope is climbable."

"I think we should trap them on the beach," Falco said. "What's your opinion?"

Falco never got to hear the noncom's reply as columns of ice shot up all around them and a Russian Sukhoi Su-25 roared overhead. It all happened so quickly that there wasn't time to do anything other than flinch. Where the hell were the good guys anyway? Did the Russians own the sky?

Someone shouted for a medic, and Falco turned to see that two soldiers were down. Falco took a quick look around. There was no cover. So the same thing could happen again. He turned back to the sergeant. "I was wrong. I suggest that you place your snipers up here, with orders to fire on the boats. The rest of us will go down to the beach. The Russian pilots won't be able to hit us without greasing their people too."

Falco wasn't army. But because he *was* a major, and spoke with an air of authority, the sergeant obeyed. "Yes, sir ... I'll give the snipers their orders."

The noncom began to place his sharpshooters while Falco led the rest of the platoon down the 75-foot slope. It was slow going. If someone fell they would land on the jagged rocks below.

The Russians were firing bow-mounted light machine guns. Bullets snapped, pinged, and slapped the hillside as the Americans slid, skidded, and in some cases fell. A woman uttered a cry of pain when a bullet smashed her left knee. She fell onto a pile of boulders.

"Take cover!" Falco shouted, as he jumped down onto the beach. "Kill those bastards!"

A tangle of sun bleached logs offered places to hide. Falco saw one of the Russian machine gunners slump sideways. Had he been hit by a sniper?

Falco thought so, as he dashed from one hiding place to another. The MP7 was practically worthless at that range. So rather than fire it Falco went soldier-to-soldier offering words of encouragement. "Pick your shots, private … That's it. Make 'em pay."

"Make your ammo last, son …"

"Target their heavy weapons. Nice! Keep it up."

And the soldiers did their best to comply. But it seemed that there weren't very many good beaches, because *more* RIB boats were arriving on the scene, and there was an increasing chance that the defenders would be overwhelmed.

Falco keyed his mike. "Attention on the net … This is Wombat with the 2nd platoon of Bravo company. We're in heavy contact on the south side of Big D, and about to be overrun. Need immediate close air support on twenty RIBs. Over."

Falco was trying to keep his voice level, but suspected he was failing, and knew those on the net would be able to hear the small arms fire. A now familiar voice came over the radio. "Geez, Wombat, are you in trouble *again?*"

"Stripper, this is Wombat. I have you Lima Charlie (loud and clear). Go with check in."

"This is Stripper and Slowboy, two F-15Es with full loads of guns and bombs ready for the target."

Falco ducked as an RPG exploded and sent shrapnel flying in every direction. "We are at the foot of the cliff on the south side of Big D, with massed infantry closing on our position. Your target is the RIBs just offshore. You are approved to attack the entire flotilla. Ordinance is up to you. Cleared to engage."

"Stripper and Slowboy in from the north. Put your head down, Wombat … Commencing engagement."

The F-15s made repeated runs with both guns and bombs. And it wasn't long before every boat was destroyed. "Stripper to Wombat, engagement complete, targets neutralized."

As the fighters raced away they left a sea of drifting wrecks, floating bodies, and bobbing debris behind them. "Wombat to Stripper ... I owe you a beer. Over."

"More like a steak. Out." Then she was gone.

Lee appeared next to him. "We have orders, sir ... We're supposed to report to Major Lawson on the west side of the island ASAP."

Falco thought he understood. After getting the situation under control, Colonel Waya was sending reserves over to meet the Russian hovercraft and the tanks they were carrying. The best time to destroy the armor was *before* it came ashore. And that was where Falco and his team could help. Falco nodded. "Come on ... We have a cliff to climb."

It took fifteen minutes for the men to pick their way up the rocky slope and reach the plateau above. "We'll head north," Falco said, "find the road, and follow it west." He began to jog and the others followed. Speed was of the essence. How soon would the tanks arrive? And would the JTACs reach the harbor first?

Falco had his doubts about that. Any general smart enough to conceive the Russian plan of attack wouldn't be shy when it came to sending the hovercraft in. So Falco ran, and it wasn't easy, since the top layer of ice was starting to melt. His boots broke through the crusty surface with each step, and it took extra effort to pull them out.

The rattle of gunfire could be heard in the distance, punctuated by the occasional crack of a grenade. That was to be expected. But in this case the sounds were coming from all around! So even though enemy soldiers hadn't been able to come ashore on Falco's beach, they'd been successful elsewhere, and dozens of firefights were under way.

The road appeared and Falco saw that troops were streaming west. Some were riding in Russian trucks, or on Russian ATVs, but most were on foot. The scene was reminiscent of WWII footage in which American soldiers trudged along snowy roads on their way to the Battle of The Bulge.

After turning onto the muddy road the JTACs went west. The JTACs were monitoring a number of frequencies and heard the news right away. The Russians had been holding most of their fighters in reserve, waiting for the right moment to strike. And now, as the hovercraft neared the coast, the Russian planes were coming in to provide air cover. Falco stopped running. "Get those people off the road!"

The team began to wave soldiers off the road. But some of them, including an army major, chose to ignore the warnings. He ordered his troops to keep going. And it was only a matter of minutes before two Sukhoi Su-25s appeared out of the west.

They came in low. Each plane was carrying more than four tons of rockets, missiles, and gravity bombs. But it seemed that the pilots were saving those weapons for later, because they chose to employ their dual 30mm cannons instead. The big shells plowed bloody furrows through the troops on the road—and turned their vehicles into flaming funeral pyres.

Shoulder launched missiles lanced up to chase the fighters, but the pilots were firing chaff, and that drew the Stingers off. After inflicting hundreds of casualties the 25s accelerated away. Falco searched the sky for American fighters but didn't see any. Either they were engaged elsewhere or had been forced to flee.

"The tanks came ashore," Oliver announced. "And they're headed our way. Along with *more* troops."

Falco swore. The Russians still had the initiative. Lee was monitoring a different frequency. "We have new orders, Major... We're supposed to occupy the knoll we camped on yesterday, and prepare the laser designator."

The laser designator was a device that forward observers and JTACs could use to pinpoint targets for laser guided weapons. That was a vast improvement over "walking" fire onto a target with instructions like, "up fifty, right fifty."

The technology had been proven in Afghanistan and other theatres. The gear was getting lighter with each successive generation, but still felt heavy. Oliver had been carrying their unit, minus the tripod, and the sacrifice was about to pay off.

Were they going to support a field gun? No, not yet. None of the big stuff had been dropped onto Big Diomede to the best of Falco's knowledge. The more likely possibility was one or more 120mm mortar tubes. They were large enough to not only fire "smart" munitions but put the hurts on a tank. That would require a direct hit of course, thus the need for the designator. "Okay," Falco replied. "Let's go. On the double."

Falco could see the rise where the team had spent the first night. As they began to close in on it he was reminded of how exposed the knoll was. A confusion of boot prints led up to the summit and that made sense. Any elevation, no matter how minor, would invite company commanders, observers, and stragglers to climb up and look around.

So it wasn't surprising to find a three-person sniper team positioned on the low-lying hill facing west. A corporal was in charge. "Welcome to Mount Evans, sir … My name is Kramer."

"Thanks," Falco said, as he dumped his pack on the ground. "*Mount* Evans? Who is Evans?"

"That would be *me*, sir," Kramer's spotter volunteered. "After conquering the mountain I named it after myself."

"What Evans means is that he happened to be on point when we walked up the slope," Kramer explained. "However, the presence of yellow snow, and lots of candy wrappers seems to indicate that Evans wasn't the first person to summit."

Falco laughed. "A company of Russian tanks are coming this way, and we have orders to set up a laser designator here. I hope you don't mind some company."

"We'll provide what security we can," Kramer responded. "Although we don't have much firepower other than Big Bertha." The weapon Kramer referred to was a .50 caliber Barrett M82 sniper rifle with a range of nearly 2,000 yards.

"Thanks," Falco said. "We'll put in a request for some back-up. Who knows? Maybe we'll get it."

There was another threat as well... What were the Russian fighters up to? Falco looked up. White contrails scratched the otherwise blue sky. It looked as though Parker and her people were on the job. In the meantime Oliver and Lee had been busy setting up without a tripod. The designator was resting on Lee's pack with the power supply in a bag right next to it. "I have a mortar crew called Steel-Three on the horn," Lee said. "They're ready to rock 'n roll."

"Where are they?"

"About two miles that-a-way," Lee replied, as he pointed east.

"Good," Falco said. "That means they can hang bombs at least a mile forward of our position."

"I have approximately two-zero targets eastbound at nine o'clock," Kramer said, as she peered through her scope.

"Okay," Falco said. "That's their screen... Thin 'em if you can."

"Roger that," Kramer said, without breaking contact with the scope. "I suggest that you hit the dirt, sir... They have snipers too."

It was good advice. After dropping down onto the icy slush Falco elbowed his way up to the designator and placed his eyes against the rubber cups. The Russians seemed to jump forward, and by making adjustments to Lee's pack, Falco could pan left and right. "They're sending a platoon forward to provide us with security," Oliver commented.

"Good," Falco replied. "The Russians are going to get real pissy when we start to drop the big BOOM-BOOMs on them. And we're sitting in plain sight."

The sound of the rifle shot was like a period at the end of Falco's sentence. "Target down," Evans said coolly.

Except for the dead man, who fell over backwards, the rest of the Russians went face down in the slush. But there wasn't any cover to speak of so they were vulnerable. "Nail the guy on the left," Evans instructed. "The one with the binoculars."

Kramer fired. Thanks to the magnification provided by the designator Falco witnessed the way the huge slug destroyed the officer's binoculars *and* his face. And that, Falco knew, could have been *him*. Which was to say any officer who was scanning the battlefield.

"Target down," Evans said emotionlessly. "They're getting up ... Wait for it. Shoot the guy with the LMG. Hit him in the leg if you can."

Another shot rang out. The machine gunner fell. A medic responded and Kramer shot him too. "*Two* targets down," Evans said. "You are shit hot, girl! That'll teach the bastards."

But it *didn't* teach the bastards. Falco saw a flash of light, heard the sharp crack of a tank gun going off, and felt the ground shake as a round landed twenty yards in front of him. The Russian tanks were visible by then. They were lined up four abreast—and coming on strong. "They're PT-76s," Oliver said, as he eyed the vehicles through a pair of binoculars. "The '76' stands for the 76.2mm guns they carry."

Falco was impressed by the extent of Oliver's knowledge, but mainly concerned with the fact that the oncoming machines could kill him and the platoon of white clad soldiers who were taking up positions around "Mount" Evans. It was tempting to call on the mortars. But Falco preferred to let the targets get a bit closer. "Contact Bomber-Three ... Ask them how many smart rounds they have."

Lee made the call, listened to the reply, and turned to Falco. "They have twenty smart rounds, sir. And that's all."

Falco did the math. Three hovercraft carrying four tanks each meant a force of twelve tanks. So with only twenty mortar bombs to call upon, there wasn't much margin for error. But, since they *were* smart weapons, there wouldn't be much wastage. *Another* shell exploded and threw a gout of icy mud up into the air. The time had come.

The PT-76 had the slightly retro appearance of machines designed in the fifties. Falco watched with considerable interest as the XM395 Guided Munition landed five yards away from the tank and exploded. A miss! Shit.

Falco was about to put another round on the target when Oliver stopped him. "They lost a track ... Mobility kill."

And sure enough ... When Falco took a second look he saw that the 76 had slewed around and been forced to stop. That did nothing to prevent the turret and cannon from swinging around to point his way however. The 76 fired and the other tanks loosed a salvo as well. Four rounds fell within seconds of each other. One of them obliterated a three person fireteam. Body parts flew through the air, and a red rain stained the white snow.

Falco brought another bomb in on the first tank, shifted left, and selected another machine for destruction. He was pleased to see a direct hit. "Two down, and two to go!" Lee shouted enthusiastically.

That was good. But it wasn't good enough, and Falco knew it. The remaining tanks were boring in, and another rank of machines was visible in the distance. It was a race. If Falco failed to kill the lead vehicles *before* they reached the knoll everyone would die. And the Russian reinforcements were firing. Shells landed on the east side of Mount Evans, and exploded without causing casualties.

Falco struggled to maintain focus. He scored a hit on one of the lead 76 which exploded. But the next bomb was a near miss. It caused some damage but that's all. Smoke trailed behind the tank as it churned upslope. When it fired the sniper team disappeared.

Shit, shit, shit! The damned thing was so close that a near miss could kill everyone on the knoll. Falco pointed the laser and called for another round. Then he closed his eyes. There was a thunderous explosion, followed by a blast wave, and cheering. Falco opened his eyes. The 76 was a burning hulk ... And he was alive.

There was no time in which to celebrate. The second rank of killing machines was closing in. Their engines roared, and clouds of black smoke billowed around them, as the Russian tank commanders sought to hide their vehicles from the smart bombs.

Falco swiveled from target-to-target, marking each, and the rounds continued to fall. Some missed. But most were close enough to inflict damage, and give the platoon's AT4 team a chance to fire anti-tank rockets at the faltering machines.

The area west of the knoll was littered with burning tanks by then. One of them rocked from side-to-side as a ready round cooked in the turret. Some crew members had survived. They spilled out of their machines, only to be cut down by soldiers armed with assault weapons.

Falco was just dimly aware of those events however. *More* Russian troops had arrived by then, and a furious gun battle was underway, as they elbowed their way through the slush. American troops fired down on them with LMGs while the Russians fired RPGs uphill.

Meanwhile the officer commanding the 76s was using the smoke produced by the burning hulks for cover as his machines crawled between them. The strategy worked for a while because

Falco couldn't target things he couldn't see. But the moment a tank came into view a smart bomb landed on or near it. Two 76s were destroyed in quick succession.

Falco felt a sense of elation, and was about to target the remaining tanks, when Oliver shouted in his ear. "That was your last round, sir... Steel-Three is empty."

Falco swore. "What about regular munitions?"

"I asked," Oliver replied. "They don't have any."

Falco stood. The last two tanks were swerving back and forth as they threaded their way between the wrecks that littered the battlefield. The Russian tankers had every reason to believe that a laser guided weapon was going to fall on them at any moment, but they kept coming anyway. Falco had to respect their courage.

"Follow me!" Falco shouted, as he ran forward. And that was a stupid thing to do since he didn't have a plan. But attacking was better than waiting, or so it seemed to Falco, as he fired short bursts from the MP7. A Russian soldier staggered and fell. Another fired and Falco felt a bullet tug at his cap. Lee was there to shoot the man in the face.

By that time it was clear that the tankers had been taken by surprise. A machine gun was mounted on the turret of each tank. But the gunners were still inside their machines. And, as the American troops surged around the tanks, their cannons were useless.

That gave the soldiers an unexpected opportunity. Most of the Americans were carrying grenades including some thermite grenades. One enterprising sergeant took it upon himself to deliver his in a unique way. First he scrambled up onto the rear deck of a 76. Then he approached the turret, lifted the hatch, and dropped a grenade inside.

At that point the noncom should have jumped clear. But, fearing that a tanker might toss the grenade back out, he sat on the hatch. No one could see what took place inside the machine.

But it didn't take a genius to figure out that the intense heat generated by the thermite grenade was responsible for detonating one or more 76mm shells. The sergeant was thrown clear when the force of the internal explosion blew the turret up off the tank's hull and dumped it onto the ground.

That left a single tank and the six Russian soldiers who were trying to protect it. They fell one after another. Then, as the last 76 rolled over the supine body of a private named Cory Trenton, he attached a block of C-4 to the machine's belly. Once Trenton could see the sky he pressed a button on his hand held remote. The results were everything Trenton had hoped for.

The charge blew a hole in the tank's hull, and detonated every shell that remained in storage. The resulting BOOM was heard miles away. *That* battle, one of many taking place on Big D, was over.

Colonel Waya appeared on the battlefield an hour later. Medevac helicopters had arrived and departed by then, but smoke continued to dribble out of a Russian tank, and the sounds of fighting could be heard to the north. Waya was riding a Russian ATV, and accompanied by green berets on identical machines. Falco was still the senior officer on the scene, and went over to greet Waya. "Major Falco, sir... Welcome to Mount Evans."

"*Mount* Evans?" Waya inquired, as he got off the ATV. "It looks like a hill to me."

"Private Evans named it after himself. He was killed by a tank shell."

Waya winced. He looked tired. "I'm sorry," he said. "A lot of good people died today. Falco? Are you the one they call Wombat?"

"Some do, sir... Wombat seems to follow me around."

Waya grinned. "Call signs do that." He looked around. "I heard about what you accomplished here, Major. And it's nothing short of amazing! Maybe I've been too hard on the air force in the past."

Falco smiled. "I had lots of help, sir ... From my JTACs *and* your soldiers. That includes a mortar team called Steel-Three."

Waya nodded. "Thanks for mentioning them ... I'll make sure that they get some recognition."

"How are we doing, sir? Do we own this island yet?"

Waya's expression was bleak. "No, Major, we don't. The Russians have a firm grip on roughly seventy percent of it. And they're making good progress on the bridge despite our best efforts to destroy it. Some sonofabitch loaded Buk surface-to-air missile launchers onto barges. They're moored next to the bridge. The Buks are so effective our fighters haven't been able to close in. The first span will be complete in a couple of days. Once that occurs the Russkies will send heavy tanks and a battalion of troops across. That's when we'll pull back."

Falco felt his spirits sink. "We aren't going to receive any reinforcements?"

Waya shook his head. "None are available. Our orders are to hold for as long as we can. Who knows? Maybe we'll catch a break."

"Shit."

"That sums it up," Waya agreed. "Keep up the good work. I won't forget what you did." And with that Waya was gone.

CHAPTER TEN

Moscow, Russia

The seemingly endless flight from Petropavlovsk to Brastic, to Tomsk, and from there to Moscow left General Anatoly Baranov feeling tired and cranky. Knowing it would be easy to set him off, Major Valery Gotov, and TASS correspondent Boris Dudin were silent as they followed Baranov off the plane.

It was dark, and made even more so by the official blackout. A precaution that most Muscovites regarded with considerable cynicism. What fool would believe that NATO forces didn't know where Moscow was? Or where the most important targets were? All of which was summed up in a popular meme: *Chinovniki boleye opasny, chem amerikantsy.* (The bureaucrats are more dangerous than the Americans.)

The Chkalovsky Military Airport was located about twenty miles northeast of Moscow. It served as an air force base and a training center for the Russian Space Program. That included learning how to murder fellow crew members aboard the International Space Station. And they had. Now the habitat was called the *Soviet Space Station.* And the station was being controlled by the Main Intelligence Agency (GRU). A ZIL limo was waiting for Baranov and his party. "Take us to the Savoy," Baranov ordered as he slid into the back seat. "And don't dawdle."

Moscow traffic was widely considered to be the worst in the world, and only slightly better at night. But, thanks to the limo's flashing blue lights, the car made the twenty minute trip in thirty. *I shall give them oil,* Baranov thought. *Oil from Alaska. Which they will waste while driving around Moscow. But that doesn't matter. Russia will be whole again ... And that is worth fighting for.*

The Savoy Hotel looked dark and gloomy without the wash of white light that normally lit the façade. Baranov left Gotov to deal with the limo driver as he got out of the car and went inside. The night manager recognized Baranov immediately, and came forward to greet him. "Welcome back Comrade General! Your suite is waiting. A courier left this for you."

Baranov accepted the envelope and tore it open. The note was from Marshal of the Soviet Union Shoygun. "Dear Anatoly please join me in my office as 0900." It was signed "Oleg."

The "please," as well as the use of Shoygun's given name, signaled that while the marshal outranked Baranov the men were friends. And they had been since attending the General Staff Academy together fifteen years earlier.

Did the appointment have something to do with the summons that had brought Baranov clear across Russia, even as his forces battled the Americans? Of course it did. And if anyone knew why Baranov had been called to Moscow it was Oleg.

Baranov tucked the card away, said goodnight to Gotov, and chose to ignore the look on Dudin's face. The only thing worse than telling subordinates too little, was divulging too much. The manager took Baranov to a suite located on the top floor. It reeked of opulence. A style Baranov associated with the oligarchs who, in his opinion, were a cancer on the body politic. But the king sized bed beckoned, and Baranov fell asleep thirty minutes later.

Baranov woke feeling groggy, ordered breakfast from room service, and placed a call to Gotov. The major answered on the first ring. "Gotov."

"Good morning, Valery. How's it going?"

Gotov knew what "it" was without asking. "Our forces control 82% of Big Diomede, General... And Colonel Yakimov believes he can drive the Americans off the island within the next 24 hours."

"And the bridge?"

"The first span is nearly complete. I understand the pontoons have proven to be unwieldy, but the navy is muscling them into place."

"Good. And the butcher's bill?"

"Two-hundred and twenty-seven soldiers killed, four-hundred and nine wounded, with three MIA."

"It could have been worse. Stay on them Valery... Don't let up."

"I won't Comrade General."

And, as Baranov hung up, he knew it was true. Gotov lacked imagination. But he was extremely loyal and efficient. And those were wonderful qualities.

Breakfast was waiting when Baranov finished his shower. It consisted of strong tea and two open faced sausage-cheese sandwiches. He consumed both while watching 1TV. As usual the government owned channel was a cornucopia of ridiculous propaganda.

One of the stories suggested that the Russian army had been able to destroy a German tank battalion without suffering a single casualty! *Wait until the bodies start to arrive*, Baranov thought. *Then they'll know the truth.*

After breakfast Baranov donned one of the uniforms Katya had been able to salvage from the wreckage of their home, and examined himself in the full length mirror. The man who stared back had neatly cut dark hair, heavy brows, and a perpetually downturned mouth.

"You should smile more," Katya liked to tell him.

To which Baranov always gave the same answer. "About *what?*"

An army staff car was waiting out front. It took Baranov through heavy traffic to the Ministry of Defense Building. The eight story structure fronted the Moskva River, and was often referred to as "The Black Hole," because most of the requests that went into the building were never seen again.

The car pulled into a courtyard where a brace of soldiers came to attention as Baranov emerged. An army captain was there to meet Baranov and escort him to the 7th floor. That's where a grim faced secretary rose from behind her fortress-like desk and led Baranov into the marshal's office.

The walls were covered with framed photos of Shoygun standing in front of famous landmarks, Shoygun shaking hands with celebrities, and Shoygun kneeling next to dead game animals. None of the pictures had anything to do with actual soldiering. And none of it bothered Baranov the way it might have. That was because Shoygun made no pretense of being anything other than a politician in a uniform.

The marshal had a round wrinkle-free face, full lips, and two chins. "Anatoly!" Shoygun exclaimed enthusiastically, as he came forward to greet his guest with a Russian bear hug. "It's good to see you." Then Shoygun went over to close the door. "Some things are best discussed in private, Anatoly, and this is one of them. Please, have a seat. Would you care for some tea?"

"No, thank you," Baranov replied as he sat down.

"All right then," Shoygun said, as he perched on the corner of his desk. "Time is short, so I'll get to the point. It's my sad duty to inform you that President Vladimir Sokolov died two days ago."

Baranov felt a sense of shock and loss. The president had been a strong proponent of reunifying mother Russia and, without Sokolov's support, Operation Red Ice would have been impossible. "I'm saddened to hear that," Baranov said. "The president was a great man. You say he died *two* days ago? I saw no mention of it on the morning news."

"No, you didn't," Shoygun agreed. "That's because certain arrangements had to be made, and key people had to be notified. You among them. The president's death will be made public at 1300 today."

"Certain arrangements had to be made." Yes, Baranov thought. *People must be silenced. Money had to be hidden. And files must disappear.* But that, he knew, was the way of things... And it would be no different if he were president. "So Toplin is going to take over?"

"Yes," Shoygun replied. "He will make the announcement."

Toplin was the prime minister, or *had* been, and would assume the presidency now. That could be a problem because unlike the past president, Toplin was a pragmatist, with little if any regard for Russia's glorious past.

Shoygun smiled. "I know what you're thinking, Anatoly... But the fact that Toplin wants to meet with you *before* he makes the announcement, signals his respect for you, and your many accomplishments."

Baranov was surprised. "He wants to meet with *me?*"

"You're too modest, Anatoly... The admiral of the Pacific Fleet outranks you. But, with that exception, you're the most senior officer on the east coast. Toplin wants and needs the army's support. *Your* support. So let's go. His residence is in Rublyovka, and it wouldn't do to be late."

A ride on an elevator and a ten minute walk took them outside, and through a passageway, to a helipad where a bright red Ka-62 helicopter was waiting. And a good thing too, since it would have taken an hour to reach the suburb by car.

Once the officers were strapped in the helicopter took off. Rublyovka was a paramecium shaped area located west of Moscow, and home to hundreds of so-called Kremliads (Kremlin whores), oligarchs of various flavors, and wealthy criminals. *Which category does Toplin belong in*, Baranov wondered. *All three*, came the answer, as the densely populated city surrendered to Rublyovka's well-manicured estates.

"There it is," Shoygun said. "The president owns 37 acres."

Baranov got a look at the stately mansion as the helicopter settled onto the surface of Toplin's private heliport. The house was made of stone. The tall windows would admit plenty of light and the onion-domed corner tower was a respectful nod to the past. Maybe there was hope after all. Toplin's black clad major domo was waiting to greet them. The man had to shout to be heard over the noise generated by the helicopter. "The president is expecting you! Please follow me."

Shoygun had used Toplin's new title earlier, and his major domo had done the same. And why not? What was, was. Or would be shortly. Toplin's importance was underscored by the presence of heavily armed Federal Security Service agents. Some were in uniform, and some wore plainclothes, but all of them had one thing in common. They were watching.

Baranov expected the civilian to lead them into the house but he didn't. A glassed in swimming pool stood behind the mansion, and that's where the major domo took them instead. The air in the pool house was uncomfortably humid. Baranov wanted to remove his heavy uniform jacket, but couldn't, not in front of the president.

He, on the other hand, was naked. Or very nearly so, since Toplin was dressed in nothing more than a posing strap and a pair of flip flops. Now, in the presence of the man, Baranov had a new appreciation of Toplin's nickname: *"Medved."* The Bear.

The moniker was clearly a reference to the man's large, mesomorphic body. But, more than that, to the wiry black hair covering most of it. And there the president was, performing curls with a barbell, as he welcomed his guests. "Marshal Shoygun, General

Baranov, thank you for coming on short notice. Please forgive me for receiving you in this manner. But, given the current set of circumstances, I must multi-task. I'm sure you understand."

"Of course," Shoygun replied smoothly. "Your health is of the utmost importance to the country."

Baranov couldn't imagine saying something like that, nor having some suck up try the strategy on him. But Toplin nodded agreeably. "Poor Vladimir ... Had he only taken better care of himself he might still be with us."

That statement hinted at a heart attack. And chances were that it had been. But Baranov was certain of one thing, and one thing only, nothing was certain. "But enough of that," Toplin said, as he began a series of deep knee bends. "I asked you to come so I could get a first-hand appraisal of how Operation Red Ice is proceeding."

Baranov knew the question was directed to him, and repeated what Gotov had told him earlier, with a strategic summary tacked on the end. "Assuming we're successful Mr. President, we'll force the Americans to pull assets away from other theatres of the war, *and* seize control of Alaska."

Toplin completed the set of deep knee bends and nodded. "Well said, General ... Those are the kind of real world objectives that make sense to me. I'll be honest ... I opposed Operation Red Ice, but Vladimir overruled me. He wanted to recreate the past, and I am more interested in the future. Once you give us Alaska, I will name you a Hero of the Soviet Union, and personally pin the medal on your chest.

"But our resources are limited, General. Use what you have, and do it wisely, because I have no more to give. And if it comes down to a choice between your adventure, and Europe, I will defend the homeland. Do you understand?"

Toplin's eyes were like black stones. Baranov understood all right ... Toplin was willing to let Operation Red Ice proceed, so long as everything went well, and there were no additional requests for men and machines. If things went poorly however, Toplin would deny responsibility for Red Ice, and denounce the former president. Would Baranov survive that? Maybe ... But his fate was by no means certain. "Yes, Comrade President," Baranov said. "I understand."

"Good," Toplin said with a smile. "Now, if you gentlemen will excuse me, I have ten laps to swim before going to the office." Toplin allowed himself to fall backwards into the water, where a powerful backstroke carried him away. The meeting had ended.

The flight from Moscow back to Petropavlovsk felt like torture. Baranov hated being cooped up, begrudged the amount of time it took to refuel during the journey, and worried about what might have occurred during his absence. Were things still on track? Or had the *pindos* (pejorative term for American soldiers) managed to turn the tables somehow?

Gotov was trying to get the latest Intel, but had been unable to reach Colonel Yakimov who, according to a junior communications officer, was in the field.

Baranov knew that he would've been worried regardless, but the conversation with Toplin had been unsettling to say the least, and there was no longer any margin for error. So while the plane flew into the rising sun, all Baranov could do was sit there and feed the ravenous creature that was Boris Dudin.

The reporter said all the right things when Baranov informed him of Sokolov's passing. But there was no look of surprise in Dudin's eyes. And that led Baranov to suspect that the TASS correspondent knew more about the president's death than *he* did.

Dudin *was* interested in the meeting with Toplin however—and Baranov chose his words with care. Toplin regretted Sokolov's premature death. Toplin was interested in the Far East. And Toplin was an excellent swimmer.

Dudin ate it up so Baranov gave him a second helping. "Yes, Boris...We are fortunate to have a leader such as President Toplin during this time of great need."

Shoygun would be proud, Baranov thought, as Dudin typed. *If bullshit was oil Russia would be a very wealthy country.*

It was dark by the time the jet finally landed, and Baranov could call Katya. Unlike her husband Katya was eternally cheerful—and had been looking for a place to live. "Very few houses are for rent," Katya informed him, "and none of them match our needs. But I was able to locate a nice two bedroom apartment. And, since we have so few possessions now, it will be more than adequate."

Baranov never ceased to be amazed at the way Katya could spin gloom into sunshine. Now, thanks to her, their loss had been transformed into a gain. "That's wonderful, *ahren* (angel)," Baranov replied. "I look forward to seeing it. But first I must take care of some business."

"When will you return?"

"I'm not sure, dear...But it might be a couple of weeks."

Katya knew better than to ask for details. "Don't forget to take your pills. Call me if you can."

Baranov promised that he would, although the only time he took the vitamins Katya pushed at him, was when she was standing next to him.

Secure in the knowledge that Katya was okay, Baranov boarded another, smaller jet for the thousand mile flight to the town of Anadyr. Then he and his party had to switch to a Mil Mi-26 transport helicopter for the 350 mile hop to the town of Lavrentiya. Baranov managed to sleep through most of the trip, and awoke when the pilot announced their arrival.

It was light out by then. And as the helicopter circled the town Baranov was conscious of the ways Lavrentiya had changed. It had been a trading center once... A place frequented by whalers and fur traders who did business with the Yupik and Chukchi peoples.

Now because of its proximity to the Diomedes islands, Lavrentiya had been jerked into the 21st century, and transformed into a military base. As Baranov peered out through a window he could see the surface-to-air missile batteries that ringed the area, row upon rows of army shelters, and the newly extended airstrip. It was home to two squadrons of fifteen fighters each, and a twelve plane bomber squadron. Would that be sufficient? It would have to be, based on what President Toplin had told him.

Colonel Yakimov was waiting when the helicopter landed. If Gotov was a screwdriver, then Yakimov was a hammer, and a heavy one at that. Yakimov had fought in the 2008 Russo-Georgian war. Later, as a major, he'd been responsible for protecting Russian air assets in Syria, and held the Khmeimim air base when a battalion of ISIS fighters attempted to capture it. And it was during that battle that a tiny piece of shrapnel pulped Yakimov's left eye.

Most men would have chosen to wear a glass eye in its place. But not Yakimov. He opted for a black eyepatch instead. To impress his troops? Certainly. And, according to the rumors, to impress the ladies as well.

"Welcome to Fort Lavrentiya, Comrade General. Major, it's good to see you again. I see that our friend Boris Dudin remains with us! Be sure to write nice things about us Comrade... You wouldn't want to hurt our feelings."

The others laughed. But Baranov knew a veiled threat when he heard one, and so did Dudin. And, since Spetsnaz (special operations) troops fell under the authority of the Main Intelligence Directorate (GRU), there was good reason for the STAS correspondent to watch his step. "Thank you for the reminder," Baranov said. "We wouldn't want to offend any of the delicate flowers under your command. I understand that you plan to give us a tour. I'm sure that Boris will be most attentive."

"The "tour" was more like an inspection, and began 300 yards to the east where a battalion of Spetsnaz troops had been assembled. The soldiers crashed to attention as the officers arrived, and Baranov passed between their ranks.

Baranov prided himself on remembering the names of soldiers he'd served with in the past, and was delighted to find that some of them were present. "Vagin! You were a sergeant when I last saw you … What happened?"

Vagin stood ramrod straight with his eyes focused on a point just above Baranov's head. "I forgot to submit a leave request, sir!"

That produced a chorus of laughs and a harsh rebuke from the battalion's Starshina (Sergeant Major). "Silence in the ranks! Or would you like to go for a swim in the bay?"

The water was extremely cold, so none of them did. Baranov smiled. "Never fear Private Vagin … The *pindos* are waiting for us. You have distinguished yourself before, and you will again."

Baranov said it loudly, so all could hear, knowing that his conversation with Vagin would soon make the rounds. Some officers gave stirring speeches. But, since Baranov wasn't very good at that, he relied on more subtle techniques to build morale.

Then it was time to board a GAZ Tigr for the drive to the site where an American F-15 had crashed, and from there to the harbor, where hundreds of pontoons were moored in orderly ranks. Baranov felt a chill wind cut through his uniform jacket as he left the vehicle—and wished he'd been smart enough to wear a parka. It wouldn't do to complain however, and Baranov didn't. Boats bobbed and the pontoons tugged at their moorings as a stiff breeze pushed its way across the inlet.

Each construct was roughly the size of a soccer field, and already equipped with painted lanes, so that when the invasion of Alaska began three columns of vehicles could cross the bridge simultaneously. And that was important, because a single line of tanks would be much easier to stop. A fourth lane would carry empty trucks and ambulances west. "So tell me," Baranov said. "How many pontoons am I looking at?"

"Eight-hundred and forty-two out of eight-hundred and fifty, sir. We lost three during a storm, and the *pindos* sank five. But most of them arrived safely. More will be destroyed during the coming days, but we only need about seven-hundred and eighty of them."

"Yes," Baranov agreed. "And the first span? How much of it has been completed?"

"*All* of it," Yakimov answered proudly. "Final testing is underway. Vehicles and troops will cross it tonight."

Baranov felt a sense of accomplishment. The battle for Alaska wasn't over, not by a long shot, but it was off to a good start. He watched as the wind strengthened and the pontoons began to pitch forward and back. "Tell me about the anchors, Colonel... The ones holding the span in place."

Yakimov understood the nature of Baranov's concern. "Two chains broke, General. One of them snapped almost immediately, and the second broke after sixteen hours of use. Alarms sounded on both occasions."

The anchor chains were a weak point. Something that *pindo* divers could attack. That was why Baranov had insisted that a live wire be woven into each chain which, when broken, would trigger an alarm. "Well done, Colonel. Instruct our naval contingent to remain vigilant. It is only a matter of time before the enemy attacks one or more chains."

Sirens began to wail. A pair of jets took off from the airstrip, and the S-400 surface-to-air missile battery located half a mile away from them swiveled to point at Alaska. "It looks like some American planes are coming our way," Yakimov observed.

"*Yebat' ikh* (fuck them)," Baranov replied. Dudin wrote it down.

CHAPTER ELEVEN

Big Diomede Island, Russia, the Bering Strait

The JTACs were huddled behind a makeshift wind break on the rise called Mount Evans when the jet fighters passed over them. They were headed west. To attack the floating bridge? Or the Russian base in Lavrentiya? Perhaps both.

Falco switched to the interflight frequency and heard Parker discussing possible threats, "playtime" (available fuel), and other matters. She was alive!

The knowledge made Falco feel good. But Parker was flying into danger, and that worried him. "Here," Lee said. "Your coffee is ready."

Falco took the mug. "Thank you, Sergeant. What will we do when you run out of instant coffee?"

"I'm going AWOL," Oliver put in, as he took a sip.

"That sounds reasonable," Falco replied. "I'll go with you."

The chatter was a way to pass the time. According to the military intelligence people the Russians had completed the first span and were busy testing it. Once the artic darkness fell they would cross the bridge in force. *Why wait?* Falco wondered. *There isn't much we can do to stop them.* But a period of darkness, no matter how brief, would give the Russians yet another advantage. And they planned to use it. The team was under orders to delay the invading force for as long as possible. Then they, and the units around them, would pull back to the east side of Big D where *something* would be waiting to take them off. No one seemed to know how the evacuation process was going to work, so all they could do was wait and see.

In the meantime the intensity of the fighting had lessened. The Russians already occupied most of the island, and they knew reinforcements were on the way, so it made sense to lay back. As for the Americans, they were trying to buy time. As much of it as they could. So both sides were content with the status quo.

The hours crept by. Falco listened to some upbeat music by Haydn. The other JTACs took naps, ate some of the MREs that fell out of the sky, and told stories. Some of them were actually true.

Finally, at 2200 hours, the sun went down. The full scale invasion began minutes later. Troops led the way and Falco received orders to target them. He disagreed. Steel-Three had been joined by Steel-Two, and the mortar teams had 25 smart rounds between them. So Falco wanted to reserve the bombs for Russian tanks.

But Major Godfrey, who was in command of the infantry battalion that the JTACs were assigned to, was of a different opinion. "I understand what you're saying, Dan," Godfrey said, congenially. "But if those troops break our line, there won't be any reason to worry about tanks, now will there?"

And, since Godfrey was in command, the JTACs had no choice but look for concentrations of ground troops and target them. Orange-red flowers blossomed in the darkness, collapsed in on themselves, and disappeared. Russians died as overlapping claps of thunder rolled across the land. That, combined with well-directed counter fire, was sufficient to hold the enemy off for twenty minutes or so.

Then the first T-14 tanks arrived. They were relatively new, and equipped with the latest technology. Each machine had a three person crew all of whom were stationed *below* the vulnerable turret, inside a well armored compartment.

The T-14s were armed with 125mm smoothbore cannons that were linked to a full array of optical sensors and capable of firing guided munitions. It wasn't long before the reality of that became painfully clear. The American mortar teams were down to seven rounds. And when they fired, the outgoing rounds were tracked by Russian tank mounted counter-battery radar systems. They calculated where the mortar bombs were coming from, and passed the information to Russian mortars, which used the data to return fire. Steel-Two and Steel-Three ceased to exist moments later. The order to fall back came shortly after that.

In the meantime a battle for air superiority was taking place thousands of feet above the JTACs. Sonic BOOMs rolled across the island as jet fighters battled for supremacy. That kept the Russian planes from attacking American troops. But it also meant that the American jets weren't available to target Russian tanks. The enemy machines continued to advance.

Suddenly, without anything to call in, the JTACs were transformed into infantrymen. Their submachine guns weren't useful for anything other than a close quarters combat, and they were low on ammo. There were things they *could* do however... Like carrying stretchers. So that's what the JTACs did as the various strands of Colonel Waya's combat team wove themselves together and trudged east.

Falco heard the crack of explosions as the Russian tanks rolled over recently laid mines, or were struck by shoulder launched rockets. That would slow the machines down, but there was little doubt as to how the situation would turn out, as Falco and Oliver carried a stretcher to the edge of the bluff. Two flares popped high above and threw an eerie glow over the road. Others were walking in front of and behind the JTACs as they made their way down to the sea. They were carrying stretchers, crew-served weapons, and field radios.

Part of that had to do with pride. No way was the combat team going to leave anything useful on the battlefield if they could help it. But the effort was a matter of necessity as well. Because after the troops arrived on Little Diomede, which lay just 2.3 miles away, the soldiers would need the things they were carrying. But how to get there?

The answer was fishing boats. At least fifty of them. Large boats, small boats, and everything in between. A call had gone out to the commercial fishing community, and the response was everything Waya could have hoped for, and more.

Flood lights dispelled the gloom as a procession of gill netters, purse seiners, and trollers lined up to take troops off the Russian jetty. Now, with twenty-twenty hindsight, it was obvious that the concrete ramp located next to the pier had been built to serve as the western terminus of the second floating bridge.

An aid station had been set up near the Russian helipad. An army doctor was in charge. She was thirty something and the front of her uniform was soaked with blood. "What have we got here?" she demanded.

"A chest wound," Oliver replied.

The doctor held a flashlight in her left hand, and felt for a pulse with her right. Then she aimed the light into the soldier's eyes, watched to see if his pupils would react, and shook her head. "He's dead. Take him over there. Next!"

"Over there," was a spot about a hundred feet away where dozens of bodies were laid out side-by-side waiting to be taken off the island. Two privates were in charge. "Remove the body from the stretcher," one of them ordered. "We might need it for someone else."

Falco was going to reply, but gave up as a Black Hawk helicopter roared overhead, and swooped in for a landing. The controllers had finished offloading the body when Major Godfrey appeared out of the surrounding darkness. He looked tired.

"There you are ... We need some help Dan. Military and civilian helicopters are flying laps overhead while they wait to land. Some have more fuel than others—and I'm worried about the possibility of a collision."

As an Air Force Special Tactics Officer, Falco was a qualified Air Traffic Controller. So the team set up well away from the noisy helipad and went to work. Falco led the effort, with Oliver as his assistant, while Lee fed them information from the aid station.

Lee's job was to find out which patients needed to go out first, and radio the information to Oliver, who chose the right moment to share it with Falco. With no computer based system to rely on, all Falco could do was scribble call signs on a tablet, as he sorted helicopters according to capacity, fuel supply, and above all speed. The most critical patients had priority for transportation on the fast movers.

There was another variable too ... Some of the incoming helos carried doctors, nurses or even dentists who had been brought in from places like Fairbanks and Anchorage.

But other choppers, like the bird that belonged to the Fish & Game people, didn't have any medical personnel on board. So it was important to put the *least* critical patients on those helos.

Meanwhile, high above, the battle for the sky continued. And it was critical. Because if the Russians won, and came swooping down, the helicopters wouldn't stand a chance. Falco knew that. And the additional pressure made his task even more difficult.

Finally, after more than two hours of work, the last medevac helicopter departed and Falco was able to sign off. Most of the combat team had been taken off Big D by then ... And fighting could be heard to the west, as Waya's rearguard fought to keep the Russians from reaching the jetty.

Falco should have been on his feet, should have been getting ready to pull out, but couldn't muster the energy. He was sitting on an ammo box, and his team was packing gear, when the doctor appeared. "Major Falco? I'm Doctor Levitt. You don't remember me, *do* you?"

Falco looked up at her. "No Doctor, I'm sorry. Have we met before?"

Levitt sat down across from him. "Yes, in Afghanistan. At FOB Hope. I taped your ankle after the strike on Hashemi."

"Thank you. I was kind of messed up at that point."

"Yes," Levitt agreed. "That was obvious. And that's why I wanted to speak with you. Two civilians died in *Em Bal*. But you saved a lot of lives tonight, Major ... I don't know how many, but a lot more than two. Remember that, Major ... Don't ever forget it. God bless you." Then she left.

Falco was dumbstruck. Lives couldn't be traded. He knew that. And the mistake at *Em Bal* couldn't be undone. But, thanks to Levitt, his failure would be easier to bear.

Falco smiled. One more wound ... That's what Levitt had seen—and done her best to heal.

"We're ready to go," Lee said, as the rearguard came galloping down the road. Colonel Waya skidded to a stop, stepped to one side, and began to wave the rest of them through.

Falco stood. "Thanks, Sergeant ... I'll give you a hand."

After carrying their gear down to the jetty the controllers were ordered onto the twenty foot open fishing boat that belonged to Sonny Toklo, a resident of Little Diomede, and the owner of a blue-eyed husky named Mack. It was impossible to see the Ingalikmiut's face because of the headlamp he wore.

"No worries," Toklo told them, as he helped the JTACs load their gear. "This is my third trip. I'll have you back in the U.S. of A. in twenty minutes."

Toklo's boat was powered by a 115hp Yamaha, sitting next to a 15hp "get me home" back-up motor. And, judging from the vessel's smell, Toklo was a fisherman.

The motor roared when Toklo turned the throttle, and the hull pounded the waves as the boat gained speed. Mack liked that, and stood like a figurehead up in the bow, where he could sample the cold air as it rushed past his black nose.

Falco had to hold on while frigid spray flew back to sting his face and the sun topped the horizon. That was when he got his first look at Little D. Having read the briefing materials Falco knew that the island was 2.3 miles from Big D, and home to approximately 120 people, most of whom made a living by harvesting polar bears, seals, and blue crabs.

Like its big brother to the west, Little Diomede had a flat top, with steep sides all around. Light spilled over the bluff to splash the seaside village of *Ignaluk* as the sun continued to creep up into the sky. Falco could see the stone jetty by then, the twin boat launches located beside it, and the brightly painted houses perched on the hillside above. Most stood on stilts, and were huddled together like seabirds on a stormy day.

Larger buildings of uncertain purpose squatted along the left side of the waterfront. A white fuel tank towered over piles of junk. Once the Russians arrived Falco figured their engineers would bulldoze a road through the village, carve a series of switchbacks into the hillside, then push the road to the other side of the island. The moment that was accomplished enemy vehicles would haul supplies east in preparation for the last span. The one that would place them on American soil.

But maybe we can stop them, Falco thought. *We have to try.* And the militarization of Little D was already underway. A steel barge had been brought in during the hours of darkness and anchored offshore. It belonged to a well-known oil company. As troops filed off a fishing boat and onto the barge, another vessel was ready to pull in. An armada of small craft ferried the soldiers ashore.

Thanks to the size of his boat, Toklo had no need to go alongside the barge, and bored straight in. The stone jetty rose to the left, as Toklo ordered Oliver and Mack to move back. That was enough to make the bow rise. And as Toklo turned the motor off and brought it up out of the water, inertia carried them in. Falco heard gravel grind under the aluminum hull as the bow ran up onto the beach and Mack jumped ashore. "Welcome to *Ignaluk*," Toklo said cheerfully. "Watch your step ... The rocks are slippery."

The water washed gravel *was* slippery. After unloading their gear, and thanking Toklo, the JTACs left the beach. A neatly dressed MP was waiting to greet them. Had he been dropped onto Little D recently? Falco thought so. "Sorry," the soldier said, as he jerked a thumb back over his shoulder. "But your destination is up *there*."

Falco looked up and back down. "*Seriously?* Won't the Russians bomb us?"

The MP nodded. "That seems quite likely, sir. Please follow the trail up past the purple house. You'll see spray painted arrows on the ground. Follow them, and you can't go wrong."

The JTACs had no choice but to comply. Others were following the path too. Men and women who were dog tired. They climbed the hill like a column of zombies, heads down, eyes on the trail.

The pathway led past the weather-grayed ruins of an old house and a neatly kept graveyard to the spot where the serious climbing began. The trail wasn't maintained insofar as Falco could tell ... That seemed to suggest the locals had very little reason to visit the windswept mesa. And if they didn't go there, why would anyone else?

The struggle continued. Their gear was heavy, and seemed to grow heavier with each passing minute, as the team plodded ever upwards. And it was getting warmer too ... Especially with high altitude jump suits on. But after what seemed like an eternity, the JTACs emerged on the mesa where they saw an unexpected sight.

Three Chinook helicopters, each with a bulldozer dangling beneath it, were hovering above the partially melted snow, and about to lay their burdens down. The CATs were bright yellow, and appeared to be new. That suggested the government had purchased them from dealers in Alaska. "Those are D-4s," Oliver observed. "They're small as CATs go, but plenty good enough for digging bunkers."

That answered Falco's earlier question. Waya was planning to dig in. Engines roared as the Chinooks left and more helicopters arrived. A 2nd lieutenant was there to greet them. She tossed a salute. "Names please."

Falco gave them and watched the lieutenant scan a Mil grade tablet computer. "The colonel is going to hold a staff meeting at 1000 and you folks are invited. See the antenna farm over there? Head for that."

Much of the winter snow had melted, leaving a slushy mess behind. Tracks ran every which way and helicopters continued to land as Falco and his team made their way to the com center. It consisted of the antennas he'd seen earlier, a cluster of tents, and a diesel generator. Keeping it fed would be no small task, but that's what the Quartermaster Corps was for.

After checking in, the men were able to snag some MREs, and recharge various batteries. Then they took advantage of the opportunity to grab a couple of hours of sleep prior to the meeting. Falco slept hard and awoke feeling stupid. A mug of Lee's coffee and a chocolate covered doughnut served to put him right. Falco could hardly believe what he was eating. And it was a good sign. If the men and women on Little D had pastries—chances were that they had ammo too.

Falco noticed something new as he followed a stream of other people to the tent where the meeting was going to take place. An ITWQ-1 Avenger anti-aircraft missile launcher was stationed about a hundred yards away, where it could protect the team's headquarters location.

That was encouraging, and Falco said as much to the army captain standing next to him in line. "And we have three more," the officer responded. "Plus enough shoulder launched Stingers to equip fifty soldiers." More good news.

There was standing room only inside the tent. Colonel Waya stepped up onto a crate so the people in back could see him. He face was shaved and his uniform was immaculate. There was no way to hide how tired he was however. There were dark circles beneath his eyes, and his face was pale. "Good morning. First I want to thank you, and your troops for all that you managed to accomplish during the last 48 hours. I know it's been tough ... But you can take satisfaction from the fact that the Russians paid a heavy price for Big Diomede. Based on preliminary reports it looks like they suffered twice the number of casualties that we did."

Someone yelled, "Hooah!" and others took up the cry.

Waya smiled. "That brings us to the present. We have orders to hold Little D, and prevent the Russians from completing their bridge. Meanwhile, resources are pouring into the village of Wales, Alaska which is located 25 miles east of here. If we're forced to fall back it will be to a position of strength. And, I'm pleased to announce that we're going to get some help."

Waya glanced at his watch before returning his gaze to the crowd. "As I speak one of our subs is launching cruise missiles at the first bridge span. If a section of it is destroyed, the Russians will need the better part of a day to replace it.

"Meanwhile *more* missiles are falling on the so-called 'port,' located on the east side of Big D. They're certain to take a heavy toll on the tanks and personnel concentrated there."

A series of dull thuds were heard and the crowd cheered. Waya nodded. "*See?* The navy *is* good for something." That provoked laughter, and Falco had to give Waya credit. He knew how to play a crowd—especially *his* crowd.

"Okay," Waya said. "Get out there and finish those bunkers, work on your defenses, and rotate through the showers. You people reek."

That was good for some additional laughs, and most people were smiling as they filed out of the tent. Falco was about to follow Oliver out when a staff sergeant appeared next to him. "Major Falco? The colonel would like to speak with you. Please follow me."

Falco called Oliver and Lee back. They followed the sergeant out through a side entrance, and over to a smaller tent. It was home to banks of com equipment and a ping pong table with a large map on top. Was it on loan from the local school? Possibly.

The JTACs saluted and Waya tossed one in return. "It's good to see you again, Major ... Who are the vagrants that you brought with you?"

Once the introductions had been made Waya wasted no time getting down to business. "I'd like to believe that the cruise missile attacks will delay the Russians for two days, but that's unlikely. The bastards are not only resourceful, they're under the command of General Baranov, a well-known hard ass.

"Plus," Waya added, "it's important to remember what the Russians are up to. They're building what amounts to a one-season military bridge. It has to be good, but it doesn't have to be perfect, so anything goes.

"In order to slow them down I had a C-17 drop two M777A2 howitzers in last night. And, since Big D is only 2.3 miles away, they can reach targets all over the island. But I want you to put most of our fire *here*."

As Waya stabbed the map with his right index finger Falco saw that he was pointing at the port. The same target that the cruise missiles were aimed at. "Fire on them around the clock,"

Waya ordered. "Disrupt their activities and mess with their minds."

Falco nodded. "Yes, sir."

"I don't have any spare artillery officers, so you'll have to move the howitzers yourself, and do so frequently," Waya told them. "Because the moment they start firing the Russians will work day and night trying to locate and destroy them. Do you have any questions?"

'Yes, sir," Oliver put in. "It will be difficult for us to spot impacts, and adjust fires from 2.3 miles away. Is there any chance of getting ahold of some Raven UAVs (Unmanned Aerial Vehicles)? They're small, they're hard to spot, and they have enough range. We'd need two of them though ... They can only remain aloft for an hour or so."

Waya nodded. "That's a good idea, Sergeant. I'll see what I can do. Is there anything else? No? I want Operation Slingshot up and running by 0800 tomorrow. Make it happen."

CHAPTER TWELVE

The Chukchi Sea

Captain Marvin Soto was sitting on his raised chair, staring out over the frost covered bow, as the icebreaker *Northern Dawn* steamed south. The hull shuddered and spray flew as the ship broke through a six-foot high roller and pitched forward. The bow sank, the stern rose, and the process started over again. Would the temporary repairs to the superstructure hold? Soto hoped so. The Bremerton shipyard was a long way off. Once the *Dawn* arrived Soto would see Maria and the children for the first time in many months. "Captain?"

Soto turned to find that the ship's first officer, Lieutenant Commander Leo Baxter, was standing next to him. "Yeah, Leo ... What's up?"

"A distress call, sir ... An air force F-15E Strike Eagle was shot down southwest of here. The pilot survived. The folks at Elmendorf want us to pick him up."

Search and rescue. That was the kind of mission the *Northern Dawn* specialized in. "The pilot is alive," Soto said. "That's good. Is he in the water? Or is he on land?"

There were islands to the southwest. Tiny things for the most part. But people were shipwrecked on them from time to time.

"In the water," Baxter replied. "But he's wearing a dry suit."

There was reason to hope. Without a dry suit the average person would perish in a matter of minutes. But, with a good suit, the pilot might last for as long as 24 hours. "Excellent," Soto said. "Set the appropriate course."

"We have," Baxter assured him. "And Lieutenant Olson is preparing to launch the remaining Dolphin. But there's a problem."

Soto made a face. "Oh goody. And what, pray tell, is *that?*"

"A Russian trawler is headed for our pilot. At its present rate of speed it's going to reach the area before the *Dawn* does. PACOM believes that the trawler is a spy ship."

Soto considered that. Had the Russians been able to eavesdrop on American radio communications? Such transmissions were encrypted, so it seemed unlikely.

But when the Russian pilot shot the F-15E down it would have been SOP for him to report both his victory, and the position of the shoot-down. If they could, the Russians would snatch the American flier, and parade him in front of their cameras. It would make for a nice piece of propaganda. Soto was reminded of the *Heath* incident. He swore. "Ask the chief if we can make more revolutions."

Baxter prided himself on anticipating such orders. "He can, sir ... But, because of the six- foot seas, it won't add more than a couple of knots to our speed."

Soto glared at him. "You're starting to piss me off, Leo ... What am I going to have for lunch?"

Baxter's face remained expressionless. "A grilled cheese sandwich, sir. And a cup of tomato soup." The bridge crew laughed.

"You got lucky," Soto said. "Increase our speed by two knots. Launch the Dolphin as soon as Olson is ready. Maybe we can snatch the pilot out from under the trawler captain's nose."

The red helo lifted off fifteen minutes later and sped away. Soto put in a call for Chief Petty Officer Wright who, along with his crew of mustachioed gunner's mates, all of whom had played important roles in sinking the Russian icebreaker *Narwhal*.

The petty officer arrived ten minutes later and, as always, appeared to be hyper alert. Soto envied the other man's square jawed good looks and natural charisma. "Good morning, Chief ... I might have a job for you. Is the 5-inch ready for action?"

Soto saw a gleam appear in Wright's eyes. "Of course, sir." The man *wanted* to fight, whereas Soto preferred not to. After listening to Soto's briefing Wright hurried away.

Soto turned to discover that 2nd officer Lieutenant Linda Penny had arrived on the bridge. He nodded. "Good morning, Lieutenant. You're early."

"I heard the helicopter take off, so I came up," Penny responded.

"Good, thank you. Please sound general quarters."

Once the recording ended Soto spoke to the crew via the ship's PA system. "This is the captain. An air force pilot is in the drink, and it's a race to see who will reach him first, the *Dawn* or a Russian spy ship. The entire crew performed admirably against the *Narwhal* ... And I expect nothing less this time. Carry on."

Once general quarters sounded, Baxter was required to leave the bridge for the secondary control station in the stern, where he would assume command if Soto was wounded or killed. Soto turned to Penny. "How long before the Dolphin arrives on scene?"

"Five minutes, sir."

"How long until we have a visual on the trawler?"

"About fifteen from the crow's nest, sir. Twenty from the bridge."

Soto went over to the check the live video feed. There wasn't much to see. Just ranks of white caps riding on an endless procession of waves. Soto could imagine how it would feel to slide down into a trough—and be buried under a ton of freezing cold water.

A swimmer would have to either hold his breath, or breathe salt water, and drown.

A squawk of static interrupted Soto's thoughts. "Bird-Dog-Two to Bird-Cage," Olson said. "We have a visual on the pilot. Standby... Over."

Soto felt a sense of relief. It was damned hard to find something as small as a human in hundreds of square miles of ocean. But pilots, especially *military* pilots, were equipped with emergency locator beacons. That meant Olson and her copilot had been able to follow the signal to its source. The final sighting was a matter of good eyesight.

"Bird-Dog-Two to Bird-Cage... We're lowering the basket. I don't want to put my rescue swimmer in the water if I can avoid it. Over."

Soto understood. Once a rescue swimmer was in the water it would double the amount of time the Dolphin had to spend over the site. "Roger that," Soto said. "Over."

"We have visual contact with the trawler," Olson said. "It's coming in from the northwest. Shit! They fired a MANPAD at us... It just sailed past."

Soto's mind was racing. "You have flare pistols... Tell your crew chief to fire them out the door. Over."

Attack helicopters could fire chaff in order to lure missiles away. But Dolphins weren't equipped for that, and so long as the helo hovered over the pilot, it was a stationary target. Would the heat generated by a distress flare be enough to draw a shoulder launched missile away? Soto held his breath.

"The flares worked! They missed," Olson said. "But we're running out of flares."

"Don't wait for the basket," Soto said. "Get the hell out of there."

Soto watched via the Dolphin's nose camera as the horizon tilted and began to swing. He saw waves, a brief glimpse of the trawler, and more waves. A second screen showed the cable slanting back and out of the frame. The air force pilot was getting one helluva ride, that was for sure.

"The trawler is in range, and Chief Wright requests permission to fire," Penny said.

Soto could imagine Wright up in the crow's nest eyeing the trawler through a pair of binoculars. "Permission granted," Soto said. "Tell the chief to sink that piece of shit."

Penny grinned wolfishly. "Aye, aye, Captain."

There was no way to know how much information the Russian captain had regarding the *Dawn* and her capabilities. But Soto figured that the 5-inch shells were a surprise. If it were otherwise, the trawler would be running like hell rather than boring in.

The gun wasn't linked to a targeting system other than Chief Wright's eyes. And even though Soto couldn't see the enemy vessel yet, the noncom could. Soto heard a dull thud as the first shot was fired. "That was over boys," Wright told his gunners. "Drop fifty."

The *Dawn* shuddered as the five-incher fired again. "That's better," Wright allowed, "but no cigars for you. Left twenty."

A *third* bang was heard as a puff of smoke issued from the five-inch barrel, and another high explosive shell flew down range. "Bingo!" Wright said. "You dropped that one onto her stern. She's turning. Right ten."

The deck gun spoke again, and *again*, as shells continued to rain down on the spy ship. Soto considered calling an end to it, and giving the Russians a chance to save themselves, but he couldn't forgive them for firing on a rescue helicopter. *I'm changing*, Soto thought to himself, as the deck gun continued to fire. *And it isn't pretty.*

Finally, after three additional rounds, Wright made the call. "The target is dead in the water. She's sinking."

"Cease firing," Soto said. "Lieutenant? What's the status on the rescue?"

"The pilot is aboard the helicopter," Penny replied. "Dr. Nelson and his team are waiting to receive him."

"Turn the ship into the wind," Soto ordered. "Then, once the Dolphin is on board, we'll search for survivors."

Soto knew the landing would delay the search, but there was the distinct possibility that the pilot was in need of medical attention. And that had priority.

The better part of twenty minutes elapsed before the *Dawn* was free to turn and crisscross the area where the trawler had gone down. The initial oil slick had broken up by then, but patches of the black stuff remained, and debris was floating on the water. There weren't any boats, rafts, or swimmers. There were bodies though … Surging with the waves. But Soto had no intention of risking lives to retrieve them.

After telling the crew to stand down Soto ordered Penny to put the ship back on its original course and left the bridge. When Soto entered the sickbay five minutes later it was to discover that Dr. Nelson was sitting in his tiny waiting room sipping tea. "It looks like your patient is doing well," Soto said.

"Yes," Nelson replied, "and no."

"Which means?"

"Which means that he's in good shape physically. But emotionally? Not so much. His weapons officer was killed—and he blames himself."

"Can I see him?"

Nelson shrugged. "Yes, but watch what you say."

"I will," Soto assured him. "What's his name?"

"Davis. Lieutenant Milo Davis."

"Okay, thanks."

A Health Services tech was with Davis when Soto entered. She said, "Hello," and left. The lights were dimmed but Soto could see. Davis had a buzz cut, dark skin, and his eyes were closed. A blanket was pulled up under the aviator's chin. Soto assumed Davis was asleep, and was about to leave, when the pilot opened his eyes. "Hello," Soto said. "I'm Captain Soto."

Davis stirred, as if to get up, and Soto shook his head. "As you were, Lieutenant. If you get up, Dr. Nelson will take my head off."

Davis produced something akin to a grin. "Thank you for coming to get me, sir ... I understand you sank a Russian trawler."

"That's true," Soto replied, as he sat on the foot of the bed. "The Russians wanted to take you home for show and tell."

Davis made a face. "I'll bet ... Well, thanks, and I'm sorry I caused so much trouble."

"Don't be," Soto told him. "That's what we're here for."

There was an awkward moment of silence. Soto stood, and was about to leave, when Davis spoke. "Are you going to submit a report?"

Soto nodded. "Yes, of course."

"You need to tell them," Davis said. His eyes were filled with pain.

"Tell them what?"

"Tell them about the pilot who shot us down. His name is Voronov. Adrian Voronov."

"Voronov? How do you know that?"

"I know because he told me," Davis replied miserably. "He speaks perfect English, and he's an extremely good pilot. Better than I am. That's why Mike is dead."

"Mike? Your weapons officer?"

Davis nodded. "Voronov was talking to me the whole time, telling me how good he is, and how he was going to splash us. Maybe he got inside my head. Or maybe he's that much better than I am. Either way he managed to get on my six. He fired a radar guided missile followed by a heat seeker. It slammed into us. We ejected. I saw Mike's chute. He was alive sir ... All the way down." Davis choked up at that point and turned his head away.

Soto waited for the pilot to recover. "I'm sorry, sir," Davis said. "Tell them ... Tell them I saw Mike hit the water. He waved at me as a wave lifted him up. Then I heard a sustained roar, and the water exploded around him.

"That's when Voronov flew over. He circled, wagged his wings, and left. I tried to reach Mike, but he was gone." The pilot's voice was tight. "He was counting on me sir, counting on me to kill the Russian sonofabitch, and I failed him."

Soto was out of his depth and he knew it. Davis needed help, but Soto had none to offer. And, in spite of the pilot's pain, there was something Soto needed to know. "Voronov waggled his wings? He knew you were alive?"

"Sir, yes sir," Davis answered. "He left me to tell the story ... To build his rep. I wish he *had* killed me. I'd be with Mike."

What Davis said made a horrible kind of sense. And Soto knew that Davis was correct. People on up the chain of command *would* want to know about Voronov. "Don't worry, Lieutenant ... I'll put everything you told me into my report. And one more thing ..."

"Sir?"

"Not long ago this ship fought an engagement with a Russian ship. Not the trawler ... A larger, more dangerous ship. It was the first time I'd been anywhere near a battle. People died. *My* people. I think about that every day. About what I should, or shouldn't have done. But ultimately I know this ... I did the best I could on that particular day. And that's all *any* of us can do. I'll bet that Mike would agree."

Davis nodded. But Soto could tell that the pilot was unconvinced, and knew that the young man would take a long time to heal.

The rest of the day passed without incident. The wind disappeared during the night and the sea looked like glass the next morning. The *Dawn* was making good time at that point, and Soto's mind was on his family, as he carried a mug full of coffee up to the bridge. Baxter was waiting to greet him. "Good morning, Captain … A message arrived from PACOM."

Something about the way Baxter said it, and the look in his eyes, signaled trouble. Soto felt a twinge of concern. "Yeah? What now?"

"I think you should read the full text, sir," Baxter said as he handed Soto a piece of paper.

Soto took it over to the raised chair where he began to read. The document was labeled "TOP SECRET," formatted as a so-called "Five Paragraph Order" except that everything after "Situation," Mission," and "Execution" was missing. And Soto saw why.

"SITUATION:
ENEMY FORCES HAVE COMPLETED WORK ON A FLOATING BRIDGE THAT CONNECTS LAVRENTIYA, RUSSIA WITH BIG DIOMEDE ISLAND AS THE FIRST STEP OF A PLAN TO INVADE ALASKA. ALL EFFORTS TO STOP, OR TO SIGNIFICANTLY SLOW THEM DOWN HAVE FAILED, AND THE ENEMY IS CONSTRUCTING A SECOND SPAN BETWEEN BIG AND LITTLE DIOMEDE ISLANDS."

Soto could hardly believe his eyes. There had been radio traffic, lots of it, indicating that something big was taking place. But a floating bridge! No, *two* floating bridges … That was news. Soto continued to read.

"MISSION:
THE USCGG *NORTHERN DAWN* WAGB-8 IS ORDERED TO PROCEED TO SPAN ONE OF THE FLOATING BRIDGES AND, BY WHATEVER MEANS NECESSARY, SEVER IT.

EXECUTION:
THE *DAWN'S* COMMANDING OFFICER, OR EXECUTIVE OFFICER SHOULD THE COMMANDING OFFICER BE INCAPACITATED, WILL DETERMINE THE BEST WAY TO FULFILL THE REQUIREMENTS OF THE MISSION— DEPENDING ON THE CIRCUMSTANCES AT THE TIME."

"Administration/Logistics" and "Command/Signal" were missing. Soto knew why—and the knowledge made him feel queasy.

PACOM wouldn't order him to ram the bridge, because that would amount to a suicide mission, and that wouldn't look good if a reporter got ahold of it.

No, it was up to him to "... determine the best way to fulfill the requirements of the mission." And, if *he* chose to ram the bridge, then that was his decision.

As for the *Northern Dawn*, well she was more than forty years old, and about to go into dry dock. So sacrificing an old icebreaker would make sense if it would slow the Russians down. Soto understood the logic even if he didn't like it. He sighed.

Baxter's eyes were waiting when Soto looked up. "I'm sorry, sir. I know how you feel about her."

"Thanks," Soto said. "You specialize in reading my mind, so what am I going to ask you to do?"

Baxter grinned. "You're going to ask me for an upside down crew list with the least critical people on top."

"Exactly," Soto said. "And don't put the cooks at the top ... They're critical to morale.

"Next I want you to work with Lieutenant Olson to fly as many people off as you can. Tell her to rotate flights with Drake and to put passengers in the co-pilot's position. Put Lieutenant Penny in the first load—with orders to organize things on the ground.

"Then I want you to check the lifeboats. Make sure they're properly equipped, and ready to launch. Is there anything else that I want you to do?"

"Yes, sir," Baxter replied. "You want me to draw up strict criteria as to what people can take with them, you want me to destroy all classified documents, and you want me to check on air cover."

"Damn!" Soto said. "I'm pretty smart. Plus there's one more thing, Leo ... Send for Chief Wright. Since we're going to do this thing, let's do it right."

Soto had no choice but to get on the PA system and inform the crew. His manner was matter of fact. "So," he concluded. "After more than forty years of faithful service the *Dawn* is about to complete one last mission. Plans are being drawn up to evacuate the crew. Please do your part to make sure that the process goes smoothly. Thank you."

Soto had been to every village up and down the coast of Alaska at least once, and that included the tiny community of Kivalina, Alaska, which lay roughly ninety miles to the east. That was the best place to send his crew. The Dolphin could make a round trip in a little more than an hour, which was important, because there was a limited amount of fuel aboard. And Kivalina was so remote that no one would realize what had taken place until the attack was over. At that point the air force could send planes to take the crew out.

And so began hours of frantic activity as the *Dawn* slowed, the Dolphin ferried people to shore, and final preparations were made. Fighters were on call, but not circling above, lest they draw attention to the ship. And the Russians were so busy trying to drive the Americans off Little D that they didn't send any planes north to look around.

By the time darkness fell 118 members of the 160 person crew had been taken ashore, and 40 of them were boarding motor lifeboats. The other two, which was to say Soto and Chief Engineer George Chang, were still aboard. Baxter shook hands with Soto prior to leaving the bridge for the last time. "Where's your dry suit, sir? Shouldn't you put it on?"

"Not yet," Soto told him. "It's too damned hot. Now quit screwing around and get the rest of our people to shore."

Baxter took a step backwards, came to attention, and popped a perfect salute. "I'll see you in Anchorage, Captain." Then he was gone.

Soto took a look around. He had the bridge to himself. The pictures were in his pocket. Maria, Emily, and Joel. He taped them to the console in front of him. Then, after taking hold of the wheel, he released the autopilot. Not because he had to ... But because he wanted to be one with his ship. To say goodbye in his own way. The phone was only inches away. Soto lifted the receiver and entered a number. He heard a click. "George? Are you there?"

"Of course I'm here," Chang said. "Where else would I be?"

"In a lifeboat," Soto replied. "And there's still time to bail out. What about your husband?"

"He's a marine," Chang replied. "He'll understand."

"Okay," Soto replied. "Give me everything you have. And I mean *all* of it."

"All of it," meant the combined power of three Pratt & Whitney gas turbines capable of pushing the ship through the water at 18 knots (21mph). And since the *Dawn* was 45 miles north of Big Diomede, that meant it would take about two hours to reach the bridge. It would be dark when the icebreaker arrived, which was perfect.

Russian radars would spot the *Dawn*, that was a given, but what would they make of her? Would the officer in command understand the threat? Or would he think the vessel was Russian? And way off course? That sort of thing could help, but Soto wasn't counting on it. All he could do was bore in and let the *Dawn* do what she did best: Break things in two.

In the meantime there was an opportunity to remember. The day he married Marie, the births of his children, and sailing on a sunny day.

There were regrets too ... Things he'd said. Things he *hadn't* said. And opportunities lost. But all in all Soto had led a happy life, and he was grateful for it.

So when the time came, and Soto saw the lights ahead, he was at peace. "George? Are you there?"

"Of course I'm here," came the same reply that Chang had given earlier. "Where else would I be?"

Soto laughed. "Nowhere my friend ... Just here. With me."

The *Dawn* shuddered and the vibration beneath Soto's feet increased as Chang gave him full emergency power. Soto saw flashes as the Russian guns opened fire, and watched the tracers arc his way. The shells looked like beads on a string. They hit hard, beating on steel hull like hammers, all searching for a way in. And some succeeded. A fire alarm bleated as a missile struck the ship, and destroyed the 5-inch gun.

But that wasn't enough. The *Dawn* was designed for pushing forward, for riding up onto thick sheets of ice, and for crushing them under her tremendous weight.

So when the guns failed to stop the icebreaker there was nothing to prevent the ship's specially shaped bow from sliding up and onto the floating bridge.

The impact nearly threw Soto to the deck but he managed to hold on. And there, dangling from a cord, was the thumb switch. The one that Chief Wright had rigged with help from one of Chang's engineers. It was a secret. *Their* secret.

Soto held it in his hand, stared into Marie's eyes, and thumbed the button. The shaped charges went off in quick succession. And, since they were attached to the *Dawn's* fuel tanks, there was a series of *secondary* explosions. The result was a flash of light and a clap of thunder so loud that people in Wales, Alaska heard it.

Elsewhere, more than a thousand miles away, Maria Soto awoke from a sound sleep. And then, for some unknown reason, she began to cry.

CHAPTER THIRTEEN

Little Diomede Island, USA, Bering Strait

The team had taken refuge in the ruins of an old tumbledown lighthouse on the west side of Little Diomede's mostly flat plateau. An army H45 space heater provided what warmth there was—and a battery powered lantern threw hard shadows against the stone walls. A camouflaged tarp served as a roof, and gear was stacked all around.

A hole in the section of the wall that was still standing allowed the JTACs to aim their binoculars and scopes at Big D. And Falco was staring out into the night when he saw a flash of light followed by a loud BOOM. "What the hell was *that?*" Lee wondered.

"I don't know," Oliver replied. "But it looked like whatever it was took place *west* of Big D. Maybe we dropped a MOAB (Mother of All Bombs) on those bastards."

"Oh yeah," Lee said enthusiastically. "Eighteen thousand pounds of whup ass! That would slow 'em down."

"A MOAB *would* clear the bridge of traffic," Falco said. "But MOABs aren't penetrator weapons. So a single bomb wouldn't be all that effective against the bridge itself. No, I'd put my money on a missile strike. But regardless of that, it's time to earn our pay. Let's launch a Raven."

After giving the JTACs their orders, Colonel Waya had arranged for two UAV operators to join the team, and supplied the group with an equal number of Ravens. Each drone had a 5.5 foot wing-span, was 3 feet long, and weighed 4.2 pounds. That made them small and hard to spot. It also made them vulnerable to winds.

The machines had a range of 6.2 miles—and a cruising speed of roughly18mph. And, thanks to the sophisticated sensor packages they carried, the Ravens could complete missions day and night.

Specialists Cooper and Jenkins were supposed to work twelve hour shifts. But both of the operators were awake and ready to go. Cooper was a twenty-year-old soldier with a tendency to refer to the air force as the "chair force," even though the JTACs were members of the branch she was poking fun at. Jenkins was forty-something, and one of thousands of reservists who'd been called up to fight. He had a calm, no nonsense manner, and Cooper called him "Dad." "Come on," Jenkins said. We'll put Mutt up and take a look around."

None of them knew why Jenkins had chosen to name the Ravens after the cartoon characters Mutt and Jeff—and none of them saw any reason to object. Cooper made a face. "I'm on a break."

"Cut the crap," Oliver said, "or I'll have the army ship you to Alaska."

All of them laughed, Cooper included, as she followed Jenkins out into the night. Either of them could launch Mutt alone, but the process was easier with two people. "Check with Slingshot-One, and Slingshot-Two," Falco instructed. "Tell them we'll have missions for them shortly."

Slingshot-One and Two were the M777A2 howitzers that Colonel Waya had brought in. They were relatively light at nine-thousand pounds each, capable of firing a variety of "smart" munitions, and could strike targets up to fifteen miles away. That made them perfect for the task at hand. "Both tubes are ready," Lee reported.

"Good," Falco replied. "Check on the D-4s too … Do operators know where the next positions are located? Are they ready to hook up?"

Once the howitzers began to fire, their shells would appear on Russian radar screens. As that occurred computer programs would calculate where the rounds had come from, and send counter-fire coordinates to artillery, tanks and/or missile batteries which would respond. That meant the M777A2s could fire a limited number of rounds before the CATs towed them away.

Falco figured that once an American gun began to fire, it would take the Russians about ten minutes to zero in on the weapon's position and attempt to kill it. Each M777 could fire three rounds per minute. So Falco figured that a tube could send nine rounds down range prior to being towed away. That's why a tractor was assigned to each unit. "The next positions have been selected, and the D-4s are ready," Lee reported.

"Mutt's up, and all systems are green," Jenkins announced, as he entered the shelter. Cooper was right behind him.

"Excellent," Falco replied. "Let's take a look at the so-called port on the east side of Big Diomede. That's as far as the Russians can go, unless they're able to put the second span in place. Maybe targets are starting to pile up there."

Jenkins sat down in front of an open case. The vehicle interface was on the left, with a laptop in the middle, and a UAV datalink positioned on the right. "A strong breeze is blowing in from the west. That's why Mutt is so slow," Jenkins explained. "But he'll be over the target area in ten minutes or so."

Waiting was something that JTACs did a lot of. Waiting for the enemy, waiting for friendlies, or waiting for the weather to improve. It was all part of the job. So ten minutes was no big deal. Falco took the opportunity to eat a trail bar, and wash it down with lukewarm coffee. Sugar and caffeine. The breakfast of champions.

Falco heard planes pass overhead and expected to hear some explosions. There were none. They were friendlies then, providing forces on Little D with air cover, or heading west to battle the Russians.

How was Parker doing? Falco wondered. Well, he hoped. He found himself thinking about her frequently, even though he knew that was stupid. The woman was a certified man magnet for god's sake. And bound to have a significant other somewhere. So the fantasies were a waste of time. But Falco couldn't forget the mocking half-smile and the quizzical look in her eyes. It was as if she wanted to know more. About *him?* Or was that too much to hope for? "We have targets, sir," Jenkins said. "A lot of them."

Falco went to look over the UAV operator's shoulder. The Raven was over Big D by then ... And as the drone followed the road west a column of heat signatures blossomed on the screen. The Russians were too professional to let their vehicles bunch up, so the targets were spaced out. But there was only so much room on the road, which meant the Americans might be able to score multiple kills. "We'll start on *this* side of the island," Falco said. "And work our way west. Lee, put Slingshot-One and Two on standby ... Jenkins, see the big blob? How much you wanta bet that's a T-14 tank? Mark the target, and send it to Slingshot-One. Lee? Tell them to fire when ready."

No sooner had the order been passed, than the howitzer sent a smart round arching high into the sky. Eight more fell in quick succession. The results were spectacular. The entire team gathered around and watched as death fell on target after target. What initially appeared as blobs of heat expanded into clouds, some of which began to merge.

A cheer went up after each hit. Then, as Slingshot-One fired its ninth round, Slingshot-Two took over. And, as the second howitzer fired, the first gun was towed away.

Just in time too! What sounded like a freight train passed overhead. That was followed by a BOOM, as the Russian shell exploded to the east of them. More rounds followed.

But Slingshot-One was not only clear of the target area, but in a new location, where it had to locate itself via GPS. That was required in order to use smart munitions, but consumed very little time. Twenty minutes after leaving its first location the howitzer was ready to sling lead again.

The Russians tried to run, but there was nowhere to go, so the howitzers had a field day. Then the one-sided battle came to an end when the Russians spotted Mutt and blew the Raven out of the sky. It was hard to say exactly how the feat was accomplished. But it was possible that the Russians had something akin to the American C-RAM (Counter Rocket, Artillery, and Mortar System) which used radar and a Gatling gun to defend against airborne targets.

That cut the group's targeting capabilities in half, and forced Falco to consider his options. Should he put Jeff up? And run the risk of losing it? Or save the Raven for later on? The problem was that Falco didn't have any clear notion of what that "later on" would be. So he went all in. "Okay, launch Jeff... But keep him low, and as far from the target as possible, while continuing to maintain contact. Maybe we can slip under their radar."

Jenkins went out to hand launch Jeff, and once the drone was in the air, Cooper took control. The drone took ten minutes to cross the two plus mile gap of water that separated the islands. Cooper called Falco over at that point. And, as the JTAC peered over her shoulder, he could see that the soldier had a fine touch.

The Raven was low, no more than fifty feet off the ground. That narrowed what they could see. Still, a target was a target, even if the entire array of possibilities wasn't visible.

Targeting information was sent to the gun crews, shells began to fall with devastating accuracy, and Jeff was flying so low that Falco feared the Raven would be destroyed by one of the explosions. Fortunately that didn't happen. What *did* happen was that the enemy spotted Jeff and shot it down.

But even though the howitzers couldn't fire with the same degree of precision, they could continue to fire, and the road was the obvious target. "Tell the redlegs to switch to regular rounds, and follow the road west, and onto the bridge," Falco instructed. "Colonel Waya told us to mess with their heads and we will. Are we using drones or not? The Russians won't be sure. We'll ruin their sleep if nothing else. Oh, and tell them to randomize their firing intervals."

Lee passed the orders and, secure in the knowledge that Oliver would be on duty for the next three hours, Falco took the opportunity to grab some shuteye. The ground was hard, but he slept like a rock, until Russian planes delivered a wake-up call two hours later. And they came in force. Bombs landed *everywhere*… It was as if the enemy was determined scour the mesa clean of all life.

It was still dark. So when Falco went outside there was nothing to see other than flashes of light as the gravity bombs fell—and the crisscrossing lines of tracer which reached up to find the enemy planes. Maybe the shells would hit something, but it didn't seem likely.

Fortunately the defenders had plenty of shoulder launched Stinger missiles plus the Humvee mounted Avenger Air Defense units to defend themselves with. Each Avenger system included two, four missile pods, and each weapon was equipped with an infrared homing package.

Missiles sleeted into the air and went looking for targets. Falco heard a succession of explosions, but had no way to know whether they were the result of hits on enemy aircraft, or bombs hitting the ground.

The air raid lasted for fifteen minutes or so and, when it finally came to an end, there was no way to know why. Had American planes chased the bombers away? Did the Russian planes need more bombs? Both possibilities were believable.

An uneasy silence settled over the mesa, as the short artic night came to an end, and the first blush of dawn appeared in the east. There were so many bomb craters that the plateau looked like the surface of the moon. Medics hiked from place-to-place searching for casualties. When two of them passed the shelter Falco took the opportunity to learn what he could. "How's it going? Did we take a lot of casualties?"

"A few," one the medics allowed. "But our people were spread out, and that kept the total number down." She jerked a thumb back over her shoulder. "They're taking the wounded out now."

Falco nodded, thanked her, and returned to the shelter. The rest of the team was inside grousing about their MREs, and trading meal components. "I'll trade you my cookies for your M&M's," Cooper offered.

"Forget that," Lee replied. "But I'll trade some cheese spread for cocoa." And so it went. In the meantime Falco was thinking. Random fire had *some* value...However, like any JTAC, Falco wanted to strike specific targets if possible. But both drones had been destroyed. So what to do? The answer was obvious. If Falco couldn't pick targets electronically, then he'd do it the old fashioned way, which was eyes-on.

After Falco finished his meal he went over to plop down next to Oliver. "I'm going to hire a boat, or try to, and see if I can get close enough to spot some targets."

"That's a good idea," Oliver responded. "I'm coming with you."

"No," Falco replied. "You aren't. I'm leaving you in charge of the shop. Check to see how much ammo the howitzers have left.

If they're running low, tell the crews to take a break. Then I want you to send Cooper and Jenkins out to beg, borrow, or steal some Ravens."

Oliver was none too happy, judging from the expression on his face. "Have fun on the boat, sir. Glory hog."

Falco gave Oliver the finger, and the NCO laughed.

Falco put a PRC-117G and a PRC-152 in a knapsack along with a bottle of water, and some snacks. He was ready to go. The clouds were low, and the air was cold. The slush had set up during the night and crackled underfoot.

The ruins of the old lighthouse marked the trail that led down to the village of *Ignaluk*. And as Falco started down it was clear that the locals were fleeing. They trudged uphill in twos and threes, all carrying packs, with children and dogs trailing along behind.

MPs were stationed along the trail and Falco stopped to speak with one of them. The soldier was filthy except for his weapon which was scrupulously clean. "What's going on?" Falco inquired.

"We offered to take the villagers out two days ago, sir, and most refused. But a bomb fell short of the mesa and destroyed three homes. Twelve people were killed. That changed some minds. There's a small helipad on the waterfront, but it doesn't make sense to lift able bodied people out two or three at a time. Once they arrive inland Chinooks will pick them up."

"Roger that," Falco responded. "Where are the men? All I see are women and children."

"Yes, sir … The menfolk are loading what they can into boats. The town of Wales is only 25 miles east of here—and they make the crossing all the time."

Falco felt a renewed sense of urgency as he hurried down the trail. What if all the boats were gone? Or about to depart? That would put an end to his plan.

When Falco reached the village he saw that both of the boat launches were backed up. A civilian helicopter sat on a pad as people helped two elders climb aboard. Another chopper was circling above and waiting to land. Both aircraft would be easy meat for a Russian fighter, and Falco had to give the helo pilots credit. What they were doing required a lot of courage. Falco stopped a villager. "I'm looking for Sonny Toklo ... Where would I find him?"

The woman pointed toward the beach. Falco thanked her and made his way down. Toklo was helping another man load boxes into a boat. Water smoothed rocks rattled under Falco's boots and threatened to dump him. "Hey Sonny ... It's me. Major Falco."

Sonny turned. There was a smile on his face. "Hey, Major ... It's good to see you. What's up?"

Falco told Toklo about the drones and his desire to hit targets on Big D. Toklo nodded. "I'd love to put the hurts to those bastards! Count me in. Look up there."

Falco followed the pointing finger up the steep hillside to a pile of smoking rubble. "Twelve people died," Toklo said. "I was related to eight of them."

"I'm sorry to hear that," Falco replied. "But I'm afraid that things are about to get even worse. If the Russians land they will level *Ignaluk* in order to make way for a road."

Toklo winced. "Follow me, Major ... We'll make 'em pay."

Toklo's boat was anchored just offshore. To reach it the fisherman summoned a boy in a Zodiac who came to get them. Transferring from one boat to the other proved to be tricky—and Falco felt lucky to make the crossing without falling in.

Toklo thanked the boy, started the engine, and ordered Falco to raise the anchor. Once it was in the boat Toklo took off. The men had no defenses other than the boat's speed and agility. Falco hoped that would be enough.

After a radio check, all Falco had to do was hang on, as the boat banged through low lying waves and Big D grew steadily larger. The top half of the island appeared to be floating on a layer of mist. As they drew closer Falco saw something that alarmed him. *Two* steel barges, both equipped with cranes, had been brought in during the night. In spite of the pounding the Russians had endured they were still grinding ahead! The next steps would be to renew the assault on Little D, seize control if they could, and bring more pontoons in.

But that wasn't going to happen. Not if Falco had anything to say about it. After establishing contact with the howitzer teams Falco fed them information about his intended targets. The wave action made it difficult to hold his binoculars steady, and the engine was so loud that he was forced to shout for Toklo to hear him. "Slow down! I need a steady platform."

Toklo cut the power by half, and the slower speed made a significant difference. The boat was still bucking, but not as violently. That enabled Falco to direct fire the old fashioned way with instructions like "Up, fifty, right fifty, and hold."

Columns of water shot up into the air and collapsed in on themselves. But with each shot the shells landed a little bit closer until shell after shell fell on what Falco thought of as barge one. The hits came only seconds apart. The barge seemed to swell in size before exploding.

There was fuel on board. And it fed an orange-red fireball that rose like a balloon before popping. Steel deck plates sailed through the air as if they were weightless, and the crane fell like a mighty tree. A cloud of steam erupted from below as the remains of the barge dived under the surface. The response was both quick and terrifying. What seemed like a hundred guns opened fire from shore. Geysers of water jumped up all around as Toklo began to jig and jag. "Stop that!" Falco ordered. "I need to hold my glasses steady."

To his credit, and contrary to all common sense, Toklo obeyed. So as Falco sent targeting information to the howitzer teams the only thing that kept them alive was good luck. Then it was over, the shells were on the way, and it was time to run. "Now!" Falco shouted, as a bullet tugged his sleeve. "Let's get out of here!"

Toklo opened the throttle, the bow came up, and the boat raced toward Little D. The small arms fire soon began to dwindle. But the larger weapons continued to fire. Columns of white water shot up all around them. Suddenly Falco had time to be scared and he was. His heart was beating faster—and he felt giddy.

Then Falco saw the Russian patrol boat. White water foamed around the vessel's bow as it surged out of the low lying mist and turned toward them. It had the streamlined appearance of something manufactured in the 50's, and Falco saw that a gun was mounted in the bow. It produced a puff of smoke—and a shell rumbled through the air.

The Russian swabbies clearly knew what they were doing, because when the shot exploded, it was close enough to drench both men with cold water. "Slow down!" Falco ordered, as he brought the binoculars up to his eyes.

Toklo obeyed and Falco began to call fire in. Thanks to the fact that the boat was no longer speeding away, the next shell landed twenty yards in front of it. Falco gave an order and both of the howitzers fired. One round fell short, but the other struck the vessel's bridge. More followed. And, when one of the shells hit a side-mounted missile launcher, there was a secondary explosion that cut the vessel in half.

The bow tilted up before sliding under the waves, even as the stern remained level and started to settle. The patrol boat's horn bleated in a futile attempt to summon help and then the vessel was gone. "Holy shit!" Toklo said, as he stood in the stern. "*That* was amazing! The sky god *Torngasoak* was with you."

"The boat is leaking," Falco observed, as water squirted through a half dozen tiny holes. Caused by flying shrapnel? Yes, it had been a close thing.

"Time to bail," Toklo said, as he tossed a scoop to Falco. "But don't count on *Torngasoak* to help with that."

Falco bailed while Toklo opened the throttle and the boat began to plane. As the bow rose some of the holes cleared the water. That, plus Falco's efforts, were sufficient to keep the bilge water from rising.

By the time the boat arrived most of the other villagers had left and a ramp was open. Toklo ran the bow up onto the gravelly beach. "I'll use some spray stuff to patch the holes," Toklo said, as they got out. "Then I'll head for Wales."

"Thank you," Falco said. "Give me an invoice, and I'll make sure you get paid."

Toklo looked hurt. "I'm an American, Major... I don't want any money."

They shook hands. "My apologies," Falco said. "You're not just an American, you're a badass American! Take care during the crossing."

"I will," Toklo promised. "You're okay for a *Qallunaat.*"

"I don't know what that means," Falco replied, "and I'm not going to ask."

Falco heard Toklo laugh as he walked away. The trail lay ahead... And it was going to be a steep climb.

CHAPTER FOURTEEN

Elmendorf Air Force Base, Alaska, USA

The sun was rising in the east, and the ground came up fast, as Parker put the F-15E Strike Eagle down with a gentle thump. "Sweet... It's almost like you've done it before," Captain Jimmy Baines commented from the back seat. Baines was a Weapons Systems Officer, or WSO, usually pronounced "Wizzo." As such he had responsibility for the plane's navigation, electronic, and weapons systems. His call sign was "Dodger." And if Parker was incapacitated Baines could fly the plane himself.

"Thanks," Parker said, as she turned onto a taxiway. The concrete path led to one of the hastily constructed revetments that lined both sides of the main runway. Now, after dozens of air raids, a single hangar remained. A bullseye was painted on the roof.

Baines wasn't one to hand out compliments for routine landings. So Parker knew the Wizzo was trying to raise her spirits. Because in spite of their best efforts, Parker's flight of four aircraft hadn't been able to penetrate the Russian air defenses.

After bringing the F-15 to a stop Parker and Baines ran through the standard shutdown sequence prior to opening the canopy and climbing out. Their crew chief was waiting on the tarmac. Her name was Evers, and as far as she was concerned, the plane was *hers*. "How's my baby?"

"Not a scratch on her," Baines replied.

"It looks like you brought the entire loadout back."

Parker knew that Evers was referring to the missiles and bombs racked under the F-15's delta shaped wings. "Yeah," she said. "Do you have a problem with that?"

Evers looked from Parker to Baines and back again. "No, ma'am."

"Good," Parker said. Then she walked away.

"Don't take it personally," Baines said. "She's pissed that's all … We didn't get through."

Evers nodded. "Sorry, sir. I put my foot in it."

"No prob. The major needs a break that's all. Gas her up … We'll do better next time."

$$* * *$$

The Russians liked to bomb Elmendorf at least two times a week, so much of the base's infrastructure lay in ruins. Parker was half-way to the makeshift Ops Shack when an army captain hurried to intercept her. "Major Parker?"

"Yes?"

"My name is Deveraux. I report to Lieutenant General Haberman. She would like to speak with you."

Parker was bone tired. *"Now?"*

Deveraux smiled. "I'm afraid so. The general rarely puts anything off."

Parker had heard of Haberman. Everyone had. And for good reason. The hard charging army officer had been plucked out of the European theatre to lead Operation Pushback and, as she told a reporter, "… to fuck the Russians up." A statement which produced smiles at the Pentagon. As Baines joined them Parker made the introductions. "Captain Deveraux is taking us to see General Haberman," she informed him. "Now."

"Uh, oh," Baines said. "What was it? The victory roll two days ago? We'll be good, I promise."

"No," Deveraux assured him. "The general will explain. Please follow me."

Parker and Baines had no choice but to accompany Deveraux to a waiting Humvee and climb in. Flight gear and all. The driver knew his way around, and felt free to take shortcuts. Like the one that cut across a badly cratered athletic field.

The headquarters building had been targeted early on, and that explained why Haberman and her staff were camped in the Officer's Club. It was surrounded by Avenger Air Defense systems. They swiveled as if sniffing the air. The officers had to pass through two layers of security before entering the building.

Once inside the aviators found themselves in what had once been the "Flight Line" dining room, but had since been converted into open office space. It was home to dozens of desks and buzzing with activity. Deveraux led them through the maze to a door with a plaque that read "Manager's Office." After following the staff officer into a spacious room, Parker saw that an entire wall was devoted to flat screens, while a second was home to a messy whiteboard, and a third could barely be seen behind a gigantic map. Colored pins had been pushed into the sheetrock beyond— and satellite photos were posted here, there and everywhere. A yellow post-it was attached to each.

Haberman was seated behind a steel desk talking on a landline. She waved her guests towards some mismatched chairs. "Yes, sir … I'll look into it. Of course, sir. You too. Goodbye."

Then, like an explosive ordinance disposal tech handling a live bomb, Haberman placed the handset on its receiver. She made a face. "That was Under Secretary of Defense Rollins. He thinks it would be a great idea to have some professional basketball players play some B-ball with our soldiers. What a pinhead."

Haberman had short hair that was, in military parlance, worn "high and tight." Her large eyes were filled with intelligence. They jumped from face-to-face. "Parker and Baines. You could open a law firm after the war. It's a pleasure to meet you. Three kills ... That would have been a significant accomplishment during WWII, but it's truly remarkable these days. Congratulations."

Is that what we're here for? Parker wondered. *A pat on the fanny? I'd rather get some sleep.* But she couldn't say that, and didn't. "Thank you, ma'am ... We were lucky."

Haberman grinned. "Modesty? From a fighter pilot? Now I've seen everything! How 'bout it, Captain? Were you *lucky?*"

"No, ma'am," Baines answered. "The major's the best we have. She shot the first plane down with an old MiG 21."

Haberman nodded. "That's what I heard. And that's why you're here. I have a job for you. A very *special* job."

Parker frowned. "Uh, oh."

Haberman laughed. "I like your style, Major ... You understand how the system works. We have a problem, and his name is Adrian Voronov. I suspect you've heard of him."

Parker knew who Voronov was. Every fighter pilot did. Voronov had shot down what? *Six* American planes? Something like that. And killed a Wizzo in the water. All of Parker's friends wanted to kill him. "Yes, ma'am. I've heard of him."

"Well, here's what he looks like." Haberman aimed a remote at the media wall and pressed a button. A face filled a screen. Voronov had dark hair and small eyes. They stared into the camera as if determined to see through the lens. His nose was bent, as if broken in a fist fight, and the disfigurement made Voronov look tough. His lips were set in a sardonic smile.

"This is his official photograph for the 2014 Sochi Winter Olympics," Haberman said. "A lot of people expected him to win the Slalom. But he got into a fight with a British skier, and was expelled."

Parker couldn't think of anything meaningful to say. "Yes, ma'am."

"Well," Haberman said, as she leaned back in her chair. "Somebody needs to kill the bastard. And we chose you two for the job."

Parker frowned. "Permission to speak freely?"

Haberman nodded. "Granted."

"That's *it?*" Parker demanded. "We go up and shoot him down? Voronov would be dead if it was that easy. Everybody's gunning for him."

"We know it won't be easy," Haberman replied. "But you're the best team in this theatre. And you understand Russian planes and pilots better than your peers do. That, plus the information we've assembled could make the critical difference.

"So, if you agree, we're going to pull you out of the normal rotation so you can bone up. Then we'll put you back on the schedule. That's when the hunt will start. Are you in?"

Parker looked at Baines. He nodded and Parker felt the first stirrings of fear. Was she truly good enough? She hoped so. "We're in," Parker said.

"Good," Haberman replied, as she pushed a file folder toward the front of her desk. "Don't take this outside the building. Park it with my adjutant when you're ready to leave. And one more thing..."

"Yes?"

"I suggest that you have a chat with Lieutenant Milo Davis. Voronov shot him down over the Bering Sea—and killed his Wizzo in the water. Maybe Davis can provide some useful information. Be gentle though... He's pretty messed up."

Parker had heard about it. Everybody had. "Yes, ma'am."

"Okay," Haberman said as she stood. "You have two days to get ready. Use the time wisely."

Parker and Baines were too tired to tackle the project then and there. So they asked Deveraux to drop them at the chow hall. After a quick meal they hitched a ride to the apartment house where they were staying. After agreeing to meet at 1600 they went their separate ways.

Parker expected to sleep well, but didn't. There were dreams. *Bad* dreams. Including one in which she and her husband Greg were riding a roller coaster when their car flew off the tracks and sailed through the air. Parker screamed, and tried to grab Greg. But he fell. And the ride continued without him.

Then the car, with Parker in it, was magically transformed into an F-15 which swooped up into the sky. An enemy pilot was on her six. He laughed manically, and Baines yelled, "Break right!" Parker woke to find that her tee was soaked with sweat, and her heart was beating like a trip hammer.

Parker lay there for a while. Light leaked in through the gap in the curtains and the monotonous thump, thump, thump of bass could be heard from a neighboring apartment. *Where was Falco?* she wondered. And why did she care? It had been awhile since she'd heard his voice on the radio. *Don't do it*, Parker admonished herself. *Don't go there. He'll get killed. And you know what that's like.*

Parker pushed the thoughts away, got up, and took a shower. Then she went out to her pickup. It wasn't much to look at, but it started with a roar, and would be good in the snow if she lived that long.

The base's DFAC (dining facility) served breakfast all day. Parker ate alone, left for the Officer's Club/Headquarters building, and went looking for Haberman's adjutant. He removed the Voronov file from a safe, asked Parker to sign for it, and told her to return it prior to departure. "I hope you nail him," the major said. "The bastard needs killing."

After commandeering an empty desk Parker went to work. The first thing on the pile was an Intel summary written by an analyst named Burke. "Based on Voronov's activities prior to war," Burke wrote, "and interviews since—there's reason to believe that he's a full blown sociopath. Voronov has no interest in the way other people feel, and no feelings of remorse when he causes them pain.

"However," Burke continued, "it should be noted that according to a doctoral thesis published by Katie M. Ragan in 2009, and titled: *'The Warfighters of Today: Personality and Cognitive Characteristics of Rated Fighter Pilots in the United States Air Force,'* the negative aspects of Voronov's personality are in some ways consistent with the attributes associated with our best fighter pilots. In her thesis Ragan points out that according to a study carried out in 2005, fighter pilots tend to have high scores relative to assertiveness, activity, and a need for achievement, but tend to score lower in agreeableness, self-consciousness, vulnerability, and warmth than other pilots do.

"So it seems fair to say that while sharing what are regarded as positive personality characteristics with his peers—Voronov's narcissism and lack of empathy serve to set him apart from his fellow aviators."

Parker frowned. Did that mean *she* was assertive and ambitious? Sure…So what? She continued reading. Based on after action reports, and military intelligence, Burke had been able to create a list of Voronov's "tendencies." He rarely flew during the hours of darkness. Did the Russian want to avoid the complexities associated with night flying? Or was Voronov hooked on watching his enemies die? No one knew.

Voronov never flew with a wingman. And that made sense. Like any egomaniac Voronov believed that he could handle everything by himself. And, due to Voronov's narcissism, there was a high probability that other pilots didn't want to fly with him. Would Voronov sacrifice them to achieve a kill? Of course he would. And so long as Voronov continued to kill Americans, the Russian command structure appeared willing to indulge the sociopath's quirks.

The next entry held particular interest for Parker. "Based on press reports, and interviews with American women who had relationships with Voronov before the war, he's extremely competitive where females are concerned. A trait that was very much on display during ski events when Voronov would challenge women to side contests that he always won.

"And where sex is concerned," Burke continued, "Voronov shows little interest in giving his partners pleasure, likes to control his lovers, and prefers positions that don't require eye contact."

Parker placed the report on the desk. What, if anything, would Voronov's misogyny mean where combat was concerned? Had he ever gone one-on-one with a female pilot? That seemed unlikely. More were being trained. But only four percent of U.S. fighter pilots were women before the war. And there were very few females in the Russian military.

Odds were that Voronov's need to compete with women would come into play the moment he heard her voice. Could she use that against him? *I hope so*, Parker thought. *We'll find out.* Her phone rang. It was Baines. "Where are you?"

Parker responded and he arrived thirty minutes later. It was more than an hour before they were slated to meet. "You couldn't sleep?" Parker inquired.

"Not very well," Baines admitted. "I see you've been reading. Give me a synopsis."

Parker told him about the contents of the report but didn't mention the misogyny. *Why?* Because she didn't want to stress an advantage that might not exist. "So this guy is a full-on fruitcake," Baines concluded, as he sipped coffee from a mug.

"*And* a hot pilot," Parker responded. "I'm going to call Lieutenant Davis. Let's see if he's willing to speak with us."

It turned out that Davis was flying a desk in the procurement office. And when he came off duty Parker and Baines were there to pick him up. Parker's truck had a crew cab, and she made eye contact with Davis, as he slipped into the backseat. Davis was a good looking kid, with even features, and mocha colored skin. "I thought we'd get a drink," Parker told him. "Does that work for you?"

"Yes, ma'am," Davis answered. "I could use one. The procurement office is a zoo."

Baines laughed. "Is it worse than flying?"

Parker knew the Wizzo meant well. But the comment served to remind Davis of the fact that he'd been grounded. His smile disappeared. "Yes, sir. It's worse than flying."

Having put his foot in it Baines sought to change the subject. The men were talking baseball when Parker pulled into the King Crab's parking lot. "Come on," Parker said, as they got out. "I'm buying."

The bar was located near the front of the restaurant and decorated with marine kitsch. Oars, brass fittings, and photos of fishing boats hung on the walls. After being shown to a well-worn booth the pilots placed their orders. "So," Parker said, as the waiter walked away. "You know why we're here."

"You have orders to kill Voronov," Davis said. "I hope you get him. For me, and for my Wizzo."

"Tell us what happened," Parker said. "Start at the beginning."

Davis shrugged. "The weather was good. After we took off we climbed to 25,000 feet and turned north. Our orders were to look for Russian shipping and a Russian spy plane that had been seen in the area. And that's what we were doing when my wingman developed a right engine control issue. He turned back, and we continued on. Voronov jumped us fifteen minutes later."

Davis looked away at that point, and Parker was about to say something, when the drinks arrived. That gave Davis an opportunity to pull himself together. "So, where was I? Oh, yeah... Voronov called me on the emergency frequency. He spoke perfect English. He identified himself as a Mud Hen (F-15E Strike Eagle), call sign Badger. Voronov said he'd been sent to replace my wingman." Davis paused at that point, and sipped his drink.

"Mike called bullshit on that," Davis said, "and told me to take evasive action. I did. We were all over the sky for a while. And it soon became apparent that Voronov was toying with me. I went to an unloaded extension but couldn't shake him."

Parker knew Davis was referring to a maneuver in which the defending pilot goes into a steep drive and applies full thrust. The purpose of the evolution was to take the g-force off the aircraft and accelerate so as to increase his or her chances of escape.

"It didn't work," Davis said morosely. "Voronov was riding my six, and critiquing my performance. Looking back I realize he was in my head.

"He could have splashed me, but he didn't," Davis added. "We played cat and mouse for what seemed like an eternity, but was actually no more than two or three minutes. I think Voronov got bored. He fired a radar guided missile. And, while I was trying to evade that, he pickled (fired) a heat seeker. It slammed into the starboard engine and exploded."

That was a common strategy, and Parker knew it could happen to anybody. "And then?"

"And then we bailed out," Davis answered bitterly. "I spotted Mike's chute. And I saw him hit the water. He waved at me. Then Voronov made a gun run. Gouts of white water shot up into the air and Mike disappeared." A tear trickled down Davis's cheek.

"I'm sorry," Baines said. "I met Mike once... He was a standup guy."

"Yeah," Davis said, as he wiped the moisture away. "And I let him down."

Parker opened her mouth to speak, but stopped when Davis raised a hand. "Don't try to make it okay, Major. The only thing you can do to make me feel better is to blow Voronov out of the sky."

"We'll do our best," Parker promised.

"He knew I was alive," Davis added. "And he let me live. So I could tell the story."

That fit everything Parker knew and she nodded. "So one of our ships managed to reach you?"

"Yeah. A coast guard icebreaker named the *Northern Dawn*."

Baines frowned. "Is that the one that rammed the bridge? And cut it in two?"

"Yes," Davis replied. "It took the Russians two days to repair the span. I hear the brass put Captain Soto in for a medal of honor. And his engineer too. "

Two days, Parker mused. *We sacrificed two men and a ship in exchange for two days. We are in some deep shit.* "Thank you," Parker said out loud. "Your glass is empty. Let's order another round." The conversation continued—but the meeting was over.

Parker slept better that night. Perhaps that was the natural result of how tired she was. And maybe a few hours of actual darkness helped. Whatever the reason Parker was in good spirits when she awoke. After a light breakfast in a nearby coffee shop, she drove on base, and made her way to the group's temporary operations center where Baines was waiting.

Then it was time to keep their appointment with military intelligence officer Mary Gooding. She was thirty-something, and had the manner of a stern librarian. Her office was located in a converted storeroom where two computer screens glowed, overlapping maps were taped to the walls, and a stick of incense burned in a tray. The reason for that was unclear as Gooding came forward to greet them. "Good morning, Major … Captain … You're on time … I like that. It's my understanding that you're here for a briefing on Russian pilot Adrian Voronov … Is that correct?"

"Yes," Parker said. "It is."

"Good," the other woman replied. "You have no idea how often people schedule a meeting to discuss subject X and demand information about topic Y."

"That would be annoying," Baines said.

"Exactly," Gooding agreed. "Now, let's take a look at the map that I prepared. The red push pins represent locations where Voronov scored a kill. The blue push pins represent an area where he was sighted, or engaged in a verbal exchange of some sort. The man loves to talk, so there are plenty of those."

"Sightings?" Parker inquired. "How so? Is there something distinctive about Voronov's plane?"

"Voronov's call sign is the Russian word for jester," Gooding replied. "And the silhouette of a jester is visible below his canopy."

"Somebody got that close?" Parker inquired.

"Yes, they did," Gooding replied, without offering any additional details.

Parker eyed the map. She was struck by the fact that most of Voronov's kills and contacts had occurred north of the Diomede Islands. That made sense since the American planes were continually looking for opportunities to end run Russian defenses. *So that's where we'll look for him,* Palmer thought. *And dance the dance.*

The rest of the briefing was focused on Voronov's ride. And *that,* Gooding informed them, was a Sukhoi Su-35. Both Parker and Baines were familiar with the planes, and had a healthy respect for them. The briefer was ready with photos *and* videos of Su-35s performing at airshows. "The 25 can carry a lot of air-to-ground ordinance," Gooding told them. "But that doesn't concern you—so I won't spend any time on it. What *does* matter is the array of long and short range air-to-air missiles Voronov will have to work with.

"And," Gooding added, "two after-action reports indicate that once you engage Voronov he will jettison his air-to-ground ordinance to lighten his plane. That's hard on Russian tax payers, but I think it's safe to say that Voronov doesn't care.

"Now, let's talk about electronics. Su-35s are equipped with Irbis-E passive electronically scanned array radars, which are integrated into the plane's fire control system. The Irbis system can detect a 32 square foot aerial target at a range of 250 miles, track 30 airborne targets at once, and simultaneously engage eight of them."

And there was more. *Much* more. And the next thirty minutes were spent listening to Gooding extoll the Su-35's considerable virtues. "In summary," she said, "the Su-35 is a match for the F-15. Yes, it's slightly slower in terms of maximum speed, but it can accelerate faster. And that isn't the worst of it. The Su-35 is definitely superior to an F-15 at lower speeds because the 35s have three-dimensional thrust vectoring. So keep that in mind if you should get a chance to mix it up with Voronov."

"Maybe we should shoot ourselves, and save Voronov the trouble," Baines suggested darkly.

"If you wish," Gooding said humorlessly. "But remember … I said the Su-35 is a match for the F-15. I didn't say it was *better*. Once you engage Voronov it will come down to piloting. And, like it or not, luck."

The rest of the day was spent in meetings with operations staff and other pilots laying out a plan and discussing the resources required to carry it out. Parker didn't get everything she asked for, but enough to do the job, and that would have to do.

Once all of the arrangements were in place Parker and Baines went their separate ways. For Parker that meant returning to her apartment to nuke a chicken and rice dinner, before paying her bills, and doing a load of laundry. Then it was time to email her mother. She couldn't tell Mary about Voronov—and didn't want to.

So she told Mary everything was fine, there was a little less daylight with each passing day, and she hoped that fuel rationing wasn't hitting too hard. Would it be the last email she sent home? Parker pushed the thought away.

After a fitful night's sleep Parker rose ready to kick some ass. And, when it came time to takeoff, her head was not only clear, but *super* clear, thanks to the adrenaline pumping through her veins. It took less than an hour of flight time to reach the area Voronov was known to frequent, climb to 40,000 feet, and fly lazy eights.

Parker was wearing a JHMCS (Joint Helmet Mounted Cueing System), which performed like a heads-up-display in her visor. The data was displayed over her dominant eye. That meant Parker could move her head in any direction and *still* see data which included her wingman, air-to-air targets, air-to-ground targets, and so on. It made cueing easy. All she had to do was lock the radar onto a bandit in an air-to-air engagement by staring at him, and using some HOTAS (Hands On Throttle And Stick).

The responsibility for navigation was shared. But ultimately Parker was supposed to get the plane where it was going, while Baines had to make sure that the coordinates for their steer points were properly loaded. And he had total responsibility for identifying all manner of targets via the Electronically Scanned Radar.

Parker's wingman was with her and following the same course. Meanwhile, down at 20,000 feet the bait plane, call sign Rubber Ducky, was pretending to fly a patrol. The hope was that Voronov would spot the Fighting Falcon and go after it. That's when Parker would fall on him like a rock.

But it didn't happen. A couple of Russian MiG-29s happened by, forcing the Falcon to run like hell, but that was all. And that left Parker and Baines feeling frustrated as they returned to Anchorage.

The following day was no better. "Maybe it's the radar that Gooding told us about," Baines said, as they continued to fly overlapping circles. "Maybe he can see us."

"I'm sure Voronov *will* see us," Parker replied. "*If* he's flying. And, when he does he'll be faced with a choice. He can go after the bait plane, or climb, in which case we'll dive on him."

"Or," Baines said, "he could come after us at 40,000 feet."

"That works for me," Parker replied. "Neither one of us can go much higher, so we'll shoot it out."

Baines had heard it before. But talking it through made him feel better. He had plenty of high tech toys to rely on including electronic countermeasures, a friend or foe interrogator, and a radar warning system that would squawk him the moment Voronov turned his fancy Irbis-E system on. At that point a cockpit display would show Baines how close the enemy plane was. Then it would be time to activate the F-15's radar and find the bastard. But not on that particular day. They returned to base.

The sky was mostly clear as they took off on the third day. Parker was alert, but less concerned than she had been previously, because she had a theory. Voronov hadn't shot anyone down since splashing Davis. Nor had he been seen, so where was the jerk?

Maybe, just maybe, Voronov had been transferred to Europe or some other theatre. And that would make sense. The bastard was shit hot ... And he'd be an asset wherever the Russians sent him.

In that case Parker was in for another boring day. And, truth be told, that would be fine. Because no one in their right mind would want to play sky tag with Voronov if they could avoid it.

But that was a private theory... One Parker wasn't going to share with anybody, lest it make her seem hesitant, or take the edge off the rest of the team.

So Parker pulled the stick back, climbed to 40,000 feet, and made the 700 mile commute to the operational area north of the Diomede Islands. As Parker and her wingman entered the area their Wizzos scanned for threats. "My screens are clean," Baines said. "Maybe Voronov is sleeping late."

"Could be," Parker allowed, hoping the bastard was somewhere else. "Keep your head on a swivel."

Time dragged, and dragged some more. After an hour and a half, and an AAR (air-to-air refueling) they resumed their previous course. Fifteen minutes passed before Baines spoke. His voice was tense. "I have an incoming target. It's at 40,000 feet, and closing on the bait plane. I have no way to know if it's Voronov."

"He knows we're here," Parker observed. "He has to ... And the arrogant bastard thinks he can splash the bait *and* kick our asses too. Tell Rubber Ducky to run ... Let's get him!"

Parker put the plane into a steep dive with Cricket off her starboard wing and slightly to the rear. Voronov began to climb as the bait plane took off. As he did so the Russian pilot was shedding air-to-ground ordinance. The mind games began. As Parker aimed the F-15 at the spot where Voronov was going to be, the Russian pilot began to talk over the guard (emergency) frequency. "Oh, my! A trap ... I'll take that as a compliment."

"Of course you will," Parker responded, as she prepared to turn in behind him. "You're a narcissist, so you take *everything* as a compliment. Like the time you had sex with Marci Owens, and she told you that it was 'Okay.'"

Voronov must have been stunned by the response, because he not only failed to respond, but wound up with *two* Strike Eagles on his tail. Parker fed him a pair of IR seeking Sidewinder missiles. Voronov fired flares that drew the heat seekers away—so

Parker kept her other weapons on the rails rather than waste them. Then Voronov was back on the air. "A woman! They sent a woman to do a man's job. Only the Americans would do such a thing. Russians love and protect their women."

"Right," Parker said, as she followed Voronov into a turn. "Like the time you beat the shit out of Mandy Mason, and left her bleeding on a bathroom floor."

Baines yelled, "Shoot!" and Parker did. The Sidewinder missed, but not by much.

* * *

Voronov was in deep shit and he knew it. The woman was on him like white on rice. But he knew a trick... A *good* trick. And one that could turn the table on the American bitch. The Cobra, also known as Pugachev's Cobra, was an extremely demanding maneuver in which a pilot raises his airplane's nose into a vertical position prior to dropping back into normal flight. The purpose of the evolution was to slow the plane down causing a pursuer to overshoot. And Voronov was flying the right plane for the job. His Su-35 was equipped with dimensional thrust vectoring which, combined with his skill, allowed Voronov to pull a flawless Cobra.

* * *

The move took Parker by surprise. And, as Voronov appeared to stall, she shot past him. Then, as Voronov came out of the Cobra, Cricket flashed past him. Voronov saw the opening and took it. Two missiles surged out from under his wings and one hit Cricket's right wing. His F-15 trailed smoke as it spiraled downwards. "You're on your own now," Voronov said, as he began to climb.

Parker knew Cricket had been hit, but couldn't allow herself to think about it, as Voronov pulled in on her six. In an effort to regain the upper hand Parker transitioned into a move called a Vector Roll.

Voronov fired an Archer IR missile but it missed thanks to the countermeasures that Baines used. Voronov fell out of position for a second, but managed to pull back in, and continue the chase. Both fighters were in a Flat Scissors flight pattern. At that point Parker had little choice but to go for a Guns-D, or Guns Jinks, which involved a series of random changes intended to throw her pursuer off.

Unfortunately the Guns-D still left Parker vulnerable to stray cannon shells and "lucky shot" hits, while doing little to improve her overall situation. She was scared and running out of ideas. "You're wasting fuel," Voronov said. "And delaying the inevitable. Bail out ... It's all the same to me."

"Forget that shit," Baines put in. "Give him a high-g barrel roll."

Parker knew it was a good call. The first step was to turn hard and pull Voronov in close, which she did, and which he perceived as an extension of the Guns-D.

Then Parker applied hard back-stick pressure and added some hard rudder to help the F-15's ailerons roll the fighter. That created the high g-forces which gave the maneuver its name.

A high-g barrel roll can be performed "over-the-top" or "underneath," which is accomplished by rolling upside-down and beginning the maneuver from the inverted position. And that's what Parker did.

Because the high-g is an energy-depleting maneuver it rarely forces the attacker out front. But it frequently results in a flight-path overshoot, or a flat scissors, either of which would give Parker a momentary advantage. "Girl skiers have a nickname for you," Parker lied. "They call you 'pin dick' because you're so small. That has to hurt."

It was hard to say if the insult caused Voronov to lose focus for a moment or the barrel roll would have worked anyway. But the result was everything Parker had been hoping for. She came out of it above and behind the other pilot. It was perfect for a guns solution. And when she pickled the plane's cannon Parker knew she had him. "This is for Davis, Cricket and Mandy Mason," Parker said as 20mm explosive rounds hit the Su-35. Then the fighter blew up.

"That was righteous," Baines said, as the plane banked. "No chute... Cricket and his Wizzo are okay... The combat search and rescue people are on the way."

"We need fuel, and we need it badly," Parker told him. "Let's find a Toad (KC-135 tanker) and gas up."

Once the fuel was on board they flew to Anchorage where, contrary to regs, Parker performed a victory roll over the strip. Baines laughed like a maniac as an air traffic controller swore at them. They were alive.

CHAPTER FIFTEEN

Little Diomede Island, USA, the Bering Strait

"**H**urry up and wait." Never had the old military axiom been truer. After destroying the Russian barges, and the patrol boat, Falco returned to Little Diomede expecting the enemy to attack within hours. They didn't.

There were various theories regarding that. Some people figured that the Russians were overextended and would have to withdraw soon. Others believed that Russia's newly named president was less enthusiastic about invading Alaska than his predecessor had been.

But there was a *third* possibility, and that was the one Falco favored. After making what they considered to be good progress, the Russians were consolidating their gains, and preparing for the next push. *Then*, in Falco's opinion, the shit would hit the fan.

Whatever the truth of the matter, the respite was an opportunity. It could have been, *should* have been, a period during which the Americans could send reinforcements to Little D. But according to Colonel Waya, there weren't any additional forces to bring in. So all his combat team could do was wait and hope. "Every day we hold Little D constitutes a victory," Waya told them.

For Falco and his team the pause was a chance to take tepid showers, eat one of the hot meals that were flown in once a day, and perform maintenance on their gear. And that's what Falco was doing when a runner appeared. The private appeared to be in his late teens—and was probably just out of boot camp. "Major Falco?"

"Yes?"

"Colonel Waya wants you to attend a briefing at 1300."

"About what?"

"I don't know, sir. I'm a private."

Falco laughed. "Roger that. I'll be there."

Finally, Falco thought, as the runner left. *We're going to do something.*

The sky was gray when 12:45 rolled around, and it was raining as Falco made his way east. It wasn't long before he fell into company with an army captain. "What have *you* heard?" Falco wanted to know. "What's Waya going to say?"

"Most people think we're going to pull out," the captain replied. "And why not? We can't hold this place. Not with what we have."

That made sense. But, if Falco had learned anything during his years in the air force, it was that things are always more complicated than they seem to be.

There was standing room only inside the tent. All sorts of uniforms were in evidence including those worn by Canadians. And that made sense. Canada was part of NATO. And, if Alaska fell, their country would be on the front line. The mood was somber and a sergeant major hollered, "Atten-hut!" as Waya entered.

Waya stepped up onto a stage that consisted of two stacked cargo pallets. His eyes roamed the crowd. "As you were. I won't waste your time with rah-rah bullshit. We're in a tough spot, and it's about to get worse. What the Intel people estimate to be three Russian attack submarines entered the strait during the last 72 hours. They have *two* objectives. The first is to shield the first span from *our* subs. The second is to protect a naval task force consisting of the Russian cruiser *Admiral Konev*, and two Udaloy Class destroyers.

"The *Konev* is a monster. Not only is she armed with anti-ship missiles, surface-to-air missiles, and an AK-130mm gun battery, she's equipped with Kashtan close-defense weapons systems that can intercept and destroy anti-ship missiles, anti-radar missiles, guided bombs, aircraft and fast attack boats. That means she's damned near unstoppable.

"It's safe to say that once the *Konev* and her escorts get here, they're going to circle Little-D the way my ancestors circled wagon trains, and try to pound us into the ground. Then their tugs will tow dozens of additional pontoons in, and work on the second span will commence."

Waya paused at that point. Except for a single cough there was complete silence within the tent. His eyes jumped from face-to-face. "General Haberman wants us to hold out as long as we can before falling back on the village of Wales. But, given how difficult the situation is, she won't order us to remain here. Any man or woman who wants to leave, and join our forces on the mainland, will be free to do so during the next twelve hours.

"Take that message back to your troops. Tell them that if they wish to withdraw they can do so starting at 1500 hours this afternoon. They are to bring all of their gear, and assemble at the helicopter pads, where Chinooks will take them off.

"Those who choose to stay will dig in even deeper and prevent troop landings until the last minute, when every effort will be made to pull them out. Do you have any questions?" There were none.

"All right," Waya told them. "Hold fast while Sergeant Major Benson reads a list of officers who I need to speak with. Thank you for your service to our country."

There was a "Hooah," but it sounded lame, and Falco wondered how many people would choose to stay. Sergeant Major

Benson read a list of seven names and Falco's was last. That forced him to wait for more than an hour before being summoned into the corner of the tent that Waya was using as his office. He threw a salute and Waya returned it. "It's good to see you, Major. Take a load off."

Waya's guest chair consisted of an upturned crate. Falco sat down as Waya lowered himself onto a rickety lawn chair. "You heard my speech, including the stuff about the *Konev*."

"Sir, yes sir."

"Good, because your job is to sink her."

Falco's thoughts started to churn. Sink her? Hell, based on what Waya had said earlier, it would be damned near impossible to put a dent in the cruiser—assuming the ship's antiaircraft capabilities were as good as advertised.

Waya raised a hand. "I know what you're thinking… There's no way to do it with what's available, and you're correct. But we have something the Russkies don't know about. It's a low Earth orbit Nuclear Spectroscopic Telescope Array called Oz. The satellite's ostensible purpose is to search deep space for black holes.

"However that's a cover for the *real* package which consists of a one-shot laser weapon code named 'Derringer.' And, according to the briefing I received six hours ago, Derringer packs a punch that could put the Konev out of action—or even sink her.

"But in order to do that I need a crazy air force major to laze the bitch, and hold the target, while the Russians throw everything they have at him! And you're the crazy major that I have in mind."

Falco felt something cold trickle into his bloodstream. The moment he locked his laser designator onto the *Konev* the Russians would get a fix on his location. And then a whole lot of bad things would start to happen. Could he refuse? Probably. But then Waya would turn to Oliver and Lee. Would one or both of them volunteer? Yes.

Falco forced a smile. "Thanks for the vote of confidence, sir ... I would like nothing better than to give the Russians some target practice. I have a question though ... What's going to happen *after* we reveal Derringer? Won't the Russians attack every satellite we have?"

Waya shrugged. "Maybe. But this mission was authorized by the Secretary of Defense. So I think we can assume that the brass are well aware of the strategic implications, and ready to deal with the blowback."

Falco hoped that was true. "Yes, sir."

"Here's how it's going to work," Waya told him. "My engineers are prepping four hardened outposts (OPs). But only one will be used. That's the one on the south shore."

Falco understood the necessity of that. The Russians were watching the Americans via satellites, spy planes, and drones. With any luck at all they would assume that the newly created OPs were part of the defensive measures to defend the entire island prior to the coming invasion. "We don't have time to start from scratch," Waya added. "That's why the engineers are putting roofs over existing ravines. They will be six feet thick."

That made sense. By placing lids over the island's many ravines the Americans could save a lot of time and effort. Plus, given the nature of the situation, the OP on the south shore didn't need to be perfect. But would six feet worth of protection be enough? Falco hoped so. "I'll need a platform to work from," he said.

"You'll have it," Waya promised. "And some help too. The brass sent an egghead to serve as a liaison with United States Strategic Command (USSTRATCOM). Doctor Moran was part of the Derringer design team, and will help you bring the weapon to bear."

That was good news since Falco hadn't been trained to call in strikes from satellites. Nor had anyone else so far as he knew. "That sounds good, sir."

"All right," Waya said. "Get together with Moran and head for your OP. The sergeant major will contact your team and let them know where to meet up with you. Based on present estimates you have about four hours to get ready."

Both men stood. Waya extended his hand. "You're the real deal, Major... I hereby retract the things I've said about the air force over the years."

Falco grinned. "I wish I could reciprocate sir, but I can't."

Waya laughed. "Take care Wombat... I'll be pulling for you." And with that the briefing was over.

Falco left the makeshift office, and was making his way to the tent's entrance, when Sergeant Major Benson intercepted him. "Major Falco, this is Doctor Betsy Moran. She's on loan from STRATCOM."

Moran was short, had a mop of graying hair, and was dressed in civilian hiking gear. Her eyes were bright. "It's a pleasure to meet you Major... I'll do everything I can to help."

Moran had a small hand, but a firm handshake, and Falco liked her straight forward manner. "Welcome to Little D, Doc. Where's your gear? Let's grab it. We can talk while we hike to the south side of the island."

Moran had a pack and metal case that held what she said was a global satellite terminal. Falco offered to carry the pack, but Moran declined. "Thanks, but it's an old friend, and I'm used to the weight."

So Falco carried the case as they trudged cross country. The sound of exploding artillery rounds could be heard from the west as howitzers located on Big D prepped the landing zone. Moran was all business. "The tricky part is making sure that Derringer is in the right spot at the right time," she explained. "In order to assure that, and to do so without attracting attention, we've been making incremental adjustments for the past eighteen hours."

"So how's this going to work?" Falco wanted to know.

"I brought the bits and pieces required to link your designator to my terminal," Moran replied. "So when you acquire the target, all you have to do is tell me, and I'll pull the trigger. Simple."

Falco hoped Moran was right, but had his doubts. No one had fired an orbital laser weapon at a moving target before, and when something *can* go wrong, it usually does.

The yellow tractors were quite visible against the white-gray backdrop of slush and sea. Engines growled and exhaust fumes jetted into the air as the machines backed and filled. An army lieutenant was there to meet them. "Major Falco? Doctor Moran? My name is Toby. I was told to expect you."

Rocks rattled as a Cat dumped a load of earth onto the OP's roof. "What's under the dirt?" Falco inquired. "Something sturdy I hope."

"We salvaged some wood beams from the village," Toby replied, "and used a Chinook to lift them out. They were laid crosswise inside the ravine. Then, after nailing sheets of ¾ inch plywood onto the supports, we laid 10 mil plastic down to keep things tidy. Now they're putting six feet of top fill over that. It won't protect you from a direct hit. But, other than that, you should be all snuggly."

If Toby was trying to make them feel better, he failed where Falco was concerned. As for Moran, she was unperturbed. "Can we go below?" she inquired. "I have tests to run."

They could, and they did. By circling around the tractors, and following the boot prints running parallel to the cliff, they were able to access the narrow trail that led down to the open end of the ravine. Moran went first. There was a sheer drop off to the right, and Falco was careful to place his feet just so, lest he slip and fall onto the boulders below.

After descending for ten yards or so Moran disappeared into the hillside. When Falco made the turn he found himself standing on a plywood platform under an eight foot ceiling. The floor was about fifteen feet wide out front, and narrowed to a third of that in the rear. Oliver was there to greet him, as was Lee, and Falco could see that the team's gear was ready to use. That included the radios, a spotting scope, and the all-important laser designator. It was aimed out to sea. "This is Doctor Moran," Falco told them. "She's on loan to the team."

Both men welcomed her, and the group went to work. The next hour was spent connecting Moran's terminal to the laser designator, and running a series of tests. Some minor software glitches surfaced but were quickly resolved.

The *Konev* was only thirty miles away by then ... And there was an empty feeling in Falco's gut. What if he screwed up? What if the *Konev's* gunners fired on the OP before he could laze the ship? Or, what if Derringer failed to work? The minutes seemed to crawl by, and Falco's nerves were frayed by the time Lee spoke. He was sprawled on the floor, and looking through a scope. "I see a ship ... One of the destroyers most likely."

Falco rolled in to take a look. A rain squall was moving across the water two miles south of their position, which meant visibility was limited. But there, nosing through the mist, was the angular bow of a warship! "We have a confirmation from Overlook," Oliver announced. "That's the destroyer *Admiral Anatoly Grishin.*"

Falco saw a flash, followed by a *second* flash, and knew that a pair of 3.9 inch shells were coming their way. Toward *him?* Maybe. But that seemed unlikely. The Russian warships had been sent to prep the island for the invasion. So it seemed reasonable to assume that they'd be gunning for the American helipad, supply dump, and air defenses.

Falco heard a series of distant thumps and knew that the shells were landing somewhere behind him. That was bad, but nothing compared to the damage that the *Konev's* 16 cruise missiles could cause. Each weapon would strike with explosive power equivalent to that of a two-thousand pound bomb.

So, tempting though the destroyer was, Falco had to save Derringer for the cruiser. The *Grishin* fired another salvo, and two additional rounds rumbled over the OP.

As the destroyer ran parallel to the coast, a dark gray shadow appeared in the distance. Falco felt a rising sense of excitement. Was that the cruiser? *Yes!* As the *Konev* cleared the rain squall, there was no mistaking the ship's towering superstructure, and the ranks of missile launchers positioned along the port side. "The target is in sight," Falco said, as he rolled in behind the laser designator.

"I'm on it," Moran said from a few feet away. Keys clicked as the civilian entered an access code into her terminal. "I have control ... Derringer is coming online."

Falco eyed the *Konev* through the designator. "Give me a signal check."

There was a pause followed by, "Signal lock."

Falco swore as missiles flashed up and away. Smoke enveloped the *Konev's* superstructure for a moment and blew away. "The Russians are firing," he said tightly, as a massive explosion was heard. The ground shook. Had the supply dump gone up? Falco assumed it had. A series of secondary explosions seemed to confirm his assumption as did the persistent rattle of small arms ammo cooking off. "Derringer is ready," Moran said flatly. "Remember the lag. You'll have to stay with the ship as it continues to move."

Falco knew that. And he knew that while he was painting the target, the Russians would detect the signal generated by his designator, and backtrack it to his location. Who would strike first? "Roger," Falco replied. "Standby ... *Fire!*"

Nothing happened. Nothing visible anyway. Falco continued to track the enemy ship. Then the *Konev* fired again. Two missiles flashed into the sky, and Falco felt a stab of fear. *No*, he thought to himself, *it's too soon. There's no way they could ...*

The cruise missile struck. There was a loud BOOM, followed by the crack of splintering wood, as the ceiling gave way and tons of dirt fell into the OP. Most of it was towards the back. Falco heard someone cry out, and felt a heavy weight land on his legs. He forced himself to focus on the enemy ship. He was staring at the *Konev* when the laser beam struck.

There was a bright explosion as the laser hit one of the launchers and detonated a cruise missile. The blast opened a hole in the *Konev's* superstructure. Flames appeared and thick black smoke trailed along the cruiser's port side. She was damaged, but still largely intact.

Falco could imagine the panic on the bridge. What had hit them? A submarine launched missile? And was another weapon about to strike the ship?

There was no way to know, so it made sense to run. And while Falco would have preferred a kill, he knew that Derringer's mission had been successful, as the *Grishin* turned back to provide the larger ship with assistance. Meanwhile a *second* destroyer had appeared in the hazy distance. Like the *Grishin* it was there to protect the badly damaged cruiser from American planes and submarines. "The *Konev* is pulling out," Falco announced. "Call it in ... Tell Overlook that we need an air strike."

There was no reply. Falco turned to see that a pile of dirt sloped up and away from him. And, rather than work the radios, Oliver was busy digging. Moran was working next to him. That was when Falco remembered hearing someone cry out. Lee ... Lee was buried!

Falco took the AN/PRC-117G radio, and carried it over to the opening. "Any available aircraft, this is Wombat."

There was a pause, followed by the crackle of static. "Wombat this is Stripper. I have you loud and clear. What kind of trouble are you in now?"

Falco felt a sudden surge of joy at the sound of Parker's voice. She was alive! "Stripper, I'm in an OP on the south side of Little D, looking south. The target is a Russian cruiser. It's damaged and trailing smoke. The target's surface-to-air system is still active in so far as I know. Can you support?"

"Copy threats active," Parker replied. "Staying five miles north. We can support. I see three ships—one is trailing smoke."

"That's your target," Falco confirmed. "Suggest missiles to maintain standoff distance."

"Stripper and Cricket will each fire one AGM-65. ETA two minutes."

"Copy, you are approved for attack, no friendlies near target, all attack headings approved."

"Stripper is in from the north."

Most of the roof was gone. Falco looked up as the first jet screamed overhead. "Visual … Stripper, you are cleared hot."

"Cricket in from the north."

"Cricket cleared hot."

After a two second pause Falco heard Parker say, "Rifle," which was shorthand for "weapon away."

Cricket spoke next. "Rifle."

Falco watched through binoculars as the *Konev's* superstructure took a direct hit. There was a flash, followed by a slightly delayed BOOM, as the sound arrived.

Falco thought Cricket had missed at first. Then came a towering explosion that broke the *Konev* in half, and sent a column of fire soaring upwards, along with pieces of what looked like confetti. Chunks of debris fell into a pool of fire. Fuel oil was burning. Thick, black smoke blew west, as the aft section of the ship sank.

Had anyone survived? It seemed unlikely. As for the destroyers, they had vanished into the haze, and were presumably running for safety. "Shack," Falco said, meaning a direct hit. "Two impacts observed, mission successful, the ship was destroyed."

"Copy the BDA (battle damage assessment)," Parker said. "I'm still waiting for that dinner."

"Never fear," Falco said. "A Wombat keeps his word. Out."

The JTAC turned and went back to where Oliver and Moran were kneeling in the dirt.

Moran had been able to expose Lee's face by then but it was too late. It looked as though he'd been struck by a falling beam prior to being buried under tons of fill. The civilian looked up at him. "I'm sorry," she said.

"Me too," Falco replied. "Come on … Let's dig him out before the floor gives way."

It took fifteen minutes to free Lee's body from the dirt, and carry it up to the plateau. Repeated trips were required to fetch all of the gear.

It was late afternoon by then, and a cold rain was falling, as the team prepared to leave. Falco was putting the laser designator away when Oliver came to join him. "Overlook called, Major. We have orders to pull out."

Falco looked at him. "Out of *here?* Or off the island?"

"Off the island," Oliver replied. "I spoke to an MP. She says our supply dump took a direct hit from a cruise missile. That forced the brass to decide between putting more resources into a losing battle, or fighting the bastards on the beach in Wales. They chose the latter."

Falco felt a sense of disappointment. After fighting hard, and holding the islands for two weeks, the brigade had been ordered to withdraw. "Okay," Falco said. "Let's make some sort of stretcher. We'll take Lee with us."

Darkness was falling by the time the team joined a column of soldiers trudging toward the ring of makeshift landing pads. The plan was to take the troops out by air, and the persistent roar of helicopter engines could be heard, as two Chinooks lifted off. One had a howitzer slung under its belly. "Where are the Russian planes?" Moran wanted to know. "Why aren't they attacking us?"

Falco was carrying one end of the improvised stretcher and Oliver had the other. Both were wearing packs which made walking difficult. "I don't know for sure," Falco replied. "But chances are that the Russians know we're leaving—and have no desire to slow us down. They want to complete the link from Big D to Little D as quickly as possible."

The scene surrounding the landing pads could best be described as organized chaos. MPs worked to divide people into loads. A graves registration team appeared to take charge of Lee's body—and Falco felt a lump form in his throat as they carried the JTAC away. He was going to miss Lee's cheerful good humor and steady determination. "Are you Major Falco?"

Falco turned to find a sergeant waiting to speak with him. "Yes?"

"The colonel wants to know if you could help with air traffic control."

Falco was reminded of the desperate scramble to evacuate troops from Big D. There was only one thing he could say. "Tell him I said, 'yes.' We'll jump in."

The noncom tossed a salute and Falco returned it. Moran was with Oliver. "The sergeant and I have a new assignment, Doctor," Falco told her. "I suggest that you buttonhole an MP and identify yourself. They'll get you out of here. You did a terrific job by the way... I'll see if we can get you some sort of civilian commendation."

Moran looked up at him. "Take care, Major... Look me up if you get to Omaha. I'll buy you a beer." Then she was gone.

It wasn't difficult to locate the army's harried air traffic controller (ATC) and join the fray. Time seemed to fly by as helicopters of every possible description came and went. All of them had the same goal, which was to get American personnel off the island before Russian troops overran it. Fighting could be heard to the west as the Spetnaz probed American positions, and Waya's paratroopers fought them off.

Then, shortly after 2100 hours the word went out for the remaining members of the brigade to pull back, and Falco was there to see dozens of exhausted soldiers materialize out of the gloom, and in some cases limp toward the waiting helicopters.

Waya was there, strolling among them, and slapping backs as his troopers appeared. "Good job, Corporal... Medic! This soldier is wounded. Sergeant Nelson... Well done, son. I won't forget."

Then, as if he had all the time in the world, Waya ambled over to where the controllers were working. "Major Falco, Sergeant Oliver, what you did to the *Konev* made my day! And made history too... That was the first tactical use of a satellite based laser weapon. And, as a reward, I'm going to let you fight the Russians when they land in Wales."

Both men laughed. "Thanks, Colonel," Falco replied. "You're all heart."

"That's what they tell me," Waya agreed. "Now get on the helo."

Once the JTACS and the ATC were aboard the Blackhawk took off. And, as Falco stood in the open doorway, he could see that a single person had been left standing on the ground below. Waya took a long look around, as if to memorize the scene, before turning to the civilian helo that was waiting for him. The battle for Little D had been lost.

CHAPTER SIXTEEN

Little Diomede Island, Russian occupied territory

Russian General Anatoly Baranov felt a sense of elation as the huge whale-shaped Mi-26 helicopter began its descent. And why not? The bridge between Big Diomede and Little Diomede had been completed during the night and, if everything went well, would be in service by 2000 hours. That, in spite of the Americans' best efforts to prevent it.

But the joy Baranov felt as the helicopter touched down stemmed not from a series of tactical victories, but from a profound sense of righteousness. Now, after more than 150 years of foreign rule—Alaska was going to be part of Russia again!

A great deal of work remained to be done. But notice had been given, and the heretofore impregnable fortress called America was about to be ravaged the way his country had been ravaged by the Mongols, the French, and the Germans. "RUSSIANS LAND ON AMERICAN SOIL!" That headline, or something like it, would be seen on the front page of the *New York Times* and TV screens in every home.

Stairs had been lowered. Major Gotov was on his feet, standing next to TASS reporter Boris Dudin, who was armed with a camera. "I'll go first Comrade General, and get a shot of you stepping down. The photo will appear on the front page of more than four thousand newspapers by tomorrow morning."

Baranov liked that idea. Not because of the manner in which it would glorify him, or the positive impact that such an image would have on civilian morale, but because Baranov knew that President Toplin would read the story—and feel encouraged. And that was important to the mission. "Yes, Boris … Please proceed."

"Try to smile," Dudin suggested.

"I'll do my best," Baranov promised, even though he knew that his best effort would produce something more akin to a grimace than a smile. Once Dudin was in position Baranov jumped down onto the slush covered ground and felt the solidity of it through his boots. It was a moment he would never forget.

But there was work to do … And it began with a tour. The boxy 4 X 4 had been brought in by helicopter and was barely large enough to accommodate the driver, Baranov, Gotov, and Dudin. The purpose of the visit was to give Baranov a firsthand look at Little Diomede, and to make his presence known. Once some of the troops saw him word would spread. "The general is on the ground." And the implication would be clear. Baranov was not only with them, but willing to take the same risks they did. Baranov's thoughts were interrupted by the sound of a distant thud. "There are mines," the driver announced. "The Americans left them along the footpaths."

Baranov turned to Gotov. "Check. Make sure that the proper orders have gone out. Don't use established trails."

Gotov nodded and spoke into a handheld radio as the UAZ bounced over some rocks. A black flower surrounded the large crater where the American supply dump had been.

And there, scattered around the adjoining helicopter pads, lay the litter of war. Baranov had seen it before. The bloody battle dressings, stray pieces of clothing, and brightly colored candy wrappers were left behind by *all* modern armies and could signal either victory or defeat.

Then they were off to circle the plateau, pausing every now and then to chat with some of the troops, or to let Dudin snap a photo. And that's what the reporter was doing when a hand cranked siren sounded and two Apache gunships roared in from the east.

Gotov threw himself onto Baranov and both officers went down. Dudin continued to stand, and was capturing the scene on video, when a rocket struck the 4 X 4. The driver was killed but the TASS reporter was untouched. He continued to record video as the helicopters flew west. "Get off of me," Baranov ordered, as he pushed Gotov away. Baranov stood. "Where are our planes? Our missiles? Someone's going to pay."

"The village is a mile or two west of here," Gotov said. "That's where we'll find the officer in charge."

That made sense. So the men trudged west. Gotov took the lead and was careful to avoid the well-trodden paths. Groups of soldiers passed them going in the opposite direction. Baranov took the opportunity to greet them. The fact that he was on foot would leave a positive impression. "And there the general was," a soldier might say. "Walking along like a man on his way to church! Why can't all of our officers be like him?"

An ominous column of smoke was visible in the distance. Were the American helicopters responsible for that? That's the way it appeared.

The men heard the sound of diesel engines before they saw the landing party. Then, as the threesome arrived at the top of the bluff, they were treated to quite a sight. The second span was more than half complete. As a tug worked to nudge a pontoon into place a sister ship continued to burn. Where were the anti-aircraft barges? The ones carrying the Buk missile systems? Four such platforms were supposed to be anchored off shore. Had that been the case the American helicopters would've been shot down.

Engines roared as two B-10 bulldozers worked to create the road that would switchback up through the ruins of what had been *Ignaluk,* to the plateau on which they were standing. "Come," Baranov said. "Let's go down and find the officer in charge."

The foot path had been cleared of mines. But it was steep, and extremely muddy, so Baranov had to watch his step. Every now and then he risked a glance at the scene below. *Zubr-*class air-cushioned landing craft were busy delivering more bulldozers, tons of supplies, and hundreds of troops. Piles of cargo containers were stacked up on the pier. Why had *they* been spared? Perhaps the helos had been on their way somewhere else, and fired on the tug because it was sitting in their path. Such were the imponderables of war.

Once the men reached sea level, Gotov wasted no time corralling an army captain. "Who's in charge?" the major demanded. "And where are they?"

The young officer was clearly frightened, and for good reason. Gotov was a very imposing figure—and a general was standing five feet away! "C-C-Captain Kharamov is in c-c-command, sir. He's on the *Bortov.*"

The captain was pointing to a nondescript navy vessel which was anchored offshore. A navy captain, Baranov thought, a rank equivalent to a colonel. Baranov frowned. "Get him on the radio."

Gotov succeeded on his third attempt. After a brief conversation Gotov gave his report. "Captain Kharamov was feeling ill. He left orders not to be disturbed, and retired to his cabin yesterday afternoon."

"And the first officer?"

"That *was* the first officer. He's afraid to disobey a direct order."

Baranov sighed. Alcohol, and alcohol abuse, was a big problem in Russian society. The military was no exception. Kharamov was on a bender. If so he would shoot the bastard in the face. "Get me a boat," Baranov ordered. "And be quick about it."

The officer took off at a run and returned five minutes later. "A boat is waiting at the foot of the first ramp, General."

"Good work," Baranov replied. "We need more like you."

The young man was still reveling in the compliment as Baranov and his companions left. The boat turned out to be a large semi-inflatable with a light machine gun mounted in the bow. A Starshina 2nd class was in charge with a single Matrose (seaman) for a crew. Judging from the petty officer's manner, he was accustomed to ferrying senior officers around. "Please make yourselves comfortable," he said. "And, should there be a need, you'll find life jackets under the seats."

Once the passengers were seated the Starshina backed the RIB boat out, turned it around, and opened the throttle. The front end came up, and spray flew sideways. Baranov was sitting next to the sailor. "What sort of ship is that, son?"

"It's a tender," the Matrose replied shyly. "For command and control."

"Thank you," Baranov replied, as the hull slapped the water, and the *Bortov* drew closer. As the RIB boat coasted in next to the ship Baranov saw that a platform was suspended just above the water—and a steep set of aluminum stairs led upward. *Thank god*, Baranov thought. *I'm not sure I could climb a rope ladder anymore.*

There was a gentle bump and a splash as the Starshina brought the boat alongside the platform—and the sailor made use of a boathook to keep it close. Gotov led the way, followed by Baranov, and Dudin. Baranov clutched cold metal with both hands as an incoming wave passed under the *Bortov* and she wallowed. It was impossible to understand why anyone would join the navy.

Baranov saw Gotov disappear from sight, climbed the last few steps, and pulled himself in over the side. Three officers were there to receive him, the most senior of which was a tall, gaunt looking captain of the 2nd rank. He saluted. "Welcome aboard, General … My name is Ivkin. I am the *Bortov's* first officer."

Baranov returned the salute. "I want to speak with your commanding officer. Four barges loaded with Buk antiaircraft systems were supposed to be anchored adjacent to Little Diomede by now, yet they're nowhere to be seen."

"Yes, sir," Ivkin said nervously. "I'm sorry, sir. The barges are moored on the west side of Big Diomede. But no one has been willing to move them without permission from Captain Kharamov. He's very strict about such things," Ivkin added apologetically.

"And he's sequestered in his cabin."

"Sir, yes sir."

"Tell me something," Baranov said. "Does the captain have a drinking problem?"

Ivkin's eyes flicked away. He brought them back. Baranov was sympathetic. He too had been forced to cover for incompetent superiors. Such things happened. But the charade had to end. Ivkin's Adam's apple bobbed up and down as he spoke. "Yes, sir. He does."

"And Captain Kharamov has been known to lock himself away before?"

"Yes, sir."

"Have your men break into the captain's cabin. And contact the officer in charge of the barges. I wish to speak with him."

Ivkin saluted. Judging from the expression on his face he felt relieved. Then he was gone. The junior officers fled with him.

Baranov turned to Dudin. "None of this happened, Boris."

The reporter's face was blank. "None of *what*, General?"

Baranov laughed. "You're a credit to your kind," by which Baranov meant Kremliads. But Baranov knew Dudin would believe otherwise. Because Dudin considered himself to be part of a journalistic priesthood charged with managing Russia's often unruly sheeple. The TASS reporter's self-satisfied smile served to confirm that thesis. "General?"

It was Gotov. "Ivkin's men opened the cabin, sir. I think you should take a look."

Baranov followed Gotov back along the side of the ship's superstructure to a hatch. It opened onto a corridor and *more* hatches. One of them was labeled, "Commanding Officer." It was open. Gotov stood aside so that Baranov could enter. It was a relatively small space—and neat as a pin. That wasn't consistent with Baranov's expectations. Where were the empty bottles? The pieces of castoff clothing? And the sweet-sour stench so often associated with alcoholics? Only one bottle of vodka was visible, and it sat on a shelf, still half full.

Baranov turned his attention to the man on the bed. Kharamov's face had the gray, waxy look of a dead man. And that was when Baranov realized the truth... The navy officer *had* been ill. And, after locking himself in his cabin, had *what*? Suffered a heart attack? Probably.

And because of the officer's well-known alcoholism his subordinates assumed that Kharamov was drunk. Not that it mattered to anyone other than the UAV's unfortunate driver and the crew on the burning tug. Kharamov had died. And so, as a result, had they. Such was the horrible warp and weave of war.

Baranov left the cabin to discover that Ivkin was waiting for him. "The barges are under the command of Captain 3rd rank Vortnik," the navy officer told him. "He's waiting to speak with you. Please follow me... I'll take you to the bridge. You can use the radio there."

The conversation was short, and not especially sweet. "It's important to respect the chain of command," Baranov told Vortnik. "But there are times when a good officer must rely on his own judgement. You were faced with such a challenge and found wanting. But there's a chance that you can redeem yourself. Reposition the barges, cooperate with the officer in charge of missile launchers, and keep the *pindos* at bay. Do all of those things and I will commend you. Fail, and you will find yourself serving on a garbage scow. Do you understand?"

Vortnik understood all right... And promised to have all of the barges in place by nightfall. So that problem was solved. Now Baranov faced a choice. He could remain on the ship, and direct efforts from there, or return to Little Diomede. The first option would be more comfortable—and the second would put him closer to the action.

Baranov was mulling the situation over when Ivkin emerged from the adjoining radio room and came over. His features were strained. "I'm sorry to disturb you, General... But Marshal of the Russian Federation Orlov is on Little Diomede Island. And when I spoke to him, he said, 'What the fuck is Baranov doing? Tell him to get his ass over here.' Sir."

Baranov was stunned. Orlov was the highest ranking officer the army had! And, under normal circumstances, at least a week's notice would precede such a visit. But Russia was at war—and security was necessarily tight. So that could explain the unannounced visit.

But there was a second possibility too. Baranov and Orlov were rivals. Or had been until Orlov was promoted over Baranov, thereby winning the final prize. What if the visit was the high level equivalent of a surprise inspection? Which was to say an opportunity for Orlov to find Baranov wanting, and relieve him, just prior to what promised to be a successful invasion? Doing so would allow Orlov to take credit for the invasion.

All of that cycled through Baranov's mind as Ivkin awaited Baranov's response. "Tell the marshal that I have completed arrangements for antiaircraft systems to be brought up from the rear, and will arrive on Little Diomede shortly, at which time it would be my honor to show him around."

Ivkin said, "Yes sir," and rushed off.

Gotov appeared. His face was expressionless. "A two-seat helicopter will put down on the ship's pad in five minutes. Dudin and I will go over by boat."

As usual Gotov not only knew what was taking place, but understood the potential significance of it. And was taking steps to make Baranov look good. "You are a marvel, Valery," Baranov told him. "And you will be a colonel soon. Thank you."

Ivkin led Baranov back to the ship's stern, where a sleek two-place helo was about to land. It was the military version of an Afalina. As soon as Baranov finished fastening his seat belt the aircraft took off. The trip from the ship to the spot where Baranov's engineers were excavating a command bunker took no more than ten minutes.

But that was too slow for Orlov who continued to pace back and forth in front of his hulking Mi-8M transport helicopter, while slapping his left leg with an old fashioned swagger stick. He was bare headed, bald, and at least ten pounds heavier than the last time Baranov had seen him. Too much time spent behind a desk could do that to a man. "There you are!" Orlov said, as Baranov approached. "Always late to class. You haven't changed. That's why Colonel Essen called you, 'The Turtle.'"

Colonel Essen had been an instructor at the Tambov Cadet Corps school, where both officers had been students in their teens. By reminding Baranov of the nickname Orlov was trying to get under the officer's skin.

Baranov struggled to control his anger. The salute was parade ground perfect. "Good morning, Marshal...And welcome to Russian held territory. Perhaps you were able to see the American mainland from the air. It's only twenty-five miles away."

The best defense is a good offense. Every officer knew that. And by reminding Orlov of where he was standing, Baranov hoped to seize the initiative. Orlov returned the salute. His words sounded stilted. "I have a message from the president. He's grateful for your service to mother Russia—and looks forward to the moment of victory."

Baranov felt a surge of pride, and a renewed sense of confidence. President Toplin had ordered Orlov to thank him! And the need to do so was eating Orlov from the inside out. Baranov smiled. "Thank you for bringing me that message comrade Marshal."

Orlov nodded stiffly. His eyes narrowed to slits. "It's nice to receive praise from the president, Anatoly. But remember ... With great responsibility comes great risk. Do not fail us, or yourself, because the stakes are high."

Then, after a long slow look around, Orlov shook his head. "Alaska is strategically important. But why does it have to be a frozen shithole? Russia has enough ice and snow. Attack Hawaii next time." And with that Orlov turned to his helicopter, mounted the fold-down stairs, and vanished from sight. Baranov felt a powerful downdraft, as the helo lumbered into the air. *I hope you crash*, Baranov thought, as he waved goodbye. *And die screaming. Our country would be better for it.*

CHAPTER SEVENTEEN

The Attack Submarine, *USS Hawaii* (SSN-776), in the Chuckchi Sea

The Attack Submarine *USS Hawaii* was lurking 150 feet below the surface of the Chuckchi Sea, about 50 nautical miles north of the Diomede Islands, when the ELF (extremely low frequency) transmission arrived. The problem with low frequency transmissions was that their data rates were extremely slow. Receiving even a single character took an inordinate amount of time. That's why ELF was used to pass simple commands like, "Come up for a message," rather than long messages.

Commander Nick Hollis was the boat's skipper. He wore an easy to maintain buzz cut, was known for his calm manner, and had been dubbed "the Super Smurf" at Annapolis. The nickname stemmed from his short stature, and determination to overcome every obstacle no matter how tall it was. Hollis was working at the fold down desk in his tiny cabin when the message arrived. "Surface to receive orders." He read the words for a second time before returning the slip of paper to the waiting electronics tech (ET). "Thanks, Evans. Pass the word to the XO. Tell her I'll be down in a minute."

Evans said, "Aye-aye, Captain," and left. Hollis took a moment to put his work away, and collect his thoughts. The last couple of weeks had been frustrating. His orders were to attack the Russian bridge. And six of the *Hawaii's* twelve Tomahawk missiles had been spent on the target without producing meaningful results.

Unfortunately each Tomahawk carried only 1,000 pounds of explosives. And that payload was nothing compared to the standard loadout for a B-52 bomber. A BUF (big, ugly, fucker) could deliver *fifty* 500 pound bombs, plus *thirty* 1,000 pound bombs, plus a shit load of missiles during a single mission. Why not use *them?* Hollis wondered. There was no obvious answer. Maybe the B-52s couldn't penetrate Russian defenses.

In any case the *Hawaii* wasn't designed for busting bridges. Every time the submarine launched a Tomahawk missile, its position was revealed to the enemy, and the *Hawaii* had to find a new hiding place. In the meantime the Russians repaired the damage. So Hollis hoped that his new orders would be more in keeping with the sub's *true* purpose, which was to destroy submarines and surface ships.

Hollis left his cabin, made his way down a narrow corridor, and followed a steep ladder to the control room one deck below. The space was very high tech, and operations were more efficient than they'd been in the past. A good example was the way a pilot and a copilot had been able to replace the dive officer, chief of the watch, helmsman, planesman, and messenger required on the older boats. *Machines*, Hollis thought. *They're going to replace all of us. Me included.*

The XO was waiting. Her presence on the *Hawaii* was yet another departure from past practices. Until recently women hadn't been allowed to enter the silent service. And Hollis thought the change was long overdue. Lieutenant Commander Emily "Em" Ochi was an extremely competent submariner, and on the short list for a command. 'Hey, Em," Hollis said. "I hear that PACOM is knocking on the door."

"Maybe it's a reminder," Ochi replied. "This *is* national chocolate chip cookie day after all." Those who heard the interchange laughed. Humor is an important lubricant on submarines.

"Does Cassidy know?" Hollis inquired.

Cassidy was the boat's senior CS, or Culinary Specialist, which made him a very important person. "Of course he knows," Ochi said. "Cookies are mission critical."

Hollis laughed. "Take her up. We'll look around. Then, assuming that everything's clear, we'll grab that message."

Rather than the old fashioned periscopes so central to WWII movies, *Virginia* Class submarines were equipped with Universal Modular Masts. They housed the antennas and sensors necessary for tactical communications, high-data-rate SATCOM messages, radar, and electronic warfare.

The deck slanted as the pilot took the boat up. As the sub rose sonar operators were alert to the slightest sound that might indicate the presence of an enemy submarine or surface ship. Once the *Hawaii* was at the proper depth the photonics mast was raised, and the top mounted sensor package broke the surface of the water. Imagery appeared on a flat screen, along with tactical readouts. By using a handheld remote Hollis could turn the photonics package back and forth, and cause it to tilt.

Hollis and Ochi saw endless ranks of low one-foot waves, a gray sky, and a smudge of land to the south. And *that*, Hollis knew, was Big Diomede Island. Their first concern was to make sure that the boat was safe. There were no vessels in sight, and as far as Hollis could tell, the skies were empty of aircraft.

While the officers scanned for threats Evans was pulling the message down via the boat's SATCOM mast. Because PACOM didn't have the submarine's exact location, it was necessary to broadcast the message to the entire fleet.

The navigator, or "gator," was a lieutenant named Gregory Gregory. But what started as a parental joke, was no laughing matter to Gregory, who'd been taking shit about his name since the third grade. He knew that the crew called him "Gigi" behind his back and resented it. The com techs reported to Gregory so it was his privilege to deliver the news. "We have the message, sir. We're printing it off."

Hollis nodded. "Thanks, Greg. Okay, Em … Lower the hardware, and take her down."

Ochi said, "Dive, Dive!" and pushed a button. A klaxon sounded.

Orders were passed, the deck slanted, and USS *Hawaii* descended into the relative safety of the sea. "Here you go," Gregory said, as he handed the printout to Hollis.

A standard header was followed by a short message: "THE RUSSIAN CRUISER *KONEV* WAS SUNK SOUTH OF LITTLE DIOMEDE ISLAND. TWO ESCORTS, BOTH BELIEVED TO BE *UDALOY* CLASS DESTROYERS, ESCAPED AND ARE STEAMING SOUTH. INTERCEPT AND SINK." That was followed by the warships' positions as of two hours earlier.

Hollis took a moment to absorb that. From the sound of it the *Konev* had been torpedoed by one of his peers. *Not Estevez, I hope*, Hollis thought. *That bastard has a big head already.*

As for the destroyers, they had a head start. Could he catch up? It seemed unlikely, but Hollis was determined to try. He looked at Gregory. "Set a course that will put us south of the Diomede Islands as quickly as possible."

Hollis turned to Ochi. "Em, let's see what we have on *Udaloy* Class destroyers. You know, prop sounds and all of that."

"Will do," Ochi replied, and stepped away.

After calculating the course himself, and checking it against a computer program, Gregory offered his recommendation. "The fastest option is to pass between Big Diomede and Little Diomede."

Hollis frowned as he eyed the course on the computer screen. "A straight line is always the fastest route between two points," he allowed. "But the islands are only 2.3 miles apart. We'd have to pass *under* the new bridge, and the Russians could have mined the passageway."

"Mines seem unlikely," Gregory replied tactfully, "given the need to move boats and pontoons around. But sonobuoys *are* a possibility."

Sonobuoys could be dumped into the water from planes or boats. Once deployed an inflatable float containing a radio transmitter remained on the surface, while a canister full of listening gear would sink to a predetermined depth. When a possible target was detected a plane or boat would be dispatched to attack it.

So Hollis was in a jam. He couldn't pass *west* of Big Diomede because of the heavily defended first span that connected Big D to the Russian mainland. And if ever there was a place where the enemy was likely to put sonobuoys that was it.

And Hollis didn't want to swing east around Little Diomede because of the shallow water there, not to mention the additional time involved. Every minute was precious. He cleared his throat. "I'm going to take the chance. Since the Russians are still putting the final touches on the span between Big D and Little D they're unlikely to have sonobuoys in place yet. Rig for silent running, and pass the word for all hands to man their battle stations."

Ochi acknowledged the order and went to work. The boat's department heads knew what to do. Crew members were to refrain from making unnecessary sounds, the submarine's speed would be reduced to minimize propeller noise, and the reactor's active cooling system would be off. That meant the sub would have to rely on water convection to cool the nuclear power plant. But, if sonobuoys *had* been placed in the passageway, perhaps the *Hawaii* would be able to slip past unnoticed.

Once the preparations were complete there was nothing left for Hollis to do other than look cool, sip coffee, and wait to learn his fate. And looking cool was of paramount importance. Prior to commanding a submarine Hollis had been a member of the crew, of *many* crews, and knew how it worked. The skipper was in charge, so the people who worked for him or her were highly attuned to the CO's non-verbal communications, and quick to notice subtle changes. And if someone said, "Did you see the captain? He looks pissy today." That perception would race from one end of the sub to the other in a matter of minutes causing morale to suffer.

So Hollis *had* to look cool. Even if his guts were tied in a knot. He knew the destroyers were opening the lead they already had. That made it tempting to order full speed ahead and take the chance. But that would be stupid. And, as his father liked to say, "Avoid being stupid. That will make you smart."

So Hollis stood there, shooting the shit with the control room crew, as the boat slipped through the water. Finally, after what seemed like an eternity Gregory cleared his throat. "We're entering the passage skipper ... So far so good."

But no sooner had the Gator spoken, than a sonar tech named Williams delivered the bad news. His voice was tense. "We have company Skipper ... The sounds match the file for *Akula* Class attack boats."

The Weapons Officer, better known as Weps, was named Alan Kirk. He was husky, balding, and known for his ability to chug-a-lug a full pitcher of beer without taking a breath. "We're working on a firing solution, sir."

Hollis felt his heart beat faster. An enemy sub had been sent to guard the passageway between Big D and Little D! *Akula* Class boats and *Virginia* Class subs had a great deal in common. The *Akulas* carried cruise missiles, and so did the American boats.

But there were differences too. Important differences where underwater fights were concerned. The *Akulas* had *four* 533mm torpedo tubes, plus an equal number of 650mm tubes. That added up to eight tubes in all. While the *Hawaii* had four 533mm torpedo tubes. And that was a serious disparity.

Moreover Hollis knew the *Akula* could dive deeper than the *Hawaii* could—although that wouldn't mean much in such shallow water. And the Russian boat was faster too, which would suck in a chase.

But there wasn't going to be a chase. Fifteen seconds had passed without a response from the enemy submarine. *They don't know we're here*, Hollis concluded, and the reason for that was obvious. Thanks to specially designed anechoic coatings and a new propulsor design, *Virginia* Class submarines had an acoustic signature lower than the *Akulas'*. But that precious advantage would vanish in a heartbeat if someone dropped a wrench onto the *Hawaii's* steel plating. Hollis pitched his voice low. "This is not a drill. Prepare to fire tubes 1 and 3."

"Tubes 1 and 3 are ready, sir," Kirk said.

Hollis took a deep breath. "Fire 1! Fire 3!"

The *Hawaii* was armed with MK-48 torpedoes. Unlike the straight running torpedoes of WWII, the MK-48s were equipped with sonar, and some artificial intelligence. That meant they could ping, analyze the returns, and make whatever adjustments were necessary.

And, if an enemy sub chose to deploy decoys, the MK-48s could differentiate between the false targets and home on the real one. The 48s were also trailing wires that the *Hawaii's* crew could use to steer the weapons. But in order to do that, they'd have to leave the bow mounted tubes open to the sea, and that would create turbulence which equaled noise. Hollis ordered Kirk to cut the wires.

"They made us," Williams warned. "Their screw is turning at high rpms, and it sounds like they're dumping decoys."

"Take evasive action," Hollis ordered.

Williams spoke again. "They fired what sounds like *four* torps, sir. About 2,000 yards and closing fast."

"Eject countermeasures," Hollis ordered. Hopefully the ECM pods would draw the enemy torpedoes away. Hollis forced himself to think ahead. The Russian sub was equipped with *eight* tubes. That meant the enemy skipper still had four weapons available to him, while Hollis was left with two. Both submarines could attempt to reload, but it was a time consuming process, and unlikely to be completed in time to make a difference.

A pair of thumps were heard. The *Hawaii* shuddered as a pressure wave hit the hull. "It sounds like our torps struck decoys," Williams announced.

Hollis felt a jab of fear. He had two torpedoes left. And if they missed the mark, his only option would be to outrun a boat he couldn't outrun. "We're going to close with the bastard," Hollis announced grimly. "Ahead, flank, cavitate." (Give me all the speed you can, and to hell with the noise.) "Prepare to fire tubes 2 and 4."

The power increased quickly, and as the *Hawaii* surged forward, the distance between the subs continued to close. "Two fish incoming," Williams intoned.

"Eject countermeasures," Hollis said.

"We're closing fast," Gregory warned.

"Fire 2," Hollis ordered, "and fire 4."

"They're running straight and normal," Weps announced.

"Don't cut the wires," Hollis added. "Stay with them … Steer them all the way in."

Hollis heard two fire control (FT) techs confirm his order—and had no choice but to put his faith in them. "Shit!" one of the sailors said, as the enemy sub took a sharp turn, and his torp sailed past.

"Stay with it Conway," Kirk ordered, as the second FT continued to guide his torpedo to the target. "Put it to those bastards!"

Conway didn't answer. A sweaty sheen covered his forehead, and his eyes were glued to the screen in front of him. Then came a thump that was considerably louder than those heard earlier, and a pressure wave hammered the sub. Hollis had to hang on, or be thrown to the deck. "A kill!" Ochi shouted. "You did it Conway... You goddamn did it!"

A cheer went up, and Hollis grinned. "Belay the bullshit people, we have a couple of destroyers to catch up with. "Take her up," Hollis added, "Let's see if there's anything new from PACOM."

Once the *Hawaii* arrived at the proper depth, the masts were raised, and Hollis eyed the photonics screen. The first thing he noticed were the pieces of debris that were bobbing up and down in the water. Video of the scene would become part of his report.

Hollis used the remote to conduct a 360-degree sweep of the sub's surroundings. He saw the humped shape of Big Diomede, the low lying bridge, and Little Diomede beyond. There were work boats in the area. Some were headed his way, but none represented a threat. "Evans pulled this down," Ochi said, as she gave Hollis a slip of paper. He read it. "ONE *UDALOY* CLASS DESTROYER SUNK BY AIRCRAFT AND ONE UNDER TOW. INTERCEPT AND SINK." The words were followed by a position and a heading.

Gregory had been the first person other than Evans to see the message. "I crunched the numbers," he said, "and it looks as if the destroyer is being towed to Lavrentiya. The Russians have a new base there."

Hollis felt a rising sense of excitement. "Can we catch up?"

"It'll be close," Gregory replied, "but there's a chance."

Hollis could imagine what had transpired. American planes had been dispatched to attack the tin cans just as the *Hawaii* had. But, after sinking one ship, the zoomies had been driven off. By Russian aircraft? Quite possibly.

If so, it seemed safe to suppose that the enemy planes were still on the job. But they couldn't *see* the *Hawaii*. And, depending on the degree of damage the destroyer had suffered, there was a possibility that the tin can wouldn't be able to "hear" the sub.

Or that the attack boat would manage to close in even *if* the enemy's sonar was operational. "Take her down," Hollis ordered. "Set a course for Lavrentiya, and put the pedal to the metal. I want those bastards."

The *Hawaii* could do 28mph underwater. And there was no way to know what kind of speed the Russian tug was capable of with a large ship under tow. Gregory had chosen to plug 10mph into his calculations. If that was correct the sub would catch up with the destroyer in an hour and fifteen minutes. But, if the tug was faster than projected, the warship could be safely anchored within Lavrentiya's harbor by the time the *Hawaii* arrived offshore.

Whatever would be, would be. That's what Hollis told himself as he challenged the Chief of the Boat to a nerf basketball game. *Look cool*, Hollis thought, *look cool*. Meanwhile, up forward, a full set of fish were being loaded into the *Hawaii's* tubes.

Hollis lost the game, much to the enjoyment of the control room crew, and the minutes continued to drag by. Eventually, after what felt like an eternity, they hit the one-hour mark. Hollis felt a sinking sensation. Now it appeared that the tug had been towing the destroyer at something like *15mph*. And the bastards were sitting around drinking vodka. Williams spoke. "I have something, sir … It doesn't match anything in our files. But it would make sense if I'm hearing *two* signatures mixed together."

Hollis felt the first stirrings of hope. According to what they had on file *Udaloy* class destroyers were equipped with four gas turbines, and *two* propeller shafts. What if one shaft was offline—and one was turning? But doing so at low rpms? That sound, superimposed over the noise produced by the tug, might generate the sort of sonic mishmash Williams had described. "The signal's getting stronger," the sonar operator reported. "We're catching up."

"Take her up to photonics depth," Hollis ordered. "Let's see what we have."

The sub rose, the photonics mast broke the surface of the water, and Hollis felt an unexpected tightness in his chest. He was looking at the destroyer from an angle. He could see the ship and the tug laboring beyond. Both vessels were headed for Zaliv Bay, and the town of Lavrentiya. "The bottom's rising," the pilot warned. "We're at one-five-six."

That depth was sufficient for the moment. "Keep me advised," Hollis replied. "Prepare to fire all four tubes."

But, as the *Hawaii* continued to close with the destroyer, an idea occurred to Hollis. He had a thing for submarine movies. *Run Silent, Run Deep, The Hunt For Red October* and *Das Boot*. He enjoyed them all, including a comedy, in which a sub sneaks into a harbor by hiding *under* an incoming merchant vessel. Was that crazy? Or could such a strategy work?

If it did, the *Hawaii* would be able to target the Russian destroyer. "Ignore my last order," Hollis said, "but be ready with the tubes. Take her down to a hundred. Is the destroyer pinging?"

"No sir," Williams replied. "But they could be passive."

Hollis figured they were. But the enemy sonar operators would hear the same cacophony of sounds that Williams had described. And the *Hawaii* was very quiet. "Take us in under that tin can," Hollis ordered. "And keep us there."

The pilot looked back over his shoulder. "For real, Skipper? It isn't very deep."

"I realize that," Hollis answered. "So tuck the bow in under the ship, with the sail just under the surface. Williams, monitor those rpms. If they drop we'll need to cut speed or we'll run into the destroyer's ass."

The pilot turned back to his controls. It wasn't long before the sub entered the turbulence created by the destroyer's hull and single screw. The hull began to shake violently. Loose items rattled. An alarm started to beep. Someone turned it off.

Hollis turned to Kirk. "Do me a favor, Weps... Pull the targeting data for the Anadyr naval base." Anadyr was 350 miles away, which put it well within a Tomahawk missile's one-thousand mile range.

Kirk's eyes widened. "Holy shit! Let me see if I understand... We're going to sneak into an enemy harbor, torpedo a tin can, *and* fire Tomahawks at Anadyr!"

The *Hawaii* stopped rattling. Hollis turned to the pilot. "How are we doing?"

"We're directly below her, sir," the petty officer replied. "In the sweet spot."

"Williams? How's it going?"

"So far, so good skipper."

"The targeting solution is loaded, sir," Kirk assured him. "We're ready when you are."

Hollis nodded. "We'll fire the torpedoes first, followed by the missiles. *All* of them. Then we'll run like hell. The Russians won't be able to respond without running the risk of targeting their own assets. As for PACOM, what are they going to do? Send me to the artic?"

Kirk laughed. "This will make for one helluva sea story."

Ochi nodded. "No one will believe it."

Hollis could hear the blood pounding in his head. His hands were trembling so he took hold of a chair to hide it. "I think we're in the bay," Williams said. "The destroyer cut power—and I'm picking up other signatures. Small craft probably, coming out to assist the destroyer."

"Back us out from under the destroyer, pilot," Hollis ordered. "I'll be filling out paperwork for years if the Russians drop an anchor on us. Once we're clear take her up to photonics depth."

Hollis turned to Kirk. "Pass the word ... Prepare to fire tubes 1 and 3, followed by the Tomahawks."

Kirk repeated the order followed by an "Aye, aye, sir."

Hollis stood waiting in front of the screen as the photonics package broke the surface. He could see the town of Lavrentiya. Cranes were visible to the left, with buildings in the middle of the screen, and docks to the right. Most of the one, two, and three story structures were painted bright colors as if to make the town more cheerful during the long artic winters.

As Hollis panned to his right he saw that some sizeable fishing boats were anchored in the bay. Targeting data appeared for each. But the vessels were too small to justify a nine- hundred-thousand dollar torpedo.

Hollis continued the turn and there she was! Gray smoke dribbled out of a black-edged hole in the destroyer's hull, and she sat low in the water, as boats swarmed around her. It seemed that none of Lavrentiya's docks could accommodate such a large ship. So the Russians were hoisting pumps on board in a desperate attempt to keep the tin can afloat.

It was tempting to take the shot. But Hollis forced himself to continue the sweep. There was nothing to see but empty water at first. Then a white-over-red cargo ship slid onto the screen! Hollis recognized the vessel as an SA-15 class multipurpose icebreaker. She was about 500 feet long, and equipped with three cranes, all located forward of the ship's superstructure. The freighter was off-loading cargo onto a barge that was moored alongside. "Check this Weps," Hollis said. "We'll sink her first. But, unless we're careful, our torpedoes will hit the barge. Make sure they're set to pass *under* it."

"Aye, aye, sir," Kirk said, before passing the word to his techs. Then, about thirty seconds later, he was ready. "Tubes 1 and 3 are ready to fire."

Hollis turned to the pilot. "Standby... Once the fish are running, I want you to turn back toward the destroyer." Then, without waiting for a response, Hollis gave the orders. "Fire 1, and fire 3."

"Both torpedoes are running straight and normal," Kirk assured him.

Hollis forced himself to focus on the *next* target... And that was the destroyer. Even as the pilot turned the boat toward the Russian warship, Kirk and his techs were targeting it. There was no need to point the torpedoes directly at the ship. "Tubes 2 and 4 are ready to fire Captain."

"Fire 2," Hollis said. "Fire 4."

"Torpedoes away," Kick confirmed. "Both are running straight and normal."

"Prepare to fire Tomahawks in sequence," Hollis said. "Fire!"

Hollis couldn't see the launches first hand, but he could imagine the way the missiles would explode up through the surface of the bay, turn, and head for the naval base in Anadyr. Each weapon would be traveling at 550mph, and their turbofan engines would be audible for miles around. Everyone, military personnel included, would ask themselves the same question: "What the hell is going on?"

Hollis heard some dull thumps. "Two hits on the freighter," Kirk said. "I think..."

Kirk never got to finish his sentence. A louder thump was heard, and a pressure wave rocked the sub. Mugs clattered and a pencil rolled onto the deck. "She blew!" Kirk exclaimed.

"I'll bet she was loaded with ammo," Ochi added.

"Only one hit on the destroyer," Kirk added, as another thump was heard.

Hollis could tell that the weapons officer was disappointed. But, as Hollis stared at the screen, he could see that the single torpedo had been sufficient. A gun turret rode a column of flame up into the air and seemed to pause there before crashing down.

The internal fire continued to burn as the destroyer settled deeper in the water. Fortunately for the crew small boats were there to take them off. It wasn't long before waves sloshed over the warship's main deck. Some of them found the interior and produced clouds of steam.

Hollis wanted to get the *Hawaii* out of the harbor as quickly as possible, but forced himself to wait, so he could capture the scene on video. Otherwise Hollis would be forced to use the words, "presumably sunk" in his report … And that would suck.

A wave rolled outwards as the warship slipped under the surface, causing small craft to bob up and down, as a large oil slick began to form. That was Hollis's cue to turn the photonics package back on the freighter. And just in time too, as the aft half of the icebreaker's hull pointed straight up, and plunged to the bottom of the bay. "Aircraft from the north!" a tech said. "It looks like someone spotted us."

The deck slanted steeply as the sub went down. The attack was far from surprising. It had taken some time for the Russians to figure out what had occurred and to put a plane in the air. But they had, and now positions were reversed. Suddenly the hunter was the hunted. "Set a course for the Aleutians," Hollis ordered, "and reload those tubes. This voyage isn't over."

But deep in his heart Hollis had a hunch that the operation *was* over. And that PACOM would order the *Hawaii* back to port to load missiles if nothing else. *Then I'm going to call Cristy,* Hollis decided, *and take a shower that lasts a lot longer than three minutes, and sleep for twenty-four hours.* And that was a lot to look forward to.

A series of thumps were heard as the plane continued to attack, but the depth charges were a long ways off, and nothing to worry about. The *Hawaii* had survived.

CHAPTER EIGHTEEN

Wales, Alaska, USA

Prior to the war the tiny village of Wales, Alaska had been known for two things: The fact that it was the westernmost city on mainland North America, and its proximity to an ancient *Birnik* burial mound. But now it was in danger of being overrun by the Russians, and people in the lower forty-eight were hearing about it for the first time.

In an effort to prevent the Russians from landing, military personnel and supplies were pouring in. And what had been a population of 150 had swollen to more than 3,000 with more people arriving each hour. There was no road. That meant everything and everybody had to be flown in—and the racket caused by the planes and helicopters was constant. A howitzer dangled below a Chinook's belly as the helo passed over Falco and Oliver.

Meanwhile off to their right a huge bulldozer was hard at work pushing dirt and the splintered remains of Inuit homes up to form a defensive wall. A thousand interlocking concrete blocks had been barged in to create ocean facing bunkers. Each was topped with sheets of corrugated metal and a thick layer of dirt.

Would the preparations be sufficient to stop the Russian marines as they stormed up the sloping beach? They'd have to get through the minefield first. Then, after cutting holes in the coils of razor wire, they would confront dozens of machine guns.

Meanwhile mortar bombs would fall all around the Russians—even as Falco and Oliver summoned planes to attack those who were still alive. So, had a frontal attack been the only option available to the Russians, the Americans would have been in a good position to repel it.

But that isn't the case, Falco thought to himself, as they walked along. *The Russians aren't stupid. They'll flank us north and/or south in an attempt to roll us up without storming the beach.* General Haberman knew that of course ... And had plans to prevent such a maneuver. But could she and her team get the necessary defenses in place quickly enough? That was an open question. All Falco could do was focus on his job.

Engines roared as ATVs, Humvees, and civilian vehicles passed by the JTACs, going in both directions. The southernmost section of the wall was complete and the controllers had been assigned to bunker FP23. Red spray paint marked each entrance.

Falco spotted 21, followed by 22, and 23. He ducked inside. What light there was entered through a water-facing horizontal slit. It was positioned low for the convenience of machine gunners and riflemen.

Ice crystals were trapped in the earthen walls. And now, as they began to melt, water was trickling down to puddle on the dirt floor. That meant the mud was about to get even muddier. Falco's boots made sucking sounds as he went forward to kneel and peer outside. Oliver joined him. "Home sweet home," the noncom said. "Aren't we the lucky ones?"

"Yeah," Falco agreed, as he eyed the beach. "The guys at Travis don't know what they're missing. This isn't going to work."

"Nope," Oliver agreed. "We can sleep in here, and take cover if necessary, but that's all. We need to see what's going on."

"Exactly," Falco responded. "So let's leave our gear here— and go shopping for some construction materials. An OP on the roof would be ideal—with cargo pallets on this floor. I don't want to sleep in the mud."

"Roger that," Oliver replied.

The JTACs had been forced to leave everything other than their radios, scopes, and the laser designator on Little D. But thanks to all the supplies that had been airlifted into Wales they had new packs, sleeping bags, a spare set of Cammie's each, some MREs and basics such as toothpaste. And, in case they had to join the infantry, they'd been issued brand spanking new M4 carbines to replace the submachine guns.

After piling their equipment on a dry spot, the men went looking for materials they could work with. Unfortunately there was a lot of competition from people with similar needs. But, by the time the light started to fade, the JTACs had acquired enough pallets to cover the muddy floor.

Then work began on what Oliver referred to as an "air force lounge" on the roof. The U-shaped enclosure was made of sand-bags and salvaged lumber. It wouldn't protect the JTACs from a full-on beach assault. But it might shield them from flying shrapnel and small caliber stuff. And the OP would offer them unrestricted views of the sky and shoreline.

With no immediate threat to worry about, Falco and Oliver joined the machine gun team next door around a campfire on the beach. It was located on the strip of land between the bunkers and the wire, which meant there was no need to worry about mines.

Other fires were visible to the north and south. Falco half expected an MP to come along and order them to douse the flames. But no one did. And that made sense. The Russians knew where Wales was—and were presumably watching from space.

As the sun dipped below the western horizon a soldier appeared on the top of the wall, and began to blow taps. Those who'd been seated stood as the sweet, sorrowful sound floated over the encampment. It was as if they were already in mourning.

Once it was over the talk was subdued as soldiers, sailors and marines settled in around their fires to eat MREs and shoot the shit. The one thing they *didn't* talk about was the coming battle. None of them wanted to consider that—or what might befall them.

People left for their makeshift beds as the temperature fell, and the campfires were extinguished one-by-one. It was warm in Falco's sleeping bag, but the pallets were hard, and he didn't expect to sleep well. Especially given the nonstop noise of aircraft passing overhead. Was Parker nearby? Or was she flying out of Elmendorf? Either was a possibility.

When Oliver woke him Falco was surprised to discover that he'd been asleep for six hours. Oliver's flashlight was on—but pointed at a wall. "Sorry, sir ... But an MP came by. The Russians are coming. I have water in the Jetboils."

Falco swore, battled his way out of the bag, and went out to visit the nearest latrine. It was cold, but the stars were visible, and that meant planes would be in the air. Thank god for that.

The hot water was ready by the time Falco returned. They had some government issued coffee, but it wasn't half as good as the packets of Starbucks Lee always carried with him, and Falco missed the other JTAC's cheerful nonsense. The two men were on the bunker's roof sitting on five-gallon plastic buckets. Falco wrapped his fingers around the mug and took a sip. "So, what's shaking?"

Oliver had the radios on, and was monitoring them. "The Russians are loading marines onto two *Pomornik* Class landing craft. Each of them can carry three tanks, plus one-hundred and forty troops. Add some BK-16s, plus lots of RIB boats, and we'll have plenty of stuff to shoot at."

"So they're not going to sneak up on us. They're coming straight in. That's a surprise."

"That's how it looks," Oliver agreed. "Their ETA is approximately one hour."

"So I have time for breakfast," Falco said, "and to freshen up. I want to look good for the Russians."

"I'm sure they will appreciate that," Oliver replied. "Plus you never get a second chance to make a first impression." Both of them laughed. The air battle started two minutes later.

Both sides were determined to own the airspace over Wales and the pilots went after each other at 30,000 feet. The JTACs watched the twisting, turning contrails as they carved scratches into the pale blue sky. They could hear a mish mash of allied transmissions, but they were necessarily brief, and disconnected from the big picture. That made it impossible to know who was winning. Falco felt his heart jump as a male voice came over the radio. "Stripper … Snowman has a bogey, visual, one o'clock, 10 miles, angels 30."

"Roger that," Parker replied. "Stripper and Cricket turning to intercept. Over."

Then her voice was gone as a third pilot spoke, and Falco was left to wonder if Parker would survive, and if they would meet again. Oliver's voice interrupted his thoughts. The noncom was holding a pair of binoculars and looking out to sea. "It's show time! Here they come."

When Falco raised his glasses he saw that Oliver was correct. He was familiar with a variety of U.S. made landing craft, but had never seen a *Pomornik* Class hovercraft before. There were two of them separated by half a mile of cold gray water. The one Falco had focused on threw spray every which way. Further back, about half the length of the hull, a small pilot house could be seen. Two massive propeller housings were visible aft of that. They were driving the monster forward at something like 60mph. That was damned fast for something so large. Automatic weapons began to chatter as the incoming hovercraft opened fire.

What Falco estimated to be 30mm cannon shells triggered mines as they marched up the beach, found the wall, and began to pound it. In the meantime rockets were streaking in and scoring hits along the defensive line. If they struck a weapon position, good. But the real purpose of the barrage was to suppress defensive fire. And there was plenty of it as American fifty-caliber machine guns, mortars, and rocket launchers opened up on the hovercraft. The combined rattle of automatic weapons and the crack of exploding rockets was nearly deafening.

Falco saw columns of white water shoot up around the oncoming landing craft, followed by at least two hits, and a sudden upwelling of black smoke. But as the hovercraft neared the beach it became clear that the vessels could take a lot of punishment.

That's why Oliver was on the horn with a pair of howitzer teams. And when they fired the results were clear to see. The hovercraft on the left survived a near miss. But the boat on the right took a hit near its stern. And when the smoke cleared the port engine and its mount were missing! The vessel veered, but kept coming, and managed to ground itself on the gently sloping beach. That's when the black air cushion deflated, a ramp fell, and what might have been two hundred people surged out onto the gravelly incline. What happened next took Falco and presumably everyone else by surprise.

The invaders rushed forward seemingly eager to attack. Then came the explosions as some of the leaders stepped on mines and were blown to smithereens. Others fell grievously wounded to lay screaming on the beach. Those who could turned, some dragging wounded comrades behind them, to gain the relative safety of the boat.

But men with guns were there to block them. The marines fired at the gravel in front of the mob and forced it to turn back. That was when Falco realized that the people being forced up the beach and into the American minefield weren't wearing uniforms, and didn't have weapons! They were civilians, or POWs, captured somewhere, and brought east for safekeeping. Or worse yet, taken for the very purpose they had been put to, which was clearing a path for Russian marines!

And sure enough, as the prisoners were forced to enter the minefield, heavily armed troops poured out of the hovercraft to follow up. Orders crackled over the radio. "Don't fire on the people in the minefield! Kill the soldiers behind them."

It was the correct order to give, but largely meaningless, as mines continued to detonate. "Bring fire in on the waterline!" Falco said, and Oliver passed the order on.

Shells rumbled overhead, fell, and exploded among the marines. Dozens fell. So many of them that the survivors were forced back. And because the ramp had been raised, all the marines could do was stand knee deep in the chilly water, and huddle around the boat's bow. Then mortar and howitzer rounds began to fall on the hovercraft themselves.

Meanwhile prisoners fortunate enough to survive the journey up through the minefield found themselves trapped against coils of razor wire. American soldiers risked their lives to go down and cut holes in the wire, even though more Russians were landing from RIB boats, and might pour through the newly created gaps.

Then the very thing that Falco had feared took place. "Overlook to all units," a male voice said. "The Russians are landing in force both north *and* south of Wales. Reserves will engage. Watch your flanks. Over."

At first Falco was only vaguely aware of the battles taking place north and south of him as he worked with Oliver to call fire in on the secondary landing craft that continued to land on the beach. The howitzers and the big 120mm mortars had plenty of smart rounds to work with. That meant the JTACs could use the laser designator to systematically target and destroy even small landing craft. And one or two rounds was typically sufficient to do the job. So it wasn't long before a dozen columns of heavy black smoke were rising from the wrecks and drifting north.

At that point Falco was able to take a moment to look around. A wild tangle of contrails was sprawled across the sky indicating that American and Russian planes were battling for control of the airspace above Wales. Suddenly Falco heard what he knew to be Parker's voice. "*Mayday, Mayday, Mayday*, Stripper with catastrophic engine failure over Wales, two people on board; *Mayday, Mayday, Mayday*."

As Falco looked south he saw an orange-red explosion at about eleven o'clock. A wing twirled as it fell. Smaller pieces of debris left individual smoke trails as they drifted down. A single chute appeared. Did it belong to Parker? Or to her Wizzo?

Falco grabbed a handheld radio. "I have to go Greg...Stay on it. I'll be back as soon as I can." Oliver opened his mouth to speak, but never got the opportunity.

Falco had his M4 in hand as he jumped down into the street. He hit hard and began to run. The chute was no longer visible. That meant someone was down. Had he or she been captured? Were they on the run? Falco prayed for the second possibility.

Falco saw a civilian ATV up ahead. It was parked next to a bunker with the engine running. Was the driver inside? Probably. After slinging the M4 over a shoulder Falco jumped on board. There was a shout as Falco accelerated away, but he didn't look back.

It didn't take long to clear the fortified area, blow through a checkpoint, and climb the hill beyond. Falco paused at the top to look down into the depression beyond. A battle was underway. It appeared that six Stryker vehicles had been brought in aboard C-17s. The eight-wheeled vehicles were heavily armed. And they, along with a large contingent of infantry, were battling a Russian invasion force. Their backs were to the sea. But precarious though their position was the Russian marines had fire support from two gunboats positioned offshore. Falco watched in horror as a Stryker took a hit and blew up.

Was the equivalent of a Russian JTAC at work? Yes, that's the way it appeared. Falco brought a small pair of binoculars up to his eyes. It didn't take long to find the spotter's location. He was where Falco would have been—which was atop some rocks near the shoreline. A spot with a good view.

And there, no more than a hundred yards away, was a parachute. It lay crumpled on the ground. Was there a body? No, Falco didn't see one. Perhaps the person the chute belonged to had been captured—or maybe they were hiding. Falco opened the throttle. Slush flew. There was no cover. So all Falco could do was use the ATV's speed to reach the pile of rocks as quickly as possible.

Falco was halfway to his destination, and closing fast, when the Russian fired at him. Geysers of mud crossed in front of the quad. That was bad, but good in a strange sort of way, because the other JTAC couldn't fire on him *and* spot for the gunboats. That would reduce the accuracy of incoming fire.

Falco braked as he neared the pinnacle, brought the ATV to a stop, and got off. Where was the Russian hiding? That question was foremost in Falco's mind as he sought cover among the rocks. It felt good to have something solid behind him as the JTAC scanned his surroundings. There were no signs of movement.

It would've been nice to stay put, and let the Russian come to him, but the clock was ticking. What if the enemy JTAC decided to ignore him? And continued to bring fire in on the Strykers? Or what if the downed aviator was wounded? There were a lot of possibilities and none of them were good. That forced Falco to move. It seemed natural to circle the jumble of rocks in a clockwise direction. He was careful to keep the M4 up—as his eyes scanned the heights above. That's where any JTAC worth his salt would be.

Falco was shuffling sideways, with his heart in his throat, when a small rock fell. It took a bounce, passed over his head, and landed somewhere behind him. The Russian stood, raised his AK-47, and fired. Bullets snapped past Falco's right ear. The JTAC was silhouetted against the gray sky. The carbine seemed to fire itself. The Russian jerked as the slugs hit him, took an involuntary step backwards, and toppled out of sight.

Target down. Falco felt a profound sense of relief as shells landed south of him. Yes, the gunboats were firing, but their spotter was dead. That meant Falco could . . .

A rifle butt struck the side of Falco's head and sent him reeling. It was a glancing blow, which was fortunate, since a solid hit might have been fatal. The Russian JTAC had an assistant! Falco should have considered that possibility but hadn't.

The thought flashed through Falco's mind as he allowed the M4 to fall and rolled to the right. Bullets kicked up geysers of slush where he'd been standing. Falco's fingers clawed at the 9mm holstered on his vest and jerked it free.

The Russian had adjusted his aim by then. He yelled something in Russian. "Eat shit and die?" Something similar perhaps. And that was a mistake. Falco fired two shots. The first bullet hit the soldier in the crotch. The second slug struck higher—but didn't have enough punch to penetrate the Russian's chest plate. It didn't matter. When the soldier released his AK to grab hold of his privates Falco shot him again. The third bullet was fatal. The body slumped to the ground.

Falco lay panting on the ground, pistol up, half expecting *another* attack. A large bump was forming on his head—and it hurt like hell. The sound of an explosion served to focus his thoughts. Parker . . . The Wizzo . . . One of them was in trouble.

Falco stood, went to retrieve the M4, and removed the PRC-152 from a slot on his vest. He keyed the mike. "Stripper? Do you read me? Over."

There was a moment of silence. The response was little more than a whisper. The rattle of gunfire was audible in the background. The *same* rattle he could hear. "*Wombat?* Is that you? Over."

Parker! She was alive! "Yes," Falco replied. "It's me. Where are you? Over."

"South of Wales," the pilot whispered. "The Russians are closing in from the west."

Falco turned to look. The pinnacle was at least a mile from the nearest fighting. It looked as though the Russians had gained some more ground, and were spread out in a line just west of the smoldering helicopter. "Where are you relative to the Chinook? Over."

"You can see it?"

"Yes. Over."

"I'm *inside* it," Parker replied. "I'm hiding just aft of the cockpit. Over."

That was a surprise. It made sense though ... Because of the smoke that continued to trickle out of the fuselage *both* sides had stayed clear of it. "Get ready," Falco told her. "I'm coming to get you. I'll be on an ATV. Over."

"Don't do it," Parker said. "You won't stand a chance."

"Get ready," Falco said. "If we don't pull you out now it will be too late."

Was there enough time to contact the Stryker commander? And what would happen if he did? Would some colonel order him to stay put?

Falco put the radio away, made a run for the ATV, and cranked it up. Then with the M4 slung over his shoulder he took off. The opposing sides were focused on each other, so Falco went unnoticed at first. Then the Russians spotted the off-road vehicle and opened fire. Falco zigzagged back and forth in an attempt to ruin their aim.

Then, as he rounded a boulder, shells rumbled overhead. The gunfire was supposed to explode in among the Strykers. But the high explosive rounds landed perilously close to Russian marines instead. And that meant the shells were striking around the Chinook! Was a company commander calling the shots? Probably.

Falco swerved to avoid a chunk of helicopter and straightened the handlebars. A shell landed to Falco's left, made a loud BOOM, and showered the JTAC with mud as he neared the wreck. Another round struck as the ATV's right front wheel dipped into a shell crater. The vehicle took a nose dive and Falco was thrown off. He landed hard. He couldn't breathe at first ... And it took a moment to recover.

Parker appeared out of the swirling smoke. Her face was dirty, her flight suit was ripped, and there was a pistol in her hand. "Were you hit?"

"No," Falco replied. "I don't think so."

"Good. Get up. We'll hide in the Chinook."

Falco rolled to his feet and followed Parker in through an open hatch. Once they were inside Parker pointed a finger to the west. "They're over there," she said, as shells continued to fall. The wreckage trembled as one of them exploded nearby.

Falco felt for his radio. The first thing to do was call for close air support. The PRC-152 was gone. Lost during the wild ride. He looked at Parker. "Lend me your radio ... I'll call for support."

"I already have," Parker whispered. "They'll come as quickly as they can. But they need to kick some ass first. And that could take a while."

Falco checked to make sure the M4 was ready. If the Russians attempted to enter he would take at least some of them down. "What are you doing here?" Parker wanted to know.

"I was in Wales," Falco whispered. "I heard your Mayday. So I came looking for you."

Parker had green eyes. They studied him. "That was stupid, but brave. Thank you. Did you see any sign of Baines?"

"Your Wizzo?"

"Yes."

"No. I saw one chute. But, there could have been a second one. Maybe I missed it."

Parker looked away. Tears were trickling down her cheeks. It seemed natural to put an arm around her shoulders. "I'm sorry."

Falco heard a shout. It was in Russian. He removed the arm and brought the carbine up. A man stepped into the cargo bay, did a double take, and raised his AK-47. Falco shot him in the face and he collapsed. *More* men appeared. Falco fired on them as did Parker. Two soldiers fell. "Into the cockpit!" Falco ordered, and gave her a shove.

They were barely clear when two grenades flew in through the hatch, bounced, and rattled across the deck. There were overlapping explosions. Shrapnel flew and Falco felt something sting his cheek. That was when a man appeared outside the transparent canopy. Parker fired three shots at him and he fell. *We're screwed*, Falco thought. *The Russians will...*

Parker's radio produced a burp of static. "Hey Stripper.... Keep your head down. Cowboy and Wizard in from the north with guns."

Falco and Parker hit the deck. Not that doing so would do much good if one of the fighter pilots missed the Russians and hit the wreck. The sound of jet engines was followed by the roar of a Gatling gun. Then the first plane was gone and the second screamed over. *More* 25mm rounds tore up the ground west of the Chinook.

Falco performed a pushup, and made his way over to the hatch, where he ventured outside. The M4 was up and ready to fire. But there was no need. Dead and wounded Russians lay everywhere. Engines growled as the Stryker battalion moved west to secure the area. A first lieutenant came forward to toss a salute. "Are you Wombat?"

"Yes."

"I'm glad you're okay, sir. The ATV thing was crazy. No offense intended. Is this yours?" The lieutenant was holding the PRC-152. It was muddy but intact.

"Yes, thank you," Falco said as he accepted the radio.

Parker appeared at his side. "I just got off the horn ... Cowboy and Wizard took care of the gunboats."

Falco realized that the shelling had stopped. "That's wonderful! Did you thank them?"

"Yes. And we owe them a case of beer."

Falco nodded. "Come on ... Let's see if the ATV will run." It did. Parker climbed on behind him. And, when she leaned forward to wrap her arms around Falco's waist, it felt good.

CHAPTER NINETEEN

Lavrentiya, Russia

General Anatoly Baranov didn't want to be in Lavrentiya, especially then, as his soldiers struggled to secure a beachhead in Wales, Alaska. But he had no choice. Admiral Maxim Zharkov, commander of the pacific fleet might be a friend. But he was a superior officer as well. And a man Baranov couldn't afford to ignore because Operation Red Ice couldn't go forward without the navy's support. So, if Zharkov wanted to speak with him in person, then speak he would.

That's what Baranov was thinking as he got off the helicopter, and made his way across the tarmac to the point where Colonel Yakimov was waiting. The one-eyed Spetnaz officer reminded Baranov of the grim faced portraits which lined the halls of the Moscow war museum. Russian war heroes were a universally glum lot, and understandably so, since many of them had fought and lost battles in the Great Patriotic War. But they were tenacious bastards … And eventually emerged victorious. Did that describe *his* situation? After failing to establish a beachhead in Wales? Baranov wanted to think so. Yakimov rendered a salute. "Good morning, Comrade General."

Baranov returned the courtesy. "What's so good about it?"

It was a churlish thing to say, but Yakimov remained unfazed. "We are alive, General … And only 2.3 miles from victory."

Baranov couldn't help but smile. "You are an optimist Colonel, and I love you for it. Has the admiral arrived?"

"Yes, sir. He's waiting."

"And how would you describe his mood?"

"He's worried, sir. About everything. Including his ass."

Dudin and Gotov were standing a few feet away. Could the TASS reporter hear what had been said? Baranov hoped not. Yakimov was an outstanding solider *and* a member of the GRU. Still, the last comment was well over the line. Baranov decided to ignore it. "Let's get this over with, shall we?"

A beat up GAZ Tigr was waiting to take the officers to Fort Lavrentiya's command bunker. The once sleepy town was heavily fortified with AA missile batteries, fighters prowled the skies above, and sonobuoys had been placed at strategic locations around the bay. A precaution Admiral Zharkov should have taken earlier. Did the loss of two destroyers and a cruiser account for the naval officer's nervousness? Definitely. Never mind the damage done in Anadyr.

But all was not lost. Troops were everywhere marching, running, and training. And once the last section of bridge was in place they would stream across the strait and take Alaska back.

The entrance to the command bunker was protected by a platoon of Spetsnaz troopers, a barbwire fence, and concrete blast walls. Guards snapped to attention as Baranov and his companions strode past—and followed a ramp down into the dimly lit room below. Orderly rows of technicians sat in front of flat screen monitors tracking ships, planes, and drones. The combined murmur of their voices had a soft, soothing quality.

A junior officer was waiting to lead the men back to the conference room where Admiral Zharkov sat waiting. He rose and came forward to wrap Baranov in a bear hug. But the navy officer looked tired, and his smile was forced. "It's good to see you, Anatoly ... Even if you resemble a horse's rear end."

"And *you* Maxim," Baranov replied. "In spite of the fact that you look like a dog's breakfast."

Both men laughed. But the moment lacked the unforced comradery of days gone by. "Good morning, Major Gotov," Zharkov said. "And it's good to see you again Comrade Dudin. Could you excuse us for a moment?" Then, without waiting for a reply, Zharkov said, "Thank you."

As the two men departed Zharkov turned to Baranov. "Give me a status report, Anatoly. And no bullshit. I want the truth! First I lost the *Konev* to some kind of orbital weapon. Then the Americans sank both of her escorts. Since then the *pindos* have destroyed *two Pomornik* class hovercraft, *two* gunboats, and dozens of small craft. This has to end, Anatoly... The Americans and their allies sank a Chinese carrier two days ago. The *Konev* and her escorts might have made the difference."

"I'm sorry to hear that," Baranov replied. "But this is war Maxim... What did you expect? Some assets will be lost."

"Some," Zharkov agreed, "but there are limits. I can't give you any more ships Anatoly."

"What about tugs? We're close, very close, and I need tugs to push section three into place."

"I will give you tugs," Zharkov agreed. "But nothing more. Not so much as a rowboat. You must finish it, Anatoly. I spoke with Marshal Orlov yesterday. He grows impatient."

Baranov wanted to say, "Fuck him," but managed to control himself. It felt as though the walls were closing in on him. To fail while so close to victory would drive him mad. "I understand, Maxim. I will finish it."

"How soon?"

"Within forty-eight hours."

"Do that Anatoly, and every Russian will know your name. I have to go now, but keep me in the loop."

"I will," Baranov promised. "I will."

Once Zharkov was gone Dudin and Gotov entered the room. "So, Comrade General," Dudin said. "How did it go?"

"It went well," Baranov lied. "The admiral is looking forward to landing on newly conquered soil."

"As well he should," Gotov said.

Baranov was barely aware of the comment. His mind was racing. The frontal assault on Wales had been nothing less than a total disaster. And his attempts to flank the American defenses had failed. What remained?

Baranov stood and made his way over to a large wall map. His eyes roamed the area around Wales, happened on two words, and paused. "Find an intelligence officer. Bring him here."

Gotov knew the order was directed to him and left. Dudin came over to stand next to Baranov. "You are staring at the map, General ... What do you see?"

"This," Baranov said, as his right index finger stabbed a spot immediately south of Wales.

Dudin moved in for a closer look. The letters were so small that Dudin could barely read them. "Tin City."

Dudin looked at Baranov. What was the general thinking?

***

Tin City Air Force Station, Alaska, USA

Tom Riley preferred to sleep in the station's equipment bay because racks of components kept it warm, and he could hear the audible alarms should any go off. The larger facility had been closed for more than 35 years, but the air force continued to operate Tin City's radar remotely from Elmendorf AFB. The "minimally attended" AN/FPS-117 radar system required regular maintenance however—and that's where Riley came in.

It was 0600 when the alarm clock beside Riley's cot went off. Russian fighters had destroyed the antenna on Cope Mountain two days earlier, but Riley was under orders to keep the rest of the system running, so he had to get up. A new antenna was to be flown in soon.

Tin City was located at the foot of the mountain. After destroying the antenna the Russians strafed the buildings that comprised the original base. But most of the structures were empty, and had been since 1983. And, as luck would have it, the low flying jets missed the nondescript concrete structure that was home to the AN/FPS-117's equipment racks as well as Tin City's sole resident.

Riley squirmed his way out of the sleeping bag, slipped his feet into a pair of fleece lined mocs, and shuffled out into the maintenance area that also served as his living room. It was furnished contractor style, which was to say poorly, with an old sofa and a stained recliner. A much abused footlocker stood in as a coffee table. It had, according to the moniker stenciled on the front of it, been the property of someone named "Denton."

Riley paused to mark the wall calendar. There were sixteen days left on his thirty day tour. Then he would go home to Cindy, and another contractor would arrive. Assuming Tin City still belonged to the US of A.

Riley entered the bathroom where he brushed his teeth and shaved. It wasn't required. Most contractors didn't. But after shaving every day of his twenty-two years in the air force, Riley couldn't imagine wearing a beard, even though he was retired and "double-dipping."

After a hot shower Riley toweled off, got dressed, and made breakfast. His fresh food was gone by then. But he liked Spam, and he liked hotcakes, so he ate some of both every morning.

By 0800 Riley was ready to run the morning check on what he thought of as his life-support systems. Those included the leaky plumbing, the electric heating, and the station's diesel generator.

Riley was halfway through the routine when the handheld radio on his belt beeped. It was connected to a relay station and an antenna near the four-thousand five-hundred foot airstrip. This enabled the duty techs in Elmendorf to reach him whenever they needed to. "This is Tin City One ... Over."

"This is Mark," a voice said. "Grab some gear and run like hell! Head for Wales ... Russian planes are headed your way!"

Riley's mind started to race. A knot formed in his belly. Mark Hanson was one of the techs at Elmendorf. "What about the system?"

"Pull enough modules to disable it, and take one of them with you. Now get ... Or would you like to spend next winter in a Siberian gulag?"

"I'm on it," Riley replied. "Thanks. Out." Riley circled the building and dashed inside. The next couple of minutes were spent jerking modules out of racks. He hid some and dumped two of them into a day pack. A handful of trail bars went on top. Then, with his bear rifle in hand, Riley took off. And just in time too, as a Sukhoi Su-25 screamed over the station, and circled the base.

There was no cover other than scattered rock piles, so all Riley could do was run north, and hope for the best. The pilot wouldn't fire on a single individual would he?

The answer was, "Yes." As Riley learned when a rocket turned the old pump shack into splinters—and a second missile struck the gymnasium. The explosion sent debris whirling into the air and started a fire.

The airstrip ran west to east. Riley dashed across the runway onto the barren ground that lay beyond. Because it was summer the contractor had to thread his way between a scattering of fresh water ponds in order to travel north. He looked back over his shoulder, saw the jet lining up for a second run, and made a mad dash for a cluster of rocks.

The Russian fired his guns, and all Riley could do was lay flat and pray. Cannon shells threw up geysers of dirt to the left and right as the Su-25 flashed over. Then it was time to get up and run some more. As Riley did so he was conscious of the fact that *more* planes were arriving on the scene. But *why?*

The answer became obvious when an Illyoshin 11-76 transport plane bored in from the west, and paratroopers tumbled out of it. The airborne troops were supposed to land, secure the airstrip, and hold it so that more transports could land. Most of the soldiers fell around the runway.

But, due to a capricious sea breeze, some troopers were going to land north of Riley. Three to be exact. And once on the ground the Russians could prevent him from reaching Wales which lay nine miles away.

Riley stopped, brought the rifle around, and dropped to one knee. It took a moment to find the nearest paratrooper's chute with his scope. Then it was necessary to follow the shrouds down to the heavily laden soldier. He was falling fast. *Lead him*, Riley told himself.

That required Riley to depress the rifle barrel even further. He took a guess, pressed the trigger, and felt the Winchester Model 70 thump his shoulder.

The .338 magnum bullet flew straight and true. Riley saw the soldier jerk and crumple to the ground. The chute billowed in the breeze. One down. Two to go.

A brass casing flew sideways as Riley worked another round into the chamber. He hurried forward. The other paratroopers were on the ground by then. Had they heard the shot? Or witnessed the killing? Riley hoped the soldiers would see the chute flapping around and rush over assist their comrade.

Riley hurried forward, took up a position behind a weatherworn boulder, and took aim at the dead body. It was no more than a hundred yards away, and well within the Winchester's reach. A paratrooper appeared and knelt next to his comrade. The .338 round knocked him over. The report was loud, and guaranteed to attract attention.

Two down, one to go, Riley thought. Then he felt something cold make contact with the nape of his neck. "Put rifle down," a voice said, in accented English. "And turn around."

Riley felt his blood run cold. The Russian had approached him without making a sound! Riley placed the Winchester on the ground and turned.

"Rise your hands." Riley did so. The paratrooper was wearing winter camos, a full combat kit, and holding a fancy submachine gun. A sure sign that Riley was eyeball to eyeball with some sort of special operator. "What *are* you?" the Russian demanded. "SEAL?"

"No," Riley replied. "I'm a United States Air Force Master Sergeant, retired." Riley flicked his eyes to the right. "Isn't that right, Nate?"

The soldier fell for it, and Riley charged straight at him. The gun went flying as they collided and the paratrooper fell over backwards. Riley landed on top of the man, managed to place his thumbs over the Russian's eyes, and leaned forward. An eye popped and the soldier screamed. Then, conscious of the need for speed, Riley stood.

It was second nature to toss the submachine gun away, and look to the south, as the soldier writhed in pain. A platoon of Russians had formed a skirmish line and were crossing the runway. Riley turned, made a grab for the bear rifle, and began to run. The pack slapped his back.

Riley hadn't gone far when he heard the rattle of gunfire. But the Russians were a long way off—and none of the bullets came close. Not so far as he knew anyway. Could he follow the coastal trail up to Wales? He would sure as hell try.

***

Baranov, Dudin, Gotov, and Yakimov were aboard the first transport to land. The airstrip was secure by then, and a major was waiting to deliver his report. He saluted. "The base is ours, sir."

"Good," Colonel Yakimov replied. "Did we suffer any casualties?"

"Two dead, sir. One man was wounded."

"*Two?* How many Americans were there?"

"One, sir."

Baranov stepped forward. "I'm sorry to hear that there were casualties. But, as Comrade Dudin knows, there's reason to celebrate. Isn't that right, Boris?"

Dudin knew a cue when he heard one… And understood what Baranov was up to. *He*, along with two-hundred and fifty Russian troops, had successfully landed on the American mainland! That was something no foreign power had been able to effectively do since the war of 1812, and it was going to be a *huge* propaganda coup.

Would the landing be sufficient to take the pressure off Baranov? And counterbalance his failure in Wales? Yes, for the time being. And that meant the general would get another chance to complete his bridge. "You are correct, Comrade General," Dudin proclaimed as he raised his camera. "Please stand *there*, with the mountain behind you, while I shoot some footage. I will upload the story within the hour. Then the entire world will witness what you've been able to accomplish."

Baranov *knew* that Dudin *knew*, and didn't care. Not so long as the reporter did his job. Once the story was aired in Moscow, Marshal Orlov would be forced to back off. And President Toplin would claim the credit. So Baranov struck a variety of poses and tried to smile. In the meantime his thoughts were churning.

Wales was *close*. Very close. Less than a day's march for crack troops like his.

They would follow the Winter Trail up to a point east of Wales and attack the Americans from the rear. Would the enemy see them coming? Of course they would. But with only hours in which to respond the enemy wouldn't have time to construct a wall like the one that fronted the beach. Nor would they be able to abandon that fortification because he planned to send *another* attack force across from Little Diomede. That would force the American general to split her forces in two. Meanwhile a company of his paratroopers would take control of the airport.

"All right," Baranov said. "That's enough posing for the camera. Colonel Yakimov... You have a map... Follow the Winter Trail to Wales. I expect to be in control of the town when the sun rises tomorrow."

* * *

After running full out for five minutes, Riley paused to look back. The pack felt heavy, and his breath came in short gasps. *I'm getting old*, Riley concluded. *And I'm out of shape. Maybe I should cut back on the pancakes.*

Riley didn't have binoculars, so he used the Winchester's scope to check his back trail. His pursuers were easy to spot. One was armed with a long gun—and the other was carrying something smaller. Another submachine gun perhaps.

Riley felt a stab of fear. A sniper team had been sent to kill him! And, because the Russians were in better shape, they were closing the gap.

Riley turned and began to jog. He was running parallel to a high bluff with the sea on his left. A steady breeze pushed rows of orderly waves in to crash against the rocks. Jets could be heard fighting somewhere above. He didn't dare to look. *Watch where you put your feet*, Riley told himself. *This is no time to trip and fall.*

The trail was faint. And that was to be expected. Contactors like Riley had no reason to make the trip north—and the residents of Wales weren't likely to visit Tin City. But the path was there. And, as a rock formation forced the trail out towards the edge of the cliff, Riley paused. After removing two trail bars from his pack Riley threw it out over the edge of the cliff.

The contractor couldn't watch the knapsack fall, but knew it would be lost in the seething surf below. That meant the Russians wouldn't get their hands on the modules. Did their experts know everything there was to know about an AN/FPS-117 radar? Probably. But it wasn't for Riley to say. His duty was to destroy the mods and he had.

A bullet kicked up dirt one foot to the right of him. The report arrived moments later. *Windage*, Riley thought, as he ran. *The wind is blowing from the west—and he didn't compensate enough. He won't make that mistake again.*

The best way to solve the problem was to kill the Russians. That much was obvious. But to do that Riley had to find a hide. A spot where he could hunker down and put the Winchester to work. But nothing caught his eye as he jogged uphill. It was easier to run without the pack to slow him down.

When Riley topped the rise he saw the gully that lay beyond. A seasonal stream ran from east to west and produced gurgling sounds as it hurried to the sea. He turned, lay on the ground, and looked south. There was nothing to see at first. Then Riley detected a flicker of movement through the scope. He brought the rifle in close and poured all of his mental resources into making a successful shot.

A soldier appeared. Only his head was visible at first. It rose and fell as the Russian ran. Then the pursuer became visible as he emerged from a dip. There was no sign of the rifle. Riley was looking at the spotter then ... And the sniper was bringing up the rear.

The wind continued to blow in from the right as Riley's index finger tightened on the trigger. It gave, the Winchester spoke, and the soldier went down. Had he been hit? Or was he diving for cover? All Riley could do was wait.

Three minutes passed. And when the second Russian appeared, Riley knew he was looking at the sniper, because he had the long gun. And he was closer than the spotter had been! Somehow, some way, the bastard had been able to cover open ground without allowing himself to be seen. Riley swore and backed away. Once he was out of view Riley jumped to his feet and ran.

The rest had done him good, and Riley gobbled a trail bar as he ran. The downhill stretch led to a stream, which he splashed through, prior to tackling the opposite slope. Had the Russian topped the last rise? If so, Riley would be visible. He didn't think the sniper was that close though ... So when Riley reached the summit he turned to look back. That was a mistake.

The bullet was low, but still on target. It struck Riley's left leg with the force of a sledgehammer blow. He fell like a rock. The pain was excruciating, and Riley whimpered as he sat up to inspect the damage. "Shit, shit, *shit!* That hurts."

The area just above his knee was a bloody mess—and Riley could see white bone through the surrounding hamburger. Blood ran out to stain the gravel. *A tourniquet,* Riley thought. *I need a tourniquet.*

After fumbling with the buckle Riley pulled his belt free. That dumped the radio onto the ground and the contractor left it there, as he wrapped the strap around his thigh, and cinched it tight. The worst of the bleeding stopped. He had some time, but not much. The sniper had seen the hit. So he knew Riley was down, but possibly alive. The man would come carefully, but he would come.

Riley grabbed the radio, stuffed it into a pocket, and elbowed his way over to a pile of loose rocks. He felt dizzy and slightly nauseous. The pain was worse than anything he'd ever experienced. Once in place Riley brought the radio out and struggled to focus on the keypad. The numbers seemed to swim in front of his eyes as he thumbed the buttons. Was the repeater still on? If so, the device could run on battery power even if the generator was off. The response was immediate. "This is Home Plate ... Go. Over."

"It's Tom," Riley said weakly. "Is that you, Mark?"

There was a short pause. "Name your favorite beer. Over."

"Corona."

"Where *are* you? What's going on? Over."

"The Russians landed in force. I capped three of them on my way out. But a sniper shot me in the leg. Patch me through to Cindy, Mark ... But don't tell her about the leg. Over."

"Hang on," Mark said. "I'll send help from Wales. Over."

"Sure," Riley said. "You do that. Now patch me through."

Mark could, and ultimately did, although the process seemed to last forever. Finally Cindy came on the line. "Tom? Is that *you*?"

Riley felt a surge of warmth and tenderness. For nearly twenty years Cindy had followed him all over the world, made homes for the two of them, and never uttered a word of complaint. Riley's leg was throbbing. He bit his lip to keep from crying out. "Yes, hon ... It's me."

"Are you okay? I heard reports of fighting in Wales." Cindy could read him like no one else. Maybe that was because they'd been married so long. Or maybe it had something to do with what he referred to as her "Cindydar."

"Yes, I'm okay," Riley lied. "I miss you that's all. And I wanted to hear your voice."

"Well, here I am," Cindy replied. "I'm glad you called."

"What are you doing today?"

"The usual. Go to the store, work in the yard, and do some laundry."

"That sounds good," Riley told her. "Listen...I'm not very good with words. You know that. But I love you Cindy, and I always have."

"*Tom?* Something's wrong, I can tell! What is it?"

Riley heard the scrape of a boot and saw the soldier appear. The Russian was a dark silhouette against the light blue sky. Riley barely had time to thumb the power button and lift the Winchester with his right hand. It seemed to weigh a ton. Then Riley saw a spark—and the pain vanished.

CHAPTER TWENTY

Wales, Alaska, USA

Falco took Parker to the airport where he had to immediately part company with her. There was a kiss however … On his right cheek. Followed by a quick squeeze of his hand. "Thank you, Wombat," Parker said. "You're a wonderful, crazy man." Then she turned and made her way out across the tarmac to a waiting C-17. Planes were coming in full, and leaving empty. That made it easy for Parker to hitch a ride.

Falco could still feel the touch of Parker's lips on his as he drove the ATV back to the bunker. It was early afternoon by that time, and the sky was gray. Oliver was there to greet him. "The prodigal returns … And just in time too. Things are heating up."

"How so?"

"The Russians landed nine miles south of here. It sounds like they're going to swing around and attack us from the east. Our planes are trying to stop them but the Russians own the sky. Meanwhile it looks like the bastards plan to land in our front yard again. So, if you survive your meeting with Colonel Waya, you'll have plenty to do."

Falco frowned. "*What* meeting?"

"The one where he rips you a new one for running off to rescue a pretty pilot."

Falco made a face. "When?"

Oliver smiled. "He said, 'Tell that sonofabitch to come see me as soon as he returns.' Or did he say, 'shithead?' It was one of the two."

Falco frowned. "You're enjoying this, aren't you?"

"Who? *Me?*" Oliver replied innocently.

"I'm sorry," Falco said. "I left you holding the bag. And that was wrong."

"Yup," Oliver agreed. "It was. Fortunately I like beer. And a case of it would go a long ways towards reestablishing my faith in your leadership."

"Done." Falco said. "I'll be back as soon as I can." And with that Falco went out to discover that the stolen ATV had been stolen! Falco swore and set off on foot. There were lots of people on the streets, and Falco noticed that the mix included many civilians. They came in all shapes and sizes and were armed with a wild assortment of weapons. As Falco passed between them he saw hunting rifles, assault weapons, and compound bows. Were things so desperate that General Haberman had been forced to bring civilians in? Or were they arriving on their own? Time would tell.

It took half an hour to find Waya. The better part of another half hour was spent waiting to be chewed on. Finally, when Falco was invited to enter the crude command bunker, the actual ass kicking was less severe than he expected. Perhaps that had something to do with the fact that Waya was tired. His eyes were red, his skin looked gray, and he was in need of a shave. "You're a major," Waya began, "rather than a lieutenant, a sergeant, or a private.

"So I expect you to understand the strategic importance of your role. Not to run off on self-assigned SAR missions, while leaving your subordinate to fend for himself. That said, I'm willing to write your stupidity off to a misplaced sense of gallantry. But I won't be so understanding if it happens again. Do you read me?"

Waya was seated. Falco was standing at attention. His eyes were focused on a spot just above the colonel's head. "Sir, yes sir."

"Good. At ease. Take a load off."

Falco lowered his weight into the sagging lawn chair and hoped it wouldn't collapse under his weight. "Here's the sitrep," Waya told him. "The Russians landed on an airstrip located nine miles south of us. It's clear that they plan to flank us. Once they're ready, they'll attack from both the east *and* the west. If they capture Wales they'll hurry to complete the bridge. Thousands of troops will stream across it. More than we can handle. So we *have* to hold. That's why General Haberman put out a call for civilian volunteers. They call themselves 'The Wolverines,' and their job is to protect our eastern flank."

Falco remembered the wild looking assortment of men and women he'd seen walking the streets. "Yes, sir."

"So here's the deal," Waya continued, "You're going to work with The Wolverines. Roughly half of our heavy mortars and artillery will be under your direct command. Master Sergeant Oliver will assume responsibility for the rest of it. His job is to keep the bastards off the beach. And remember … Most of the civilians don't know jack shit about the military—and won't understand your role. That makes the possibility of a friendly fire incident extremely high. Do you have any questions?"

"Yes, sir. How much time do we have?"

Waya looked at his watch. "Two hours if the Russians attack this evening. And, given how long the days are, that's what we expect them to do. You will report to a retired general named Gooding. He's something of a character, but he has a good rep, and he knows Alaska."

"What about air support, sir … Will we have any?"

"Maybe," Waya replied. "But the Russians outnumber us in the air. And they have a full court press on. Do the best you can."

Falco stood, and threw a salute. "Yes, sir."

Waya nodded. "Go get 'em, Major ... We can win this thing."

Falco thought about Waya as he left. *Hang in there, Colonel ... We need you.*

There was a lot to do and very little time in which to accomplish it. The first step was to hurry back to the bunker where Oliver was waiting. After agreeing on which frequencies to use, and dividing the available firepower between them, the JTACs began the task of contacting the batteries and bringing them up to speed. The changes were no big deal for half the teams.

But those selected to defend the brigade's eastern flank had to turn their weapons around and reorient themselves. Once the logistics were complete, it was time for the JTACs to part company. "Try to stay alive," Oliver said. "I want my case of beer."

"Don't drop a shell on the command bunker," Falco replied. "I'm in enough trouble already."

Both men laughed and Falco left with his M4 in hand. His next task was to find General Gooding and check in. Waya had granted him permission to direct fire as he saw fit. Would Gooding see it the same way? And what if he didn't? Falco made his way east.

Like a lot of military people Falco had a tendency to view civilians as being unorganized. So he was expecting to walk into a chaotic mess. But that wasn't the case despite the snarling sled dogs, the tendency to organize around family groups, and the visible consumption of alcohol.

The defenders didn't have enough time to put up a defensive wall like the one fronting the beach. But a small track hoe was being used to dig tidy six-person fighting positions along a line that led from the north end of Wales, to a section of high ground that looked down on the Winter Trail.

All of which was explained to Falco by an enthusiastic young man named Roy. He was dressed in head-to-toe hunting camos and armed with an AR-15. "Come on," Roy said. "I'll take you to the general."

Roy led Falco south onto the high ground. Patches of snow were hiding in the nooks and crannies that the gradually setting sun hadn't been able to find and penetrate. Roy was following a set of tracks too narrow to have been made by a tractor or personnel carrier. And, as they topped the rise Roy said, "There he is! That's General Gooding."

The general was seated on an all-terrain tracked chair. A scabbard was strapped to the side of the rig and a rifle butt could be seen protruding from it. Gooding was sporting an Australian style bush hat with one side folded up. The retired officer was glassing the area in front of him with an enormous pair of binoculars. A gray mastiff rose to stand stiff legged and growl at the newcomers as they arrived. Gooding lowered his glasses and turned to the dog. "At ease, Sergeant."

The mastiff whined submissively and lowered himself onto the ground. "Major Falco, I presume," Gooding said. "Colonel Waya said you'd be by." Gooding's face was long, thin, and deeply lined. There was no need to salute a retired officer, especially one in civilian clothes, but Falco chose to do so anyway. "It's a pleasure to meet you, sir."

"Excuse me if I don't get up," Gooding said with a wry smile. "I see that you're acquainted with my grandson."

Falco looked at Roy and back. "Yes, sir. Roy was kind enough to bring me over."

"He's my aide, nurse, and bodyguard," Gooding said. "Not that there's much left to guard. So here's the situation. A couple of Russian scouts are out there—watching us from that pile of rocks off to the right. There's no point in killing them because the Russkies would send more. And who knows? The replacements might be more competent.

"The rest of the bastards will arrive in less than an hour. Then we'll be facing about two-hundred and fifty men. That doesn't sound like a lot, but here's the thing... All of them are Spetsnaz. That's like being attacked by two companies of green berets."

"But Spetsnaz or not, they're still human," Gooding observed. "And when they arrive, it will be after a nine-mile march, and an even longer day. And rather than face what they expect to be ineffective civilians, they're going to fight some of the meanest bastards in the world! Which is to say my fellow Alaskans. We ain't pretty," Gooding added, "but we have teeth. Isn't that right, Sergeant?" The mastiff heard his name, and growled.

***

Baranov was exhausted but determined to conceal it. How long had it been since his last nine-mile march? Ten years? At least. And he wasn't carrying a pack. Dudin by contrast was carrying his own gear—and appeared to be fresh as a daisy.

But we're almost there, Baranov assured himself. And, based on the latest Intel reports, the Americans are desperate. Civilians were brought in to help defend the village. The Spetsnaz will cut through them like a hot knife through butter while our marines land on the beach.

The prospect pleased Baranov. But the pleasure was short lived. A scream was heard from up ahead—and it wasn't long before word came back. One of the soldiers had stepped on a bear trap! His right foot was hanging by a thread. "It's an old trick," Gotov growled. "The presence of animal traps can sow fear... And when a soldier is injured, a medic must help. Combat related wounds might go untreated as a result."

"Not to mention the fact that it takes two soldiers to carry a stretcher," Baranov added. "Pass the word... We will establish an aid station *here*. Once the battle starts helicopters will arrive to evacuate the wounded."

"Yes, sir," Gotov agreed, as he turned to his radioman.

For his part Baranov was determined to finish the march—*and* watch where he placed his feet. Had more traps been laid? Baranov assumed the answer was yes.

***

Falco found a home for himself in a recently dug fighting position already occupied by three men and a woman. She was pretty in a hard edged way, and introduced herself as Yukon Jane. Falco wasn't sure if that was a stage name or a radio handle.

Jane was helping Falco settle in when the Humvee mounted ADMS Avenger (Air Defense Missile Systems) that protected the town began to spit fire-and-forget Stinger missiles into the air. Falco saw a flash of light and knew that a Russian plane had been hit. But what *kind* of plane? And were more of them on the way?

The answer came in the form of a steel rain. At least one-hundred gravity bombs fell in quick succession. By listening to the radio traffic Falco was able to get a feel for the big picture. The first bombs landed in the water where they exploded harmlessly. But the rest were right on target. Columns of gravel and earth shot up into the air. Gaps appeared in the defensive wall. And Falco heard what sounded like rolling thunder, as the bombs leveled homes, destroyed a missile battery, and laid waste to the airport.

Jane raised her head to look and Falco pulled her down as one of the weapons landed 200 feet east of them. There was a tremendous BOOM, followed by what felt like an earthquake. There was nothing the Russians wanted or needed in the town of Wales. So they had every reason to carpet bomb the area. And more than that, to prep the battlefield for the soldiers who were on the way.

Falco heard what sounded like a clap of thunder and looked up in time to see pieces of fiery debris tumble out of the sky. He was reminded of a 4th of July fireworks display in his home town of Eugene. It was impossible to know how many civilians had been killed or wounded during the attack. But Falco figured casualties had been high, and wondered how long the defensive line could hold. "Here they come!" someone shouted, and the Russians attacked.

Falco was standing on an improvised firing step and looking downslope. Very little daylight remained, and the Spetsnaz were wearing artic camos, so Falco would have to turn his night vision gear on soon.

Rather than charge up the hill en masse, the Russians came forward a dozen at a time, dropped to the ground, and opened fire. That was the signal for *more* troops to dash forward. It was good soldiering, and what one would expect of the Spetsnaz.

But most of the Alaskans didn't know what good soldiering was, nor did they care. They wanted to win, and didn't care how that was accomplished. And, thanks to Gooding's leadership, there were a variety of surprises awaiting the Russians.

Falco heard someone yell, "Roll the barrel bombs!" The JTAC had to stand aside as two of his companions muscled a fifty-gallon oil drum up onto the edge of the fighting position and set it free. He watched as the barrel rolled and bounced down the hill. "It's half full of gas," Jane explained. "And rigged with C-4. The general has the remote."

Falco saw the container take another jump, and land two feet further on. The drum, plus a dozen like it, were in among the Russian troops when Gooding pushed a button. Some of the bombs went off with no noticeable effect. Others exploded near clusters of soldiers, tore them apart, and sent body parts whirling through the air.

The assault stalled. But Falco could hear orders being shouted and knew the enemy was going to launch a second attack. And that was the perfect time to drop some mortar bombs on them. He called on his batteries, gave a series of orders, and was pleased with the results.

Flashes of light marked the spots where the bombs fell. Each hit produced a crack-BOOM which, taken with the rest of the noise, became part of a hellish symphony. It was difficult to carry out a realistic damage assessment. But Falco felt sure that the bombs were making a significant difference. Still, rather than expend all the ammo the mortars had, Falco called a momentary halt. Once specific targets were visible the bombardment would resume.

* * *

Meanwhile, on the west side of town, an amphibious assault was underway. That gave Oliver reason to worry. The Russians were arriving in dozens of RIB boats. And while they were susceptible to mortar fire, the targets were too small to target with the M777A2 howitzers.

The noncom wasn't about to let the big tubes go to waste however, so when the marines began to bunch up, he was ready to laze them. "Mark," Oliver said. "Fire when ready."

A shell rumbled overhead, struck the beach, and produced a resonant BOOM. "Bingo!" Oliver exclaimed. "Right on the money!"

* * *

Falco's attention was on the slope in front of him as the Russians opened fire with LMGs (light machine guns) and soldiers charged up hill. Some of the attackers were backlit by pools of burning gasoline. That made them easy meat for the Alaskans, all of whom were experienced hunters.

But there were a lot of Russians. And as the machine guns continued to chatter, entire fire teams were killed as RPGs flew up hill. Falco had his night vision gear on, and was firing the carbine by then. He dropped a soldier, followed by another, and was about to target a third—when an order was shouted. "Release the dogs!"

Falco had noticed the dogs earlier—but assumed they were pets. Now he realized that Gooding had yet another unconventional weapon up his sleeve. Dogs snarled as they went up over the top of the fighting positions and raced down the slope. Some of the Russians fired right away, and sent furry bodies tumbling. But most of the enemy soldiers were too slow.

Russians were thrown to the ground by a husky, a German Shepard, or a mongrel … All hardened by lives lived in the wild. Screams were heard. And, as the Spetsnaz shot at the dogs, some of their bullets struck fellow soldiers, and cries of "*Medik!*" were heard.

Logic suggested that Falco take advantage of the situation to bring more fire in. But even though most of the dogs were going to die anyway, Falco knew their owners would be furious if his mortars were the cause, and understandably so.

However as a military officer Falco felt a strong need to do something more than watch the mayhem. So he went up over the top. "*Follow me!*" Falco shouted as thousands of officers had before him, and skidded down the slope.

An incoherent cry went up all around him as the surviving civilians came boiling up out of their fighting positions, and swept downhill. The Russians, some of whom had been wounded by the dogs, tried to fight. One took an axe to the head and fell with it embedded there. Another was thrown backwards by the full force of a double barreled shotgun blast to the chest. And when a third trooper rose to block Falco's way, the JTAC shot him in the face. "Kill them!" a woman screamed shrilly. "Kill *all* of them!"

Meanwhile, at the top of slope, Gooding sat and cried. Sergeant had gone into battle with the rest of the dogs, never to return. The general's heart was broken.

* * *

There was nothing Baranov could do but watch in horror, as a madman led an army of rabble down the slope to battle his men. Rather than pull back, as they should have, the Americans were attacking him! The tide of oncoming civilians came close to the front line but was forced to pause when the Spetsnaz rose to oppose them. There was no place for either side to take cover behind. A woman leveled a seal harpoon and charged. Baranov raised his pistol and shot her in the face.

The Russian line was beginning to fall back, and Baranov was forced to do likewise, as Gotov delivered the news. According to radio reports the situation on the seaward side of town was grave as well. After coming ashore, and surging through gaps in the American minefields, a team of marines had managed to cut a hole in the razor wire.

A platoon following along behind them had been able to reach the foot of the defensive wall. Charges were placed and detonated. A hole opened up and marines rushed through. That had put them in an enemy bunker, and only steps from the street beyond.

Then 155mm shells fired from deep inside American territory had fallen on the bunker and destroyed it. Suddenly it became apparent that the enemy had allowed Baranov's marines to enter the fortification for the express purpose of killing them! What should Baranov do? Fight a losing battle? Or save what he could? The answer was obvious.

An American flare went off, followed by another, and the full horror of the scene was revealed. The dead and dying from both sides lay everywhere—often separated by no more than a few bloody feet.

Yakimov was nearby exhorting his troops through a bull-horn. "Fight, damn you! They're civilians. Kill the *pindos*!"

"Colonel!" Baranov shouted, as bullets snapped past his head. "We will withdraw. Wounded first."

"*Tak tochno* (Yes sir)," Yakimov replied. He went to work.

"Air support is on the way," Gotov announced.

Baranov nodded. "Good. Come…We will help the wounded."

The wave of Americans couldn't sustain itself, broke, and had to pull back.

Jet engines were heard as Russian fighters swept in. Baranov felt a surge of hope. Maybe the planes could turn the tide! But the incoming aircraft were met by salvos of Stinger missiles. And when a bright flash strobed the barren countryside Baranov knew that a fighter had gone down.

Baranov was duty bound to remain until Yakimov pulled the last of his soldiers back to the Winter Trail. Then, with the Alaskans nipping at their heels, the Russians began the long and hellish withdrawal. They were already exhausted. And many of those called upon to fight a series of rearguard actions had been wounded earlier in the battle.

Again and again Baranov, Gotov, and even Dudin were forced to pause and fire at their pursuers who, rather than take heavy casualties, were content to harass the fleeing Spetsnaz. It was a nightmarish journey, and one Baranov would never forget.

Finally after hours of struggle Baranov and his men arrived in Tin City where two transports sat on the runway. Baranov forced himself to wait until the first plane was loaded and in the air, before following Yakimov up the ramp into the Antonov An-22, where he fell into a seat.

Baranov closed his eyes as the plane raced down the bumpy airstrip and lumbered into the sky. All of his hopes and dreams lay in ruins. But the inner fire continued to burn. He would regroup in Lavrentiya, pull what remained of his brigade together, and launch a final attack. But it would have to be done quickly—before news of his defeat could reach Moscow. *Dudin,* Baranov thought to himself. *I need to do something about Dudin.* Then he fell asleep.

CHAPTER TWENTY-ONE

Wales, Alaska USA

Falco was in his sleeping bag, curled up in a corner of the bunker he shared with Master Sergeant Greg Oliver, when the MPs came for him. He awoke to scuffling sounds and saw a blob of light wandering around the floor. "We're looking for Major Falco," a voice announced.

"He's the one pointing a pistol at your head," Oliver replied. "You might want to knock next time."

The light moved, found the .9mm, and followed an arm up to Falco's face. The JTAC blinked. "Aim the light somewhere else."

"Yes, sir...Sorry, sir," the MP said, as the light flicked away. "Colonel Waya sent us. He wants you to attend a staff meeting at 0400."

Falco looked at the luminous dial on his watch and swore. It was 0330. He put the pistol away. "What the hell for?"

"He didn't say," the MP replied. "But I can tell you this much...Something big is afoot. They gave us a long list of people to notify."

"One of them will shoot you," Oliver predicted.

"The meeting will be held in front of the command bunker," the MP said, as he backed out into the night.

"Have a nice time," Oliver said, pulling the bag up around his shoulders. "I'll be right here—holding the fort."

"Bullshit," Falco replied, kicking his sleeping bag off. "You're coming with me, and that's an order."

"I don't like you anymore," Oliver whined, imitating his daughter's voice. "I want a *new* major."

Falco laughed. "Submit a request, and wait in line."

Even as Falco pulled his boots on he could tell that the anonymous MP was correct. Something *was* up. Helicopters clattered overhead, engines roared as vehicles passed by, and snatches of radio traffic could be heard as a squad of marines walked past.

And, when Falco stepped outside the bunker, he could *feel* the sense of urgency in the air. But *why?* None of the passersby knew.

Officers and senior noncoms were streaming toward the command bunker. The JTACs tagged along. A much trod path led them to an open area where a large shelter had been erected, and miracle of miracles, urns of hot coffee stood waiting! Boxes of doughnuts had been flown in, and were open on a folding table. "Now *this* is worth getting up for," Oliver proclaimed through a mouthful of chocolate doughnut. "Life is good."

Falco wasn't ready to go that far, but had to admit that the pastries were excellent, and even better with hot coffee. Waya was smart enough to let the assemblage feast for ten minutes before making an appearance. His stage consisted of two stacked cargo pallets. The buzz of conversation came to an end, as an army captain yelled, "Atten-hut!"

That was impossible for most of them to do, while holding coffee and doughnuts in hand, and none of them wanted to let go. Waya took them off the hook. "At ease." He was holding a wireless mike, and his voice boomed from speakers located around the meeting area.

"First," Waya began, "I want to congratulate each, and every one of you, for holding Wales and pushing the Russians back."

Someone yelled, "Hooah!" A cry echoed by the rest.

Waya smiled. "'Hooah,' indeed. But our work isn't done. Operation Boomerang is getting underway."

"Uh, oh," Oliver said, sotto voce. "I don't like the sound of that."

Falco knew what Oliver meant. He was filthy, and bone tired. The last thing he wanted to do was take part in a new operation. Unfortunately neither of them had a choice. Waya nodded. "I know what you're thinking. When is this going to end? And that's a good question. The answer might surprise you! Operation Boomerang, and our part in it, will end when we take control of Nunyamo, Russia."

The statement was followed by a moment of stunned silence as tired minds struggled to process the news. Then someone said, "Holy shit! We're going to invade Russia!"

Waya smiled. "Bingo! Give that man a doughnut."

Falco's mind was churning. Of course! At some point General Haberman, and or the brass in D.C. had seen the opportunity to turn the situation upside down by using the bridge *against* the Russians! But it would only work if the Americans could hold onto Wales, and prevent the enemy from securing a beachhead.

Others had arrived at the same conclusion and there was a growing murmur of conversation. "As you were," a lieutenant colonel ordered. "You'll have a chance to shoot the shit when the briefing is over." The talking stopped.

"The initial discussion began shortly after the Russians completed the first span of the bridge," Waya informed them. "The idea seemed like a pipe dream back then. But General Haberman believed it could be done, and convinced a whole lot of people that she was right. And *that*, ladies and gentlemen, is why we never used B-52s or B-2s to bomb the bridge. We *wanted* the Russians to complete the project, but slowly, so we'd have time to assemble the troops, ships, and pontoons required to use the span ourselves.

"And yes, we have newly manufactured pontoons of our own! They will be used to replace those destroyed during the last few days. The replacements will arrive this morning, along with the navy ships required to protect them.

"Once that's accomplished," Waya continued, "we'll fight our way across the strait to Nunyamo, and across the bay to Lavrentiya, where we'll capture the town's airfield. Shortly thereafter the newly formed 11th Mountain Division will be flown in.

"Do we intend to push deeper into Russia?" Waya inquired rhetorically. "I have no idea. That's above my pay grade. But I know this... By invading the Chukotka Peninsula, we will force the enemy to defend the east coast, thereby sucking resources away from the western front. And that alone is enough to make the effort worthwhile.

"All right... That's the thirty-thousand foot view. Now, get ready to take notes on the operational stuff. This is about to get real."

***

Lavrentiya, Russia

General Anatoly Baranov had taken over Yakimov's office—and was sitting at the colonel's desk. Baranov was not only exhausted, but depressed, and desperate to turn the situation around. Now even *more* bad news had arrived. *Pindo* ships were steaming north... And some of them were towing pontoons! Others were thought to be carrying marines.

It seemed that the Americans intended to not only repair the bridge, but to use it as the means to invade mother Russia. And if that was allowed to occur his name would become permanently associated with a blunder so horrendous it might become synonymous with military stupidity. And his dream of reclaiming Russian lands would end in failure.

That hasn't happened yet, Baranov assured himself. *I still have time. But only if I can keep this mess out of the headlines long enough to turn the situation around. Otherwise President Toplin will send some asshole in to relieve me. I control all of the communications that enter and leave Lavrentiya... So none of Dudin's recent messages have been sent.*

Baranov's thoughts were interrupted as a Starshina entered the office. "Comrade Dudin has arrived, sir."

"Good," Baranov replied. "Send him in, and notify Major Gotov. I want him to join us."

The noncom said, "Yes, sir," and withdrew.

Baranov took a moment to review the plan. Once Dudin was in the office Gotov would enter and close the door behind him. Then, while Baranov spoke to the reporter, Gotov would shoot him. After Dudin fell, Gotov would place a pistol by the reporter's hand.

Soldiers would hear the noise and rush in. That's when Gotov would point at the handgun and accuse Dudin of attempted murder. Would such a scenario hold up in Moscow? No. But they weren't in Moscow, they were in Lavrentiya. And it belonged to him.

Once Dudin was out of the way, Baranov would muster what resources remained to him, and fight the Americans to a standstill. "Good morning Comrade General," Dudin said, as he entered the office. "I brought Colonel Yakimov with me as you can see. I hope you don't mind."

Baranov *did* mind, but couldn't say so. He forced a smile. "No, of course not. The colonel is always welcome."

Yakimov will toe the line, Baranov assured himself. *What else can he do? Side with a reporter? Never.*

Baranov invited the men to sit down. Dudin shook his head. "No, Comrade General, I can't stay for long. I have a plane to catch."

Tomorrow would have been too late, Baranov thought. *Here's Gotov, thank god. He knows what to do.*

Gotov entered the office, and was just about speak, when Dudin shot him. Once in the face, and once in the chest, just as the instructors at Russia's Main Intelligence Agency (GRU) had taught him to do. The weapon was a short barreled OTs-38 double action revolver chambered for the silent SP-4 cartridge. It produced nothing louder than a click when fired.

Gotov collapsed. "Kill the dog first, *then* the master," Dudin said. "It's safer that way. Especially when the master is planning to kill *you.* You look surprised, Anatoly... Do you believe that President Toplin, Marshal Orlov, and Admiral Zharkov are fools? They sent me to keep an eye on you, and yes, I have a sat phone. So they know about the debacle in Wales."

Baranov felt a nearly overwhelming sense of shock. Dudin was more than a reporter! Why hadn't that possibility occurred to him? *I was too trusting,* Baranov concluded. *And too focused on my mission. So it's over. Or is it?*

Baranov looked at Yakimov. The other officer was expressionless. "So you're part of this, Colonel?"

"Yes," Yakimov replied flatly. "You've done more damage to Mother Russia than the *pindos* have. We took thousands of casualties, and for *what?* For your dream. Or was it your ego?"

Baranov had a backup plan of sorts. His right hand was under the top of the desk holding a .9mm pistol. It was pointed in Dudin's direction. But, since Baranov couldn't aim properly, he would most likely miss. Still, the shot would cause Dudin to flinch if nothing else. And that would be Baranov's chance to pull the weapon up and aim. Could he accomplish that *before* Yakimov drew his sidearm? Yes, he could. Because Yakimov would have to undo the flap that protected his sidearm before he could draw his weapon and fire.

Dudin smiled, but there was no humor in it. "Are you holding a pistol, Anatoly? I think you are." The revolver produced a series of clicking sounds.

***

Baranov felt the slugs slam into his chest. They sent his chair rolling backwards. His pistol clattered to the floor. The ceiling was a blur. *Russia ... My beautiful Russia ...* Then he was gone.

***

Dudin circled the desk to check on Baranov's pulse. There was none. "The General was killed in action," Dudin said. "And Gotov committed suicide. Both bodies will be cremated later today."

"Yes, sir," Yakimov said stoically. "My men will handle the details."

"I'm sure they will," Dudin replied, as he reloaded the revolver. "And *you* will take charge of Baranov's brigade. The Americans will attempt to capture Nunyamo. Don't allow that to happen."

***

Near Lavrentiya, Russia

A green beret threw up when the *Morskaya Rakushka's* (Sea Shell's) stern rose, forcing her bow down into the cold waters of the Bering Sea. After pausing there for a moment, as if considering a dive to the bottom, the 67-foot trawler's bow came back up. The soldier barfed the rest of his breakfast into a plastic bucket located between his boots and wiped his mouth. Falco didn't blame the man. *His* stomach felt queasy—and the smell didn't help.

The fishing boat's captain was a bushy bearded Russian national named Igor Zukov. He stood with sea boots spread, staring at a dimly lit compass. He was a CIA contractor, and to Falco's way of thinking, untrustworthy. Was Zukov steering the proper course? Or guiding the Americans into a trap?

But Oliver was down in the cabin, hanging out with the rest of the special ops team, and tracking the boat's progress with a GPS receiver. And if Zukov veered off the correct course, Oliver would shoot the Russian in the head. Unfortunately none of the Americans had any experience steering a fishing trawler through frigid artic waters. That meant the solution to the problem would give birth to another problem.

Falco sighed. While Operation Boomerang looked good on a PowerPoint, it had all the hallmarks of a grade "A" shit show. Everything had been thrown together on the fly, was generally late, and poorly resourced. The lack of an experienced seaman being a good example of that. And there was more. The "fleet" of ships Waya had promised consisted of *two* vessels. An aging destroyer called the *USS Ramage*, and a minesweeper named the *USS Scout*.

The latter had been charged with the dangerous mission of removing mines from the approaches to Nunyamo, while the *Ramage* was tasked with providing fire support. That made the destroyer Falco's most important weapon until American planes could claim air superiority.

The *Sea Shell* heaved, spray flew back to splatter the windows, and the Russian made a small course correction. "We enter bay soon," Zukov said. "Calm there. You leave."

"That sounds good," Falco said, knowing full well that the team wasn't going to release Zukov or the *Sea Shell* until Lavrentiya was secured. The trawler wasn't much of an escape plan. But it would give them something to run to should the shit hit the fan.

As the hours of darkness came to an end, and the sky began to lighten in the east, Falco could make out the dim outlines of headlands to his right and left. True to Zukov's word the wave action decreased moments after the *Sea Shell* entered a tiny bay.

Falco had studied the maps, plus satellite photography of the area, and knew that the town of Lavrentiya was located five miles to the north. Would the Russian military notice the fishermen coming ashore? No, Falco didn't think so. But anything was possible.

As the light level continued to improve, Falco was able to make out the two fishing boats already anchored in the bay. Half a dozen ramshackle buildings were arrayed at the top of a steeply sloping beach. The only building of any size was the remains of a Russian Orthodox church.

Zukov put the fishing boat's single screw into reverse for a moment prior to switching neutral. "You go now," Zukov said. His eyes widened as a pistol barrel made contact with the nape of his neck. Sergeant Nathan Kirby had recovered from his seasickness by then, and had a businesslike demeanor.

"There's no reason to be concerned," Kirby assured the Russian in his own language. "We won't harm you. But we need to maintain an escape route. So you, Corporal Smith and I are going to remain here, and make sure that the *Morskaya Rakushka* is ready for sea. Now, clasp your hands behind your neck. I'm going to pat you down. Then we'll go forward and drop the anchor."

Falco accepted the pistol and two knives that were hidden beneath the Russian's clothes. He tossed the weapons overboard on his way to the stern, where the rest of the special operations team was wrestling a gray RIB boat into position. The group consisted of Oliver, a marine Joint Fires Observer by the name of Staff Sergeant Sam Purdy, and two green berets. Larry Yussef was going to accompany the JTACs, while Corporal Milo Smith had been assigned to stay, and help Kirby guard Zukov.

All were dressed like the fishermen they were supposed to be, and looked the part, as they swung the RIB boat out over the water. Falco eyed the beat-up outboard mounted on the stern—and hoped that it was in good working order. The beach was a long way off, and there weren't any oars.

Yussef went over the side and entered the boat once it was in the water. The duffle bags that Oliver lowered down to him were old and frayed, just like the ones fishermen might have. Falco turned to Smith. "You know the frequencies. Monitor them. And, if things go south, haul ass. That's an order."

Smith nodded. "Yes, sir. But they won't."

Falco went to the side, threw a leg over the bulwark, and lowered himself into the waiting boat. The motor was making a steady putt, putt, putt sound. Yussef had the tiller. "Take us in," Falco ordered. "And remember ... No English. Purdy will do the talking."

Like Kirby, Purdy spoke Russian, albeit with a Ukrainian accent. But something was better than nothing.

The trip went smoothly. Waves rolled in to push the boat along, sea birds wheeled overhead, and a man emerged from a building that fronted the beach. He was brushing his teeth. A muted roar was heard as a pair of jet fighters took off from the airfield to the north. Falco eyed his watch. Six a.m. straight up ... The battle had begun and it was important for the team to reach the airstrip as quickly as it could.

Yussef opened the throttle all the way, cut power, and brought the engine up. The inflatable surged forward, and rocks rattled as the bow pushed up onto the beach. "Everybody out," Falco whispered, knowing that voices could carry. "Let's take the boat up above the tideline."

With two men on either side, they carried the boat up the steep slope and put it down. The man with the toothbrush spit a mouthful of water onto the ground, and made use of a hairy forearm to wipe his face. He was dressed in a stained tee shirt and a pair of baggy pants. He said something in Russian. Purdy responded in kind. "What did he say?" Falco inquired, as the fisherman disappeared into the building.

"He asked if his friend Igor is okay. I told him yes, assuming that a really bad hangover is 'okay.'"

"Good work," Falco said. "Let's grab the gear and get moving. Keep those MP5s handy." Each man had an easy-to-conceal submachine gun hidden under their jackets.

The road meandered north. There was no vegetation to speak of. Just rocks, patches of unmelted snow, and occasional streams to cross. The track followed the coastline for the most part, but was forced to swerve inland, whenever an inlet blocked the way. But never for very long.

Falco caught the occasional glimpse of waves breaking over rocks off to the right and gave thanks for the bay where the *Sea Shell* was anchored. He figured that the men and women who cleared the trail hundreds of years earlier had a good reason for living along the coast. Their food came from the sea—and the search for it never ended.

A sonic BOOM rolled over the land, and a pair of antiaircraft missiles streaked across the sky, where they disappeared into the clouds. The air war was heating up. Was Parker up there? Falco feared that she was. "Uh, oh," Oliver said, as a vehicle topped the rise in front of them. "Here comes trouble."

Judging from the top mounted LMG the boxy 4 X 4 was military, and probably on patrol. "I want everyone on the west side of that truck," Falco said. "And be ready."

The men understood. If they stood on *both* sides of the vehicle, and a firefight began, they would wind up firing at each other.

The truck bounced through a gully, growled upslope, and jerked to a stop. It carried *three* soldiers. A driver, a top gunner, and a passenger who might be a noncom. The man certainly *acted* like a noncom as he dropped to the ground, and gave what sounded like an order.

Purdy answered in Russian but, judging from the noncom's expression, the soldier didn't like what he'd heard. Not only that, but the gunner was bringing his weapon around. "Kill them!" Falco said, as he brought his submachine gun out into the open.

His first priority was to shoot the gunner. The initial burst of bullets was too low. But the Russian jerked spastically as Falco walked his fire up to the correct height.

Meanwhile a hail of machine gun fire from the other team members took care of the noncom and his driver. The entire incident lasted less than ten seconds. Had anyone heard? That seemed unlikely. "Hide the bodies," Falco ordered. "Check the truck. Can we use it?"

They could, and Falco decided that the team *had* to take it, even though the vehicle could attract the wrong sort of attention from both sides. Because if the Russians happened across the shot-up 4 X 4 all hell would break loose.

Once the bodies were hidden behind a pile of rocks Falco ordered his men to get aboard. Oliver was at the wheel. "Turn it around," Falco ordered. "We'll drive it a few miles up the road, look for an inlet, and push it in."

The plan worked perfectly. The narrow bay was both deep, and open to the sea, which sent waves rushing in to explode against the rocks. After the truck hit the water it disappeared without leaving a trace. Falco felt confident that although someone would discover the bodies eventually, the 4 X 4 would never be found.

They were within a mile of Lavrentiya by then, and the sounds of distant fighting could be heard. Falco led the men off the road. "Over there," he said, pointing west. "On the high ground. That's where we'll set up."

The airstrip was visible in the distance. Engines roared as a Russian transport lumbered down the runway and took off. It was flying low and headed out over the strait to avoid the air-to-air combat above. Were VIPs on board? Escaping to safety? Or did the flight have another purpose? Falco would never know.

The rocky slope led up to the top of the low lying hill. A fifteen-foot tall granite obelisk stood atop the high ground and pointed at the sky. There was a plaque, but it was in Cyrillic. Broken vodka bottles, cast off candy wrappers, and used condoms lay on the ground at the foot of the monument. A place to party then ... When the weather allowed.

. "Yussef will provide security," Falco said, "while you guys set up."

"Roger that," Purdy replied.

Falco removed a small pair of binoculars from a pocket. He began the scan on the far west side of town. A Buk Missile system stood ready to defend Lavrentiya from American planes. Troops were visible, but not many. Most were on the other side of the bay, trying to defend the bridgehead.

Then, as Falco panned to the right he saw some colorful buildings, fishing boats, and *another* Buk. A cluster of cranes marked the location of the local freight terminal.

The airfield appeared next. A number of aircraft were visible including two civilian prop planes, an attack helicopter, and two Sukhoi Su-25s—both waiting to take off.

The jets would have been good targets had there been enough time to bring fire in on them. That wasn't the case however. Engines roared as the fighters hurtled down the runway and took off to the east.

Falco's glasses skimmed the blue waters of Zaliv Bay to the settlement of Nunyamo off in the far distance. And *that*, Falco knew, was the western terminus of the floating bridge, and the spot where Russian ground forces were trying to stop American troops. The rumble of artillery could be heard, and clouds of smoke billowed up into the sky.

The visual tour came to end as Falco's binoculars came to rest on the spindly control tower that marked the east end of the airstrip. Falco planned to take that down first, because by doing so, he could disrupt flight operations and communications. "We're ready," Oliver informed him. "Let's do this thing."

Falco turned to Purdy. The noncom was thin, wiry, and badly in need of a shave. Under normal circumstances the marine would have been part of a Naval Shore Fire Control Party, under the command of a naval Gunfire Liaison Officer.

But these weren't normal circumstances. Like the mission itself, the team had been thrown together on the fly, and Falco had to make it work.

"Here's what I have in mind, Sergeant," Falco said. "I'll pick the targets and pass them to you. Then, since you speak swabbie, you'll translate what I say and give orders to the *Ramage*."

Purdy looked pleased. "Yes, sir. You can count on me."

Falco turned to Oliver. "I'm depending on you to handle whatever air support becomes available. But pay attention to the naval stuff … I don't want to double up on targets unless there's a good reason to do so. And Greg …"

"Yes?"

"Don't let our jet jockeys bomb the airstrip. Waya will take me off at the ankles if they do."

"Got it," Oliver said with a grin. "No BOOM-BOOM on the runway."

Falco looked at Purdy. "See what I put up with? Okay, call the *Ramage*. Let's put those swabbies to work."

The *Ramage* was an *Arleigh-Burke* Class guided missile destroyer. The tin can had been launched way back in 1994, but Falco didn't give a shit, so long as the *Ramage* could deliver the goods. That meant missiles and 5-inch shells when he asked for them. "I have the *Ramage* on the horn," Purdy announced. "They're standing by."

"We're going to drop the control tower first," Falco announced. "You have the coordinates ... Request two Harpoons."

The *Ramage* was cruising fifteen miles offshore—and her arsenal included eight active radar-homing, over-the-horizon, anti-ship missiles. Except the Harpoons were going to be used against shore targets instead of enemy vessels.

After some routine back and forth with the destroyer's command center, the missiles were launched. Falco took comfort from the fact that the radar-homing weapons were flying just above the surface of the sea, which would make them damned hard to hit.

The bad news was that the missiles' relatively puny 488-pound warheads might lack a sufficient amount of punch. Accuracy would be everything. "They're running hot and straight," Purdy reported.

There was no reason to wait for the moment of impact, so Falco gave Purdy a new target. "There are two Buk anti-aircraft missile systems in front of us. Let's assume that both have active radar. Hit the one on the right."

Yussef had been silent so far. "The attack helicopter is spinning up, sir."

Falco swore. The Russian helo might be headed for the bridge, where a hellacious battle was underway, or some other destination. But what if the helicopter was supposed to locate the missing 4X4? That would put the team under the helo's flight path as it flew south. And the MP5s would be worthless against a Mi-24 gunship. "Oliver! Put out the call ... We need help, and we need it *now.*"

That was when Falco heard a two explosions, and raised his glasses in time to see the *second* Harpoon hit the control tower. The explosion blew a hole in the column, and sent debris flying, but left the structure standing. "Tell the *Ramage* to use her 5-inch gun on that sucker," Falco ordered. "Maybe that'll bring it down."

Purdy nodded as the Buk launcher blew up. The second explosion was like an echo of the first. A column of dirty grey smoke twisted up to mark the spot. "Notify the *Ramage*," Falco said. "Target destroyed."

Purdy nodded, and was speaking into his mike, as the Mi-24 lifted off. Falco swore as the insectoid looking helicopter turned and headed towards them. "Disperse!" Falco shouted. "And take cover!" A pile of rocks offered a place to hide.

Falco was crouched between two boulders, looking up through the crack that divided them, as the gunship clattered overhead. *Keep going*, he prayed, *head south*. But God must have been attending to someone else's needs at that moment, because the Mi-24 entered a wide turn, and bored in. That's when the Gatling gun in the ship's bulbous nose opened fire. The slugs took the top of the obelisk off. And, as the large chunk of granite fell, 5-inch shells began to rain down around the control tower below.

The helo continued to speed away before circling back. As the noise level dropped Falco could hear Purdy walking the 5-inch shells in. "Up ten! Right five! Fire!"

"They're coming in again!" Yussef warned. "Put your heads down."

The pilot fired rockets this time. One of them scored a direct hit on Purdy's hiding place. The bright red explosion killed him. A second missile struck a pile of rocks and sent shrapnel scything through the air. Falco heard it clatter around him as Oliver uttered a joyful shout. "Hang on! A guy called Boss Hog and his wingman are rolling in from the north!"

Falco dared to take a look, and saw that two A-10s were coming his way. The Mi-24 tried to run but that was a waste of time. There was an orange-red explosion as Boss Hog blew the Russian out of the air. Bits and pieces of fiery debris rained down as the A-10s turned north to lend assistance there.

Shells continued to fall around the tower as Falco made his way over to where Purdy lay. He barely knew the marine. But during the short period of time they'd spent together Falco had come to appreciate the jarhead's can-do spirit. He swore under his breath.

"Two hits!" Yussef exclaimed. "There it goes!"

Falco looked up to see the top half of the tower break off and fall free. The column shattered as it hit a taxiway. *You did it Sergeant,* Falco thought. *You killed that sonofabitch. And I'm going to put your ass in for a medal.*

Most of the targets had been accounted for, but one remained. "Tell the *Ramage* to shift fire." Falco ordered. "See the Buk system at the west end of the runway? Order them to put two Harpoons on it."

Oliver passed the word. Shortly after he did so, a call came in. "Boomerang-Five to Red-Eye-Six. Do you read me? Over."

Falco took the mike. "This is six. I read you five-by-five. Over."

The words were followed by two overlapping explosions as the Harpoons raced in from the Bering Strait to score direct hits on the Buk system. A dark mushroom cloud floated up into the air. Boomerang-Five was still on the horn. "What's your status? Over."

"All of our primary targets have been destroyed," Falco replied. "Over."

"Excellent. Stand down. Phase two is about to begin. Out."

Falco looked at Oliver. "A whole lot of people are about to fall out of the sky."

The noncom nodded. "That's a good sign! Things must be going well on the bridge."

"Let's pack up," Falco said. "Our job is done."

The fighters arrived first, and began to circle at 15,000 feet. Transport planes appeared next. Tiny stick figures spilled out into the air. Parachutes blossomed, and most of the soldiers landed on the airfield. A few rangers went astray though—and Falco saw one of them splash into the bay.

The Americans didn't land unopposed however. Most of the Russian troops were fighting on the north side of the bay, where Waya's forces were trying to come ashore, but the airport's security force put up a fight. They were badly outgunned however, and the battle was over fifteen minutes later.

Falco, Oliver and Yussef took turns carrying Purdy down the winding trail to the edge of town. Falco was on point. A waist high stone wall wandered across the hillside. It was gray and covered with lichen. Falco led the team down the path and through an open gate.

That was when Falco heard a pop, followed by a loud bang, and a feeling of incredible lightness. *This is what it feels like to fly*, Falco thought, as his body was thrown into the air. Then he fell, and the ground came up hard. The world ceased to exist.

CHAPTER TWENTY-TWO

Eugene, Oregon USA

After exiting the two-engined plane, and passing through the busy terminal, Parker found herself in Eugene, Oregon. The college town where Falco had been born and raised. She felt a host of conflicting emotions. Three months had passed since the Americans had taken control of the Russian made bridge, repaired it where necessary, and crossed into Russian territory. More than a thousand lives were lost in the process.

After capturing Nunyamo, *and* the town of Lavrentiya, the Americans settled in. There was no strategic reason to occupy the surrounding wastelands and they didn't. The whole idea was to score a psychological victory, create a nearly impregnable fortress, and pull Russian resources away from the war in Europe. The same strategy the Russians had been hoping to employ. And it was working.

Meanwhile as the arctic winter set in, most of the bridge had been destroyed. Ice floes slammed into it, storms tore at it, and the Americans made no effort to intervene. Nor was there a reason to. They could resupply Firebase Waya by air, so long as American fighters kept their counterparts at bay, which they had. And Parker had been part of that effort.

Now she was on leave. And, rather than go home to Spokane, Parker had chosen to visit Eugene instead. *Why?* Because of Major Dan Falco, that's why.

After stepping on a mine in Lavrentiya, Falco had been airevaced to the hospital at Joint Base Elmendorf-Richardson, and from there to David Grant USAF Medical Center at Travis AFB in California. Parker knew that, because she'd been in touch with Master Sergeant Greg Oliver, and he kept her apprised of Falco's condition.

And the situation wasn't good. The JTAC's left leg had been blown off—and seventeen pieces of shrapnel had been removed from various parts of his anatomy. That, Parker imagined, was why Falco wasn't responding to her emails. He was going through the emotional upheaval that most people experience after a traumatic amputation.

According to what Parker had read, a person in Falco's situation was likely to experience grief, anger, and withdrawal. So why was Parker standing in the cold, outside the terminal in Eugene? Did she pity Falco? Had she come to provide the comfort he hadn't requested? Or, was it because she *wanted* him? Maybe. Realizing that they barely knew each other. *Still*, Parker thought, *we had something. Or the beginnings of something.*

A ride share car stopped in front of her. That was popular now … And ride share drivers could buy a larger allotment of gas. Parker opened the back door, placed her carryon inside, and slid in next to it. The driver was an older man. He eyed her in the mirror. "Yes, ma'am … Where to?"

According to Oliver, Falco was staying with his parents, and waiting for a medical board to decide his fate. He wanted a return to full duty. To be a JTAC again. That was unlikely. But, after the upcoming bump to lieutenant colonel, the air force could utilize Falco's talents in other ways. *If* he was willing. Parker read Falco's address off her phone. "No problem," the driver said. "I know where it is."

Parker watched the scenery slide by as the car left the airport. *This is either the stupidest thing you've done,* Parker thought, *or the smartest. You'll know soon.*

As the car passed through the suburbs, and continued into the countryside beyond, Parker saw apple orchards to the left and right. That was a revelation. *Falco's a country boy,* Parker thought. *And it fits.*

It took fifteen minutes to reach their destination, and pass under the sign that read, "Falco Farms." A curving driveway led up to the dignified farmhouse on top of the softly rounded hill. There was a barn too... And farm equipment. Parker's heart was beating faster. Was the visit a mistake? Would she be sorry?

"That'll be thirty-six dollars," the man said. "Sorry, but gas is expensive."

"No problem," Parker replied, as she handed the money over. "Do you have a card? I might need a ride to the airport later today."

He turned to look at her. "Are you here to see Danny?"

"Yes. Do you know him?"

"Of course," the driver replied. "Danny and my son Larry were best friends in high school. Larry's in the marines now, serving somewhere in Africa."

Parker swallowed. There were so many young men and women serving overseas. And all of them were in danger. "Everyone has someone in the war," Parker said. "I'm sure Larry will be fine."

"I hope so," the man said. "As for Danny, well, he's been down lately. A pretty face might cheer him up."

Parker opened the door, got out, and leaned over to get the bag. "Thanks for the ride. Maybe I'll see you later."

Gravel crunched under Parker's feet as she made her way up a short flight of stairs to the wraparound porch. The screen door made a squealing sound as a woman pushed it open. She had carefully kept gray hair, a kindly face, and Falco's mouth. "Yes? May I help you?"

"My name is Parker, Kathy Parker, and I'm a friend of Dan's. We served together in Alaska. Please excuse my unannounced visit. I tried to contact Dan by email, but couldn't reach him."

The woman nodded. "I'm Nancy, Danny's mom. What you *really* mean is that Danny didn't reply to your messages. He's been moody lately. Please come in."

As Parker followed Nancy into the house she half expected to see Falco sitting on a couch with his prosthetic leg up on a hassock. He wasn't there. The living room was furnished with a carefully conceived mix of old and new items. The result was both stylish and comfortable.

A tall, rangy man entered the room from the kitchen. He was in excellent shape, and something about the way he moved, reminded Parker of Falco. "This is my husband, Ralph," Nancy said. "Ralph, this is Kathy Parker. She's a friend of Danny's."

Ralph had piercing blue eyes, and a firm handshake. 'It's a pleasure to meet you Kathy... Are you a JTAC?"

"No," Parker replied. "I'm a pilot."

Ralph's eyes lit up. "A pilot! What do you fly?"

"I fly F-15s right now."

Ralph nodded. "Danny wanted to fly, but he didn't make the cut. He took it well though, and we were proud of him."

"*Are* proud of him," Nancy put in pointedly. "They gave him a silver star for what he did in Alaska."

"And he deserved it," Parker said. "Dan is a brave man. He saved my life."

Nancy eyed her. Parker could see the wheels turning. And could imagine what the other woman was thinking. *Who is this woman? A friend? Or something more? And how will her visit impact my son?*

Parker forced a smile. "Is Dan around?"

"Yes, he is," Ralph assured her. "Danny's supposed to do exercises, and walk as much as he can. He's out in the orchard. Follow me ... I'll point you in the right direction."

***

The sky was clear, the sun was up, and the air was crisp. Falco had completed his morning exercises, and was bent over, peering into the shallow creek that trickled through the orchard. It was something he'd done countless times as a child. Crayfish lived in the cold water, and he liked to watch them scuttle around.

Falco straightened up. The stump hurt, the way it *always* hurt, but less now. And that was a good thing. The medical board was coming up, and he needed to show progress in order to reclaim his life. More than that his identity, and his reason for being.

Falco's combat honed senses were still quite acute. He heard a twig snap and turned. He was looking east, into the sun, and it was difficult to see. Was that his father? Coming out to check on him? No, this was someone shorter. A person wrapped in a halo of orange-yellow light. Then the truth dawned on him. "Kathy? Is that *you?*"

Parker stopped. "Yes, it's me. Hello, Dan ... It's good to see you."

Falco felt a surge of embarrassment. "I'm sorry, Kathy. I got your emails, and I read each one of them at least twenty times. But I didn't know what to say. I have drafts though ... Lots and lots of drafts."

"It's okay," Parker replied. "I understand."

Falco limped forward. "*Do* you? I don't want to be your friend. I never did. And I don't think that's what you had in mind either. Not then. But now, with *this*, I'm not the same man."

Parker smiled. "Oh, I get it ... You were planning on a career as a ballet dancer."

It was hard edged humor, *military* humor, the kind common to every branch. And there was no pity in it. Falco laughed, and it felt good. He moved closer. "I dreamed of you."

Parker looked up at him. Her eyes were big. "And I of you. That's why I came. I want you to buy me to dinner. I want you to tell me about everything and nothing. And I want you to kiss me Wombat ... *Now*, on the lips."

Falco took Parker into his arms and felt her hands touch the back of his neck. Their lips met and seemed to fuse. The moment was accompanied by a sense of completion, as well as an abiding hunger, which was waiting to be satisfied.

Suddenly, in place of what had been lost, Falco had something of even greater value. Their lips parted and their combined breaths fogged the air as they smiled. "Come on," Falco said, as he took her hand. "I'll give you the tour. I hope you like apples. Dad would be pleased."

***

Nancy Falco was watching from an upstairs window. She couldn't see everything. But she witnessed the kiss, and felt a sense of joy. The doctors had done their best. But it was Kathy Parker who could put her son back together. And for that she was extremely grateful.

Praise for the America Rising series

"*Into the Guns* doesn't waste a second getting going right out of the gate... By the time you get to the last page, you're out of breath. But things are only getting started."—Pulp Fiction Reviews

***

ABOUT THE WINDS OF
WAR SERIES

In **RED DAWN**, volume two of the *Winds of War* Series, WWIII rages on as secret service agent John Blue-Crow strives to protect the American president from harm.

But President Alfred Hayden has a secret, one which only the Russians know and, when they threaten to expose the president for what he truly is, Hayden commits a series of acts so heinous that a special team is formed to hunt him down.

Crow is assigned to that team, as is DEA agent Cissy Jones, and together they must not only survive attacks by a shadowy group known as the 5th Column, but go rogue in an effort to track Hayden down. Nothing less than the outcome of the war is at stake.

RED DAWN will be released in the Spring of 2019.

***

ABOUT WILLIAM C. DIETZ

For more about **William C. Dietz** and his fiction, please visit williamcdietz.com. You can find Bill on Facebook at: www.facebook.com/williamcdietz and you can follow him on Twitter: William C. Dietz @wcdietz